THE LIVERPOOL BASQUE

Manuel Echaniz is a Basque. Now an old man, he is living in British Columbia, far from the city of his birth — Liverpool. This is the story of Manuel's childhood and coming-of-age in the teeming streets of Liverpool's docklands. Brought up by women while the men are at sea, Manuel grows up with a fierce pride in his heritage and a powerful will to survive in an era of deprivation. Against all odds, he gets himself an education of sorts, and sets off on the long voyage of his life that will lead to Canada.

SPECIAL MESSAGE TO READERS

This book is published under the auspices of

THE ULVERSCROFT FOUNDATION

(registered charity No. 264873 UK)

Established in 1972 to provide funds for research, diagnosis and treatment of eye diseases. Examples of contributions made are: —

A new Children's Assessment Unit at Moorfield's Hospital, London.

•

Twin operating theatres at the Western Ophthalmic Hospital, London.

•

A Chair of Ophthalmology at the University of Leicester.

•

The establishment of a Royal Australian College of Ophthalmologists "Fellowship".

You can help further the work of the Foundation by making a donation or leaving a legacy. Every contribution, no matter how small, is received with gratitude. Please write for details to:

THE ULVERSCROFT FOUNDATION,
The Green, Bradgate Road, Anstey,
Leicester LE7 7FU, England.
Telephone: (0116) 236 4325

In Australia write to:
THE ULVERSCROFT FOUNDATION,
c/o The Royal Australian College of Ophthalmologists,
27, Commonwealth Street, Sydney,
N.S.W. 2010.

I've travelled the world twice over,
Met the famous: saints and sinners,
Poets and artists, kings and queens,
Old stars and hopeful beginners,
I've been where no-one's been before,
Learned secrets from writers and cooks
All with one library ticket
To the wonderful world of books.

HELEN FORRESTER

THE LIVERPOOL BASQUE

Complete and Unabridged

CHARNWOOD
Leicester

First published in Great Britain in 1993 by
HarperCollins Publishers
London

First Charnwood Edition
published October 1994
by arrangement with
HarperCollins Publishers
London

British Library CIP Data

Forrester, Helen
The Liverpool Basque.—Large print ed.—
Charnwood library series
I. Title II. Series
823.914 [F]

ISBN 0–7089–8789–3

Published by
F. A. Thorpe (Publishing) Ltd.
Anstey, Leicestershire

Set by Words & Graphics Ltd.
Anstey, Leicestershire
Printed and bound in Great Britain by
T. J. Press (Padstow) Ltd., Padstow, Cornwall

This book is printed on acid-free paper

This novel is dedicated to my friend,
Doroteo Vincent Elordieta,
a Basque from Liverpool,
whose wonderful stories about the city
inspired me to write it

This is a novel and its characters are products of my imagination, its situations likewise. Whatever similarity there may be of name, no reference is intended to any person living or dead. The loss of the ship, the *Esperanza Larringa*, in 1920, is part of the history of Liverpool, and I have allowed one of the characters I have created to die in it.

Just as the twig is bent the tree's inclined

Epistle i, line 149
Moral Essays
Alexander Pope, 1688 – 1744

1

IGNORING the pouring rain, he came out of the house, and then turned to check that the front door had closed properly behind him. Satisfied, he walked slowly down the path between the flowerbeds, empty except for a few winter aconites cautiously beginning to open.

When he reached the two steps which led down to the pavement, he paused before carefully descending them. As the wind off the Strait caught him, his shiny black oilskin flapped against his lean frame. A fringe of white hair fluttered round the edge of the black beret set firmly on his head; the beret had been arranged so that it had a small peak to protect his forehead and encourage the rain to fall down his cheeks instead of veiling his sight.

Safely on the narrow pavement, he lingered for a moment to look across the Juan de Fuca Strait. The Olympic Mountains were obliterated by the downpour, but nearer to hand a freighter was stubbornly butting its way through the sheeting rain towards Victoria Harbour. With a seaman's eye for weather, he looked up at the louring clouds, pursed his lips and muttered, "Cold enough for snow."

Water was trickling down his neck, so he heaved his collar up higher and then proceeded along The Esplanade towards the cemetery. He walked with his head bent, his shoulders slightly hunched, as if expecting to hit his skull on a door frame if he straightened up. Though his gait was light and steady, his old Wellington boots made an intermittent squishing sound as he slopped through muddy puddles.

In the large inside pocket of his oilskin was a single pink rose wrapped in damp tissue paper. He had bought it yesterday from the florist in Cook Street; throughout the winter he had a standing order with her, to purchase the flowers four at a time. He kept them fresh in a cut-glass vase on the dining-room table, and, regardless of the weather, he took one each day to the cemetery to lay on the grave of his wife, Kathleen.

Sometimes the florist was not able to obtain the pink or white blooms which he requested, and he would have to make do with red ones, which Kathleen had not loved quite so much. In summer, he cut roses in shades of pink or cream from the bushes which she herself had planted in their garden when first they had retired to Vancouver Island. While she had the strength, she had tenderly pruned and fertilized them herself. Then, when she had begun to fail, he had pushed her wheelchair on to the lawn, and had learned to look after them for her, doing his best to hide from her the agony of mind he had felt, as he watched her suffer the multiple infections to which leukaemia laid her open.

Seamen don't get much chance to garden, he ruminated, as he gazed down at yesterday's offering, which lay, tattered and sodden, on the grave in front of the memorial stone. But

Kathleen had loved her garden, and every day he made this small pilgrimage to tell her that he was caring for it and for her household icons, and that he loved her still. Mostly, however, he came to ask her forgiveness for having failed, when she was so ill, to keep her out of pain. Mixed with the rain, tears ran down his face; no matter how the years since her death rolled along, they failed to obliterate from his mind the torture he had watched her endure. There were, of course, days when he took the walk to the cemetery from force of habit; but all too often he went in the hope of easing his own haunting memories. Today, his nightmare was very close.

He bent down carefully to avoid the dizziness which, nowadays, sometimes bothered him, and picked up yesterday's battered bloom. Regardless of its wet condition, he stuffed it into his outside pocket. His chest felt tight, and he paused to take a few short breaths of the cold, damp air, before slowly opening his oilskin to retrieve the slightly flattened fresh rose from his inner pocket. He unrolled the tissue paper from it and laid the flower in front of the headstone. The wind was strong and capricious, so he picked up a small rock and laid it on the stalk to hold it down. Most people had a vase into which they put their flower offerings, but he laid them on the ground; in his mind's eye he always saw the roses as lying between his wife's perfect white breasts.

Then he addressed the marble headstone. He did not see the words cut into it, *In loving memory of Kathleen Echaniz, beloved wife of Manuel Echaniz, born 3rd June, 1914, died 20th January, 1984. At peace.* His first words were, as always, "Forgive me, my darling, forgive me." He paused, as if waiting for a reply. Then he swallowed hard, and lifted his head a little, to look out towards the heaving waters of the Strait. He saw his wife's smiling face, her eyes unclouded by illness; he felt her fullness beneath him, before suffering reduced her to a skeleton; and, as he had always done, either by letter from distant ports or when they lay comfortably in bed together, he told her all that had happened to him in the previous twenty-four hours, all the funny things, all the small disasters. Today, he said that he had washed her Royal Doulton figurines in the cabinet in the sitting-room and had set them back exactly as she had left them, that last night he had cooked himself some fish for supper, and that Veronica Harris, her friend from next door, had brought him in some homemade cookies, as she did each week.

The soft words came out like a litany, not in Kathleen's native English, but in a strange evocative language known only to a few, a language which Kathleen had never been able to master.

He spoke in Basque, a unique language of farmers and shepherds in the enclaves of the Pyrenees, of fishermen in the Bay of Biscay, of iron workers and factory hands in big cities like Bilbao and smaller ones like Guernica and Pamplona; it was also spoken by lonely, elderly shepherds and their descendants in Nevada,

Utah and Arizona, and by small groups of emigrants in Eastern Canada. It was a language so old that it was unrelated to any other language in the modern world, preserved by people shielded by nature's walls, the Pyrenees, between France and Spain. It had the advantage that anyone in the cemetery who heard his words to his wife would not understand them.

Manuel Echaniz was a Basque. Though he also spoke Spanish quite fluently, he seethed with anger when he was frequently mistaken for a Spaniard. He would occasionally flare up and say that though General Franco had, in the Spanish Civil War, bombed into submission his grandparents' native city of Bilbao, he had never succeeded in making its Basque inhabitants into Spaniards, any more than Roman and Moorish invaders of Spain had been able to do so in much earlier times.

He himself had been born in England, in the port of Liverpool, and he spoke English with a pronounced Liverpool accent. Nevertheless, he would affirm indignantly that, like his father and grandfather before him, he was a Basque and very proud of it. For the benefit of Canadians, he would add, also, that he was proud to be a Canadian citizen — but he was still pure Basque!

He had married Kathleen Weston, a Vancouver Island girl, whom he had met, during the war, in Halifax, Nova Scotia. She had tried several times to learn his native tongue, but had finally given up, arguing that his command of English was so good that they could communicate perfectly in that language. Because he had spoken to her consistently since babyhood only in Basque, his daughter Faith understood the language — but she would always answer him in English. As for Lorilyn, his only grandchild, now aged nineteen and doing her first year at the University of British Columbia, she would laugh and tell him to stop 'talking funny' and speak English.

Sometimes, without his Canadian Kathleen to support him, he wondered why he stayed in Victoria. He frequently longed for the familiar dockside streets of Liverpool, for the warmth and friendliness of the Baltic Fleet or the Flags of all Nations, both pubs that he remembered as being packed with an international gathering of seamen, all talking exuberantly at once. And he wanted to hear again St Peter's church bell calling him to Mass, a Mass celebrated in Latin. He could go to Mass in Victoria; he could even ease his soul by going to Confession; but it would all be in English, as lately ordained by the Vatican, and would have little of the comforting magic of a Mass chanted in Latin, as it had been when he was young. The Latin Mass, untouched by war or pestilence, unchanging like God himself, had been a dear familiar ceremony, no matter how strange a port his ship had been tied up in. If he had to listen to Mass in the vernacular, he wanted to hear it in Basque — and for that he would have to return to Vizcaya, the province of his forefathers.

He sighed as he turned from Kathleen's grave and began slowly to make his way homeward under the dripping pine trees. Both Liverpool and Vizcaya were a long way off; journeys to either of them were not to be undertaken lightly by an eighty-four-year-old. Then there was Faith who lived with her Canadian husband, George McLaren, in Vancouver; she was his living link with Kathleen. She did come occasionally, with her family, to visit him, but never frequently enough. He would smile when he thought of her and try to shake off his depression. Yet, sometimes when he could not sleep, a fearful inner loneliness would overwhelm him to the point of terror, and older voices called him, voices of others whom he had loved, Basque voices, Liverpool voices, people who were part of his very nature, people he had not been able to tell Kathleen much about.

He knew that he dreaded dying in this pretty city on the west coast of Canada, even if they laid him beside Kathleen. It was too lonely — a single Basque name in a cemetery full of British pioneers. Kathleen was amid her own, but he would not be.

He wanted, at least, to lie in a Liverpool churchyard or cemetery, surrounded by headstones with Basque names on them, to be laid to rest by Basques speaking either the thick colloquial English of his childhood friends or the language of his roots, Basque.

As he pushed to one side a rain-dropped branch of Scottish pine, he considered soberly how strange it was that, when he thought about his own death, all that had happened to him in Canada was wiped out of his mind, even the long, contented years with Kathleen. What was left — the essence of himself — was Liverpool Basque; and he wanted to lie with his parents and grandparents and friends in a corner of Liverpool they had made their own. Afterwards, he wanted toasts to his memory drunk in wines familiar to him and funny stories told about him in pithy Basque phrases.

Back on the pavement that led to his home, he shivered. It was not easy to have a conscience formed by Jesuits in the back streets of Liverpool. They taught perfection — but an ordinary man could do only his best — and he had done his best for Kathleen.

2

ALTHOUGH the morning's winter storm had been so intense and Victoria's Scenic Drive had been, for once, deserted, Manuel's expedition had not gone unnoticed.

Seated in the bay window of the bungalow next door, Sharon Herman, daughter of an old friend of Veronica Harris, had noted with mild interest the very old man going for a walk despite the inclement weather.

She was a nurse who specialized in the care of the terminally ill, and she had just arrived to take up a position in a local hospital about to open a palliative care ward. Her interest in the elderly pedestrian was kindly and caring — she felt he should not be getting soaking wet at his age.

She turned towards Veronica, who was seated at her computer across the room, trying to unravel the complexities of Townsman's Tailors' accounts outstanding. An elderly widow, who lived alone, she earned her living by keeping the accounts of small businesses in the neighbourhood. Today, she was finding it difficult to work with someone else in the room, though she did not grudge, in the least, offering her friend's daughter temporary accommodation until she found herself a flat conveniently close to the hospital.

"Veronica, who's the old man next door? He's just gone out — in this weather! He'll get soaked

— hasn't he got a car?"

Veronica turned impatiently towards Sharon. Then she glimpsed through the bay window the bent figure plodding up the road. Her expression changed, and she smiled. "Oh, that's Manuel Echaniz — Old Spanish, Kathleen's husband. She was the friend I told you about — died of cancer."

"Is he Spanish?"

"No. Kathleen told me he was born in the UK. She said he's a Basque, whatever that might be. He speaks English and Spanish — and his own language, which only Faith seems to understand — that's his daughter, you know." She paused to rub her eyes, tired from concentration on the computer screen. Then she said, "He'll be going up to the cemetery."

"Does he work there?"

"No. He goes up every day to put a flower on Kathleen's grave. I've never known him miss a day since she passed away — must be eight years now."

Sharon laughed. "You're kidding?"

"No, I'm not. You should've seen them together. They were great!"

Sharon moved uneasily in her chair by the window, and her book slid off her lap. She bent to pick it up. "He could take some flowers up every week — it would save him time. Or he could drive up on a day like this."

"Well, he does have a car — he doesn't use it much, though." She smiled indulgently. "Weather never bothered him — I guess because he went to sea for years. And as for going every day, he told me once he wanted her to know that he thought of her each day." Her smile faded, and she sighed a little despondently; she had often wished that Manuel would think of her every day. He still seemed to her an attractive man, with his wide smile and twinkling black eyes. His finely lined face was still healthily tanned, and the long, narrow shape of it, with its flat cheekbones, still had the firmness of a much younger man.

"Sounds like an old movie," Sharon was saying, as she put her book on a side table. "Do you think he's got a screw loose?"

"Not him! He's in his eighties now, but there's nothing wrong with his brains — and I've never known him be sick." She hesitated, and then added, "He's a great old guy."

Sharon made a wry mouth. "Veronica, you're too sentimental," she teased. "Men aren't like that. Do you think he feels guilty about her in some way?"

The question irritated Veronica. Sharon, still smarting from a recent divorce, might be bitter about men — but she was, Veronica felt, being very unfair to Manuel.

"You've read too much pop psychology," she responded huffily, and swung her chair round to face the computer screen again. "I would have thought that you, with your special training, would know how long a person can grieve."

The rebuke, from a woman who was usually very mild-mannered, jolted Sharon. She realized that the question had arisen from the resentment she still felt as a divorcee. Veronica was right;

each individual needed his own time in which to recover from bereavement.

Ashamed, she inquired in a conciliatory tone if Veronica would like her to make a cup of coffee. Privately, she thought how glad she would be to begin her new job on the following Monday; it would take her mind off her own troubles.

Thankful to get her guest out of the room for the moment, Veronica said politely that she would like a cup very much, and the coffee was on the bottom shelf of the cupboard next to the sink. She wished heartily that the rain would ease, so that Sharon could resume her hunt for an apartment.

In the cluttered kitchen, Sharon put a clean filter in the coffee maker, followed by spoonfuls of coffee. She swore softly as the old kitchen tap spattered water over her when she turned it on. After filling the pot, she stared with some despair through the kitchen window at the sweeping rain. The weather was as cold and dismal as she felt herself; her only consolation was that Winnipeg, from which she had come a couple of days before, would be suffering infinitely worse temperatures. In her pocket lay a well-thumbed last letter from her lawyer, enclosing his final bill for negotiating a parsimonious settlement with her husband. The letter wrote *Finis* to a whole segment of her life.

Divorce had been much more painful than she had expected. After seven difficult years of a childless marriage, she had anticipated a sense of joyous freedom; instead, she felt a numbing sense of loss. Was this how one felt after a bereavement? Was this how Old Spanish felt? God help her, if she still felt like this at the end of eight years. One thing was certain, *her* husband would never waste time putting flowers on her grave.

She had worked all her married life. Now, she was going to start anew, away from the people who had known her when she was married. It was the kind of work which would demand a great deal from her, as she dealt with the dying and with their grief-stricken families; yet, she knew from experience that the close relationship between patient and nurse was not a one-way situation; at no time did one come so close to a person as when that person was on his or her deathbed. Beside that experience, she considered as the coffee percolated, what was a divorce? Particularly when there were no children involved.

She carefully poured the coffee into two mugs, and told herself sharply to cheer up. After the coffee, she would go out to look at the apartments she had marked in the newspaper rentals column. Blow the rain. She took Veronica's mug to her, and drank her own coffee despondently in the kitchen. Then, she quickly put on a raincoat, and took Veronica's umbrella off a hook in the hall cupboard. Opening the door into the living-room a crack, she called to Veronica that she was going to look at an apartment and that she was not to bother about lunch for her. Then, map in pocket, she went firmly out into the rain.

The rain was lessening and the umbrella

hardly necessary. She remembered suddenly her parents still living together in their Florida condominium and managing to keep extraordinarily well for their age, under the Florida sun. Married for thirty-five years, she considered with some wonderment, as she crossed the road at a traffic light. How did they do it? Old Spanish must have been married at least as long. Some people had all the luck.

But was it luck? Or was it some secret formula that the older generation used to build a happy marriage? Cynics said they stuck together because women had no means of earning a living, but it could not be that alone, because even slaves in the States who had no hope at all used to run away.

She looked up to check the street number of an apartment block and then absently pressed a bell marked *Building Manager*. No matter what the secret is, this is where you begin all over again, she told herself as she waited for a response.

3

UNAWARE of the interest he had sparked in Sharon Herman, Old Manuel stood in his narrow back hall and shook the rain off his beret and oilskin before hanging them to drip in a small washroom by the kitchen door. Without them, dressed in a white shirt and sleeveless pullover, he seemed extremely frail and thin. As he paused for a second to watch the water running down the oilskin, he smiled to himself; his daughter, Faith, was always warning him to keep himself warm and dry. At his age, she told him, he must take care not to get wet.

He would always tease her by replying that Basques had been pounded by rain in their native mountains for at least five thousand years, and they were immune to it.

He slowly heaved off his Wellington boots and laid them neatly in a boot tray. Like many men who had been to sea, he was extraordinarily neat, because he was used to making the most of the tiny space of a ship's cabin.

In his thick white socks, he padded into the kitchen to find something to eat for lunch. He slapped a cheese sandwich together and then plugged in the kettle to make some instant coffee, and looked forward to the nap he always took after the midday meal.

As he put his plate and coffee mug down on

the kitchen table and pulled out a chair, he asked himself ruefully, "Manuel, my lad, what have you come to, when all you look forward to is having a nap?"

The answer was a resigned shrug of one thin shoulder; he had sensed lately that his time was running out.

He decided that after he had slept a little, he would ring up his friend, Jack Audley, and suggest that he should come over for a game of pool on the billiard table in the basement family room. Jack was twelve years younger than he was, but they shared a common interest in fishing and ships — Jack had been a merchant seaman, too.

To help him get through his days without Kathleen, Manuel structured them as meticulously as he could, so that all the necessary domestic tasks and the garden were attended to. Sometimes, however, a thoroughly wet day upset the schedule.

If Jack was not at home, he thought, he would write to his young Liverpool cousin, Ramon Barinèta. He had already, on the first of the month, written to his oldest and dearest friend, Arnador Ganivet, another Liverpool Basque, who had been a Professor at the University of Liverpool, and he smiled gently at the recollection. Between himself and Arnador there was a frankness and concern for each other which probably exceeded that which might have been built up had they both spent their lives in Liverpool; the older they grew, the richer became the correspondence.

After supper each day, he added a page or two to the memoirs of his early life, which he was writing for the benefit of his granddaughter Lorilyn. He had a vague hope that, when she was older, she would read them and become interested in her Basque forebears. At times, her youthful scorn at his pride in his ancestry had hurt him so much that he longed to slap her; her ignorance of the world and its people, despite thirteen years of education, was absolutely abysmal, he fulminated. In frustration, he took to buying her, for her birthdays, books on European and Asian history. As far as he could tell, she never read them; the books were put on the bookshelf in the McLaren family room, their dust-jackets unbesmirched by handling, their pages stiff from never having been turned.

He never quite gave up on her immutability, though he had long since done so in the case of her mother.

He had remarked to Faith's Grade Six schoolteacher that the child seemed to have no interest in her family's past or their customs. The schoolteacher, who was an immigrant from Scotland, had tried to comfort him by saying that first-generation Canadian children were often so busy trying to be like the other children that they tended to discard, as much as possible, any trace of their immigrant origin. "It's your grandchildren who will be passionately interested in where they sprang from; they'll feel more secure," she had assured him.

But now, in Lorilyn, he had a grandchild, and

she never read any book that she did not have to for her university courses. And what was she proposing to study? Engineering, God save her! Not a decent womanly occupation, like nursing or teaching.

While strolling along the cliffs with Jack, one fine summer day, when the gorse was in riotous yellow bloom and the bees were humming like tiny dynamos, he had broached the subject of human roots.

He said, "You know, Jack, people move around too much. A lot of 'em never see another relation, even their grandparents. Come to that, they don't see much of their mum and dad either, in some cases."

"You're right."

"All they've got is kids the same age as themselves or television to set the pace. They've no idea that we've learned ways to endure bad times — cope with difficulties — take disappointments in our stride. And the first time things don't go just right — well, they're sunk."

He paused to watch a small yacht trying to tack against the wind, and muttered irritably, "He'll drown if he don't watch out." Then, picking up the original subject again, he went on, "There's nothing much to make kids feel safe, no standards, no customs. They get no religion even — our Lorilyn's never seen the inside of a church since she were christened — and I wouldn't like to offend her father by askin' what she's doing with that young man always hanging around her." He gave a barking laugh.

Then he added, "There's no family discipline — I wouldn't like *my* grandfather to see her; he'd have made her toe the line a bit, and he'd have had the backing of everybody else. Sometimes I feel like a voice in the wilderness. Do you?"

Jack's round red face wrinkled up in a wry grin. Before he answered, he stopped to strike a match and light his pipe, shielding it from the wind with his curved palms. Then, as the pipe glowed and they continued to walk, he nodded agreement. "I used to slam my kids when they needed it. It didn't do much good, because I wasn't around that much — the wife had to manage while I was at sea." He drew slowly on his pipe. Then he continued, "And things seemed to be changed almost every time I came home. Nobody else's kids were going to church any more — so ours wouldn't. Discipline in school went out, and drugs came in. Like you say, the kids went around in herds all the same age — and there were no cow hands to keep them in line. And God help a cop who boxed their ears for them. I knew what I wanted for my kids, but I didn't have much luck putting it over."

Manuel dropped his cigarette butt and ground it out with his heel. "Seems to me that when we were having Faith, nobody dared touch a child — even to bath the poor little bugger — unless they had read at least three books by experts! Kathleen had a row of books."

Jack laughed. "Same with us. It was like learning to dance from books — as if we'd no ideas of our own. My mother never needed a book to tell her what to do, and we all grew up knowing what was right and what was wrong — even if we weren't perfect. I wish my mother had been around when our lads were growing up." His red face under his straw hat was filled with pain.

Manuel could have kicked himself for bringing up the subject of children. He had, for the moment, forgotten what a bitter disappointment both Jack's boys had been to him. They seemed to lack motivation and found it difficult to keep jobs — like homing pigeons, they came back from Vancouver every few months, to live on their father.

Jack was saying bitterly, "I wish I'd taken a shore job, so I could've been home more."

"It's not your fault, Jack. I'm sure of it. It's the way things are. They're treated as kids for far too long. In the old days, by thirteen or fourteen, they would've been learning a trade under a weight of older men, who'd have kept them in line; and they'd have learned there's a limit to what you can get away with."

"Jobs are different now. How many of them ever go to sea?"

Manuel snorted. "Maybe we should send the whole pack of them to sea for a bit," he suggested, trying to lift Jack's spirits. "They'd either drown — or learn their responsibilities mighty fast."

Unexpectedly, Jack chuckled. "They'd soon learn who's boss."

Manuel began to laugh. "Oh, aye, they would.

It would be great to see some of the little bastards in a force ten gale, telling the Old Man they were as good as him — or arguing they had rights, while waves as high as the mast were coming at them!"

"Mannie, they don't know nothing about natural things, like waves."

"I wouldn't put it past our Lorilyn to explain the physics of a breaking wave to me!" responded Manuel.

This made Jack really laugh, as they plunked themselves down on a bench, two old men silhouetted against the rippling sea, which had taught them most of their skills with an iron discipline.

"Are you glad you went to sea?" asked Jack from behind a cloud of tobacco smoke.

"Never dreamed of doing anything else. Not till I met Kathleen, that is; she'd got her eyes on a shore job for me. After we was married, she kept on her nursing and she put me through college, and I come out a marine architect. We had a good life — but I missed the sea."

"Humph. My dad was a fisherman, and he took me out to sea when I was nine or ten. I was wet and cold and seasick, but I felt I was a real man. At fourteen, I was a deck boy." He made the statement with pride, and then a grin flashed across his face, as he added, "I'd never heard of being a teenager; I was a lad learning to be a man under real men. Had some good laughs, though."

"Oh, aye. I were happy when I were a little kid, too, with me dad and me Uncle Leo coming and going from sea — and being took down to visit their ships, and listen to them grumble and laugh. And getting a bit of pie from the ship's cook." He paused to light another cigarette, and then went on. "And in the house, there was me granny and grandpa to tell me stories. After me mam slapped me for being naughty, me gran would wipe me face — and explain why I got the slap!" Both men were silent, as they smoked and contemplated the sea and the mountains before them. Then Manuel said in a puzzled way, "Our Lorilyn never seems to need a grandpa at all."

While he recalled this rambling conversation with Jack, he took the handmade patchwork quilt off the bed and folded it carefully and laid it on a chair, and sighed. Though he had tried, he did not feel that he had been a very good grandfather — unlike his own grandfather, Juan Barinèta.

He sat down on the side of his bed, pulled a faded crocheted shawl out of the drawer of the bedside table, and slowly eased himself down on to the bed until he lay on his back. He paused for a moment, while every bone and muscle in his body flashed with sudden aches, then he laid the shawl over himself, clasped his hands over his chest and thankfully closed his eyes. In the moment between waking and sleeping, he remembered Kathleen upbraiding him for resting on top of the patchwork quilt. Although he was tired from a very scary wartime voyage, he had pulled her down on top of him. They had forgotten about keeping the bedspread pristine, while they spent until nightfall making love so satisfactorily that even now, nearly fifty years later, he remembered it with awe. Had he really been that strong? And she so responsive?

After her death, he had come across the old quilt folded away at the back of the linen closet. Still beautiful, its colours muted by many drycleanings, it had been like meeting an old friend again. In a way, it had comforted him for the emptiness of the other side of the bed.

He had returned to his ship on the day following his happy afternoon with Kathleen, and her letter telling him the news about her pregnancy with Faith caught up with him in Galveston, Texas.

He remembered how excited he had been about the child, overwhelmed by the divine mystery of its existence and the sense of responsibility that it had laid upon him.

He had shouted the news to the few members of the engine room crew who had not gone ashore, and they had congratulated him on his sexual prowess with explicit pithiness. His news broke the astonished silence which had seemed to grip them at other news they had received that morning. The Yanks had dropped an amazing bomb on the port of Hiroshima and blown the whole city and its inhabitants to bits. The city was known to most of the crew and they had found it hard to accept its death — even if it was supposed to shorten the war. It was a port — like Liverpool!

He had immediately scribbled a few lines to Kathleen, expressing his pure joy at her news. After she was dead, he had found the letter in her jewellery box; she had kept it all her life.

He had also written to his mother, Rosita Echaniz, in Liverpool, urging her to come on a visit as soon as the war was over, to see the babe as yet unborn.

He had hoped for more children, but Kathleen had been adamant about limiting their family. "How will we ever afford to send them to university?" she had asked. "And if you go back to college after the war . . . ?"

Manuel was still uncertain that he himself wanted to return to college, and had never considered that a real university might be within the reach of any child of his, so he had reluctantly said he did not know.

The family remained at one.

* * *

The rainstorm which had swept the Juan de Fuca Strait came to an end. The sudden quiet woke the old man from his nap. He rose stiffly and put the shawl which had been keeping him warm back into the bedside drawer. With an amused awareness of his own finickiness, he carefully replaced the bedspread on the bed.

When he phoned Jack Audley, Mrs Audley said he had gone to Vancouver for the day.

* * *

Before going to his old-fashioned roll-top desk to write to Ramon in Liverpool, he went into the kitchen and took down from a cupboard a bottle of wine, already opened. He poured a glass of it carefully, so as not to disturb the sediment at the bottom of the bottle. Then picking it up, he went to the window and stood idly twirling it in the light of the first rays of the sun to pierce the rain clouds.

Instead of his own long, gnarled fingers holding the stem of the glass, he saw, with unexpected clarity, his grandfather's huge paw holding a wine glass under his nose, to savour a bottle of a new year's crop smuggled into Liverpool from Bilbao.

Those early years in the safety of his grandfather's great shadow had been good years, he thought wistfully. He remembered how the old man's beard waggled when he laughed, and when his grandfather picked him up it was like being hugged by a friendly bear.

He took his glass of wine into his den, where he had a small desk piled with notes and exercise books. Above the desk hung a ship's chronometer, put there, he had told Jack with a laugh, to remind him that his time was short.

He put his glass down on the desk, drew up a chair and sat down. With slightly trembling fingers, he sought for and found a well-thumbed school exercise book. In it lay the life of a Basque; in fact, the lives of many of them, set down in the hope that Lorilyn would, one day, be interested in some of the men and women who were the cause of her existence. Like many Canadians, she shared a Scottish origin, too; but not everybody in the world is Scottish, considered Manuel tartly. He wanted her to know that she had roots in the oldest culture in Europe, going far back beyond written history. He wanted her to preserve something of it within her own being.

So that she would understand, he wrote in English, in an old-fashioned, neatly sloping, cursive hand. He poured out to her, as best he could, the story of his childhood and what little wisdom he felt he had acquired in the long years of his life, especially during the time that he had been part of a Basque community; he did not feel that he had to include much of his life with Kathleen — Lorilyn understood Canadian life — and the finale of Kathleen's existence was, in any case, too painful for him to write about.

It was dark by the time he had to stop because of fatigue and he had forgotten, for the moment, his intention of writing to Ramon. He leaned back in his chair to stretch himself. His eyes were watering and his shoulders ached from the concentrated effort he had been making.

When he looked again at what he had written, he wondered suddenly what lay behind his own boyhood memories. What was going on amongst the grown-ups, who surged in and out of his grandparents' kitchen-living-room? Were they happy?

It took a minute or two for him to bring himself back from Wapping Dock in Liverpool, and when his mind was clear of it, he was left with an aching longing to go home to it, to shake Arnador's hand once more and see Cousin Ramon, and speak Basque with both of them.

Although Faith will have a fit, if you suggest

that you want to do such a long air journey, you *could* do it, he told himself. And perhaps you should, before it's too late!

He grinned wickedly. This summer, he promised himself. And don't tell Faith until it's too late to cancel the flight.

4

PORTS from which men go to sea are matriarchal societies; it is women who are in charge. They have to have their babies without any support from their husbands; and they have to teach their sons, as well as their daughters, to behave and mind their manners. Father is not at home frequently enough to take a strap to a delinquent lad.

Manuel, aged eighty-four, was trying hard to explain to Lorilyn, aged nineteen, that, even before feminism was invented, some women ruled their families.

In our house, he scribbled, it was Grandma Micaela Barinèta who was the undisputed boss. She was my mother's mother, a shrunken ball of energy, always clothed in black, a piece of knitting, with a cork on the end of the needles, usually tucked into the pocket of her black apron. Even to me, when I was only three or four years old and all grown-ups seemed very tall, she appeared too little to possibly be the mother of my two uncles, one of whom, Leo Barinèta, lived with us. Whenever they had done something of which she did not approve, she lashed out at them with her tongue and scared them into line. She would not tolerate any nonsense from me, either, though I was only a toddler; and I soon learned to sit quietly, while the priest droned through the Mass, or to run away and play if she was gossiping with a neighbour.

Of course, Grandpa Juan Barinèta, who no longer went to sea, believed that he ruled the three generations in the house. He certainly received first consideration from Grandma — and from my mother, Rosita Echaniz, who always seemed to be in league with Grandma. Nevertheless, it was the two women who collected the men's earnings from them and the rents from the emigrant lodgers, and laid out the family income to the best of their joint abilities. They bargained in the market for food, decided when new clothes would be bought, purchased coal for the fires, and paid the rent each week; they put every penny they could into three old biscuit tins under Grandma's bed, until a few shillings had been accumulated to put into Post Office savings accounts.

If I had been good on the day that Grandma decided to go to the post office, she let me accompany her, and I had the honour of licking the savings stamps, which she purchased from the postmistress to put into her savings books; I must have licked pages and pages of sixpenny stamps, as Grandma laid away money, first for a rainy day, then for clothes, especially boots for all the menfolk, and finally for education.

The Basque community, nestled by the dock road, was united in its belief in education for their children; and the whole family was determined that the second child, which Mother was expecting, and I, should both go to a good private day school, rather than to the local

Catholic school. In this emphasis on their children's future, they differed somewhat from their polyglot neighbours, who tended, simply, to be thankful if their children managed to grow to adulthood in noisy, polluted Liverpool, knowing enough reading and writing to get a job in the docks or as deckhands.

I grew accustomed to hearing my future discussed, over many a glass of cheap, smuggled wine, by Grandpa, Uncle Leo, and my father, Pedro Echaniz, when he was home. Words like 'university' . . . 'doctor' . . . 'solicitor' whizzed over my head, strange words rarely used in our street.

At the beginning of each voyage, Father arranged with his employers for Mother to receive part of his wages each week. This was called an allotment, and, together with Grandpa's and Uncle Leo's earnings, was used for living expenses.

Grandma gave back to the men a little pocket money for wine and tobacco, both discreetly brought into the country by Basque seamen lucky enough to be sailing to and from their homeland, Vizcaya, in Spain.

A meal isn't complete without wine, my grandfather would often say. Smuggled wines were cheap, and, on the whole, the customs officers did not worry too much about collecting duty on a few bottles of our native wines, as long as its illicit importation was on a very small scale.

Though ours was a very united household, it was not a placid one. Argument, debate were the salt of life, and, in addition, there were all kinds of small vendettas within the Basque community. The community became a solid block, however, whenever it felt it had, as a group, been insulted. The supreme calumny was to be referred to as *Spaniards*! Such a blunder was frequently made by our cheerful, easy-going fellow Liverpudlians, especially the Irish, who seemed sorely lacking in a knowledge of Iberian history, and by English clerks behind official counters, who didn't really care what we were.

Amongst the men gathered round our kitchen table for a smoke and a gossip, such an allegation produced a glowering animosity; they sputtered like half-lit sparklers, and muttered about the improbable origins of all the accursed Spaniards they had ever met. Many of them spoke Spanish as well as they did Basque, and they could be equally rude in both languages; even in English, the English of the back streets, they could be quite lurid. My knowledge of lively curses in all three languages began at an early age.

So, from the time I was big enough to be carried around on Grandpa's or Uncle Leo's shoulder, I learned that I was a Basque and to be proud of it. I learned to speak Basque first; it was the language which flowed around my small world of kitchen-living room and brick-lined backyard; I learned good Castilian from the Spanish priests of St Peter's Church — they were frequently in and out of our homes, to counsel or console, their lean, dark figures the epitome of God's authority over little boys. And I learned English from my playmates in the street.

Grandpa had a beard heavily streaked with grey. His head was bald, except for a thin ring of neatly clipped black hair. Most of his teeth were deep-stained by tobacco, but a missing one had been replaced by a gold tooth which flashed as he talked; I was fascinated by it and my first ambition was to have a flashing gold tooth for myself. He had gone to sea in the days of sailing ships, and was proud to say that he had several times breasted the storms of Cape Horn, a place of terror at the most southerly point of Chile, where many a ship was lost before the advent of the Panama Canal gave a safer entry to the Pacific Ocean. "They don't know what seamanship is, nowadays," he would grumble testily to my father, when he told of *his* adventures in a steamer.

For many years now, Grandpa Barinèta had held the agency for Basque emigrants passing through Liverpool on their way to Nevada, Arizona, California and Washington. An Agent was essential to protect such travellers from exploitation in a strange port, where their language was not spoken. He saw that they were housed and fed, while they waited for their ship; he kept their luggage safe, and delivered them to the correct ship at the right time. It was his pride that, to his knowledge, he had never lost even a piece of luggage, never mind an emigrant.

Many of these people were lodged in our

own house, which was a large eighteenth-century dwelling, and I was quite used to our home being suddenly filled with strangers, who equally suddenly vanished a few days later. Even as a little child, I sensed how touchingly thankful they were to be in the hands of a fellow Basque, who took care that they were not robbed or cheated by local rascals who made a living by preying on confused travellers trying to get to the New World; and I will never forget Grandpa's slow smile of satisfaction when he could close his ledger after a boat sailed, and sink into his carving chair at the kitchen table to enjoy a quiet glass of wine with Grandma and Mother.

These transitory invasions made our house a very lively one, and a centre for resident Basques, who often drifted in to hear recent news of Vizcaya from the emigrants. The house was opposite the Wapping Dock, except that across a narrow street, the tall flat-iron building of the Baltic Fleet intervened. This public house was a popular meeting place, almost a club, to the Basque community, and emigrants often took their ease there, too. My mother told me that she sometimes went for a drink there with my father, and that she used to park me, sound asleep in my pram, by its ample walls, while she went inside. No wonder it was one of my favourite pubs when I grew up!

* * *

As I grew a little bigger, my greatest ambition became to climb into the toast-rack horse-bus, with its little canopy over the rear seats, and have a ride with the emigrants down to the big ship which took them over the ocean to the New World. On the bus's side was the name of a steamship company, and on a grubby white board at the front was the name of the ship on which the emigrants were booked. The bus was drawn by two patient, blinkered work horses, heads hanging and untidy short manes blowing in the sea wind, as they waited for the harassed, worried emigrants to be loaded.

"Grandpa! Let me go down to the dock — please, Grandpa. I'm five now. I'm big enough," I pleaded, one sunny September day in 1913.

He stood on the pavement, between our front door and the horse-bus, in his hand a piece of board with innumerable sheets of paper pinned to it, his peaked cap pushed to the back of his head, while he supervised the people climbing on to the bus. I clutched at his long, serge-covered legs, and peered up at him to catch his eye.

He looked down at me impatiently. He was fond of me, I knew, but at that moment I was a nuisance, as round him swirled an anxious group of heavily laden men, women and children, all of them desperately dependent upon him.

"Manuel Echaniz! The bus is too full," he responded with exasperation. "Go and see your mother in the kitchen." As I reluctantly let go of his leg, his voice rose to a shriek. "Mind out! You're too close to the wheels. Get out of the way, boy."

My face fell. I wanted to cry. At five, I felt

I was grown-up enough to be able to keep out of the way of wheels and horses' feet. But when Grandpa spoke like that, everyone obeyed, even Mother and Father. Sullenly and with difficulty, I turned away and pushed myself between long, trousered legs and flowing black skirts issuing from the house, an incredible stream of people. A white-faced little girl, with whom I had played for the past week, said shyly, "Goodbye, Manuel," as I shoved by her. I did not reply, as I fought my way kitchenwards. Through my ill humour, I smelled the emigrants' underlying fear, and it made me uneasy, as baskets, bundles tied in old shawls, and the bare feet of small children carried in their parents' arms brushed or bumped my head.

When I was a little older, I was able to visualize more accurately the discomforts of the long voyage in steerage still faced by our visitors, and could understand their dread. Meanwhile, infected by their fear, I almost ran down the deserted back part of the passageway leading to the kitchen and safety, while Grandpa, his pencil tucked behind his ear, continued to cope with the travellers.

Grandpa had a habit of rubbing his short beard when hard-pressed by nervous questions from his charges. Already tired from the journey from Bilbao, and distressed at leaving home, however poverty-stricken, the emigrants seemed to find great comfort and reassurance from the self-confident old man. Now, at the time of parting from us, some of the women were invariably near to tears; not only did they have yet to face the long voyage to New York, but also a long train journey to the West, with children and husbands to keep fed and happy. In some cases, they had to sustain a pregnancy and, at the end, a confinement amid strangers.

On the other hand, there was always a group of young, single men, excited, strung-up and sometimes drunk, for Grandpa to control; on each he pinned a numbered identity disc, while they laughed and joked, and talked of making a fortune in their new land. Not for ever would they tend other people's sheep in Nevada, they assured each other.

In the big, stone-floored kitchen-living-room, with its high ceiling covered with a century of soot, my comfortable, plump mother took no notice of my entry; she was holding her youngest brother, Uncle Leo Barinèta, tightly to her and was weeping bitterly.

Frightened, and not a little jealous, I paused in the doorway.

Uncle Leo was saying, "It's not for ever, Rosita. I'll come back." His voice rose with false cheerfulness. "Come on. At worst, a seaman can work his way home again — even from Nevada! Don't cry, Rosita."

Mother leaned back in his arms, to look up at his face. "You've got a home with us," she wailed. "You can go on sailing out of Liverpool. Why move? Nevada sounds a godforsaken place."

"Tush, Rosita. I want to better myself. There's land there, almost for the asking." He dropped his arms to his sides in a hopeless gesture, realizing that land meant nothing to her.

She drew away from him, and wiped her tears on the corner of her white apron. "Mother's broken-hearted," she reproached him.

I watched wide-eyed. Uncle Leo was an essential part of my small world; it was frightening that he should be about to vanish like all the other emigrants. People poured in and out of our house, but the family members always came home; as seamen, Uncle Leo and Father, even Uncle Agustin, reappeared regularly, armed with presents for small boys. But Mother's tears told me that this departure was very different.

"Mam!" I cried in a strangled, scared voice, and ran to her.

Mechanically, she picked me up and held me against her shoulder. I felt her slump slightly, and turned my face towards hers. Her pretty, little mouth was drooping, her whole expression woebegone. She was gazing at Uncle Leo as if she could never take her eyes off him. "I'll miss you so much," she whimpered. "And Mother's nearly out of her mind, up there on the bed."

Uncle Leo swallowed, and I thought he was going to cry; it was a new and scary idea to me that a young man could cry. He controlled himself, however, and, instead, he put his arms round both of us together. He kissed my mother's cheek and then I felt his lips on the back of my own head. He loosed his hold on us, and said, "I know. Mam's been upset about it for weeks. Comfort her, Rosita — I feel bad about it. But I'll be back, never fear."

He turned abruptly and went out through the

hallway to say farewell to his father and to join the embarking throng.

It was over nine years before I saw Uncle Leo again.

Mother stood silent for a moment or two; then she seemed to gather herself together and become aware of my own trembling. Through her tears, she smiled at me. She said brightly, "Pudding's got a great surprise for you. Come and see."

* * *

I missed Uncle Leo for his own sake. But, as I grew up, I learned that the loss of a man from a family weakens that family immeasurably. No one knew it better than Basque mountain farmers and their descendants, who dwelt in the rocky, inhospitable Pyrenees, between the French and the Spanish. For century upon century, they had to watch their younger sons leave their stony fortress, because the land could not feed them; they became famous mercenaries in foreign armies, or fishermen in the Bay of Biscay or iron workers in the foundries of Bilbao. When the New World opened up, they took their skills as shepherds and as seamen to it, and Uncle Leo, full of hope, went with them.

* * *

Mother slowly slid me to the floor. As she tried to control her grief, I saw her fine, round breasts rise and fall quickly under her black blouse, and I knew that Uncle Leo's departure must be something very disturbing to her.

My childhood fears soon gave way to curiosity, as she led me to a small cupboard beside the big kitchen range on which she and Grandma cooked. The door was open, and she squatted down beside her. "Have a look," she urged me.

I approached the small, dark cavern of the cupboard with caution. Pudding was a very large, black cat with expressionless pale-green eyes; she was quite capable of giving a small boy a sharp clawing, if she felt her dignity was at stake.

She was curled up on a piece of grubby blanket in the darkest corner. Her green eyes flashed as she looked up quickly at her visitors, while round her crawled four tiny black bundles. Surprised, I put out my hand to touch one of them. Pudding peremptorily nuzzled my hand away.

In some astonishment, I turned to Mother. "Kittens! Where did she find them?"

"She had them inside her. They came out in the night."

The reply was so unexpected that I knew my mother was teasing me. I looked at her knowingly, and laughed. "They couldn't. How would they get out?"

Mother hesitated, before she replied. Then she said, "Pudding won't let me touch her at the moment; she's tired. Tomorrow, I'll lift her up and show you."

Though she had been born in Bilbao, my

mother had close relations who lived in the countryside, where, as a matter of course, children saw animals born and die. It had apparently not struck her that her little son was ignorant of birth — and, possibly, also of death.

5

LADEN with greyish sheets to be washed, Grandma Micaela came slowly and heavily down the stairs, and, as she entered the kitchen, I looked up from watching the kittens. A shaft of sunlight from the tall, narrow kitchen window lit up her paper-pale cheeks, wet with tears.

I was shocked. Grandma never cried. The worst she ever did was scold; and she was my rock, my safe refuge, when both Mother and Father were cross with me. Now, as Mother scrambled hastily to her feet, Grandma looked imploringly at her and quavered, "I can't make myself go out to see him leave. I can't bear it. I'll never see him again!" She dropped the sheets on to the stone floor; her hands, heavily veined, and scarlet from too much immersion in hot soda water, dangled helplessly at her sides.

Mother ran to her and took her in her arms. She patted her back and rocked her, just as she did me when I had hurt myself. "I know, Mam. I know," she crooned. "I can't go out, either."

"He's my baby," cried Grandma, with a further explosion of tears.

I stopped stroking Pudding, and interjected, with some derision, "Uncle Leo isn't a baby — he's a big man."

Obviously startled, both women turned to look down at me, as I knelt by the open cupboard.

Grandma was the first to recover. She swallowed a sob, and then laughed through her tears. She slowly nodded her white head, and responded tenderly, "You're right, my precious dumpling." She let out a long sigh, and lifted a finger to touch Mother's round, pink cheek, a tiny, loving gesture of affection. She said, "He's right. I mustn't forget it. He *is* a real man — and I have to let him go." Then her tired voice rose, as she added, "But it hurts, Rosita. It hurts." Tears again trickled down her cheeks.

Mother hugged her, and said determinedly, "We'll pretend he's simply gone to sea again — on a long voyage. It'll help. And he'll write to you."

Did grown-ups have to pretend things? I wondered uneasily. Like small boys do?

"And, next month, Agustin should put into Liverpool. That'll be nice for you — for all of us." She was referring to my elder uncle, who was an able seaman in a freighter which docked periodically in Liverpool with cargoes of iron ore. Between voyages he lived with Grandpa Barinèta's brother and his two motherless daughters in Bilbao, because he himself was still a bachelor.

"Yes," agreed Grandma heavily. Uncle Agustin was a dark, silent man, not nearly so exuberant or lovable as his younger brother, Leo. But Grandma smiled, and I felt better when I saw it.

My mother began to pick up the sheets that Grandma had dropped on the floor. "Let's put these to soak — we can boil them later on this afternoon. Let's do the bedrooms now. Would you like a glass of wine or a cup of camomile tea to carry round with you?"

Grandma sniffed. "No, thanks," she replied with a sigh. "I'll have something at teatime."

* * *

Uncle Leo was the first person to pass out of my childhood. For months, Grandma watched for his letters, but he wrote only two from Nevada, to which she replied immediately. Since she had no other address except the one he had given her in Nevada, she continued to write to him there, and she was always the first to reach the front door when a letter slid through the letter box and across the cracked tiled floor. But no more letters arrived, and she mentioned her son less and less and ceased to hope.

Unaware of the despondency the lack of news from Uncle Leo caused her, I regarded her as my own special property, always there to dispense comfort, wipe my nose and wash painfully grazed knees when I had fallen down.

Unlike Uncle Agustin, Uncle Leo and I had been born in Liverpool, and we spoke the thick catarrhal English, with a strong tinge of mixed Irish accents in it, that was current in the streets around the docks. Uncle Agustin spoke only Basque and Spanish.

It had been Uncle Leo's custom during times of unemployment to go to Spain, to his maternal grandfather's small farm in the Pyrenees, to work there in return for his food. It was there that he learned to care for sheep; and it was this skill that he hoped to build on in the United States. I had heard him discuss this with his father on a number of occasions, and I knew that he hoped eventually to have his own sheep farm.

Though he did not say much in the two letters Grandma received, I learned later that he had set his expectations of Nevada too high. Ashamed to tell his parents that he had not done too well, he put off writing to them, and moved to Arizona and, later on, wandered through Utah and Colorado. Grandma's replies to his letters never reached him. He always told himself that he would write when he was settled, but as the years went by and memories of Liverpool dimmed, he had nothing very hopeful to tell his parents so he did not write.

I forgot him.

⋆ ⋆ ⋆

With a steady, though small family income from Grandpa's activities amongst the emigrants and from my father, we were able to visit Spain occasionally. Carrying our own food in a big market basket, we sailed for Bilbao in Basque-owned fishing boats or small freighters. In part-return for our passage, Grandpa worked as a member of the crew. In Bilbao we stayed with Grandpa's brother and his daughters, and, occasionally, our visit coincided with the homecoming of Uncle Agustin. A more rapid form of transport was sometimes used by both families, if they felt the need to see each other on some urgent matter; they went by rail. They caught the train from Liverpool and went to Dover, crossed on the Channel ferry to Calais, and took the train from there to Bilbao. This, however, was considered very extravagant because eight pounds had to be expended on the fare — and why part with hard cash, when you could go all the way by sea for almost nothing? Grandma's sense of economy was almost as well developed as that of Mr and Mrs Wing, who owned the Chinese laundry and were the parents of one of my best-loved playmates, Brian Wing.

My childhood memories of Spain are faint, evoked mainly by the smell of baking bread and of farm animals, or the heavy odour of newly harvested hay, and a sense of having been particularly happy there, blissfully unaware of the hardship and oppression endured by the grown-ups. I took for granted callused hands and bent backs, chilblained fingers and toes, rooms where one moved like a small snake amid people, because homes were so crowded. In fact, the closeness in which everybody I knew lived was very comforting to a small boy.

As I grew bigger, I would, after a few weeks in Bilbao or up in the mountains with my father's family, the Echanizes, and another bumper crop of Barinèta second cousins, suddenly feel homesick for Liverpool. Healthy from the mountain air and the coarse fresh food stuffed into me by endless loving relations, I longed to return to the lively world centred on the Wapping Dock. I wanted to play with a shoal of small friends, Malayans, Chinese, Irish, Filipinos, and black people both from Africa and the Caribbean, as well as one or two Basque boys who were a little older than me and sometimes condescended to let me join in their games. We darted like minnows in and out of dark, familiar narrow lanes and alleys, Brian Wing and I at the end of the line because we were the smallest. The black and bleak city, rich with the smell of horse manure, vanilla pods, fish and raw hides, was to us a wonderful playground. We barely took note of the racket of horses' hooves and steel-bound wheels on the streets' stone setts or the constant roar of machinery in the workshops round us; it was simply part of everyday life.

Despite our diversity of race and religion, all my small friends had two things in common: as the children of dockers, shipyard workers or seamen, our lives were inextricably bound to the sea; and we all shared a true Liverpool sense of humour — life was intrinsically so hard that one learned early to make a joke of it. How we laughed, Lorilyn! Deep belly laughs that I rarely hear nowadays.

* * *

After seeing off the emigrants on the day of Uncle Leo's departure for Nevada, Grandpa Juan Barinèta came slowly into the kitchen and dropped his papers and house ledger on to the well-scrubbed deal table. His wooden chair, which he had made himself, scraped on the stone floor as he pulled it away from the table and wearily flopped into it. He said heavily, to nobody in particular, "Well, that's that lot."

Mother and Grandma Micaela had just come up from the cellar, after putting the sheets to soak in the copper before scrubbing and boiling them.

Seeing his wife's red-rimmed eyes, Grandpa said kindly to her in Basque, "The boy's going to be all right, never fear, my dear." He turned to my mother, and asked her, "Rosita, get out a bottle of wine — if there's anything left after last night's party. Let's all sit down and have a drink."

The reference to the previous night's send-off party for Leo made even Grandma smile, though rather wanly.

Already packed with emigrants, the house had been further jammed as Basque neighbours dropped in to say farewell.

Uncle Leo and Jean Baptiste Saitua, who lived up the road, both had excellent singing voices, and they had sung all the old Basque songs they could remember, vying with each other in a good-humoured way.

Sitting on Mother's lap, leaning on her swollen stomach and clinging to her so that I did not accidentally slip off, I had watched the oil lamp light up her bright red curls. Then, as I had listened, I had turned slightly to watch the spell-bound faces crowding round us; loving faces, cunning faces, fair faces, mahogany faces, bearded, sad old faces, young bright faces; not a dull or stupid face amongst them.

In this magic circle of friends, I must have fallen asleep, because I have no memory of being put to bed, only of being surrounded by warmth and lovely sounds of singing.

6

MANUEL put down his pen and took off his spectacles, to rub his eyes. He stretched and yawned. He had better make some supper. Mechanically, he felt in his shirt pocket for his cigarettes, took one out and put it between his lips. He was just feeling in his trouser pocket for his matches when he heard the front door bell ring. Patting his empty pockets, he rose stiffly from his chair and looked up at his chronometer. "Five o'clock," he muttered irritably. "Must be Veronica." Veronica Harris was a creature of habit.

Outside, on his doorstep, Veronica, with a plate poised on one hand, turned to Sharon and said cheerfully, "He never answers on the first ring — I don't think he hears all that well."

"Maybe we shouldn't disturb him now." Sharon felt a little embarrassed at being coerced into calling on someone without first telephoning.

"Oh, he's used to me running in and out. He won't mind." She pressed the bell again.

Manuel stood in the middle of his den and wondered if she would go away, if he stayed perfectly still. Veronica was kind, but he had never liked her very much; he was uneasily suspicious that she would have enjoyed taking Kathleen's place, an idea which made him shudder. Since Kathleen's death, he had been distantly polite to her, and reluctantly accepted her baked offerings because she insistently pressed them upon him to the point of rudeness.

He never went to her home; in fact, since Kathleen's death he had rarely visited any of their friends. Their abounding energy made him feel tired. In nursing Kathleen for months, his strength had been sapped, and all he wanted was to be left alone with his grief.

He stood perfectly still in the back of the hall, but the bell was rung for the third time.

"Why not leave the plate on the doorstep?" suggested Sharon, who had already done an eight-hour shift in the Palliative Care Unit and found her feet to be aching abominably.

"The dogs might get it," Veronica replied shortly.

Resigned, Manuel put down his unlit cigarette on the hall table and answered the door. As he opened it, he did his best to show pleasant surprise. He wondered who the other woman was — not a bad-looking judy.

Without hesitation, Veronica stepped into his hall, and he backed hastily. "Ah!" she cooed. "I thought you'd never hear me. How are you doing?" She half-turned towards Sharon, who was still teetering on the step. "I want to introduce you to Elaine's daughter — you remember Elaine? She's staying with me until she finds an apartment. Come in, Sharon."

Old Manuel gave up.

He retreated further into the little hallway,

while Sharon, loath to intrude, stepped into the doorway.

Who, in the name of God, was Elaine? Old Manuel could not remember.

Blithely oblivious to the lack of welcome, Veronica moved firmly through the archway that led to the sitting-room. "I've brought you some cold roast beef," she announced. "I got a roast when I knew Sharon was coming — and it's too much for us, isn't it, Sharon?"

Sharon smiled, and fidgeted uncertainly. What was she supposed to say?

Veronica was asking Manuel if she should put the meat in the refrigerator for him. He hastily took the plate from her. He had no desire to have her poking through the entrails of his refrigerator.

"No. That's OK. I'll take it. I'll put it on the table here." He darted through the opposite arch, which led into the dining-room, with an alacrity surprising for a man in his eighties. If he were quick enough, he thought, he could shoo her out of the door again quite rapidly.

He was too late. Veronica was already seated on the flower-covered settee in the sitting-room, and was patting the cushion beside her to indicate to Sharon that she, too, should sit down.

From the archway, Manuel viewed them both with trepidation, while Veronica chirruped on about Sharon coming to nurse in the Palliative Care Unit, and wasn't it great that they would have such a unit in their closest hospital? Such a shame that there had not been one when Kathleen was so ill.

Manuel stiffened. He was not too clear what exactly a Palliative Care Unit was meant for; but he certainly did not feel like discussing Kathleen in front of a stranger.

The lack of welcome was all too obvious to Sharon, and her colour rose as her embarrassment increased. She glanced directly up at him, wondering how to retreat with grace. What she saw in his face was the closed-off look of suffering, all too familiar to her in her work.

She got up immediately and filled the gap in the conversation which Manuel's silence had caused. "It's suppertime, Veronica," she said firmly. "We should leave Mr Echaniz to enjoy the beef, and perhaps we could meet again another day." She held out her hand to Manuel, and, since Veronica had not introduced her properly, she added, "I'm Sharon Herman. It's nice to meet you."

The relief which flooded Manuel's face was so blatant that she wanted to laugh. Her eyes must have twinkled, because there was the hint of an answering grin suddenly flickering round his wide, thin mouth.

She let go of his hand, and bent to help a disconcerted Veronica up from the low settee.

God's blessings on the girl, the old man thought, as he assured her that he was pleased to meet her.

With her hand under Veronica's elbow, she steered her towards the front door, which was still open, and guided Veronica down the steps. Not too sure what was happening to her, Veronica did her best, and said to Manuel, "I hope you'll like the meat. You can bring the plate back another time."

In her heart, she knew that he would never bring the plate back — the next time she called it would be sitting on the hall table, in a paper bag, waiting for her to pick it up.

He nodded agreeably to both of them. Then he shut the front door after them. He stood leaning against it for a moment, as if to make sure that they would not come back in. Veronica had been Kathleen's devoted friend, he reminded himself for the umpteenth time. "And for her sake, I must be pleasant to her — even if she's a real cross!"

As he retrieved his unlit cigarette and started back to his den to find some matches, he looked down at the plate of meat. He had a great urge to empty it straight into the rubbish bin — but she did mean kindly, and the young woman with her had understood well enough to take her away. Furthermore, it would save him cooking for himself.

He laughed at himself as he put the plate in the refrigerator, and then went to get his long-delayed smoke.

Nice young woman, he considered, as he thankfully drew on his cigarette. Just what does she do in palliative care?

* * *

Outside, as the women went down the steps to the pavement, to walk round to Veronica's house, Sharon said soothingly, "He looked so exhausted and so upset when you mentioned Kathleen, I thought we'd better not stay."

"Oh? I didn't notice." Veronica's expression was puzzled. Then, accepting Sharon's explanation, she said, "Well, I suppose at his age . . ." And left it at that.

* * *

As he smoked, Manuel stood staring out of the window, rocking slightly on his heels, as if he were in a boat and must keep his balance. He did not notice the two ladies pass beyond his budding lilac tree. His mind had reverted to the memoirs he had been writing for Lorilyn, before the visit.

He smiled slowly at a sudden remembrance of a ship's master saying to his Grandfather Barinèta that his crew were a lot of 'hard cases'.

"Oh, aye," he muttered to himself, "So were me granddad and me dad — tough as old boots. They could fight anybody if they had to — even other 'hard cases' out on a spree of a Saturday night."

Very thoughtfully, he stubbed out his cigarette in an overcrowded ash tray, and then stood absently rubbing his nicotine-stained thumb and forefinger together, as if to erase the yellow stain on them.

Was he remembering correctly? Had his life

in Liverpool really been as golden as he had described? Had the other boys with whom he had played been as good mates as he remembered? While he played or went to school, safe in the shelter of his ferocious old grandfather, what was going on between the adult members of the family?

7

MANUEL would soon be six years old, a thin streak of a child, tall for his age. Filled with resentment, he was clutching his bag of marbles to his chest for fear that Andrew would snatch them from him.

Seven-year-old Andrew had just won his best blue-streaked ollie from him, and Manuel felt sure that Andrew had cheated him, but he was not certain how. Tears of rage sprang to his eyes at the smug look on Andrew's face as he stowed the disputed marble in the pocket of his ragged shorts.

"You don't play fair," he yelled. "I'll tell my dad of you!"

Andrew's lips curled. "Who's afraid of your dad? He's not home."

"Me dad's a Master Mariner, and he'll get you when he does come home," cried Manuel furiously. "So there!"

The youngest of five unruly boys, Andrew was the offspring of a Filipino and an Irish girl, who lived in a nearby street. Nearly a year older than the young Basque, he enjoyed lording it over the smaller lads in the vicinity. Now he made a lewd gesture. "My dad's a stoker, and he's stronger 'n yours. He's stronger than anybody in the world!"

Too angry to care that he was probably stirring up a hornet's nest, Manuel went a step closer.

He thrust his chin towards Andrew and ground his teeth menacingly. He snarled, "No, he isn't! And you cheated! I want me bluey back."

Andrew pushed his face close to Manuel's. Blue eyes, bloodshot with conjunctivitis, glared into clear brown ones, as Andrew made the worst grimace he could conjure up. "You're not getting it back, see. You shut up, or I'll put me brothers on to you!" He stepped back, and grinned. "Me dad showed us how to break a man's arm real quick last night." To demonstrate, he did a vicious twist with his right hand.

Apprehension cooled Manuel's rage; he was scared suddenly of being beaten up by five known bullies. He glanced quickly around in search of adult help. None was visible.

Brian Wing, even younger than Manuel, had been watching Manuel's defiance of Andrew in silent astonishment. Now, he squatted quickly down on his heels and began to pick up those of his marbles still on the pavement. Deftly, he shovelled them into a cotton drawstring bag. Manuel knew that he was preparing to run back home to the laundry, if a fight should start; Brian did not worry about being called a cowardy custard. When trouble threatened, he was the first to vanish. At this moment, as he rose to his feet, he was beaming amiably at both prospective combatants, his eyes thin slits above pudgy cheeks.

Manuel glanced again at Andrew. With a satisfied smirk, the bigger boy had taken the blue out of his pocket, and was holding it up to the sunlight. Manuel snatched unsuccessfully at it, and Andrew laughed.

Brian fled.

From round the curve of the street suddenly floated Grandma Micaela's strident voice. "Manuel! Manuel Echaniz! Where are you?"

With total relief, Manuel edged back from Andrew, and shrieked, "Coming, Grandma!" Then he turned and ran for home. It left Andrew in command of the field — but, Manuel solaced himself as he tore back to the safety of Grandma, he now had nobody to play with.

Thanks to Grandma's calling him, his retreat was an honourable one; even Andrew would admit that. When mothers called, you responded fairly promptly. If you did not, you got soundly slapped the minute you showed your face at home — and there was always the overwhelming threat from the females of the family, "When your dad gets in, I'll tell him about you!" Fathers whacked much harder than mothers did; they sometimes took their belt to you.

Grandma bent to catch him in the curve of her arm. "Come along, dumpling," she said in Basque. "We're going up to the market. Your dad's docking tomorrow; and your mam wants to have chicken ready for him when he gets home."

"Do I have to come?" asked Manuel in a whining voice. He had been to school, had his tea, and had then gone out into the street to play, only to find himself up against Andrew. He was tired, and the thought of the long, boring walk up to St John's Market made his legs ache.

"Yes, dear. With Auntie Maria only just out of hospital, she can't watch you. Who'll take care of you while we're out? Your grandpa's gone over to the Baltic for a game of chequers and a drink."

With the threat of Andrew and his brothers still in his mind, Manuel saw the point of this, and made no further demur.

* * *

On her return from the hospital the previous day, Manuel had watched his spinster Aunt Maria being laid carefully on the old sofa in the big kitchen-living-room, so that Grandma and Mother would not have to run up and downstairs to and from her bedroom while nursing her.

She was his mother's elder sister, and she and Manuel were great friends. She had taught him to play snap and snakes and ladders, and she usually took care of him whenever the others were out.

Now, back home, she was exceedingly quiet, her face white and haggard, except for a single hectic pink spot on either cheek.

It was called convalescence, which Manuel understood was another word for getting better. But he had noticed that all the ladies who had crowded in to see her during the last twenty-four hours looked sad, and sighed. "TB's a terrible thing, God save us," they had murmured to each other. Then they had spoken to Auntie Maria in bright, artificial voices.

Even seventy-eight years later, as he wrote about them in his Canadian home, for Lorilyn, he could still remember clearly the black-clad women, their arms wrapped in their woollen shawls, despite the summer heat, while they smiled determinedly and chirruped like birds, as they bent over the stricken invalid.

* * *

Grandma took his hand and led him up the worn sandstone steps into the soot-blackened house, to see if his mother and two of her Basque friends were ready to set out.

Rosita was just wrapping Manuel's new baby sister, Francesca, into the folds of the black shawl she wore. He felt a sting of jealousy at the baby's privileged position in his mother's arms; she had usurped his place. Admittedly, Grandma had been particularly kind since Francesca's birth — but Grandma was kind to the baby as well.

As he waited in the crowded kitchen-living-room for the women to marshal themselves, Aunt Maria put out a bone-thin hand and held his fingertips, as she smiled up at him. Manuel looked down at her. Neither said anything, but Manuel found it consoling that he still appeared to be his aunt's favourite; she had never even held Francesca in her arms, as far as he was aware.

It was always a matter of earnest debate between Grandma Micaela, Rosita and Aunt Maria whether it was better to go to the market early in the morning, when there was lots of choice; or to go at the end of the day, when it was possible to beat down the prices of wares which vendors did not want to have to take back home. Since a live chicken was as fresh in the late afternoon as it would have been in the early morning, they had decided to go at the last possible moment.

Aunt Maria felt well enough to be disappointed that she would miss the excitement of the market, and she said wistfully that she wished she had an invalid chair to go out in.

Grandma grunted. Invalid chairs were beyond the dreams of avarice, so she said comfortingly, "Never mind, dear, save your strength for tomorrow. We'll get you up and dressed in time to greet Pedro when he arrives. He'd be so happy to see you up and about — so you mustn't tire yourself today."

Mollified, she allowed Grandma to prop her up with another cushion and put an extra shawl around her, though the day was warm. With a glass of water, her spectacles and her rosary on a stool by her couch, she settled down resignedly to await their return.

By the time the four chattering ladies reached the beginning of the narrow lane at the back of the market, where poultry was sold, Manuel's feet were dragging through the straw which littered the cobblestones. Fine beads of perspiration lay on his forehead, and he clutched Rosita's black skirt, in order to keep up with her. The smell of poultry droppings and other manure lay like a blanket over the crowded lane, and was not improved by the intense odour of dozens of unbathed women, who sat amid their goods for sale. He felt stifled and began to grizzle.

Amid the din and the thick black skirts flapping round him, his wails went unremarked. Men and women shouted, puppies yapped, ducks quacked; fouled in their own excrement, kittens mewed pitifully and scratched at the bars of their cages; next to a cage of clucking hens, a lone goose hissed at passersby. Only rabbits crouched quietly, their quivering noses a tiny indication that they were still alive, despite the heat.

The approach of a small group of Basque women, chattering loudly in their own peculiar language, did not raise the hopes of the purveyors of poultry. They, too, were hot and weary. An impending Basque invasion made their spirits wilt: if the women bought anything, it would only be after strenuous bargaining; it would surely make any stallholder they fastened upon late home for his tea.

After strolling the length of the still busy lane, the target of the Basque attack became a small cage holding three hens, which appeared not to have sold because they were rather scrawny. Before showing any direct interest in the birds, Grandma Micaela led a distracting minor scrimmage by examining carefully a pair of rabbits. She poked at them through the bars of their cage, and they stared back at her without hope. She drew Rosita's attention to them, and she also poked disparagingly at them. Rosita's two friends, who had accompanied them, pursed their lips and agreed loudly with one another that they weren't worth sixpence each. The man in charge of them said something inaudible under his breath.

Sighing, they looked desultorily at a pair of slaughtered hens, not yet cleaned or feathered, hanging heads down in front of the next small stall.

"Here ye are, ladies," called the stallholder, beaming at them. "A real nice dinner. Good fat birds. One and sixpence each. Feather 'em yerself." He unhooked the hens and held them against his forearm for inspection. Four ladies pinched the hens' breasts and declared in chorus that they had no fat on them.

The man lost his amiability as quickly as it had been assumed; the price he had asked was fair for two good birds. "Pack of bloody Israelites!" he muttered, and turned angrily away to accost another shopper.

Though Grandma's eyes were weak and she could not see any of the products very well, prompted by Rosita, she opened negotiations with the man who had three live hens. They were, apparently, the last of his offerings for that day; several empty cages had already been piled on a hand-cart behind him.

"What do you think, Mother?" Rosita asked.

Grandma bent down to squint carefully at the hens. One of them tried to peck her, and she hastily drew back. She nodded her head negatively, and said dolefully, "They might make good soup. Nothing on them for anything else."

She glanced up at the vendor. "How much do you want for them?" she inquired, her English difficult to understand.

"How much?" interjected Rosita. Her two friends stood behind her, politely silent, ready to murmur approbation or denigration, as required.

"A bob each," he told her, hoping to get rid of three birds in one sale, so that he could wander off for a much-needed pint of bitter, before going home.

Rosita translated the price, and Grandma's heavy eyebrows rose, as if in shock. "For those?" She turned to their silent friends for confirmation of her horror at such an outrageous price. Like a Greek chorus, they nodded agreement and stared coldly at the stallholder. Still holding his mother's skirt, Manuel scrubbed one small boot against another, and sighed; he had seen this pantomime so often. He watched a woodlouse, surprised by his shuffling feet from under a few wisps of straw, hasten into hiding beneath a couple of feathers.

Meanwhile, the face of the chicken vendor went as dark as an angry cockerel's comb. "Wass the matter with 'em?" he asked indignantly. "Best roastin' chicken you could buy. Why, one of 'em would feed six, easy."

Manuel saw his mother's generous chest expand, as she readied herself to dive into the fray. It was going to be a long and boring battle. He let go of her skirt and wandered down the sloping lane for a few yards, to look at ugly white dishes laid out on straw; they were tended by three Irish women from the north end of the city.

"Mind your clumsy feet!" one of them shouted at him, as he stumbled over a cobblestone. He backed hastily away; to a small boy, they seemed very big and threatening.

Further down, towards Elliott Street, there were still a few puppies for sale, and he paused to watch them, as they stumbled over each other in the dirty cage. In the background, he could hear his mother arguing volubly, as she sought to bring down the price of the hens; she was demanding that they be taken out of the cage, so that she could feel how much flesh there was on the unfortunate creatures.

He was wondering if he could persuade his father, when he came home, to get him a puppy, when there was a chorus of female shrieks accompanied by a roar of male anger. He jumped, and whipped around to see if his mother was all right.

His view was blocked by a large woman with a shopping basket on her arm. He tried to edge around her. She looked down kindly at him, and said, "Careful, sonny, mind the pile of saucepans behind me." Then, at a slight noise, she glanced back. "Holy Mary!" she cried shrilly, and jumped to one side, sending the pile of iron saucepans in all directions, so that cursing market women leapt to their feet to avoid them.

Flapping awkwardly on clipped wings, a terrified, squawking hen sailed over their heads. The poor bird was unable to gain any height and came down to earth, momentarily, in front of Manuel. He laughed, and instinctively grabbed at it. It managed to scuttle a few feet away from him towards Elliott Street. Then, seeing a break in the highly amused crowd, it took off again in a series of desperate hops and flaps.

Manuel forgot his mother. Hens lived in cages, so this one must have escaped. In high glee, he scampered after it, dodging in and out between piles of kitchenware and ironmongery. He bumped into two young men entering the lane. "Watch it, kiddo!" one shouted after him, irritably.

Driven by panic and despair, the hen managed to soar upward a little. Absorbed in the chase, Manuel ran faster.

As the bird descended, to perch for a moment on top of a fire hydrant in busy Elliott Street, the boy plunged across the pavement towards it, tripping up and confusing the crowd of office workers hurrying homeward. A young clerk made a playful grab at the bird, to the amusement of the girl accompanying him. The frantic hen immediately hopped off its perch on the edge of the pavement, and staggered into the heavy traffic, as if to cross the road. Intent on catching it, Manuel shot after it.

The hen ran directly under a work horse pulling a small cart. The horse reared in fright. The cart skidded past Manuel. It missed him by a hand's breadth, as the carter swore and fought to rein in the animal. A few yards behind came three errand boys on their bicycles, hurrying to finish the last deliveries of the day. They swerved to avoid the child. Two of them collided and tumbled off, the packages in their front baskets scattering amid both lines of traffic; the third boy managed to reach the gutter, and dismounted; he yelled imprecations at a heedless Manuel, while more cyclists wobbled and dodged around the two bikes tangled in the middle of the lane. Two chauffeur-driven private cars came to a screeching halt, and the drivers impatiently blew their klaxon horns.

All traffic was coming quickly to a halt; and harsh words were exchanged between drivers and carters in the near lane, as horses, set to breast the upward slope of the street, were hauled to a clattering stop, their shoes striking sparks from the setts, and foam from their mouths splattering passersby.

Nobody attempted to rescue Manuel — or the hen.

At the sight of the traffic coming the other way, he had, in the middle of the street, suddenly ceased his headlong chase; he could see that, on the other side, the hen had found a safe perch on the high windowsill of a bank.

With disorganized traffic still edging past him, both before and behind, he was suddenly very frightened. As he stood frozen, at the back of him the driver of a carriage with two ladies in it, leaned down, whip in hand, and shouted at him, "Gerroff the street!" He glanced up over his shoulder, and the high wheels, far higher than him, rolled past him dangerously closely. He turned back towards the opposite pavement. A tram, unable to stop quickly, rolled slowly past him on its rails. It was followed by a brewer's dray which had been successfully slowed by the drayman; it was pulled by two huge horses and the dray itself was piled high with barrels of beer. Though the upward slope meant it would be hard to start the horses again, the driver drew to a careful stop, thus blocking any further traffic in that lane. He stood up and called to the frightened child, "Get on pavement, luv. Quick, now."

Though all Manuel could see was the slavering mouth and huge, bronze-coloured legs of the lead horse, he heard the voice, and he obediently trotted, almost under the great animal's nose, to the safety of the pavement.

As the traffic began to move again, he stood, bewildered, on the kerb, and looked up at the hen. From the safety of the bank's windowsill, the hen opened its eyes and looked down at him with grave suspicion; then, the lids closed again.

Distraught, the child began to cry.

Standing against the bank wall, an elderly newspaperman was calling to the homegoing crowd of pedestrians, "*Echo! Liverpool Echo!* Read all about it!" Perspiration was running down his bulbous red nose, as he shoved a neatly folded newspaper into any hand proffering the necessary coppers for it. On a blackboard beside him was scrawled the day's headline, *Countess of Derby Opens Crippled Children's Hospital*.

He glanced down at the weeping child, while saying to a customer, "Fourpence change, Sir. What's to do, lad?"

"I want me mam," howled Manuel, hastily taking refuge beside the news-vendor's second blackboard, which proclaimed in white chalk, *Big Fire at Huskisson Dock*. "And I can't reach me hen!" He pointed upwards to the refuge on the windowsill.

The newspaperman squinted quickly upwards, and grinned. The hen had squatted down, eyes still closed, and looked like a bundle of feathers. "That's yours? Not to worry, lad. Soon as this little rush is over, I'll get it for yez. It don't look like it's goin' to fly away."

Manuel nodded, wiped his nose on the sleeve of his jersey, and continued to weep, though at a lower pitch. He had no idea where he was, and he didn't really care what happened to the hen; all he wanted was his mother.

Meanwhile, Rosita and Grandma had assumed that Manuel was still in the market lane, looking at the pets for sale, and had contentedly bought the two remaining live hens. The stallholder, still fuming over the loss of the third hen, sullenly wrung the birds' necks, while Grandma went to the nearest greengrocery stall by the door of the main market, and bought onions and garlic.

The crowd in the lane was thinning rapidly; the Irish women were packing up their remaining plates; some of the disconsolate, unsold pets had already been whisked away. Manuel was not visible, and Rosita became anxious.

To save her carrying the baby around unnecessarily, her two friends ran the length of the lane, but there was no place in which he could have hidden. They came back panting and gesticulating.

"Who you lookin' for?" asked a young woman, hooking a cage of kittens on to the handlebars of a bicycle, near the Elliott Street entrance.

Rosita told her.

"Oh, aye," she replied readily. "He were nearly run over, he was. You'll mebbe find 'im across the road. I'll bet you'll find 'im in the station there — kids love trains." She smiled, and mounted her bike and wobbled over the cobblestones in the general direction to which she had pointed.

"Oh, goodness!" Rosita exclaimed, her face paling, as, united, the four women pushed their way to the edge of the Elliott Street pavement. A break in the traffic revealed Manuel, with his mouth as wide as a choir boy's singing a Te Deum, shrieking, "I want me mam."

Rosita's expression changed immediately to one of parental outrage. With baby Francesca bouncing on her chest and followed by the other three, shawls flapping like the wings of angry magpies, she surged through a break in the traffic, to face her tearstained son. Before the child could do more than turn his face to her and reduce his sobs, she scolded him, "What do you mean by running off like this? We bin scared stiff for you. I'll tell your dad about you, when he gets home!" With her free hand, she grabbed him by the shoulder and shook him.

Far from being more upset by this, Manuel recognized the typical reaction of a mam who had indeed been scared. His sobs became sniffs, as she alternately cajoled and scolded again.

Meanwhile, Grandma Micaela, who was feeling extremely tired, looked on silently, and the news-vendor asked her, "Do you want the 'en, Queen?" He pointed up to the bank windowsill, on which the hen lay inert.

Grandma blinked, and her eyes followed the line of the man's finger. She peered at the bank wall. Halfway up, she saw a vague, copper-coloured lump. "On the windowsill," the man said impatiently.

Grandma was under five feet tall; the sill was impossibly high up for her. "Could you possibly reach it?" she asked shyly.

The man grinned. "Anything to oblige a lady," he responded with sudden gallantry. He reached up and managed to gather the bird into his hand. After inspecting it dubiously, he said, "It looks like dead, Missus."

"It's fresh enough to cook," she told him, with a little laugh. Her faded blue eyes, though partially clouded by cataracts, still had a twinkle in them, and the news-vendor returned to his pitch feeling pleased with himself.

Grandma laid the hen on top of the other two in her calico bag. Rosita had finished her scolding and was wiping Manuel's face with the corner of her apron. Her friends stopped gossiping about the high price of rabbits — and the party straggled down Hanover Street towards home.

At home, the oil lamp had been lit. Grandpa was seated at the kitchen table, writing in his ledger. Behind him, on the wall, the huge map on which Pedro recorded his voyages, glimmered softly, the net of inky lines linking the ports of call looking like a tangled mass of black cotton thread.

As the shoppers entered, he closed the book wearily. He nodded to his wife and to Rosita, as they entered and thankfully plonked the shopping bags on the draining board by the kitchen sink. The baby was beginning to whimper from hunger, and Grandma said she would make a pot of tea before starting the evening meal. Rosita nodded agreement, and sat down in a rocking chair. She unbuttoned her black blouse and modestly arranged her shawl round the baby's head and her breast, while she fed her new daughter.

Manuel slunk to the other side of the fireplace, where Aunt Maria had, in their absence, established herself in an easy chair. He leaned against his aunt, who put down the knitting she had been struggling to do and put her arm round him. He was grateful for her presence; he had missed her during her stay in hospital.

He could not have articulated his sense of desertion as he watched his mother feed the baby. He only knew he longed to be cuddled by her and to lay his head on her milky breast. Not even when she called him her *big* boy, and sent him off to school with a loving pat on his behind, was he comforted.

Auntie Maria suddenly began to cough. She withdrew her arm, and fumbled for her handkerchief in her dressing-gown pocket. She put it to her mouth, and tried to smile at Manuel over its folds.

As she had taught him, he stepped back from her while the spasm lasted. "I don't want to splutter all over you," she had once explained to him. "It's not very nice."

Aunt Maria's cough was part and parcel of Manuel's childhood; he slept in the same room as she did, and the sound of it comforted him when he woke in the night after a bad dream; it meant that she was awake, and if he were very scared, he could scramble out of bed and run to her. It puzzled him, however, that, unlike his mother, she would never let him into her bed, however much he was shivering with fright; and she was the only one of his doting relations who did not kiss him; even Grandpa kissed him sometimes. He occasionally thought that he would never understand the idiosyncrasies of grown-ups.

After feeding Francesca, Rosita laid the dozing child in Manuel's old cradle, near the fireplace, but far enough from it not to be spattered by the fat in which Grandma was frying fish for tea. She then unpacked the three hens and took them out into the brick-lined backyard, to feather and singe them. Though the stallholder had obligingly wrung the necks of the two hens, he had complained sourly that he would not have lost the third one if Grandma had not insisted on the cage being opened. He could not run after the flying bird himself, he said bitterly, because it would have meant leaving his stall untended in an area where petty theft was a fine art.

After the meal, the hens were brought in and drawn on the draining board, giving Manuel an early lesson in anatomy, as he watched the operation.

The naked birds were then washed and hung up in the larder overnight. Manuel stared up at them, and decided they did not look much different from Francesca, after she had been bathed in front of the kitchen fire.

That night he dreamed that he had been hung up in the larder, by his feet. He was too terrified even to run across to Auntie Maria's bed, and he lay quivering under his cotton sheet until sleep overtook him again.

8

IN the golden summer days of 1914 his view of his world was that of a child, considered Manuel. His was a permanent world which Grandpa Barinèta would rule for ever. Ample food arrived on the table at least three times a day, and boys did their best not to offend Grandma Micaela or Mother, who ruled the kitchen-living-room like royal queens.

Close by his home was the world of school, where nuns in white wimples and long black dresses talked of eternity and the need to be a good Catholic boy; so that when one died — an event which would take place so far ahead that one could not envision it — one could, in a state of grace, enjoy eternity sitting on the right hand of God, where, hoped Little Manuel fervently, there would be no nuns with sharp voices and spanking rulers to tell you that you had been naughty again. He had secretly wondered if God liked nuns. Old Manuel reflected that the latter thought had seemed so wicked that he had hastily stifled it and had hoped that St Peter would not make a note of it.

At the edge of his world, not counting St John's Market, lay St Peter's Church in Seel Street, where, every Sunday morning, he went to Mass with either Grandma or his mother. Though the conversation of the congregation was split between Spanish, Basque and English, the Mass was said in Latin; his father said that it did not matter which port he was in, the Mass was always there, always the same — in Latin. Little Manuel began to think that there was something magical about Latin.

Some of the priests were Jesuits and good scholars. Scholarliness was not something particularly appreciated in the dockside parish, but the Jesuits' awesome reputation as missionaries, many of whom had come to untimely ends in foreign parts, gained them a grudging respect. They always made Little Manuel feel nervous. They seemed so disciplined; and he could not imagine them sneaking off to see a music hall show or having a drink in the local, like any normal human being.

At home, he took for granted the constant work which engaged Grandma and his mother, how they washed and scrubbed and cooked, knitted and sewed, in a house with one cold-water tap and no electricity or gas. In addition to their usual chores, they endured the house being periodically filled with emigrants, all wanting to prepare food, wash clothes and cope with husbands and babies.

He never considered that his grandfather might be very tired and long to retire, but could not because he had never been able to save much; or that he might be homesick for his native country. It never occurred to him that his father had any feelings beyond affection for his son — and a curious desire to lie on her bed with his mother, with the big iron key turned in the doorlock.

It seemed a very safe world, though Mother sometimes announced herself worried. Exactly what she meant by that, Little Manuel was not very sure, except that it manifested itself in the form of a sharp slap if he did not come straight home from school, and an irate warning never to go with a strange man or accept a sweet from one; the vague warnings of dire results, if he ever took a sweetie from a stranger, remained with him long after he understood what lay behind them, so that even as an adult he always refused a proffered sweet.

The fear of unemployment must have haunted his father, considered Old Manuel. Some of his friends' fathers were out of work from time to time; and their mams grew short-tempered, and hoped they would not have another baby that year.

Mr Connolly, who lived next door with his wife, Bridget, and little Mary and Baby Joey, was periodically without employment. But he was more cheerful than his neighbours, and he would sit on his front doorstep and play simple hand games with Manuel and Mary. It was he who taught the little boy how to catch and throw an old tennis ball. He was so good at lip-reading that it was a long time before Manuel understood that he was deaf, the usual fate of ships' scalers, who spent their working lives inside ships' boilers chipping away at accumulated scale, a job which created tremendous noise.

Pedro was fortunate in being steadily employed by a small freighting company sailing out of

Liverpool, though he always hoped that when times improved he would get a better ship. When he was at home for a few days, he would take Manuel swimming, or up to the park to play ball. Sometimes, they walked down to the Pier Head, and, looking out across the river, he taught his small son how to identify the ownership of the vessels plying the river, by the colours of their funnels. Manuel also learned that each country had its own flag fluttering from ships belonging to it; when he and his father got home, they found the countries on the big map pinned to the wall of the kitchen-living-room.

Pedro had a shrewd eye for what might interest a boy and told him stories about the ports he had visited, including small details which Old Manuel still remembered, like the kind of sweets on sale in the streets of Bombay or the kind of clothing that ladies in Yokahama wore.

"You'll see them all yourself, one day," his father assured him, certain that his boy would follow in his footsteps, though with better qualifications.

* * *

As he wrote for Lorilyn, Old Manuel wondered if Faith would remember him with the same uncritical love with which he remembered his father. He doubted it; his Canadian wife and child seemed to live lives crammed with commitments. They were far too busy to spend much time listening to what had happened to him in his last absence from them; they appeared to exist deep in a women's world of school, voluntary work, dancing classes, music lessons, skating classes, teas and ladies' bridge parties. Sometimes, Kathleen did a spell of nursing which gave her a whole new collection of women with whom to become involved. Men seemed to be expected to keep to their world and not intrude — even to their half of a room, if they were at a party, Manuel remembered with a rueful smile.

Perhaps it was his own fault, he thought. Even when he had become a marine architect, he had sometimes been away for weeks. As a seaman from a family of seamen, this had not appeared unusual to him; but it had probably made Kathleen and Faith cling more closely to each other for support.

He sighed, and paused in his writing to light another cigarette. He had got to know Kathleen in her final illness better than he had ever known her before, and, in his current loneliness, he regretted that he had not tried harder to be closer to her in their earlier married life. They had not been unhappy, he considered, just not quite as happy as they might have been.

In marrying a Canadian and settling in Canada, Manuel had achieved a much higher standard of living than he could have reasonably hoped for if he had stayed in Liverpool. After qualifying as a marine architect, he had worked in Montreal, and he had had to acquire a working knowledge of yet another language, French; it had added to the difficulties of adjusting himself to North American life.

After enjoying the close support of an extended Basque community in Liverpool and Bilbao, he had been, for a time, intensely lonely. It was some time before he met anyone who knew what a Basque was, and he remembered his intense thankfulness when he met a sprinkling of fellow Basques and could speak his own language to them. His neighbours were supremely indifferent that he could switch in and out of four languages — being multilingual was something that born Canadians were not supposed to worry about; English-speaking Canadians seemed to take it for granted that even their French compatriots would be able to speak English — just as the Spaniards expected the Basques to be competent in Spanish, thought Manuel tartly.

Though sometimes he tripped up, for Kathleen's sake he made a great effort to sink into her world. He had, however, done his best to teach Faith to speak Basque, and as a little child she had always spoken to him in that language — until she went to school, when, under the tight conforming pressure of her school life, she had soon discovered that it was convenient to forget that her father was an immigrant.

As he worked on his notes for his granddaughter, Old Manuel wondered if his quiet, capable father felt like a stranger in his own home, when he carried a kitbag full of grubby clothes up the steps of Grandpa Barinèta's house, at the end of long boring weeks at sea in a tramp steamer.

Was it difficult for Pedro Echaniz to

re-establish a rapport with his wife and mother-in-law and his rather forbidding father-in-law, all of whom seemed to talk to him at once?

Mulling over his memories of his father sitting in the crowded kitchen-living-room, smoking his pipe and listening to the chatter, Old Manuel realized that, sometimes, it may have been quite hard; only when he was alone with Little Manuel had the dam burst, and Pedro himself had talked and talked, creating a fabulous world of distant places and homespun philosophy for his small son. God keep him, prayed Old Manuel, with a surge of love.

* * *

The day after the three chickens had been carefully prepared for cooking, Pedro had run up the steps of his father-in-law's house. The front door was hospitably ajar, and through it wafted an excellent smell of cooking — olive oil, garlic, onions, herbs and chicken. How good it would be to eat some decent food!

In the narrow hall, he slung his kitbag to the floor and threw down his heavy jacket and peaked cap.

"Rosita!" he shouted, over the clamour of the riveters in the workshop immediately to the rear of the house. Dear God! How could she stand that kind of noise all day long? "Rosita!"

She heard him and came running, plump face beaming and blue eyes flashing, her mass of wavy red hair bouncing round her shoulders. She flew into his arms, and, over the odours of cooking and babies, he smelled the freshness of her. He always swore to himself that every time he returned home he fell in love with her again.

Before the family caught up with them, he hugged and kissed her, cupping one breast in an eager hand, feeling the dampness of her milk soaking through her starched flowered pinafore. She giggled happily; seconds of privacy were precious in a house full of relations — and often with emigrants as well.

He dropped his hand, as his tiny mother-in-law came pattering after her daughter, followed closely by Grandpa Juan Barinèta. Behind them, Manuel stood shyly by the kitchen door, waiting to be noticed.

Over his wife's head, Pedro greeted his parents-in-law; he was struck by how old they seemed suddenly to have become. He was fond of both of them, and was thankful that Rosita had their company while he was at sea.

With a twinge of anxiety for the old people, he loosened himself from Rosita, to bend and kiss Micaela's cheek. He then embraced Juan.

"It's been a long time," Grandpa said, keeping his arm round the younger man's shoulder. "Come in, boy. Come in."

Pedro moved down the passage, and then saw Manuel. He stopped and squatted down close to him. "How's my big lad?" he asked, and opened his arms to him, and the boy went joyfully into them. There was the feel of his father's beard on his cheek, the smell of sweat and tobacco and wine, the total comfort of his being.

Manuel chuckled in his father's ear, and said shyly that he was all right.

In the steamy kitchen, Pedro stretched himself and looked around the familiar domain. Auntie Maria shyly and carefully rose from her chair to greet him; she was dressed in her best black skirt and black silk blouse. Jet earrings hung against her cheeks.

"Maria! You're up and about!" exclaimed Pedro, as if he had already been primed by Grandma what to say to the stricken woman. Without hesitation, he went to her and put his arm protectively round her shoulders, as she subsided again into her chair, and kissed her on both cheeks. "I thought you would still be in hospital."

She glowed, as she looked up at him with frank yearning. Why tell him that she was at home because the doctors could do no more for her?

"I'm doing quite well," she affirmed. "I can sit in the yard — or on the steps, and I'm hoping to walk out soon."

He looked into the big blue eyes turned up towards him, so like his wife's but without her beauty; and he knew that she was lying. He played up to her, however, and joked about all the young Basques who would ask her out when she could get about again. Manuel came to lean against her, so as to be included in his father's attention. He realized that nobody but his father ever kissed Auntie Maria, and he sensed his aunt's pleasure at being so closely touched by another human being, though he did not yet fully understand her inner loneliness, caused by other people's fear of catching her dread disease.

Grandma Micaela turned quickly away from the little group, and went to fetch some wine glasses from the dresser. There was a lump in her throat and she wanted to cry. With Leo gone and Agustin rarely in Liverpool, her daughters were doubly precious to her, and yet she had to accept that Maria was preparing for a much longer journey.

She took a big breath, and, with her hands full of glasses, she turned back to the family. "Let's have a drink," she suggested gaily. "Juan, dear. Get a bottle out for us."

As Grandpa produced a bottle of good Basque wine, Rosita said cheerfully to Pedro, "You haven't met your daughter yet!"

She bent down and scooped the child out of her wooden cradle, and thrust her into her father's arms. Francesca stared up at him with some perplexity. She opened her tiny mouth to cry. Pedro suddenly laughed, and said to Rosita, "She's the dead spit of you. Look at her! Blue eyes and all that red fluff on her head."

His wife playfully shook her red mane over the baby's face. "She's goin' to be just like her mam, aren't you, luv," she said to the child, and Pedro's loins ached, as the creamy skin of his wife's neck came close to him.

The baby whimpered uncertainly, and Rosita snatched her back. Manuel promptly eased himself on to his father's knee. Over his head,

Pedro asked her, "Did you have a bad time with her?"

"Not too bad," she told him.

He took a sip of his wine, and looked wickedly over his glass at her. She flounced provocatively away from him to return the child to her cradle, and stood, hand on hip, watching him, as she rocked the cradle with her foot to soothe the baby.

The kitchen fell silent after this as everyone sipped their wine, and listened to the tolling of the bell of the dock railway train, as it passed along the street under the overhead railway, and to the usual turmoil of the machinery in the buildings at the back of the house.

While the train clattered rhythmically on its way, Pedro stared at his half-empty glass and wondered what to say. Once greetings had been exchanged, he had to pick up the threads of his life ashore; it was like trying to understand the gist of a novel after commencing to read it in the middle of the volume.

Rosita wrote to him regularly during his absences, though, occasionally, he received the letters only when he returned to Liverpool; in any case, they did not really convey to him the daily ups and downs of the family. It took time to understand all the references made in the course of the family's conversations.

There were times when Pedro felt that his shipmates were closer to him than his family was; they certainly knew more about each other than their families did. He had sailed with some of them for years. Yet he loved Rosita; and

Manuel was someone to boast about through many a monotonous day at sea. He felt guilty that his first inner reaction to the new baby had been that it would be something to tell his mates about when he returned to sea — another beautiful redhead. He ran his fingers through his roughly cut hair; it was sticky with salt. He could use a good scrub down in the old tin bath; but he could have it only when all the family had gone to bed, and he could have the privacy of the empty kitchen-living-room. He sighed, and puffed at his pipe.

The awkward silence was broken by Manuel. With his head against his father's shoulder, he asked shyly, in Basque, "What've you brought me, Daddy?"

Pedro immediately snapped out of his reverie and put down his pipe. "Aha!" he exclaimed mysteriously. "Wouldn't you like to know?" He clutched the boy tighter, enjoying the child's warm trust.

Manuel giggled and pushed himself off Pedro's knee. "Let's see," he urged, and trotted towards the kitbag, still lying in the hall.

Underneath all the impedimenta of a seaman's life, just when it seemed to Manuel that his father must have lost the gifts he had purchased, they unearthed a cream jug in the shape of a cow, for Grandma to add to her collection of little jugs, and a big tin of good Virginia tobacco for Grandpa.

A parcel, wrapped in tissue paper, was handed to Rosita, who cautiously peeped into it, and then blushed and giggled when she discovered a lace-trimmed petticoat. She hastily wrapped it up again, while Manuel's mouth drooped and his eyes grew wide with disappointment. A further burrowing in the bag produced a pretty pair of hair combs for Auntie Maria.

Pedro glanced up at Manuel, as he felt down to the bottom of the bag. "I hope I haven't lost it," he said, with mock anxiety. He pulled out an old sweater, and then another one. But the second sweater was wrapped around something.

Very carefully, Pedro loosened the bundle and lifted out a model yacht, its mast and sails folded flat. He handed it to his son. "Guaranteed to sail — and not to sink," he told his son.

Manuel took it gingerly from him. Nobody amongst his school friends had anything to equal it — he was sure of that. "Will it really sail?" he asked, as he twisted it round to have a better look at it.

"Given a decent breeze it will — like a real one. Tomorrow, we'll go up to the park and try it on the pond. You'll soon get the hang of it."

The pond? That was where grown-up men took their model yachts, yachts carefully pushed through the town in old perambulators, because they were too big to carry.

The child's face was beatific. He determined that he would never let Andrew get even a glimpse of the little boat; he was not going to chance its being taken from him.

Grandpa leaned forward. "Let me see it, Mannie."

Manuel used both hands to pass it to his grandfather, and the old man took a closer look at it: the brass rails, the finely polished wood, and the correct rigging. "Nice piece of work," he said. "Must've taken a while to do that."

"Aye, it did. It's to scale."

Juan handed the boat back to his grandson. "You don't take that up to the park by yourself," he instructed. "When your dad's away, I'll come with you." He, too, was aware of the predatory children, some of them homeless, who ran wild in the streets.

Manuel promised.

Rosita bent over them, to admire the little vessel, and Pedro slyly pinched her bottom.

She shot a shocked glance of reproof at him. "Not in public!" she hissed, trying to look suitably outraged.

A further diversion, which relieved Pedro's feeling of strangeness in his own home, was created by the sound of hobnailed boots in the hall, as Jean Baptiste Saitua and two of his sons stepped tentatively through the open front door; it did not take long for the Basque community to learn through the grapevine any bit of news, like a return from sea, and these old friends of the entire family felt free to step in and inquire how Pedro was.

Grandpa leaned back in his chair to look down the hall. "Come in," he shouted. "How are you, Jean — Domingo — Vicente?"

They tramped in and shook Pedro's hand and slapped him on the back, while Rosita quietly slid over to the fireplace, to remove the chicken casserole from the oven and place it on the warming shelf above the fire; she winked at Aunt Maria, sitting quietly watching the scene. "Heaven only knows when we'll get our tea," she muttered to her sister. "Would you like another glass of wine?"

Maria smiled gently and nodded. "Yes."

Grandma, equally resigned to a long session of male reminiscences, was already getting more glasses and another bottle of wine. Jean Baptiste was a bosun with a small Basque shipping company sailing out of Liverpool; he had a couple of nights' leave. Domingo was a ferryman, and Vicente was in his last year at school. After much joking, Vicente was allowed a glass of wine, though Jean Baptiste said his mother would probably be after him, if she smelled it on his breath.

The cakes intended for dessert were brought out and handed round, and the party became quite merry. Pedro abandoned hope of a bath that evening, and Rosita was beginning to wonder if she could stretch her chicken casserole to feed three extra men, when Maria began to cough violently. The hilarity ceased immediately, and Grandma said, "Don't worry. I'll take her upstairs — it's just the smoke."

Fat, jolly Jean Baptiste quickly rose from the table, however, his heavy jowls suddenly drooping. "Ah! I forgot!" He looked round the room, thick with blue tobacco smoke. "I'm sorry, Maria." He turned to Grandpa, and said, "We can meet in the Baltic later on; some of the other lads'll be sure to be there."

With grave dignity, he eased himself and his sons out of the crowded room, calling his thanks to Grandma for the wine and cake.

His sons clattered down the steps to the pavement, while he paused at the top, to speak to Juan and Pedro. "The wife told me Maria was back home. I thought she must be well again. How is she?"

Grandpa's shoulders went up in a hopeless shrug. "They can't do anything for her — but you mustn't worry about the tobacco smoke; she loves to be part of what's going on. If we put her upstairs all the time, she'd die of loneliness."

"Of course, poor girl. It must be a terrible worry to you."

He turned to Pedro. "See you later, lad."

And Pedro, who simply wanted to go to bed with his wife, nodded agreement.

9

WHILE Micaela unbolted the back door to open it, to let out the tobacco smoke, Rosita quickly filled a glass of water and handed it to Manuel. "Give this to Auntie; it'll help her stop coughing."

The little boy obediently took the glass over to his struggling aunt. Rosita leaned over the sink to heave up the sash window; it had been partially open during the Saituas' visit; now she struggled to push it up further, but after a couple of inches, it stuck in its rotting wooden frame. "Blast," she muttered, "I'll have to tell the rent collector when he comes."

Micaela pushed her slightly aside, so that she could damp a towel under the tap. As she turned and wiggled her way between the scattered kitchen chairs to get to Maria, she said grimly, "You can tell him — but don't expect him to do anything. Better to get your father to have a look at it."

Maria had been coughing so violently that she had not been able to take the glass of water from Manuel; he was standing by her, wide-eyed, not knowing what to do.

The sick woman held a big man's handkerchief over her mouth to catch the blood-streaked phlegm which she was coughing up.

"It's all right, Mannie, dear. Put the glass on the little table, and go and help your mam."

Micaela gently wiped her daughter's face with the damp cloth, and, as fresh air entered the room, the coughing lessened enough for Maria to be eased on to the oil-cloth-covered sofa and be propped up with a myriad of patchwork cushions. Her mother covered her with a knitted shawl, and persuaded her to take a sip or two of water.

After chatting for a minute or two with Jean Baptiste Saitua, Juan and Pedro sat down on the front doorstep to continue their smoke. They remained there, in companionable silence, until Rosita called them in to eat.

While Rosita took a bellowing Francesca out of her cradle and put her to the breast under the cover of her shawl, Micaela served the family. She put a plate of food in front of Rosita, so that she, too, could eat, while nursing the baby.

Before sitting down, Pedro looked across at his sister-in-law, lying limply on the sofa. "Sorry the smoke made you cough, Maria. Cigarette smoke's the worst. I'll smoke outside in future."

The kindly meant words spoken softly in Basque brought tears of weakness to Maria's eye. She made a small gesture with her hand, as if to say it did not matter.

Micaela took a little bowl, put a spoonful of rice in it, and covered it with a ladle of gravy from the casserole. Very slowly, teaspoonful by teaspoonful, she got the food into the invalid. Only then did she sit down to eat herself.

Pedro had been praising the dinner to Rosita, and she smiled happily, while she shifted the baby to the other breast. She remembered suddenly what had happened when she had bought the hens in the market, and she told him the story of the third hen, retrieved from the bank windowsill.

Juan was silent during this recital. He carefully masticated his last piece of chicken and swallowed it, and, with his fingernail, released a bit of meat that had lodged between his front teeth. He did not laugh at the story; he sounded grumpy, as he said, "I hope you paid for that chicken?"

Rosita laughed. "We paid for the two we bought."

"The third one was dead when we found it," Micaela told him. She obviously expected Juan to shrug and say no more. But the old man stiffened up. He rubbed his beard, as he always did when thinking something over. "So you didn't pay for it?"

"Well, of course not. We just found it dead." She put down her fork.

"But it was still good enough to eat?"

"You've just eaten it! Rosita wouldn't cook anything that had gone bad."

Grandpa looked at her frigidly. "In that case, shouldn't you have gone back and paid for it?"

Micaela was annoyed at this. She replied huffily. "It was lost — and we found it. Anybody else who'd found it would have taken it."

"But you asked for the cage to be opened. If you hadn't, it would not have been lost."

Manuel realized that a sharp family tiff was

in the offing, and he wondered if he could get down from the table, without first asking Grandpa. His grandfather was looking extremely grim, however, and he decided he had better sit very quietly and not draw attention to himself.

Micaela tossed her head. "Tush!" she exclaimed. "The poultry man must've believed it had got crushed underfoot in the crowd — or in the traffic. He'll never know we found it."

Juan's long, dark face darkened further, his beard tilted up as if in pride. Pedro discreetly kept his mouth shut.

"My dear, it should be paid for; it was our fault it was lost." Though the words were not unkind, it was an order.

"Juan! You're being unreasonable. You really are." Impatiently, Grandma made to rise from the table. "He'll have forgotten about it by now."

"I want it paid for. He won't've forgotten that the whole hassle was caused by a bunch of Basque women, and he'll talk about it. We've got to *live* here; and we Basques have a good reputation — and it's small things that keep that reputation up." He slapped his hand crossly on the tabletop. "And what will your grandchild think? That if he can get away with something, it's automatically all right?" His gold tooth flashed between his beard and his moustache. "Not on your sweet life! What a Basque takes, he pays for."

"Really, Juan!" Grandma was trembling now, her face flushed, her fingertips on the table to steady herself. Rosita opened her mouth to join in, but was quelled by a look from Juan.

"Listen to me. You and Manuel — I want him to go, too — go back to the market tomorrow and pay for that bird."

"But, Papa . . . "

"Tomorrow!"

Grandma took a big breath, and then said, "Well, if you feel that strongly about it, Manuel and I can walk up and do it." Then she spat out, "But I think you're being terribly fussy!"

Grandpa got up from the table. "I know what I'm about," he growled. "Come on, Pedro, let's get down to the Baltic; Jean Baptiste'll be waiting."

10

CALMLY clipping the hedge in the early-morning peace of his Victoria garden, Old Manuel smiled over this episode, which he had included in his notes for Lorilyn as an example of the stiff honesty of Basques; and wondered if he should also include what extraordinarily able smugglers they were.

"What are you laughing at?" asked a cheery voice from behind the hedge.

Surprised at his peace being intruded upon, he told Sharon Herman that it was a memory of his childhood; and continued clipping along the hedge, while he asked politely how she was.

Sharon had a plate of buttered toast in her hand, and as she followed him down the hedge, she continued to eat. "I'm just fine," she told him. "Got myself an apartment, but the possession date isn't for a month. So Veronica says to stay with her till it's ready."

"She's very kind," Old Manuel replied dryly, and put his shears down, while he pulled at an old bird's nest tangled in the hedge.

"She is, isn't she?"

I wish Veronica wasn't so persistent, thought Old Manuel. High above his neighbour's roof a gull soared effortlessly and he speculated idly that in another few seconds it would dive to snatch a piece of Sharon's toast. But she turned suddenly towards him, and the gull flew swiftly seaward.

"Tell me what you were laughing at," she demanded playfully.

He told her the story of the lost hen. "My grandfather knew that it isn't enough to be honest — if you were foreign immigrants, like we were, you've got to be seen to be honest."

As he slowly clipped his way down the length of the hedge, he told her of his Basque origins and the tiny community near the Wapping Dock. Then he paused, to hold his shears in his left hand, while he carefully stretched the fingers of his right hand. He saw her glance at his hand, and said, with a rueful smile, "It's a touch of arthritis. Hurts sometimes."

She nodded sympathetically, and he went on, "I never thought of being foreign — I were born in Liverpool and christened in St Peter's. All the little kids I played with were born there — though their dads came from all over the world — as near as Ireland or as far as the Philippines."

"Like Canada." Sharon bit into another piece of toast with strong, even teeth.

He agreed. She looked much healthier than she had done when Veronica had brought her to his house, and he was glad. Her fair skin had acquired a slight tan, and her blonde hair was blowing in a wild tangle in the wind. She wasn't exactly pretty, but she had a pleasant open look about her and her figure had a cuddly roundness which reminded him of his mother. She was very likeable, he decided. Easy to talk to.

"I've got to get to work," she told him briskly, and his wise eyes nearly vanished amid the wrinkles, as he smiled goodbye to her.

* * *

The next time he saw her she was seated on a huge log on the beach, staring disconsolately out on to a placid pale-blue sea. She was obviously crying, her shoulders heaving under her sweater.

He hesitated in embarrassment. They were the only people on the shore that morning. She must have felt sure of her solitude to cry so openly, he debated uncertainly with himself. Should he go to her or not?

Aware of a sense of inadequacy at the idea of dealing with a young woman's tears, he decided to avoid invading her privacy, so he curved up the beach to pass well behind her. He was sure that she had not noticed him, but the crunch of pebbles under his feet drew her attention, and she turned a woebegone face towards him. She lifted a hand in slow salute and, embarrassed, he waved back, continuing to plod slowly on his chosen route.

She quickly took a paper handkerchief out of her pocket and wiped her face and blew her nose. He had only just passed her when she shouted, "Are you walking home?"

He stopped, and nodded his head a little guiltily.

"Wait a minute, and I'll walk with you."

"I'm rather slow," he called back. Though

her distress troubled him, he hoped she would change her mind and allow him to go on walking alone. She ran lightly over the pebbles, however, until she reached him.

He looked her up and down in a bemused way. She had cried enough to make her face swollen and her eyes mournful; yet she did not seem to want to hide it. "I guess you didn't hurt yourself, if you can run like that," he remarked tentatively, to give her an opening if she wished to explain her distress.

As she fell into step alongside him, she asked with a tight, wry grimace, "You mean you thought I was crying because I'd fallen or something?"

He considered her query, and then said, "Well, I didn't know. I didn't want to intrude. I thought I should let you be."

She sighed. "I'm OK. I was feeling a bit down, that's all — a bit lonely in a new place, I guess."

Walking on pebbles was tiring him, and he wished he had taken the path at the top of the cliff. "You're working in the new ward at the hospital, I think Veronica mentioned?"

"The Palliative Care Unit? Yes."

"Patients who are going to die are put in there? Must be hard on you."

"Not really." She went on to tell him how worthwhile she thought her work was. Her enthusiasm surprised him.

Though he was interested in what she was saying, he began to feel that he must sit down to rest; there was an unpleasant tightness in his chest. He stopped, and said, "At the top of the cliff staircase here, there's a little park kiosk that sells coffee. Would you like a cup?" He was panting slightly and his speech came slowly. "We have to get up the cliff, somewhere, to get home."

She looked at him with concern. "Could you climb the steps all right?"

"If I do a few at a time."

She was immediately practical. "Let's sit on the bottom steps for a few minutes — until you get your breath."

Manuel thankfully sat down suddenly on the steps, and they listened to the waves lapping on the beach for about ten minutes. Then she asked, "Have you seen your doctor lately?"

Manuel's mouth turned up in a quick grin; he was feeling better. "Saw him in the winter. He always says the same thing — you're in great shape — for your age! He's a nice kid."

She laughed. A wonderful old dear, gentle to the point of passivity.

She judged him wrongly. Manuel was feeling a little exhausted — but he was cussing inwardly at his weakness. He got slowly to his feet, and looked down at her quite blankly. What was the girl's name? For the life of him, he could not recall it.

Unaware of his dilemma, she took his hand to help him up the wooden staircase.

"I'm all right," he told her a trifle peevishly, and she quickly withdrew her hand. Old people could be quite tetchy about being helped, she knew.

Over coffee and muffins, which he insisted on paying for, he sat quietly for a few minutes, thinking that Jack Audley would be highly amused when he told him that he had, that morning, taken a bright young thing out to coffee!

"Why were you crying?" he finally asked her baldly, and then felt that he was being inquisitive and should not have said anything. She answered him without hesitation, however, and told him, "We lost a patient last night, not unexpectedly. It was her widowed daughter's reaction that got me. She had lived with her mother for years. She's got no children; and she was beside herself." She paused, her expression desolate. "I guess I could relate to her feeling of being bereft."

"How do you mean?"

"The feeling that nobody is left to care what happens to you."

"Tush. A bright young woman like you must have lots of friends — and even parents still alive!" He tried to sound cheering.

Sharon bit her lower lip. "Well, you see I'm divorced, and I don't have any kids — and Mum and Pop live in Florida; I'm their only child." She sighed. "When I was married, I went to live in Toronto. My husband wasn't the social type, so we didn't make any friends to speak of. I was a fool to marry him. We weren't really suited to each other from day one."

He nodded understandingly. "So what brought you here?"

"Well, I need to work — and I'm a qualified

nurse. I saw the ad for this job at the hospital, and applied. When I was a very little girl, I lived here — and it's such a truly beautiful place. I'm glad I came — but I've got to start again, making friends." She smiled suddenly, and said, "At least I've made one, haven't I?"

Manuel gave a little chuckle. "Of course," he assured her. Loneliness makes strange bedfellows, he thought with amusement; then decided hastily that 'bedfellows' was not quite the word — not at your age, old boy, he told himself.

She caught the smile that flicked across his face. "Now, what are you laughing at?" she demanded, smiling herself.

"I don't think I can explain it to you," he replied with a chuckle. Then he laughed.

Laughter is infectious and soon they were giggling like a couple of children, about nothing.

Nevertheless, when he got home, he was thankful to crawl on to his bed. But he was still smiling to himself.

11

IN June 1914, Rosita announced that she wanted Pedro's family to see Francesca, who was their first granddaughter; Pedro himself was at sea, but to Juan and Micaela it seemed a good opportunity to take a holiday, so a visit to Spain was arranged. Little Manuel was thrilled.

Juan tried to persuade Maria to accompany them. "You could go up into the mountains with Rosita to visit the Echaniz family, while your grandmother and I are in Bilbao. It would do you good to breathe mountain air," he told her.

Maria was feeling a little better and, at first, had been tempted to make the journey. Then, when she discovered that the family would be travelling by sea, she said she could not face being seasick.

Though horribly disappointed, Micaela said she would remain at home to care of her.

Rosita looked at her mother's bent, tired figure and, at first, said nothing; instead, she went to see Bridget Connolly next door. Rosita often looked after Mary and Joey, when their mother was helping to nurse a sick neighbour or delivering a baby. Now, she asked a favour on Micaela's behalf.

Would Bridget keep an eye on Maria, if Micaela went to Spain for three weeks in July? If

Bridget could watch her during the day and cook for her, she thought that Mrs Saitua's daughter, Panchika, could be persuaded to sleep overnight in the Barinèta home and give Maria a bit of breakfast.

"Panchika doesn't have to be at work till eight o'clock," she explained to Bridget. "She's got a daily job as a cook-general in a fine house in Princes Road, with very nice people.

"Maria can get herself to the can in the yard, now," she added. "And she can keep a fire going, if someone'll bring in the coal for her and start it each morning. And she can wash her hands and face at the kitchen sink. But she's not strong enough to stand and cook — or go to the shops, or anything like that."

Bridget was seated by her own fire, sipping a mug of vintage tea — it had been simmering on the hob for hours. At Rosita's suggestion, she nodded her head; her black hair was done up in untidy, coiled plaits, from which the hairpins constantly threatened to fall out; before answering Rosita, she absently pushed one back into her hair.

Plump, patient and very knowledgeable about the needs of the sick, she looked up at her neighbour, and said, "Oh, aye, I could do that, if you could manage to pay for the food I'd give her. It'd only be the price of a potato or two and what we're havin' ourselves — me housekeeping won't stretch to feed another." At the latter statement, her voice was full of apology.

"I'd get the coal up from the cellar for her, Mam," her daughter Mary volunteered; she had been listening avidly to what Rosita had had to say. "And I could chop some wood chips for her every day — and put it all in the hearth. It wouldn't take a minute, then, for Panchika to make her fire for her."

Panchika Saitua, a grumbling, middle-aged spinster, was ordered by her mother to sleep in her neighbour's bedroom and to get up half an hour earlier, so that she could build Maria's fire for her and give her tea and bread and margarine for breakfast.

Although she had not seen so much of her since she had been in service, Panchika knew Maria quite well; her working day was long and exacting and the idea of making the effort to visit someone, except, perhaps, on her Sunday off once a month, filled her with added gloom.

In the event, however, she thoroughly enjoyed her time with Maria, away from under her mother's thumb. They spent an hour or two each evening before bedtime contentedly commiserating with each other; so much so, that, even after the family returned from Spain, Panchika discovered that she could endure to walk down the road in her carpet slippers, in the late evening, for an hour's visit to Maria.

Maria was very appreciative of her visits, and missed her sorely when she failed to let herself in and come through to Rosita's busy kitchen, to sink on to the chair by the old sofa, and gasp, "Ee! Me pore feet!"

* * *

Once the trip to Bilbao had been arranged, the family looked forward to it very much. The summer of 1914 was a gorgeous one and they could hope for a pleasantly calm passage. Grandma included in the food basket a gift of fresh eatables for the crew, whose diet was very monotonous. The present was much appreciated.

It was clear that Juan enjoyed such temporary returns to sea. It gave him a fresh audience of younger Basques, to whom he could relate stories of his early days sailing before the mast, when they had none of these new-fangled steam engines. "Seamanship was seamanship, in those days," he told them. "Rounded the Horn four times, I did, in storms like you'd never believe — and the cold!" He shuddered.

This time, one young man told him, with equal pride, that he'd gone through the Panama Canal on an experimental voyage the previous year. "We were scared stiff," he said, "because we were afraid landslides would block us in, and we'd die of fever if we had to come out overland."

"Oh, aye. You're right about the fever. That canal's a waste of good money. Whole crews'll get fever going through it — like the navvies building it get sick and die."

When they arrived in Bilbao, they were met by Juan Barinèta's brother, who looked even tougher and older than Juan himself. Little Manuel viewed him with awe. Rosita said he worked in an iron foundry, and that that accounted for the mass of white scars that crisscrossed his hairy arms, his hands and his face. "They're from burns," she explained.

Great-uncle was a widower. His two single daughters looked after him; they also took care of Uncle Agustin, Rosita's brother, when he was in port or out of work. Both young women did piecework at home, and their eyes were black-rimmed and bloodshot from long hours spent peering at the silk shawls they embroidered. They were gentle creatures, who, much to Manuel's annoyance, adored baby Francesca and presented her with an exquisitely embroidered bonnet which they had made for her. They patted him on his head and exclaimed at how much he had grown; then they encouraged him to go out into the street to play with another small boy, who had wandered in from next door, to stare at the new arrivals.

In the narrow, medieval street sloping down to the river Nervión, he felt, at first, closed in, and unnerved at facing a number of strange urchins, who looked him over as if he were a peculiar animal of some kind. When the boys discovered, however, that he had never tried to play pelota vasca, they produced a rock-hard ball and showed him how to hit it against a wall with his bare hands. They approved of him when he bore stoically the pain of it, and he was almost overwhelmed by their friendly advice and instruction; he went back to his great-uncle's house with several self-appointed coaches in tow, and badly bruised hands.

Before the evening meal, his hands were washed and regretfully cooed over by his two second cousins. Grandpa laughed, and said they would soon toughen up; he showed Manuel two of his fingers which had been disjointed when he had played as a young man.

At the end of a week, he was leaping about in front of the wall with the same abandonment — and lack of finesse — as the other youngsters. Then he was told that he and his mother and Francesca would be going up into the mountains to see Grandpa and Grandma Echaniz, while Juan and Micaela remained in Bilbao.

As a baby and a toddler, he had already made three journeys to Spain, but he had few clear recollections of them. Going first by train and then in a rickety donkey cart up narrow roads into the foothills was a new adventure. He tucked his small aching hands underneath his jersey, and was relieved not to have to play pelota that day.

Grandpa and Grandma Echaniz were younger than Micaela and Juan Barinèta, and Little Manuel noted that they did not talk so much. They greeted the little family, however, with bear hugs and kind kisses; small in stature, sun-burned and stolid, they were not otherwise particularly demonstrative, but it was obvious that they were fond of their beautiful daughter-in-law and very taken by Francesca's blue eyes and red hair.

Rosita explained to Manuel that, once upon a time, his father had had two brothers to play with up here in the mountains, but they were now with God. Later, Manuel felt that perhaps the loss of her two middle sons accounted for Grandma Echaniz's affection for himself. She took him into the big living-room of their wooden house and made him her special companion. He had a great time, helping to punch down bread dough and learning how to milk a cow — he had stood, astonished, watching a pail slowly fill with milk. His grandmother let him try to milk a particularly patient cow; and he was wild with excitement when he managed to spray himself with milk. She gave him a small basket and showed him where to find eggs from the hens and ducks. He was warned not to go too close to a nanny-goat tethered to a tree in case she butted him. He discovered with amazement that she also produced milk.

The donkey lived under the house, in a small stable, next to a series of storerooms, though, since it was summertime, it was left to graze in a little field near the house; his grandfather amused him by giving him a ride on it occasionally.

While Rosita sat on the high front steps in the sun and nursed Francesca, Grandpa Echaniz took him, one morning, further up the mountain to see his father's surviving elder brother, Uncle Vicente, who was shepherding the family's flock of sheep. The climb made all the aches he had acquired playing pelota ache a lot more.

At first, he was nervous of the sheep, which looked quite large to him, despite the fact that they had been sheared of their winter coats. The bellwether ram lifted its nose out of a weed patch and looked him up and down with cold brown eyes. Then, satisfied, it returned to its grazing. When Manuel moved, the other sheep bounced away from him, towards the bellwether, whose bell tinkled as he led the flock a little away from the strangers.

They approached a series of rough shelters, fronted by a stone hut, but could not find Vicente. While his grandfather looked for him further up the mountain, Manuel turned to look back along the path they had just traversed.

Far below him lay the valley dark with trees, interspersed with tiny fields nearly ready for harvesting. From the chimneys of toy houses curled the smoke from kitchens like Grandma's. He could see a whole village, with a church spire, and a road winding through it. It was very quiet, except for the occasional jingle of the bellwether's bell and the shush-shush of the sheep as they followed him. To a child brought up amid the constant racket of machinery and traffic, it felt unearthly, and he was relieved when Uncle Vicente shouted that he was coming down; he had been sitting on a promontory further up, from which he could see the whole flock at a glance. When Manuel looked up, he saw a tall, lanky man coming slowly down towards his grandfather, who had climbed a little way to meet him. From under the man's black beret fell the same golden hair as his father had, and the sun glinted on his beard, stained with tobacco smoke just as his father's was.

Vicente greeted his father, and then came running down the slope towards Manuel. He flung down his staff and picked the boy up to toss him in the air with a friendly shout. Then he put him down on his feet again, and, while he held the child's hand, he looked into his face. "You look exactly like my mother," he announced. "Her dark hair and eyes. Doesn't he, Dad?"

Grandpa Echaniz chuckled and agreed.

"When's your dad going to come up and see us?" Vicente asked Manuel, as they turned towards the stone hut.

Manuel smiled shyly. He did not know what answer to give and looked towards his grandfather for a reply.

Grandpa said, "He'll try to get up here next time he docks in Bilbao. Last time he only had an hour or two ashore, Rosita says, so he went to see the Barinètas."

The shepherd nodded. "Come on in," he said, as he led the way into the stone hut. He pulled off his beret and threw it on to a wooden bench against the wall. Then he mopped his face with a red cotton handkerchief from his trouser pocket.

After staring round the little hut, Manuel found his voice, "What about the sheep, Uncle Vicente? Won't they get lost?"

His uncle looked down at him and laughed. "No," he assured him. "Come and see." He took him to the door, and pointed with a stubby, brown finger. "Look past the sheep, right over there."

Manuel looked and saw nothing but sheep, sparse grass and rock. Then he saw a slight movement a little above the sheep's sheared bodies. "Is that a dog?" he asked.

"Yes. It's my sheep dog. He won't let any of the sheep wander very far."

"He can't talk to them," responded Manuel rather scornfully.

"He barks at them — and runs round and round until he gets a stray back with the flock."

Manuel felt a little sceptical at this; it was his experience that grown-ups sometimes told tall tales. He was too polite to say anything, however, and allowed himself to be sat up on the table, while Uncle Vicente got three grubby mugs down from a shelf, and Grandpa slung a bag he had been carrying on his back on to the table beside him. "Brought you some bread," he announced to Vicente. He took a bottle of wine out of his pocket and placed it by the bag.

While Uncle Vicente rifled the bag of food his mother had sent up, and took out a knife to cut the bread, Manuel looked round him.

Grandpa Echaniz had picked up Vicente's staff and brought it into the hut. It was now propped in a corner beside a heavy cudgel. From wooden pegs driven between the stones making up the wall hung the shepherd's leggings and dark-coloured cape. A narrow wooden bed, with a couple of coarse blankets on it, lay against another wall. A stool and a bench made up the furnishings. A chipped enamel bowl flanked by a large tin of tobacco stood on a shelf, with a bar of soap in a saucer, a candlestick and a lantern. To Manuel it did not seem much more bleak than one or two of the rooms he had seen round Wapping Dock, when he visited some of his playmates, except that it had no fireplace — and no stout mam presiding over it.

Vicente handed him a slice of fresh bread with a piece of hard cheese on top. He poured wine into two of the mugs. Then he put a little into the child's mug and added a ladle of water to it from a jar covered by a cotton cloth, which Manuel had not noticed before. "Mustn't send you home drunk," he remarked, as he handed the mug to his nephew.

Manuel smiled up at his new uncle, and Vicente chucked him under the chin. "You're a great lad," he told him. Then he took his own drink and sat down on the bench by Grandpa. "Pedro's lucky," he said, and lifted his mug towards his father before taking a sip.

The old man lifted his own in return, and said, "You'll do as well yourself one of these days. You'll have this farm."

"I suppose," replied Vicente. "But I'd like a girl who wants to marry me, not the farm!"

His father laughed, and bit into his bread and cheese.

With his scratched and aching legs dangling from the table top, Manuel copied his uncle's movements exactly, lifting his mug to drink from time to time and eating his bread. He listened, while the two men discussed a modest increase in the price which they had got for their fleeces. They speculated that the increase might be due to a sudden demand in Europe for woollen cloth for army uniforms, as a result of war threatening to break out. Far from the political turmoil of Madrid, they scented profit, if the Spanish government had enough sense to remain neutral.

"God give them enough sense to stay out of it," said Grandpa Echaniz fervently.

Grandpa's prayer proved most effective. The Spanish did remain neutral throughout the conflict, and Bilbao and its hinterland profited exceedingly well.

After making the acquaintance of Uncle Vicente's dog, who wagged his tail at them absently, but never took his eyes off his sheep, Grandpa and Manuel walked companionably back home. Manuel wondered if Uncle Leo, far away in America, had a stone hut with lots of sheep nearby, and a lovely black dog.

* * *

All through his life Manuel remembered the quiet of the mountain shepherd's surroundings and their beauty. Not even a whole range of Rocky Mountains could take the belief from him that his father came from the most beautiful place on earth.

When he was grown-up, the Second World War provided him with greatly increased wages, but it cut him off from visits to Spain; meeting Kathleen in Canada and marrying her had added to the separation. He rarely saw *his* mountains again.

When adding to his memoirs in a fit of deep nostalgia, he described for Lorilyn the perfection of this moment of his life when he fell in love with a place, not a person. Then he closed his exercise book. His Echaniz grandparents died of influenza after the First World War, and Uncle Vicente took over the farm. When Uncle Vicente's grandson finally inherited, Manuel lost touch with the family. But he never quite forgot them.

⋆ ⋆ ⋆

It was the declaration of the *First* World War, however, which cut short his childhood stay with Grandma and Grandpa Echaniz.

When he and his grandfather walked into the farmhouse, after visiting Vicente and his sheep, the carrier had brought a message to Rosita telling her to return to Bilbao as soon as she could, because Grandpa Juan Barinèta wished to sail home to Liverpool, before hostilities cut them off.

Manuel's narrow, sallow face had grown brown in the mountain air, and his flat cheekbones had a healthy pink in them. To Rosita, looking at him as she passed on Grandpa Barinèta's urgent message it seemed as if he had suddenly grown from being a toddler into a boy, so much so that she unhesitatingly plonked a fretful Francesca into his arms, while she resumed packing their valise, and then bundled up napkins, still warm from drying in the sunshine, into an old shawl. She tied the shawl up with sharp hasty tugs.

"Why can't we stay up in the mountains?"

he asked, wanting to cry and to put down Francesca, who was heavier to hold than he had imagined.

"And who will look after your Auntie Maria, if we get marooned here — or your Papa, hm? And him in a British-registered ship!"

Manuel could not see the significance of his father's being in a British ship — what was so wonderful about that? He always sailed in the same boat. He put the question to Rosita, as he staggered to a footstool, to sit down and lay Francesca across his lap.

"Because the Germans might sink it!" his mother replied testily. She was not feeling well. She was pregnant again and it was not improving her temper.

Manuel felt sick; he knew that when ships went down men sometimes drowned. He was not too sure what drowning entailed, but he knew men went to be with God after it. He shivered and clutched the baby tighter. Francesca gurgled at him and the tiny mouth formed a smile; at that moment she became a person to him, and he began to lose some of his jealousy of her. It was comforting to hold her, while he tried to come to terms with the sense of panic that swept him, at the idea that his father could be in real danger.

They said farewell to Grandma in her big kitchen and asked her to give their love to Vicente, since there was no time to go back up the mountain to give it personally. Grandma clung to the little boy. She had already lost two sons, and she had seen immediately the threat to Pedro's life now that the British had declared war, and she was inwardly terrified of losing him.

She watched the little donkey cart wind its way down the narrow mountain road, waving until it vanished round a bend. Then she went silently back to her washboard to scrub her husband's shirts.

Grandfather Echaniz delivered them safely to the house in Bilbao. He stayed only long enough to have a glass of wine with the Barinèta brothers, before starting back to his farm. "Got to get the hay in," he said.

The Liverpool family was to sail early the following morning, and the sun was barely up when Rosita called Manuel to get ready to leave. There was a second flurry of hasty packing of baby clothes in a shawl, and to help his mother, Manuel bumped a valise down from stair to stair and then ran up again to get the shawl bundle. "When will we have breakfast, Mam?"

"In the ship," she responded morosely, as she buttoned up her blouse after feeding Francesca. She was feeling a little sick and dreaded the discomfort of the voyage home.

When he came downstairs for the second time, he found Grandma Micaela in the hall. She was wrapped in her shawl and was sitting on a suitcase. When he had put down the bundle, she handed him a mug of milk. "Your auntie brought this for you, luv."

He thankfully took the milk from her and drank it, while she observed his forlorn expression.

"What's the matter, dumpling?"

He laid the empty mug in the corner of one of the stairs, and went to her, his bottom lip trembling. He put his arm round her neck and laid his head on her shoulder. "It's Daddy. I'm so scared."

"Oh, dear. What are you frightened of?"

"Mam said the Germans might drown him."

How could Rosita be such a fool! She embraced the child, and assured him that Pedro was fine. The Germans were not going to waste ammunition on a little old freighter.

"Mam's frightened. I'm sure she is."

"Well, a war is a shock to us all," his grandmother admitted. "But when you get as old as me you know you can get through them all right." She pushed him away from her a little, so that she could look at him. She laughed, and then added, "Your dad's a great swimmer!" She continued to hold him close to her, while the family slowly gathered by the front door, waiting for a friend of his great-uncle's to bring his horse and cart to take them down to the dock, where lay the small freighter on which Grandpa Barinèta had secured a passage for them.

It was his great-uncle who lifted him on to the cart and told him to hold the side tightly. He helped Rosita up, so that she could sit beside the driver, and handed Francesca up to her.

"Take good care of yourself," the second cousins cried to her in chorus. "You mustn't lose it." They giggled together, as they stood back from the horse.

While Manuel watched the street of fine old

houses roll past and waved farewell to new friends, the old people walked behind the cart. They did not say much to each other; they did not need to.

At the wharf, Juan's brother clung to Juan's and Micaela's hands, as if loath to let them go. In their earlier life in Spain, they had had plenty of experience of turmoil and strife; and it was as if they all sensed that this newly declared war would be extremely bitter. "You could be better staying here," he suggested to Juan. "There'll be plenty of work, if Spain stays neutral."

Juan sighed. "We don't know yet. Let's see what happens." He held his brother's hand closely and put his other arm round him in an embrace. "If it were only Micaela and me — we'd stay here. But I have to think of Pedro and Rosita — and Maria, not to speak of the kids. I'll wait till Pedro comes home, and talk to him."

* * *

The voyage was fairly placid, until near the Isles of Scilly where they hit choppy waters. Though a queasy Manuel and an equally uncertain Grandma Micaela, carrying Francesca, managed to go on deck, to sit in a protected corner, Rosita lay on a bunk and heaved helplessly into a rusted enamel basin. Not only was she sick, but she was also short-tempered — her current pregnancy was sapping her strength. It had come too soon; she still felt tired from having Francesca. Micaela, who had every sympathy for her, did her best to keep Manuel and Francesca away from her.

She assured Manuel that his mam was not seriously ill; she would be better the moment she was on land again. He was relieved to hear Micaela say this; mams could die, too.

Grandpa Barinèta sat cross-legged by him on the deck and told him seamen were rarely sick, which was far from true, and taught him how to tie several complicated knots. "When you go to sea, when you're a big man," he said to the boy, "you'll need to know knots." With a couple of pieces of string in his hand, Manuel sat by Micaela and practised them assiduously. She praised his efforts and hoped he would do better in life than go to sea.

When they reached the beginning of Liverpool Bay, the sea was calmer, and a shaky Rosita was able to crawl up on deck, to sit cross-legged with them. Manuel thankfully curled up by her, grateful that she seemed more herself.

As they waited for the pilot to come aboard, Micaela began to worry aloud about Aunt Maria.

"I hope she's all right. It's a pity she couldn't come with us."

Rosita pushed her red, windswept curls back from her face. "She didn't want to come. She hates boats — even going on the ferryboat. And, you know, neither she nor I really belong in Vizcaya. Maria's always saying that she belongs to Liverpool — and I feel like that, too."

"You were glad enough to come to Vizcaya!" Her mother's voice was unusually sharp.

"Well, of course I was. It's lovely to go for a holiday, and Pedro's family was very good to us. And they loved seeing Francesca. But I mean, not to go for ever."

Grandma felt too old and tired to argue. She would have liked to have gone to see some of her own relations, in Santiago de Compostela, while they were in Spain. But they had had to keep the cost of the visit to a minimum, so she had not mentioned this desire to Juan. Now, she wondered if she would ever see them again. She was painfully homesick, and was upset at her daughter's lack of attachment to her homeland. She pursed her lips in disapproval.

Beside her, Manuel lay flat on his back and watched the seagulls swoop and climb above the boat. The sun shone warmly on him. The chatter of the crew, standing at the rail while they watched the approaching pilot boat, came to him as a comfortable male buzz. He had not been listening to his womenfolk's conversation; reassured about his father, glad to see his mother on deck, his mind was a contented blank.

Far away in Canada, Manuel remembered those golden moments, lying contentedly on the deck. They were his last truly happy moments of childhood before his sense of total security was shattered.

12

ON his return to Liverpool, Manuel quickly discovered that his playmates were not interested in his adventures in Spain; most of them had exotic grandparents on the male side, anyway. Andy Pilar was bursting with the news that he had had the measles. "Me ma had to get the doctor, 'cos me temperature was a hundred and ten! You should of seen me spots — all over me stummick, they was!"

More temperately, Brian Wing told him that he had had the measles, too, and that Mrs Connolly had remarked that, as a result of the disease, he might have to wear spectacles — as soon as his father could afford them, that was.

"I feel I'm in a bit of a fog," he explained to Manuel, as they amiably swopped cigarette cards. He had to peer closely at each card, which Manuel found most peculiar.

At the tea-table that evening, Manuel mentioned Brian's need of spectacles. Grandma Micaela immediately suggested that he tell Mrs Wing that the pawnbroker sometimes had second-hand glasses for sale; so, after the meal, he ran along Mersey Street to the tiny laundry to inform her of this.

He found her surrounded by piles of dry washing, busy damping and rolling each shirt or sheet, preparatory to ironing them. Several irons were hooked into the bars of the fire-grate to heat; and in a corner the copper heaved and bubbled with further washing. The tiny room was stiflingly hot.

On a bench against a wall sat Mr Wing, his older son, Fred, and Brian, each with a coarse pottery bowl in his hand. With a dexterity which mesmerized Manuel, they shovelled rice from the bowls to their mouths with a pair of sticks.

Manuel blinked, and turned to Mrs Wing to give the message about the glasses. She smiled and bowed over her ironing table, though it was doubtful if she understood what he was saying. Mr Wing understood, however; and the kindly thought behind the message.

"Please to thank respected grandmother," he said to Manuel; his English came slowly and was pronounced with difficulty.

Manuel nodded. "Can Brian come out to play?" he asked.

Brian must finish his tea, first; then he could go out for a little while, Mr Wing said gravely. He would come to Manuel's house.

Grandma Micaela was seated on the front step, when Manuel returned. He sat down by her, to wait for Brian, and repeated Mr Wing's thanks to her.

She gave a slow, sweet smile; it was nice to be called 'respected', even if it was only by a Chinese.

"Why doesn't Fred come out to play, Granny? He never plays with anyone. Is he too old, do you think?"

"I don't think he's too old," responded

Grandma. She spoke, as usual, in Basque. "I've seen the lad carrying huge bundles of laundry on his back, along South John Street, and, once, pushing an old pram full of it, in Princes Road. It's my guess he delivers and collects washing from little hotels and cafés, for his dad. He won't have time to play."

Nor energy, she thought with a sigh. When she considered the abject poverty of the Wing family, she knew she was rich. She hugged her grandson to her and thanked God that he was well fed and clothed.

* * *

The hot weather concluded with a heavy thunderstorm, and the drainpipe at the back of the Barinètas' house collapsed. Micaela asked Juan if he could repair it.

"If we wait for the landlord to do it, we'll wait for ever," she told him. "The water's trickling from the gutters all down the walls — there's a real puddle, even in the cellar. The coal's getting damp."

Juan had not been very busy with emigrants during the summer: the threat of war had made people hesitant to travel overseas; its outbreak, and the subsequent sinking of three British cruisers by a single German U-boat, had, apparently, confirmed the nervous fears of many who had intended to emigrate; they deferred their crossing of the Atlantic in a British ship.

Juan was, therefore, thankful to be given something to do. He got up from his chair, opposite Maria's couch, and, on the top bar of the fireplace, knocked the dottle out of his clay pipe. Maria was thankful to see him go. The smoke from his pipe had been bothering her; but nobody dared to tell Juan that he could not smoke in his own kitchen-living-room; he had a fixed idea that only cigarette smoke was bad for Maria. Maria sometimes wished fretfully that he would go back to sea and take his pipe with him.

In the rain-soaked, brick-lined back yard, Grandpa viewed the damage, while Grandma stood behind him, her arms crossed over her stomach. The rain had stopped, but both could clearly see the water dripping from the hole left in the gutter after the collapse of the drainpipe. Below it the rainwater barrel was brimming, a length of drainpipe protruding from the water. At a point level with Grandpa's eyes, a further piece of pipe was still fairly firmly affixed to the wall by a clasp. A third piece, rotten from rust, had fallen into the yard, and Manuel joyfully picked it up and staggered round the yard, blowing into it as if it were a trumpet.

The old man peered up at the sodden wall. "Tush," he exclaimed irritably. "The whole pipe must be absolutely rusted out — and that wall needs repointing. You'd best tell Fleet, when he comes for the rent — show him it." Though his words were firm, he knew and Micaela knew that the landlord's agent would never do anything about it. He and Leo had done innumerable repairs themselves; now he wished the younger man was still at home, to get out the heavy ladder, mix the cement, try to find a reasonable piece of piping in some builder's yard and fix it up. He was acutely aware of his own ageing, his lack of physical strength, as he turned towards the back door.

Micaela looked up at the louring sky. Though she was resigned to the house being persistently damp, she knew that the loss of the drainpipe would rapidly worsen it.

"It looks as if it's going to rain a lot more," she said doubtfully to her husband's back. "Couldn't you somehow knock the pieces together — use an old tin to join them and some rags for binding them — just to hold it for a few days? I'll ask Roy Fleet when he comes next Friday." Her husband had stopped and turned to face her, a hand on the doorjamb. She urged him again. "More water in the cellar's going to soak the coal — not to speak of the kindling I've got down there."

He did not reply, and she realized suddenly how he had aged recently, but she continued, "With the wall so wet, the plaster'll fall off the big back bedroom — it's got holes in it already."

Manuel had paused in his trumpeting, to listen to his grandparents. Now he said generously, "I've got an old pineapple tin — my spare marbles're in it. You can have it." He looked eagerly up at Juan; helping Grandpa mend a drainpipe could be fun.

Juan glanced down at the boy, and grinned. Then he shrugged, and said to his wife, "All right. Get me some rags — and plenty of string.

Manuel, you get the tin — I'll need more than one — and I'll see what glue or paint I've got to hold it all together. Have you got any more tins, Micaela?"

Grandma and Rosita hoarded everything; very little was ever thrown away. It did not take them long to produce a large ball of string, made up of short pieces knotted together into one strand, a remarkable pile of rags, neatly torn into squares for patching or for dusters, and three largish, round tins, in which they had been storing bits of candle grease for starting the kitchen fire, a button collection and Grandma's hairpins. While they scraped out the grease and found another home in old jam jars for the buttons and the hairpins, Juan fetched an extendable wooden ladder from under the lean-to next to the lavatory in the yard. He extended it to its fullest length, and, in the narrow space between the house and the brick-walled lavatory, he managed to lean it against the wet wall.

"I'll take a look at the gutter itself, first — before I put a lot of work into mending the pipe — it's probably rusted, too — it mayn't take the weight of the tins and the rags, as well as the drainpipe."

He climbed slowly up, while Micaela held the bottom of the ladder, and Manuel watched, fascinated. Rosita, busy peeling potatoes, tried to look upwards through the kitchen window.

Through the open back door, she and Maria heard her father call down fretfully, "It looks too far gone to do anything about." A small hail of rusty bits of metal descended past the window, as he felt along the gutter. Micaela looked up and stepped back hastily to avoid getting flying bits into her eyes. Her husband leaned over and gave a sharp tug to the gutter a bit further along. It held.

"Humph," he grunted, and shifted his weight on the ladder.

"Watch out, luv," shrieked Grandma suddenly, and Manuel, alarmed, ran back towards the kitchen door.

There was a cracking sound. Not a big sound, recollected Old Manuel, but a deadly one, as the three top rungs of the ladder came out of their sockets.

Grandpa's wet boots slipped, and the ladder swayed badly. He grabbed at the gutter. It came away in his hand. Wrongly pitched in the narrow space, the ladder swayed outwards from the wall. Grandma leapt away, as Grandpa came crashing down. As he fell his head hit the edge of the slate-tiled lavatory roof, cutting off his scream. He slid down the sloping roof and landed on the ground with a heavy thud and a splash of water from the puddles. His head lay at an impossible angle.

Micaela did not cry out. A paralysed Manuel watched her sink slowly to her knees by the stricken man. Very gently she lifted his head. As she touched him, his life went out of him and his body relaxed. As a horrified Rosita squeezed her way past a clutter of chairs in the crowded kitchen and Maria cried out in alarm, she curled her arms tenderly round his face. "My dear," she whispered. "My dearest dear."

Manuel awoke from his shock. "Mam," he yelled to his mother. "Mam!"

A frantic Rosita had caught the bow of her apron on the knob of the dresser drawer. She tore at the apron string, freed herself, and pushed Manuel to one side, as she flew into the yard, to stand, appalled, looking down at her parents. Micaela lifted a face to her so empty of expression that she might have been dead herself. "The ladder gave way," she said simply. "He's gone."

Rosita wanted to scream. She swallowed hard, trying to control her panic, and fell on her knees by Micaela. "Are you sure?" she asked her mother desperately.

"Yes."

Manuel began to whimper. His mother turned her head towards him, and said as calmly as she could, "Auntie Connolly's out, I know. Run up to Mrs Saitua's and tell her Grandpa's had an accident. Ask her to come quick — and to bring any of her boys who are home. Understand? Don't cry, luv."

Manuel nodded, and began to move towards the door. "Wait a minute," Rosita called. "Then I want you to go across to the vicarage, and ask Father Felipe to come — or any of the priests. Run, sweetheart."

As if he had not heard her properly, he paused to stand and stare at her, not understanding why Grandpa lay so still. His mother's face, however, was a ghastly white, and she was trembling. He himself began to shake.

"Run, dear. Run, quick. It's urgent!"

He dragged himself uncertainly through the kitchen door. Then, ignoring his aunt's cries of, "What's up?" he made himself run, through the house, down the steps, round the curve, pushing past three girls bouncing a ball against a wall. He ignored their furious cries as they retrieved the ball from the flooded gutter, and panted his way up Corn Hill.

He paused for a second in front of the Saituas' open front door, to get his breath, and then took the two front steps at a bound.

Mrs Saitua was scrubbing the living-room floor, her black skirt hitched up and tucked into its waistband. Her fat bottom was draped by her grubby white petticoat and from under it protruded the dirty, callused soles of her bare feet.

At Manuel's precipitous arrival, she sat back on her heels, and quickly turned a scarlet face dripping with perspiration.

At the sight of the gasping small ghost of a child, she dropped her scrubbing brush and stumbled to her feet. "What's up, duck?" she asked.

"It's Grandpa. And me mam says will you come quick." He paused to gulp a breath. "And bring Domingo and Vicente with you."

Madeleine Saitua had already shoved her feet into a pair of down-trodden carpet slippers, and, before he had actually finished speaking, she was shouting up the narrow staircase for her boys to get up quick. "Something's happened at the Barinètas'," she yelled.

Manuel was already on his way out of the

front door, when she turned back to him to say, "Tell your mam I'm coming." She was hastily straightening her bundled-up skirt.

"I've got to get Father Felipe," Manuel panted.

"Jesus Mary! What happened?"

"He fell off a ladder," replied Manuel, and flew down the steps, to race up the slope to the vicarage.

As he stood on tiptoe to bang the knocker on the priests' door, he was sick with fright. He leaned against the wooden door, and nearly fell in when it was opened by the housekeeper.

"Be careful, lad!" she snapped, as the child caught at her black, serge skirt to steady himself. She spoke in Spanish.

He looked up at hard brown eyes in an equally brown face, and burst into tears.

In Basque, he howled, "I've got to get Father Felipe."

"Be quiet. Father's busy. What's the matter?"

Manuel's Spanish was, as yet, limited. He did his best to control his sobs and to gather the words he needed, but they would not come. He continued to howl and the housekeeper continued to scold in Spanish.

The ruckus brought a priest from a back room. Manuel did not know him, but the long cassock and sandalled feet were comforting. "It's Grandpa," he wept to the young man. "And me mam says to get Father Felipe quick."

The housekeeper grudgingly gave way to the priest, who squatted down on his heels until his face was level with the child's. "Don't cry," he said in stiff English. "Tell me what happened."

"He fell off the ladder — and he's lying in the yard — and Mam says to get Father Felipe."

The young priest's face immediately became very grave. "Wait here a minute," he said. "I'll get Father Felipe. What's your name?"

Manuel told him.

Father Felipe was commendably quick. He gathered what he needed in order to administer Extreme Unction, took Manuel by the hand, and together they hurried down the narrow, black streets. "Did your mother send you for the doctor?"

"No," panted Manuel. He was a little surprised at the question; when you fell down Mam bandaged you up — or, maybe, Mrs Connolly, who was very good at it.

The priest's dark face looked suddenly more lined than usual; he glanced compassionately down at the child who held his hand so confidently; the death of the man of the house in this desperately poor neighbourhood was a particularly terrible loss. He hoped he was in time to administer the Last Rites.

13

AS she knelt beside her mother, Rosita's stomach heaved and she feared she would vomit. Her breath came in short gasps, as she made herself cautiously slip her hand under her father's pullover to feel for a heartbeat. She could not find one, so she took his limp wrist to feel his pulse.

Nothing.

She put her arm round her mother's bent back. "I'm sorry, Mam," she said brokenly.

Her mother did not answer her; it was as if she had forgotten her daughter's presence. Even when Maria, clutching her flannel nightgown modestly round her, crept into the yard in bare feet and knelt down on the other side of her, Micaela seemed unaware of her daughters. Her whole being was focused upon her husband, as if she believed that if she kept on crooning to him, he would come round from being stunned; yet it was clear from what she had said that, somewhere in her shocked mind, she understood that he was dead.

"What happened?" whispered Maria. She was shivering with cold and fear. "Is he dead?"

Rosita nodded. She laid her cheek on her mother's back, and hoped she would not vomit; her current pregnancy was not proceeding as comfortably as the earlier ones had and, most mornings, she felt nauseated.

"Please, Madeleine, come quick!" she prayed, as she waited for Madeleine Saitua to arrive.

Maria began to cry, the slow, helpless crying of the very weak. Through all her painful, hopeless illness, her father had been the pillar of her life; her mother nursed her, but her father had ungrudgingly provided a home for her. "Even extra milk," she moaned aloud.

A little startled, Rosita lifted her head. Maria saw the movement, and rubbed the tears out of her eyes, as she explained. "He thought of everything for me — even more milk."

"He did," replied Rosita in a low voice. "He looked after us all." She hugged her shocked mother more tightly, while beyond the brick wall of the yard, the riveters continued their merciless clangour, and beneath her the puddle in which she was kneeling slowly soaked through her heavy, serge skirt. Would Madeleine never come?

Her agitated thoughts leapt fearfully to the future, as the import of Maria's words sank in. Pedro would now be the sole breadwinner; he would have seven people to maintain, if she included the baby now on its way.

Still in her carpet slippers, Madeleine Saitua laboured up the front steps and ran through the open front door and through the kitchen-living-room to the back door. She was a heavy woman, unused to moving fast, and she had to pause for a moment to catch her breath, as through the back door she observed the three women kneeling round Juan.

"Looked like something out of a church

window, they did — and him so peaceful," she said that night to an acquaintance in the Baltic, while she enjoyed a sustaining glass of port and considerable attention from other customers, always interested in a tragedy.

Now, however, she was forced into action.

At the sound of the scurrying flip-flap of her carpet slippers as she descended the back steps, Maria shuffled round on her knees to see who was coming; through her flannel nightgown the rough bricks hurt her knees, and her whimpering became a loud wail.

Very shaken, Madeleine peered down at Juan and at her old friend, Micaela. There was no doubt in her mind that she was looking at a dead man; the angle of his head indicated that quite clearly.

Rosita scrambled to her feet. She was so white that Madeleine was immediately alarmed that she would miscarry.

She did not want another catastrophe on her hands, so she said sharply to her, "Take Maria in and wrap her up by the fire. And get yourself a glass of water — and sit down. I'll take care of your mother — the boys'll be here in a minute — they're just putting their kecks on — lucky they're both home — Domingo's on the evening shift this week — and there's no hurry for Vicente on a Saturday."

She bent over Micaela who had ignored her arrival. She said soothingly, "We're getting help, luv. It won't be a minute."

Taking Rosita's place, she squatted down on her heels and put her arm round the mourning woman. Then she leaned forward and firmly closed the dead man's eyes. She looked up at Rosita, who had taken her shivering sister's arm and lifted her to her feet. "You'd better call the doctor," she advised.

"It's too late," responded Rosita dully. She tugged Maria's arm. "Come on, now. Be brave. Come on — indoors."

Still wailing, Maria turned towards the house. Rosita bent down to stroke her mother's white hair, trying frantically to think how to comfort her. "Manuel's gone to fetch Father Felipe, Mama," she told her, her voice choking on the words.

Her mother made no response. She continued to sit with her husband's head in her lap and to stroke his cheek, while she muttered brokenly, "My dear, my dear."

Mrs Saitua sighed. She did not argue about the need for a doctor, though she knew someone would have to tell the coroner of the accident; Juan was, indeed, beyond medical aid. In a minute or two reality would strike Micaela; she would be wild with grief; and there was the chance, also, that Rosita might begin to miscarry. She hoped there was some whisky or brandy in the house. Maybe Father Felipe would insist on the doctor's being called, she thought anxiously, as she muttered to Micaela, "There, there, luv. There, there."

She was thankful when, almost immediately, there was a distant knock on the front door, followed by the tramp of hob-nailed boots. Her sons burst into the yard, one of them still struggling into a navy-blue pullover.

"Christ!" Domingo exclaimed. "What's to do, Mam?"

Their mother looked up at them fiercely. "Hush!" she admonished. "Juan's had an awful accident. Lift him into the house — put him on the couch in the sitting-room. Gently, now!"

She turned back to Micaela. "The boys are going to carry Juan into the house, dear. They'll be very careful of him. Now, you come along of me." She put her hand under her friend's chin and made her turn to look at her. "Come on, luv. The rain's starting again."

The shaken young men edged round the two women. Domingo very cautiously lifted the dead man's head away from Micaela's lap. Micaela glanced at him in bewilderment.

Madeleine stood up and put her hands under the armpits of the tiny kneeling woman; then, bracing herself, she eased her to her feet. It was like lifting a sagging sack of potatoes. Micaela's eyes were on the boys, who were used to shifting heavy weights. As they picked up her husband she saw the pity in their eyes. The agony of her loss struck her and she opened her mouth and screamed.

The terrible shrieks roused her neighbours. They whipped their shawls over their shoulders and shot out into the street. Bridget Connolly was standing on her step, about to open her front door. She froze at the sound of the scream.

"Holy Mother!" exclaimed young Peggy O'Brien from two doors down the street. "What on earth was that?" She and two other women rushed towards Bridget. "Which house was it?"

"Micaela — Rosita, I think!"

She ran down her steps and up the Barinètas' steps. Followed by the other women, she burst into the narrow hallway, to find her way blocked by Domingo and Vicente turning into the parlour with their heavy burden. Behind her, women crowded up the steps, their speculations cut short by a glimpse of the young men's grim faces.

The little crowd fell back, to allow Father Felipe, with Manuel clutching his hand, to enter a house close to pandemonium. Already terrified, Manuel clung to the priest.

As the cleric's presence was realized, people began to quieten. Space was made for him to squeeze into the small parlour, leading the child with him.

They were both faced with the dead man clumsily propped up on the horsehair sofa; Micaela was on her knees, her face buried in his lap as she loudly lamented something about a drainpipe and that it was all her fault.

While Manuel hid his face in the priest's coarse robe and clung to him, Father Felipe resolutely took command. He recognized most of those present, including Maria still in her nightgown, though someone had thrown a shawl over her shoulders. The other daughter, Rosita, looked as if she would collapse at any moment, as she turned magnificent, sorrowful blue eyes upon him. In the distance, he could hear a baby shrieking, untended. At the back of the tiny room, two young men — the Saitua boys — and their mother stood uneasily watching the scene. Three other women had crowded in; and, when entering, he had pushed past three more, whispering at the foot of the front steps.

His first thought was for the terrified child clinging to him. He recognized Bridget Connolly standing to his left; Bridget, he knew, had a lot of experience of children and nursing. He bent and picked up Manuel, as he spoke to her. "Could you take Manuel and look after him for a little while?" he asked in stilted English.

She automatically opened her arms to the white-faced little boy, who showed no signs of wanting to go to his mother. "Of course. Now, you come with Auntie Bridget, me dove. Father Felipe's going to do what he can to help your granddad and grandma — and your mam." She hugged the boy to her, and wrapped her shawl round him. "You come and have some dinner with our Mary and Joey." Space was made for her, as she eased through the parlour door. "And then you can have a little play together in our yard, till your mam comes for you." Her soft Irish voice and familiar red face were comforting and normal, so he went with her without demur; Grandpa looked so peculiar and everybody had obviously been making such a fuss before the arrival of Father Felipe that the instinct was to escape. He knew from experience that Auntie Bridget always gave you a straight answer — she never said 'perhaps' or 'maybe' — so if she said that Mother would come for him, Mother undoubtedly would.

As they squeezed past him, the priest patted the child's back and smiled at him, "Well done, Manuel," he said. "You were a clever lad to bring the message so quickly."

Manuel smiled wanly back; only later did he appreciate that he had been praised by a priest; it was like being praised by God himself, he decided; it was something good shining through an awful day.

Father Felipe turned to Mrs Saitua, who seemed calmer than the other women. "Has a doctor been sent for?" he inquired.

She looked across at Rosita. "No," she said.

Rosita said, "He's dead."

"You should get a doctor immediately, Mrs Echaniz."

Rosita nodded helplessly, her strength nearly gone.

"I'll go," Domingo told her, and thankfully left the room.

* * *

Puzzling over his notebook seventy-eight years later, Old Manuel wondered how to explain to Lorilyn the trauma of that week, how his childhood home had been invaded by an unknown something called Death. Grandpa had simply fallen off a ladder, and had in a second or two gone to God. It was called dying. Nobody had tried to hide it from him; in fact, he had been called upon to help — he had run to get Mrs Saitua and Father Felipe.

In the sanitary world of North America, at the

age of nineteen what would Lorilyn have seen of death, other than through the monstrosity of television? Would she have any idea that the victim's pain and death would be an agony to those who loved him?

Nowadays, on the whole, people lived long lives. Pain and death were dealt with by hospitals and batteries of doctors and health-care workers; even the carnage of the streets was quickly shovelled into ambulances and the streets washed down, so that no one would be offended by the sight of blood. At the end you lay in a mortuary until you had been tidied up and made fit for public inspection.

Would she even know how to lay out a loved one, as he knew his mother and grandmother had done for his grandfather? Would she sit a whole night by her dead father as Maria had done, saying her rosary over and over again? Doing all of it as a final outpouring of affection?

He knew that she would not.

It was a sore point with him that he himself had not been allowed to lay Kathleen out. Faith had been on her way to visit her mother, that morning, and had used her own key to enter the house. She found him sitting by the bed in the sitting-room, holding her dead mother's hand, and she had immediately taken charge. Her face stony, she had consulted the yellow pages of the telephone book, called a funeral director, called her husband, asked if he had had any breakfast, insisted on his moving into the dining-room and having some coffee. He was so exhausted that he obeyed her. The only thing he had said to her was, "Call the doctor."

He had not finished the coffee Faith had thrust into his hand, when the doctor arrived, followed closely by the funeral director. They held a committee over poor Kathleen's body, and then, while the young general practitioner came to sit with him for a few minutes, Kathleen was removed.

He half rose from the table in shock, when he saw what the funeral director and his men were doing. He looked in bewilderment at the doctor, but words would not come to him — he was so tired. He wanted time with Kathleen, but the doctor grasped his arm firmly, and said kindly, "Everything's been taken care of — you must rest now. Faith will deal with everything."

His rage at his daughter's quiet efficiency had simmered in him throughout the funeral and for long afterwards. He never considered that she was holding in her own grief, while she tried to make things easier for him.

Since there was no reason to stay in his own house, he went home with her for a few days and slept most of the time, until the coroner released the body and they went back to Victoria for the funeral.

People swarmed through his bungalow, drinking coffee and wine and eating cocktail-type nibbles. But when the ladies, including Veronica, had washed up the last cup and saucer and put them back into the china cabinet, he saw them all to the door. Faith had protested that he should come back to her home in Vancouver. Her big kindly husband had assured him he would be most welcome.

But he wanted to be alone with Kathleen's ghost, even if everybody else considered that a funeral finished everything. As far as he was concerned it did not.

He sat alone on the bed, which had been heaved back upstairs and into his bedroom by three male neighbours, and stared out of the window, while he mentally beat himself for allowing her to suffer so much — and at the end be so tired that he had not protested at her hasty removal.

Bearing in mind his own pent-up wrath, perhaps it was as well that Lorilyn had been in Europe, at the time. She was doing a special, high-powered course in French. Faith told him that she had written to her daughter telling her that, since she could do nothing for Grandma, she should not return for the funeral, but, instead, should take her impending exam.

And yet?

Not do anything for Kathleen? Weren't prayers and paying one's respects something? At the time, he hated his phlegmatic daughter — and his granddaughter for not disobeying her mother. Furious, he had shut himself up for weeks, frequently refusing to answer the doorbell or the telephone. He had never gone back into the social circle to which Kathleen and he — well, mostly Kathleen, he admitted — had belonged; and it had taken the best part of a year before he could do more than simply endure his daughter's and granddaughter's visits, when they inspected the food cupboard and the freezer to make sure he had enough to eat.

Then, slowly, sanity returned. He realized, shamefacedly, that both women — and his son-in-law — had done their best for him according to the society in which they lived, and that it was grossly unfair of him to expect anything different.

The more he thought about that time, the more he realized that Faith had shown the same calm, stolid endurance of grief that his own mountain grandparents would have shown. She had, indeed, done her utmost.

As for himself, it slowly dawned upon him that he was far too like Grandpa Barinèta, who, when he was angry, had always had a real tantrum, stalking round the kitchen like an enraged cockerel until he had extracted apologies from everybody in sight.

However did Kathleen put up with me? he wondered.

14

ALTHOUGH Manuel had allowed himself to be taken by Bridget Connolly to her house, while Father Felipe dealt with his stricken family — when a priest gave an order, you obeyed — he was very scared at being removed from the scene of the action; he could not put his fears into words and he wished suddenly that his father was there; he longed for his quiet orderliness; he would be able to explain what was truly happening.

But his father was at sea on the other side of the Atlantic and had no inkling of the disaster in his home.

When, in addition to midday dinner, Bridget kept him for tea, he protested strongly, crying that he wanted his mam. He quarrelled with Mary and Joey, who were very possessive of their territory and few toys; he was not a big child for his age, and they tended to treat him with the condescension usually reserved for a much younger playmate; it confused him even more.

With a sigh, Bridget picked him up as if he were, indeed, still a toddler. With him straddled on her hip, she struggled to make ready her husband's tea. Manuel found her closeness and warmth comforting, and his loud crying became soundless sobs, which made Bridget want to weep herself.

When Pat Connolly arrived home from work, his wife shouted into his ear the reason for Manuel being unexpectedly in their care.

"Juan had a bad accident," she told him briefly, since she did not want to emphasize in front of her children exactly how deadly the accident had been.

Her loud voice frightened Manuel even more, though he knew Mr Connolly could not hear properly. He cried helplessly, making no attempt to rub his eyes clear of tears.

She turned back to the child. "There, there, Mannie, luv. Your mam'll come soon," she soothed, wondering at the same time how his bereaved family was getting on.

Pat Connolly made no response to Bridget's explanation. He swept one of Pudding's granddaughters off a battered easy chair, and sat down suddenly and closed his eyes. The dislodged cat eyed him malevolently from under the deal table. Mary brought him his slippers, but he made no attempt to take them from her. She set them down by his feet and crept away.

As he watched him from the safety of Bridget's broad hip, Manuel's tears tailed off. Mary and Joey's dad looked so different from his own father. He smelled different, not only of old sweat. He had a curious metallic odour as well. He was practically bald, with a grey fringe round the sides of his head. A day's beard glinted whitely on his chin. The lids of his closed eyes were bright red, as was his nose, and the rest of his skin was an unhealthy yellowish-white, whereas Manuel's father had skin the colour of a ripe hazelnut and a thick thatch of fair hair — *and*, Manuel thought, *his* dad did not come home to sit silently in a chair; he first hugged and kissed his mother and himself.

Only when he was a little older, did Manuel understand from the conversation of adults the appalling conditions under which men like Pat worked and their absolute exhaustion by the end of the day. As Mr Saitua once remarked, "You have to be a bloody contortionist to do that job. Never mind the racket!"

Bridget swung the boy round towards the table, while she poured a mug of tea, which had been simmering on the hob for some time. She picked up a tin of condensed milk from the draining board by the sink, and let a generous amount trickle into the black brew. Then she spooned some sugar out of a small blue bag on the table. She stirred everything up vigorously, then picked the mug up and said to her weary spouse, "'Ere you are, luv. Lovely and hot, it is."

The scaler opened his eyes and there was a hint of a smile in them, as he accepted the tea. As he drank it, he began to relax and become his usual amiable self.

"How was your back today?" she inquired.

He sighed, and then said, "It weren't so bad as yesterday."

"I'll rub it again tonight for yez. Nothing like a bit of Sloane's liniment for backs." She noticed that Manuel had been diverted by the cat leaping quietly over the fender, to curl up close to the fire, so she slid him down by it. He knelt down and put his hand over the steel bar, to stroke its black satin back. The warmth of the blaze was comforting, and the cat stretched itself under his careful hand. He laid his cheek on the warm fender just above the animal. His stroking became slower and, despite the hardness of his pillow, he fell asleep.

Bridget paused in her bread-cutting to look down at him compassionately. "Poor little bugger," she mouthed at her husband, careful not to wake the child. "He were proper upset. Terrible for him to see his grandpa killed."

Pat understood what his wife was trying to convey. "Oh, aye," he agreed softly, some of his exhaustion receding as he rested his legs. "It isn't going to be easy for them, without the Ould Fella; he did well, he did, with his emigrants and all." There was no hint of shock in his voice; his fatigue was too great. Juan was an old man; his time had come.

"This is where they could use Leo."

"The lad what went to America? Oh, aye. Young Pedro will have his hands full, feedin' a houseful of women and kids."

* * *

When Manuel woke up, he was startled to find himself in his own bed, Pat Connolly having kindly carried the sleeping child in for Rosita. Across the room, Auntie Maria was seated on the edge of her narrow, iron bed, telling her beads by the light of the moon filtering between the window curtains. She wore a black shawl over her heavy, flannel nightgown, and her old carpet slippers on her feet. She was crying.

Manuel struggled to sit up; he was still in his jersey and shorts, but his boots and socks had been removed. "Where's Mam?" he asked immediately, and yawned.

Aunt Maria gave a big sob. "She's downstairs with your granddad and grandma — and Peggy O'Brien is with them; she'll watch all night with them."

"Why? It's dark — it's bedtime." He pushed off his blankets, as if to get out of bed.

Auntie Maria immediately put down her rosary, got up clumsily and shuffled over to him. "No, no, dear. You can see your mam in the morning."

Manuel remembered suddenly his grandfather hurtling through the air, and the sickening crash as he hit his head on the tiled lavatory roof; and then Father Felipe and Mrs Connolly.

He shivered. "Is Grandpa very hurt?" he asked, knowing in his heart that something much worse than being hurt had happened, though he could not put a name to it.

Aunt Maria loomed over him like a dark ghost, as, for once, she bent to kiss him on the forehead. Her face against his felt wet, as she quickly pulled herself back.

"Yes," she said softly. "He's gone to God." She pushed him gently back on to the bed and lifted his bedclothes over his shoulders.

"Does that mean he's dead?" Manuel asked tentatively, afraid of the reply.

"Yes." The single word came out slowly, like the beginning of a long lamentation.

"So Mam and Granny have to stay with him?"

"Yes. Tomorrow, Grandma and I'll sit with him, so your mam can get a little sleep — and Peggy O'Brien will go home. Maybe Mrs Saitua will come to sit for a little while to be company for Grandma and me."

"Doesn't Granny want to go to bed?"

"I don't think so, luv. She'll want to be with Grandpa."

"Is he lonely because he's dead?"

The question was almost too much for Maria. She clapped the back of her hand to her mouth, to stop herself from crying out. She did not answer, while she sought to control herself, and then she said softly, "We don't really know, dear. But we think he might be."

"While he's waiting for his Guardian Angel?"

She smiled faintly through her grief. "Yes, dear."

To his knowledge, Auntie Maria, like Bridget Connolly, rarely lied, so he was satisfied that Grandpa would soon be taken wonderful care of by his own private golden guardian, complete with wings, to bear him to Heaven. Still very weary, he turned over and was soon asleep again.

His aunt went back to her bed and her rosary. Her belief was almost as literal as the child's, and she was comforted by the reminder of a heavenly being standing close to each one of us. She would miss her father dreadfully, but it was nice to feel that he would be looked after, and that, despite dying unshriven, he could hope for a seat in Heaven, because he had been such a good parent.

15

THE day after Juan Barinèta's unexpected death, Manuel was sent back to school. He wore his Wellington boots and a macintosh, because the rain was sheeting down; it was as if winter had suddenly set in. His mother had silently given him his porridge and milk and, equally subdued, he had eaten it. Grandma and Aunt Maria did not appear at all; he guessed that they were both in the parlour, the door of which was firmly closed.

Rosita sat by him at the table, a cup of tea in front of her, and suckled Francesca. Her magnificent red hair had not been combed and, in the light of the kitchen fire, it shone like a halo. Her expression was such that Manuel had a scared feeling that the last thing she was thinking about was a jittery small boy.

When he was ready to leave, however, she handed him two biscuits for his elevenses, wrapped in a piece of paper saved from a cereal box. Then she squatted down in front of him, kissed him and told him he was being a very good, helpful boy.

He felt better and grinned shyly at her. She patted his bottom, and sent him on his way. She did not want him at home when the undertaker, alerted by Vicente Saitua, came to measure her father's body for a coffin later that morning.

* * *

On the previous day, the doctor had come immediately in response to Father Felipe's request. The accident was explained to him and the broken ladder shown to him. He wrote an appropriate certificate, and told Rosita gently, "I have to inform the Coroner's Office, and they will probably send someone to look at your father. If the coffin arrives before they do, please do not put Mr Barinèta into it until they have made their examination; they will want to see the body — and the ladder."

At this intimation of an invasion of their privacy, Rosita had looked so defeated that the doctor had to reassure her that the official would probably be both compassionate and brief. "And you should lie down for a little while," he advised. "Mrs Saitua said you were expecting — and you don't want to lose the child."

She merely shrugged; there would be other pregnancies.

"Would you like to ask Mr Biggs to look after the body for you?"

"You mean now? Give Father to the undertaker?"

"Yes. You might feel a little better to be relieved of it."

"Good Heavens! No! Mother's broken-hearted enough already."

* * *

Watched by Maria, Micaela, Rosita and young Peggy O'Brien had tenderly washed and shaved Juan and laid him out as soon as the doctor and Father Felipe had departed. They had wrapped him in a clean sheet and bound his jaw closed with a strip torn from another one. Two copper pennies were laid over his closed eyelids to keep them shut.

To keep him flat and straight, before rigor mortis set in, Domingo and Vicente had opened up the folding flaps of the parlour table and had laid him flat on his back on it. The women did not attempt to straighten his neck, in case the Coroner demanded further medical examination.

"When they hear about a man being suddenly dead, they always think he's been in a fight — especially when it's down in the docks," Peggy remarked sagely. "That's why they want to take a look — 'cos then it would be murder. Lucky we are, nobody called the police, or we'd have had them on our backs as well." She had been practical and calm, and, before she hurried home to her out-of-work husband and her babies to give them their tea, Rosita had hugged her and thanked her.

"You're so young to face all this," she told her. "But I couldn't ask Bridget, because she's minding Manuel."

"It's not so bad for me. Me mam was like Bridget, and she taught me. As a young girl, I often helped her bring a kid or lay somebody out." She wrapped her shawl round herself, and added, "When I've got the kids to bed, I'll come back and sit with you for a spell."

After Peggy had departed, Rosita felt suddenly very alone. There was much to do. She must first persuade her mother and Maria to eat something — and she had better have a bite to eat herself — what with Francesca not yet weaned and the demands of the child inside her. The nappies hadn't been washed, the fire needed remaking — it was nearly out; and she must do Juan's job of bringing some buckets of coal up the cellar step, not something she *wanted* to do while pregnant. And Manuel would be back soon, she supposed. She hoped Bridget had given him some tea.

In the event, it was Peggy who carried up the coal. She returned more quickly than Rosita had hoped. And it was she who took Manuel's boots and socks off before Pat slipped him into his bed still sound asleep. She stayed until early the next morning when she had to go to attend to her own children.

Not only Peggy and the other women had proved their worth on that awful day. Father Felipe remained for a while with Micaela. Though Spanish, he knew enough Basque to speak comfortingly to the distraught woman in her own language. Firmly, gently, he helped her to regain control of herself. He had remained with the family until after the doctor's call and the removal of the body from the sofa to the table, where it was temporarily covered with a sheet. Rosita brought them both wine, and the priest and the broken old woman sipped it together. It was he who suggested to Rosita that, to give themselves strength, they should eat before formally laying poor Juan out.

Micaela smiled dimly at this, but as soon as Father Felipe left, she insisted that the laying out be done right away. Wearily, Rosita agreed, but said she must feed a screaming Francesca first.

Working neatly and carefully, as she always did, Micaela had seemed better as she gave the last service she could to a well-loved husband of forty years. Within, she was beating herself because she had asked him to do a job, at his age, which involved climbing a ladder; it did not help her to remind herself that he had spent his youth climbing the rigging of sailing ships and had always had excellent balance.

Afterwards, she had eaten a little, as did a tear-sodden Maria. Then she had gone into the parlour, rosary in hand. Maria had determinedly blown her nose and had followed her in, to sit with her until Peggy returned to join them. Dry-eyed and drained, Rosita had settled Francesca for the night and washed a couple of nappies, ready for the morning. She was thankful when, later, Manuel was brought in sound asleep.

She was worried about the strain on Maria, already so weak and frail, and, as soon as she could, she had gone to take her place in the parlour. "Bed, Maria," she had ordered briefly, as she took out her rosary. "You must keep your strength up." So, protesting feebly, Maria had gone upstairs to the bedroom she shared with Manuel and had wept very quietly so that she did not wake the child.

* * *

Only a few minutes after Manuel had been sent to school the following morning, Ould Biggs, the undertaker, presented himself. He was brief, obsequious and politely sympathetic. He delicately inquired if they had Burial Insurance.

As Rosita led him into the parlour, she assured him that they had and that it was paid up to date. He nodded his head in acknowledgement of this welcome news, as he approached Micaela and took her hand and silently held it for a moment.

Then he briskly whipped out his tape measure and measured Juan. He was respectful of a man who had given him a lot of work for his horse buses when dispatching Basque emigrants and he did not touch the body.

He then turned back to Micaela and, taking her hand again, he asked her very kindly if she would like to step round in the afternoon to choose the kind of coffin she wanted. "You and your daughters, like. And a memorial stone — I've got a nice line in them — and I've several beautiful coffins in stock."

The candle on the table at the head of the corpse flickered from the weight of the sigh that Micaela let go, before she whispered her agreement to the visit. Tears rolled slowly down her cheeks to drop on her black apron. Maria, seated on the horsehair sofa, put her head down on her knees and wept, her silver and ebony rosary dripping from her fingers in the candlelight, as if its tiny glitter were tears and that it wept for her as well. The doctor had left a sedative for her to take, but she had not swallowed it. It lay forgotten on the mantelpiece.

Rosita had hardly ushered him out of the front door, when a grand gentleman caused a stir in the street by arriving in a motor car, a contraption rarely seen by the local inhabitants. He announced that he was from the Coroner's Office, and Micaela, wearied from mourning and lack of sleep, managed to rouse herself sufficiently to give him a fairly coherent description of the accident. He inspected the offending ladder and the broken drainpipe, while rain poured down on his bald head; he had, of course, removed his bowler hat on entering the house. He assured Micaela that she had nothing to worry about and that she could go ahead with arrangements for the funeral. The Coroner's Office would see that Mr Biggs was informed that all was in order for him to proceed.

Just before Manuel was due back from school for his midday meal, Madeleine Saitua dropped by to deliver a piping hot rabbit pie, which she put into the kitchen oven to keep warm. Rosita seized the opportunity to ask her if her boys would help her to rearrange the parlour furniture, after Juan had been coffined, so that the coffin could be supported by a chair at either end, and the neighbours could move round it when they came to pay their respects.

Madeleine gazed compassionately at the white-faced younger woman, and said, "Of course, luv.

Just send Mannie up with a message when you're ready. And you try to get some rest, luv."

Rosita agreed that she would and saw her out with an expression of thanks for the pie. She was still watching her plod up the street, when Peggy came by on her way to the corner grocery. She asked if Ould Biggs had been yet, and when Rosita said he had, Peggy remarked, "Manuel'll be able to see his granddad when he's all peaceful in his coffin — with flowers round him. Frannie'll be too young to remember him, more's the pity."

Rosita had not yet had time to weep herself and, at this remark, she felt suddenly choked with grief. She managed, however, to answer her kindly, blundering neighbour, by saying cautiously, "If the boy would like to."

⋆ ⋆ ⋆

After doing his best to describe the loss of his grandfather to Lorilyn, Old Manuel leaned back in his chair and gazed abstractedly out of his study window at the distant mountains of the United States on the other side of the Strait of Juan de Fuca. He could only guess at the sorrow and despair of his grandmother, his mother and his delicate aunt; they had done their best to swallow their own grief and reassure their frightened little boy.

16

THIS was the second year during which Manuel had attended St Peter's Catholic School, and he was accustomed to its highly disciplined system. He knew that when he was bigger and more able to travel safely by himself, he would be sent to St Francis Xavier's, a Catholic Grammar School, and, there, his real education would begin.

On the morning after his grandfather's death, when he pushed open the wrought-iron gate and entered the asphalted school yard, the atmosphere of the school seemed, unexpectedly, very peculiar; the children were too quiet. Instead of rushing about to make the most of their last moments of play before they were sent indoors, they were hanging about uneasily.

Andrew Pilar, usually belligerent, came with a crony to stare at him; Manuel tried not to cringe, as he prepared to slap away hands which often pinched him cruelly in his private parts.

To his surprise, Andrew simply snorted and turned away, followed closely by his slouching friend. Then Miss Carr, usually so brisk and acid-tongued, took him by the hand and put him quietly in the line being formed by the youngsters in his class, preparatory to being marched into their classroom. As if he did not know that he was supposed to line up, he thought bewilderedly. Behind him, Andrew in the next higher class, was given short shrift and pushed into his proper place. No child spoke to Manuel, though many stared at him.

Miss Carr stood in front of the ragged lines. In response to a sharp command, the children shuffled to align themselves by stretching out their left arm to put their hand on the right shoulder of the person next to them.

Four lines behind him, there was a small sob and a girl began to cry. Miss Carr blinked behind her pince-nez. She said kindly, "Rosemary, come and stand by me, child."

Manuel did not dare to turn his head, as the children behind him made way for Rosemary, who was one of the *big* girls, aged ten. This morning, her straggling flaxen hair was even more untidy than usual, and her white pinafore, worn over a navy-blue serge dress, was crumpled from being used to mop up floods of tears.

"Come to me, dear," Miss Carr said softly, her own mouth quivering. She put a protective arm round the girl's shoulders and held her close to her, as she quickly glanced up ferociously at her other charges. "Stop shuffling," she ordered. Then Manuel was aware of her worried frown, as her gaze rested on him for a moment.

She gave a deep sigh, and ordered, "Standard One! Attention!"

She successfully marshalled her charges into the hall of the school for the morning Assembly. On a small platform stood the Headmaster, flanked by some of his teachers. Behind them hung portraits of George V and Queen Mary.

In addition to the usual hymn, announcements, prayers and short homily, the pupils were ordered to pray for the soul of Rosemary's father and for all The Fallen; Manuel was far from sure who or what The Fallen were. Could you lose your soul without being dead, perhaps? If, however, praying for Rosemary's father would cheer her up a bit, he was willing to do it.

He felt that if one was supposed to pray for The Fallen, it was very disappointing that the Headmaster did not order prayers for Grandpa. With a sigh, he assumed that it was because he had only fallen off a ladder and that that did not count.

On their way home for their midday meal, he discussed this a little anxiously with Joey and Brian Wing, and they agreed that since Grandpa did, indeed, fall, he must be one of The Fallen. Manuel began to cry helplessly, and Joey and Brian became scared, because they barely understood what had happened to his grandfather; they were relieved when they reached the Echaniz doorstep and could leave him.

When he entered the kitchen-living-room it was so quiet that he could hear Pudding energetically washing her face. His mother sat at the table, writing a letter. Two addressed envelopes were propped against the milk jug. Though the fire had been lit before he left for school, there was none of the usual smell of dinner cooking.

At his entry, Rosita looked up. "Hello, darling," she greeted him absently, and then continued to write. He heaved off his Wellingtons and flung them into the boot cupboard by the fireplace, where Pudding usually gave birth to her kittens. He took off his macintosh and hung it on the back door — he had to stand on tiptoe to reach the wooden peg.

"Where's Granny?" he asked. "And Auntie?"

His mother signed her name at the foot of her letter, and folded it carefully. As she slipped it into an envelope, she replied, "Grandma's resting on her bed for a bit, and Auntie Maria is sitting in the parlour by Grandpa — Madeleine Saitua's there, too."

As she licked the envelope to seal it, Manuel watched her, trying not to grizzle; he was disconcerted at the lack of the usual bustle surrounding the production of the midday dinner.

"Hasn't his angel come yet?" he inquired cautiously.

Taken aback by the question, Rosita paused in her sealing of the letter. She looked down at her son, and saw the traces of tears. He had put his hand on her lap, as if to concentrate her attention on him. When she did not answer him immediately, he explained, "Auntie Maria told me that Grandpa's Guardian Angel would come to take care of him."

Rosita put down her letter, and lifted the child on to her knee. She felt guilty that she had paid little attention to him since her father's accident; Francesca had, of a necessity, to be fed and her napkins changed, or she would have screamed steadily; but her quiet eldest child had been fobbed off on to Bridget next door.

As he curled up thankfully in her lap, she struggled to keep her voice normal, as she replied, "The angel bore his soul away when he fell, dear. We've only to take care of his body. Grandma's having a beautiful box made for him to rest in, and we'll put lots of flowers round him, and Father Felipe will help us to say prayers for him. Then he will be laid in the cemetery under the trees, where it's quiet and peaceful. We think he'll like that."

With his head against his mother's shoulder, Manuel considered this explanation, and then looked round the kitchen-living-room. "I'm awfully hungry," he said heavily.

Rosita gave a broken laugh. "I haven't forgotten your dinner, luv. I've a nice piece of rabbit pie waiting for you in the oven. Mrs Saitua brought it just now — wasn't it kind of her?" Manuel slipped off her lap, as she rose, and she went on, "Grandma says she's going to cook something hot for us for tea."

It was suddenly infinitely comforting to hear that Grandma would be undertaking some of her usual tasks. He ate his rabbit pie, and went back to school feeling better.

His mother, who had not shared the meal with him, walked part of the way with him; she had to post the letters she had written to Pedro, to Great-Uncle in Bilbao and to Leo. She had addressed the latter to Nevada, in the hope that it would be redirected to Leo wherever he might be. She sighed, when she thought about her brother; he was barely twenty, completely alone in an area of the States noted for its lawlessness. He was hardly literate, but she wondered if he realized how thankful his mother would be to have even a couple of lines from him regardless of whether the news was good or bad.

She promised herself that that evening she would tackle letters to her elder brother, Agustin, and to the Echaniz family on their farm in the Pyrenees.

Leo never received his letter, and Pedro was given his only when his boat docked at Liverpool two months later.

* * *

That same day following his grandfather's death, Bridget invited Manuel over to play with Mary and Joey after tea. "It will keep the kid occupied — keep his mind off things," she told Rosita.

The two little boys were swopping cigarette cards on the mat in front of the Connollys' blazing fire, when Manuel's mystification about The Fallen was clarified a little.

Bridget was washing the dishes and Pat was reading the back page of the newspaper, where the sporting news was usually featured. "Proper awful about Frank Abbott," she shouted.

"Eh?"

"You know, Frank Abbott. He's a stoker in the Royal Navy — on the *Abouki*."

"Oh, aye. Something happened to him?"

"The Jerries sunk his ship. She got the telegram yesterday evening, poor soul. And her with three kids."

Pat put down his newspaper, and nodded. "There's going to be a lot of them," he prophesied.

Joey interrupted. "Is that Rosemary's dad?"

"Yes, luv. She'll have to go into service or summat. No more school for her — or the two boys either — they'll have to work."

"Why, Auntie Bridget?" This from Manuel.

She looked kindly down at the boys, while the sooty water from her saucepans ran slowly down her fat arms. "Well, when you haven't a dad there's no money coming in. Even if their mam can find work, it won't be enough."

Pat had caught the gist of her remarks, and he said, "Ethel Abbott'll get a bit of a pension."

"Ta, ever so," replied his wife with heavy sarcasm. "With a bit of luck it may feed the cat. And him serving his country, and all."

Pat made a wry face. "It's true. They don't care a tinker's cuss about folk like us. Dying for your country! That's a joke." He returned to his sporting news.

So if you were drowned at sea, you had died for your country and joined The Fallen. He swallowed. The idea frightened him — Papa was at sea. And Grandpa, who had been king in his own home, would not be there any more; the thought gave him a dreadful, empty feeling in the pit of his stomach. The news that, because Rosemary's father had been killed in the war she would have to go into domestic service, did not help. All Basques knew that to be a servant in a private house was humiliating in the extreme; Panchika Saitua was the only person, with whom he was acquainted, who served in a private home — and Grandpa had always said that Saitua's daughter was the stupidest woman he had ever met — which probably accounted for her situation.

* * *

Dying for your country did not help your family, ruminated Old Manuel. He had certainly learned that from Rosemary's tragedy, and, in adulthood he had borne it in mind — not that it had done him much good; his legs ached every day of his life from the effects of another war, another time.

He remembered Miss Carr again — and the other anxious teachers. For years afterwards, as men were lost at sea or killed in their thousands in the trenches of France, those women must have tried to comfort their pupils, while their own brothers and sweethearts were constantly at risk. He still recollected them with respect.

17

THE cost of Grandpa's funeral was paid from his Burial Insurance with the Prudential. Their representative, a small, neatly dressed man in a bowler hat, brought the money and delivered it to the widow with some ceremony. He had been coming to the house for years to collect sixpences as premiums. His appearance in the street always caused the same worry and, occasionally, consternation to housewives that the rent man did; nobody missed paying him if they could help it; the thought of being condemned to burial in a pauper's grave was too terrible to contemplate. He was a kindly soul, however, and had been known to help out a harassed family by putting their contribution in himself, hoping that they would pay him later, in a week when there was more work in the docks.

It was with genuine sympathy that he sat with Grandma for a few minutes, conveying his condolences and that of his company, as he passed the cash to her. "Mr Barinèta was a grand man, Missus. We shall all miss him," he told her, as he took out a handkerchief, grey with much washing, and blew his nose hard.

She smiled dimly at him, and Rosita pressed a glass of wine on him. When he rose to leave all three women thanked him effusively for coming so promptly.

He insisted that Manuel should see him out, which the boy did, while the pound notes slipped from Micaela's lap on to the rag hearth mat, as she turned to cling silently to Rosita, and Maria wept.

Carried by his mother, Manuel was taken into the parlour to say goodbye to Grandpa, before the coffin was finally closed. He had been nervous about this, because a girl at school had told him that she had been made to kiss her dead aunt in her coffin, and her cheek felt cold like a frog and she smelled horrid.

No such gesture was expected of him.

Grandpa looked strangely young, not really like the volatile old man he had known; he had a bandage round his jaw, which made him look odd. He said, "Goodbye, Grandpa," and slipped down from Rosita's arms, to run back to the warm familiarity of the kitchen.

He remembered the funeral itself quite clearly. His mother, Grandma and Auntie Maria wore black headscarves, and their blouses, skirts, shoes and stockings were the same dead colour. He himself wore his best black Sunday suit, which was rather short for him at the cuffs and ankles. The elaborate, horse-drawn hearse was followed by numerous women, their flowered pinafores doffed for the occasion, so that they, too, were in black. Those few men who were not at sea, or who were not working that day, followed the women; they, too, wore their black Sunday suits with black berets on their heads; some were very old and limped along with the aid of walking sticks; Manuel did not know many of the latter — they were the men with whom Grandpa had played dominoes in quiet corners of the Baltic Fleet. At the end of the procession, two Irish neighbours, both of whom worked a night shift, followed respectfully; they were distinguished from the Basque community by their flat caps and grubby grey raincoats. Both of them had a band of black ribbon sewn around their left sleeve, to indicate that they were in mourning.

Next to the hearse in the procession was a carriage for the immediate family. Auntie Maria had insisted on being dressed and accompanying her mother, so Mrs Saitua came in the carriage with them, to help Maria in and out and generally sustain everybody. Nobody spoke. As they passed up the street, any men who saw the procession, whether acquaintances or strangers, took off their hats as a mark of respect to the dead. A sprinkle of newly uniformed soldiers saluted the hearse, rather than doffing their caps.

After the funeral, everybody crowded into the Barinèta home for cakes and sandwiches made by Rosita and her neighbours, washed down by all the wine in the house and by strong black tea for those who liked it.

It was not as grim as Manuel had expected. The kitchen-living-room was filled with men, smoking like fireplaces on days when there was an east wind. They talked quietly in a mixture of Basque and English. They sometimes laughed as they recalled amusing stories of the dead man.

Grandma Micaela's rocking chair had been

moved into the parlour, the two chairs which had supported the coffin having been hastily moved back to the kitchen-living-room.

Surrounded by a phalanx of women, she sat with Francesca sleeping soundly on her lap, and received, with bent head, the commiserations of her friends and neighbours. To Manuel, she seemed to have become suddenly very old, with none of her usual sprightliness and quick movements. Beside her sat Auntie Maria, coughing, and weeping steadily into a black handkerchief.

Rosita, aided by Bridget Connolly and Madeleine Saitua, patiently filled cups and glasses, put out a number of saucers to act as extra ash trays, and accepted, with gratitude, small gifts of food or wine brought by kindly neighbours.

* * *

Old Manuel put down his ballpoint pen, and stretched himself stiffly in his swivel chair. Having been bereaved of Kathleen, he now understood something of his Grandmother's despair. For a while, after the funeral, she had been almost completely closed into herself — terribly lost to the world continuing to struggle round her — as if her mind had ceased to function. She would do slowly and mechanically anything Rosita asked her to do, and, when it was finished, would sit in her rocking chair, her hands in her lap.

It was Rosita, who, with a worried frown, took

on the difficult task of making Pedro's allotment stretch to cover all the needs of three women and two children. She tended to be short with her son, and he was glad to go to school, he remembered.

Rosita herself felt far from well. As the weeks of her pregnancy progressed, she ceased feeding Francesca herself, and gave her bottles of diluted cow's milk and bits of mashed up vegetable from her dinner plate.

In those early weeks, without the weekly sum handed out by Juan Barinèta from his cash box, they had had to augment the housekeeping by taking money out of the boxes under Micaela's bed, money saved for clothes, for extra coal for bitter winters and other small emergencies. This worried Rosita desperately.

She had hoped that her father had something still in his cash box, kept at the back of the wardrobe. Sometimes, after a group of emigrants had passed through, it could be expected to hold quite a sum. When she and Micaela opened it, however, it proved to have very little in it. It dawned on them that they had not had any lodgers for some months before Juan's death. He had mentioned that the threat of war must have made would be emigrants nervous about taking a long sea journey. He had joked about it, but, as they surveyed the small pile of silver and a few pound notes, they realized that he must have been very worried about his financial situation; yet, he had not bothered them with it. "Perhaps he was thinking of going to sea again," suggested

Micaela. "That's what he would have likely done in time."

Rosita nodded. It made no difference now. With the money they managed to buy a new jersey and boots for Manuel at the beginning of the school term — the child had grown out of his current garments. They also bought three months' supply of coal, before the price went up for the winter months.

They did their best not to touch the Post Office savings account in Micaela's name — because that was intended, in the long term, for school fees. They were driven eventually to draw enough for two weeks' rent, rather than get behind with such an essential payment.

Rosita wrote to Pedro again, care of the company, asking if he could increase his allotment. She hoped that the owners of the tramp steamer, of which he was first mate, would be aware of at least one of the ports which the boat would touch, and would forward her letter to their agent there.

"That's the worst of tramps," Rosita remarked to Bridget Connolly, who met her on the way to post the letter. "Even the owners often don't know, for sure, where a ship is — wandering from port to port, picking up and putting down — and not getting back to Liverpool until God knows when."

Bridget hugged her shawl round her. There had been a bit of a frost that morning, and she had been thinking how nice it would be to have a real overcoat — with a lining to it.

She said doubtfully, "Pat mentioned that your Pedro was trying for a berth with Larrinaga's. It would be proper nice if he could get one — at least you'd know when he was likely to be home."

Rosita shrugged. "I wish he could. I haven't heard from him yet in reply to my letter about my dad. And I wrote to him earlier that I'm expecting again. He writes to me, but he isn't getting my letters."

"Aye, luv. Try not to worry. At least he's in work. Have you heard from Leo?"

"Not for a long while. I can't imagine what's happened to him. I worry myself sick sometimes. And my other brother, Agustin — he's in a tramp steamer, like Pedro — and my uncle in Bilbao — Agustin lives with him — doesn't know where the lad is going, half the time." She paused, and then added grimly, "Agustin's lucky, though — his ship is Spanish-registered — nothing to fear from the Germans."

"So he still lives in Bilbao?"

"Oh, aye. He's been courting a Bilbao girl for years. They're waiting on a house in the same street as Uncle, so the girl will have plenty of company, while he's at sea."

"So you can't expect much help from him — or your uncle?"

"No. They have a struggle."

"Well, let's hope Leo comes home."

Rosita's lips trembled. "I wish he would, Bridget. I wish he would."

* * *

Unaware of Rosita's financial worries, Manuel played with Brian Wing and Joey Connolly, whipping in and out of the alleyways in wild games of tag or cops and robbers, or plodding up to Princes Park to collect conkers from the horse chestnut trees. The chestnuts were put in corners of the kitchen fireplace to dry out. A hole was then carefully bored through the centre and a piece of string inserted. After that, a boy was fully equipped to play conkers for months, until all his chestnuts had succumbed to hits from those of the other boys, after which everybody had to wait for next year's crop of nuts.

When he felt the need for male support, Manuel gradually turned to Pat Connolly. He learned that if he faced the deaf man squarely, Pat could read what he was saying from the way his lips moved, a discovery which made Manuel feel very clever. Pat himself got pleasure from playing with him and with Joey.

⋆ ⋆ ⋆

One winter afternoon, when Grandma had been invited to a glass of wine with another Basque lady, equally wizened, Manuel unwillingly accompanied his mother down to the shipping office to collect his father's allotment, which was paid out to her each week.

"Auntie Maria isn't feeling too good, but she's going to watch Francesca for me, and I don't want her to be bothered with you, too."

Manuel had not the slightest desire to visit the

shipping office, and he whined fretfully that he was fine with Joey.

"Joey's mam's delivering a baby," Rosita told him shortly. "Peggy O'Brien is watching Joey. She doesn't need anyone else cluttering up her kitchen."

Manuel resigned himself to a boring walk down to Water Street.

Instead of the usual acne-covered clerk, Rosita was dealt with by a bald, older man, who was obviously unaccustomed to the task of coping with the wives of ships' crews crowding round his beautifully polished counter; the wives were interspersed with noisy toddlers, who tried to see what was going on by scrambling up the ornamentation of the counter; they left dirty fingermarks all along the top of it and scratches on the customer's side. Enough to drive a decent man out of his wits.

As he carefully checked his account book, one woman called teasingly, "What's happened to our Charley? Why isn't he here?"

The clerk looked up and answered sourly, "He's volunteered — and about time."

The woman grunted, and made a face at the wife standing next to her. "There's a lot as has done that."

"This country has to be defended, Madam. It is the duty of all men — of the right age — to join the colours." The remarks sounded like a reproach to the menfolk of the waiting women, and a whispering grumble went through them. Didn't he know that they all had menfolk at sea, who were in constant danger from German attack? However, none of them dared to respond to his remark; you never knew how word might get back to the managers, and a job be lost in consequence.

Rosita had intended to ask Charley which would be the best port to write to and what the agent's address was, in order to get a letter to Pedro; but she was unnerved by the portly man she faced. She picked up the money he threw down in front of her, signed for it, and then counted it carefully in front of the clerk. He sucked through his teeth in irritation at the delay.

Flustered by his aggressive stance, Rosita counted it again. "I'm short a joey," she said finally, a tremor in her voice.

"You telling me I made a mistake?"

"Yes," she whispered.

"I don't make mistakes."

Faced with such male intransigence, Rosita prepared to sacrifice a threepenny piece she could ill afford, when the woman behind her, braver than the rest, addressed the cashier. "There's a joey underneath your cuff, you stupid bugger. I seen it roll. Slap money down like that and it'll fall all over the place."

Rosita glanced round. A heavily built, middle-aged woman, her black shawl decently draped over her head and shoulders, was glaring at the discomfited clerk. She had a face like a bulldog, and at the moment it was flushed red with indignation barely suppressed. "You don't have to put up with the likes of him," she assured Rosita roundly. "Youse right. And there's the joey." A fat forefinger shot over Rosita's shoulder to point at the tiny silver coin, which lay where a second before the clerk's arm had rested.

As if it were something dirty, the clerk flicked the coin across to Rosita with his thumbnail.

At this further display of discourtesy, a murmur went through the crowd of women.

Rosita picked up the coin and put it carefully into her change purse. She turned to smile at the woman who had been so helpful. The woman gave a wide grin, displaying a mouth empty of teeth, except for one incisor. "We're going to miss our Charley, aren't we, duck?" she remarked loudly.

Rosita agreed, and small titters at the clerk's discomfiture were audible amongst the onlookers.

"What's volunteered, Mam?" Manuel asked, as they went slowly down the stone steps of the shipping office.

"It means Charley's gone to be a soldier."

"What for?"

"To fight the Boche in France."

Manuel considered this information for a minute or two. Then he asked, "But why, Mam?" There was general puzzlement in the small boy's tone.

The brush with the cashier had upset Rosita, and she answered him impatiently. "For goodness' sake, stop asking silly questions. I don't know."

And when, later on, she considered his question, she really did not understand *why* Britain had gone to war. Let the damned Frogs look after themselves, she thought bitterly, as long as Pedro comes home safely.

As she turned the handle of her front door, she paused, her head against the woodwork. She felt exhausted, and the immense courage she had shown since her father's death suddenly deserted her. The bullying in the shipping office, the sense that Charley would probably get himself killed, the fear that Pedro was in danger, her unwanted pregnancy, and the loss of a good and well-loved father all came together. Her underlying grief finally exploded. She burst into wild tears.

"Mam," cried Manuel in alarm. "Ma, what's up?"

"It's all right. I'll be all right in a minute," she gasped.

18

MICAELA had returned from her visit to her Basque friend. Now, seated in her rocking chair with her sewing box beside her, she was stitching a button on to the neck opening of one of Francesca's vests. She whipped round when she heard the hysterical crying.

Both Manuel and she were filled with consternation, as Rosita threw herself on to her knees and buried her face in her mother's lap to weep broken-heartedly.

Micaela dropped the little vest on to the floor. "My dear! Whatever happened?" She lifted her daughter up to embrace her.

The boy was appalled. He had never seen his mother cry before. In dismay, he bawled, "Grandma!" and crowded close to her as if to displace his mother and crawl on to her lap. Grandma was *his* lap, *his* rock, not his mother's or Francesca's. He, too, began to cry, as Micaela put out an arm to him.

"It's Father!" Rosita sobbed. "What shall we do without him?"

Their joint grief came out in a flood of tears, and it washed away some of both women's misery.

As their weeping began to subside, Micaela slowly let go of both Rosita and Manuel. She lifted the corner of her flowered overall and wiped Rosita's swollen eyes, and then did the same for her scared, woebegone grandson. As she wiped her own face, she smiled slightly at Manuel, and said, "My goodness! We're worse than a wet week, aren't we?"

She sounded a little more like the Grandma he had known before his grandfather was killed, and he smiled weakly back.

Rosita stumbled slowly to her feet. "I'm sorry, Mam," she said to her mother. "The clerk in the shipping office was as rude as hell — he wasn't the usual one — and it was the last straw."

Micaela pulled her handkerchief out of her sleeve, and handed it to her. "Never mind, my love," she comforted. "A good cry can set you up again." She tightened her arm round Manuel, and planted a firm kiss on his cheek. She then got up, her rocking chair swinging behind her with the suddenness of her movement. "Now, what we need is a good, strong cup of tea, and we'll all feel better." As a faint wail came from upstairs, she added practically, "You'd better get Frannie up from her nap."

"Can I have a cup of tea?" asked Manuel, with a sudden desire to be promoted to more grown-up customs. "I'm six, now."

"Yes," agreed Grandma, as she filled the kettle from the single kitchen tap. "You're a big boy — you can have tea."

With Francesca on Rosita's lap, contentedly sucking at an old ink bottle filled with milk and with a rubber teat on it, and Manuel sitting with them at the table, manfully sipping tea out of a mug, the women began to discuss what they could do to improve their financial position.

As the house was quite big, they agreed that a couple of rooms could be sublet. "It would help to pay the rent," admitted Rosita, with a dry sob left over from the intensity of her weeping.

Content that life seemed suddenly to be a little more normal, Manuel left half his tea and slipped down from the table to go out to play.

Still anxious about Rosita's storm of tears, Micaela tried to focus her eyes upon her daughter's face, but it was difficult to see quite straight these days; everything looked slightly misty. She wished heartily that Pedro or one of her sons would dock. Why hadn't Juan insisted that Leo stay in Liverpool? A home needed as many men as possible.

Since Leo had left for Nevada, she had had only two letters from him, both of them not long after his departure. In neither of them had he seemed very happy about what he had found in his new country; he had said sarcastically that if he were to be a shepherd all his life — which seemed to have been the fate of other Basques he had met — he might just as well keep sheep in Vizcaya.

After Juan's death, Micaela watched eagerly for a letter; surely he would reply to their letters to him about the accident, however bad he normally was at correspondence. But there had not been a single word from him. Had something awful happened to him as well? And no one in Nevada to write to tell her about it?

She forced herself to turn her attention to her immediate worries.

"There might be a decent Basque boy who'd be glad of a clean place to lodge," she suggested to her daughter.

Rosita responded glumly. "I haven't seen a new face round here for months — the lads are probably getting ships out of Bilbao — they'd be safer in neutral ships. And some of them'll be working ashore — places like Uncle's foundry in Bilbao must be that busy with armaments, they'd take on anybody who came through the gates."

Micaela chewed her lower lip. She nodded agreement.

The hinges of the front door squeaked, as the door was pushed wide, and they both turned as they heard the slow dragging steps of Maria coming down the passage. After Micaela had returned from her visit, Maria had slipped out for a gossip with an old acquaintance, who lived just round the curve of the street. Now, as she returned, she threw back her shawl from her greying, sandy head to survey them with sombre, watery blue eyes. She was swaying with fatigue from her tiny walk. As she noted the two women bunched closely together at the table, she inquired nervously, "Anything wrong?"

Both women smiled, and Rosita said calmly, "No, we were talking, that's all. Like a cup of tea?"

When Maria had slowly seated herself on the sofa, and, with a thankful sigh, put her feet up, Rosita set a cup of tea on the small table beside her, and Micaela said, "We were thinking we could rent a couple of rooms — to help out. What do you think?"

"Oh, aye," Maria responded, as she stirred her tea and eyed them suspiciously.

Because she was sick, they did not habitually discuss family problems with her — as if, from her place on the sofa, she did not see most of what went on, she considered sardonically — and she resented this; she wanted to be part of the living world as long as she could. Though, at the moment, she was very tired, Micaela's remark gave her a chance to be included, so she continued aloud. "Well, now, I've been up with Mrs Halloran, to see how her Eileen is — I don't think her Eileen's long for this world — and she mentioned that they're going to extend the blacksmith's workshop behind her house — and they're going to pull down some houses at the back to do it." She put her cup down in her saucer with a loud clink, as if to express anger, and added, "No thought of the families living in the houses, of course!" She paused, to ruminate.

"Mother of God!" exclaimed Micaela. "As if there isn't enough racket already! Yesterday, the steam hammers started up and shook the table so much that the sugar basin was nearly jiggled off it — I caught it just in time."

"Oh, aye. It's bad," agreed Maria. "And it'll be worse. Just listen to the horses' hooves at this minute. There must be half a dozen drays in the road — and every horse'll have left us a little present, I'll be bound." They all listened as, through the open front door, came the shouts of the draymen and the clack-clack of their clogs or hob-nailed boots.

"Phew!" exclaimed Rosita, and went to shut the door as the strong odour of new manure swept into the house, mixed with the permanent fishy smell from the sardine-packing plant nearby. "Those that go to sea don't know what they're missing!" she said with a laugh, as she sat down again.

Aunt Maria finally picked up again the original thread of her discourse. "Because of the new workshop, Mr Halloran's brother, George, and his wife, Effie — you know Effie — have got to look for a place. Works for a brewery, he does — drayman on deliveries. They'd pay their rent, they would." She put down her teacup and coughed politely into her hanky.

"Well, that's an idea," Micaela replied diffidently. Having a woman in the house would mean her cooking on Micaela's own kitchen range — which would cause problems.

Maria was, however, secretly filled with glee, when Micaela reluctantly took her advice and arranged to rent the large first-floor room to Effie Halloran. Both the Halloran sons had volunteered for the Navy, so the couple felt that they would have plenty of space in such a big room.

* * *

Once they had moved in, there were the usual complaints between the women about the sink in the kitchen-living-room being full of each other's sooty saucepans after cooking, and arguments about who was responsible for this or that bit of cleaning.

Regularly, Effie would announce loftily and tearfully, "I'll look for something else, I will. I'll get out of here." But Mr Halloran would point out to his wife that cheap housing was almost impossible to find.

"You can talk," Effie would spit back at him, her dark, careworn face wrinkled up in disgust. "Youse at work all day. It's me as has to put up with Them."

Them, in the shape of Grandma, trying hard to get a grip on life again, insisted on a cleaned-up sandstone sink and fixed hours for each of them to use the kitchen oven. A disgruntled Effie held her tongue, as far as she could, and acceded.

Though the women got on each other's nerves, there were days when they would sit comfortably on the front step in the autumn sunlight, to discuss the latest hurried marriage in the neighbourhood, or the tragedies of local men killed — or worse, missing, presumed killed — in France or at sea.

Effie Halloran could not read and Micaela read English only with difficulty, so Rosita would often read the *Evening Express* to them, after George Halloran had finished poring over the sporting pages to see if the horses he had backed had won.

The reading, added to the gossip which George picked up, as he drove his cartloads of barrels of beer from public house to public house, meant that the women probably knew as much about the war as most local people did.

As he hauled the empty barrels out of the pubs' cellars, and then carefully rolled the full ones down to the pot boy waiting in each cellar, George heard, at second hand from the pot boy, numerous seamen's stories of what was happening at sea; and he sometimes regaled Effie with them, as he ate his tea. Occasionally, an innkeeper would stand him half a pint of beer to replace the perspiration he had lost in heaving heavy barrels about, and they, too, would pause to discuss the latest news.

"We don't know half of what They're up to," George would often say sagely to his wife. "They don't tell us nothing."

Though George Halloran was much surlier and less knowledgeable than Grandpa, he was stout and reliable-looking, and Manuel adopted him as part of the family. He also enjoyed being petted by Effie.

Effie missed her boys. "It's as if something's been cut off me," she would explain wistfully to anyone who would listen to such an insignificant shawlie.

Micaela and Rosita regarded her as much beneath them; they had considerable pride in being Basques, and in being literate. Poor Effie's pride consisted in keeping her room well scoured and being able to boast that both her boys were in the Royal Navy. She kept her head bowed and hoped only that her lads would survive the war.

Rosita admitted to Maria that she had been

correct in saying that the Hallorans would pay their rent. Effie knocked at the kitchen-living-room door every Friday night, and silently proffered the opened rent book, with five shillings in silver balanced precariously on it.

* * *

In late October that year, when Manuel was beginning to look forward to Guy Fawkes Day, a weary and dirty Pedro walked into his home. Hastily stuffed into his back pocket were Rosita's letters; they had been brought on board by the Mersey pilot, who had come to take his boat up the river to Liverpool. Already exhausted by a long, difficult voyage, he was greatly upset by the letters' contents.

As he entered the kitchen-living-room, he was greeted and fussed over by his womenfolk — even Maria broke her iron rule and clung to him and kissed him again and again on the cheek. He sat down thankfully close to the fire to rub his icy hands by the blaze, and accepted a mug of tea, heavy with sugar, as yet unrationed.

He was surprised when tiny hands grabbed his serge trousers, as Francesca crawled towards him and tried to pull herself up to stare at the new arrival.

His mind cluttered with weariness and bad news, Pedro stared back. Then a delighted grin creased his face, as he looked down at a tiny replica of his Rosita with the same wide blue eyes and tiny tendrils of bright-red hair.

He forgot his fatigue, put down his mug and grabbed her up to hug her with joy, despite a sopping wet nappy. He looked over the child's head at his wife, and both of them laughed.

"She's the spitting image of you," he told her. And then he asked, "Where's Mannie?"

"He's playing next door. He'll be in for his tea in a minute."

Micaela laughed when Pedro ruefully realized how wet his daughter was. She said to the child, "Come to Grandma, and I'll change you. You're making your daddy all wet."

Rosita came over to stand by him; she felt shaky with the relief of his safe return after such a long voyage. She gently caressed the back of his neck. "Where've you been?" she asked. "Did you get our letters?"

"The pilot brought them aboard today," he replied heavily. He looked at Micaela. "I'm so sad for you," he said to her, and stretched across the fireplace to catch her hand in his. "It must have been awful for you. I nearly had a fit when I read your letter, What happened exactly?"

Micaela did her best to control a fresh bout of tears, while behind her, Maria, humped up on the sofa with two shawls round her, bent her head over her teacup and shook with suppressed sobs.

Pedro looked anxiously at them. Both women looked as if a good gale would blow the pair of them to Kingdom Come. Even Rosita didn't appear too well. What a bowl of trouble it all was. He wanted to weep himself; but men can't cry. He badly needed a good meal and his bed, and some clean clothes to put on — he had not had his clothes off for days.

"It was a true accident," Micaela told him dully, her veined eyelids drooping to hide her agony of mind. She was still haunted by the fact that it was she who had urged Juan to do a job which, she felt, should have been done by a younger man.

After Micaela's cracked voice had faltered through the story, Rosita took Francesca from her, and herself changed the child on the table. She glanced back at her husband and said, "You look as if you've been in the wars. Where've you been, luv?"

Pedro picked up his mug of tea again, and drained it. "All over the bloody Atlantic," he told her exasperatedly. "Afraid of subs — and miles off course. They shouldn't have sent us to New York in the first place."

"New York? I thought they always did the west coast of Africa, and that way?"

"Oh, aye. Most times that's what we do. Not this time! We went from New York up to Halifax and Montreal. Then back south again to Charleston and then to New Orleans. I've been down as far as Argentina. The fellas were getting desperate that we'd never get home again, with one thing and another." He rubbed his tired eyes. "The war's changed everything." He felt in his pocket for his cigarettes, took one out and lit it, while the women watched in silence. Then he said, "Finally, we got a cargo for Liverpool, and were we thankful! But we had such foul weather and were blown so far south that the Ould Man was worried about coal being enough, never mind whether we'd be spotted by German subs."

Rosita was worrying about what she was going to give the unexpected arrival to eat, but she said, "You poor dear. Was the ship damaged at all?"

"She's got one or two nasty cracks in the deck. She needs a good overhaul. The Ould Man and the Chief are talking in the office now — and they'll not be mincing their words. She's that old, she's near falling apart, she is. They want a refit."

Rosita was still holding Francesca. She put her free arm round his shoulders, and he leaned against her. He wanted her.

"The company'll fire them for speaking up like that," Micaela said nervously. "Even a ship's master must mind what he says."

"Not nowadays," he said with a sudden grin. "They're getting short of men. Too many gone into the Navy — called up from the Reserve."

Rosita put Francesca down on the floor again and the child crawled away on her own small voyage of exploration. Her mother was anxious. It was unlike Pedro to complain seriously about anything. He carped occasionally, like all seamen did but it did not mean much; like his mates, he had a doglike patience and endurance, an acceptance of the dangers of his calling and of company parsimony. Now she felt sick at the thought of enemy submarines meeting a boat that probably could not travel at more than ten knots; it would be a sitting duck. As if in agreement with her apprehensions, the baby within her kicked quite energetically.

She pulled herself together, and said firmly, "I bet you're hungry. I haven't got a lot in the house, but I've got bacon and eggs — and fried bread?"

He nodded. "That sounds good," he assured her.

Manuel came wandering in in search of tea, and greeted his father exuberantly. Now Daddy was home everything would be all right, and Aunt Maria would stop bursting into tears every time you looked at her.

Micaela made herself get up briskly. "What about a wash and a shave," she suggested, "while Rosita gets the tea?"

"Oh, aye," Pedro responded, with feeling. He put his young son down from his knee. "Go and get the bucket from the outhouse," he told him. "We'll fill it from the oven tap, and I'll go up and have a good wash."

Obediently, Manuel went to collect the enamel bucket always used for this purpose and set it in the hearth under the shiny brass tap of the hot water tank. He squatted down and turned on the tap; it belched a thin stream of nearly boiling water. While he watched it trickle into the bucket, he wondered what his father had brought him this time.

Later, Micaela refilled the tank with cold water from the tap over the sink because Pedro forgot to do it.

"How long will you be home, Pedro?" Micaela asked, as she stretched upwards to lift some dinner-sized plates from the dresser shelf.

"Depends on what the Ould Fella fixes with the bosses," he responded morosely. "Maybe a few weeks."

A few weeks!

Even the threat of temporary unemployment if the ship were laid up made Rosita pause, frying-pan in hand. Despite Effie's rent, the best she had been able to do with her housekeeping was to avoid drawing further from the Post Office account and keep herself out of debt. Saving was impossible. A spurt of deep anxiety broke through her general relief at having her husband safely home, and a shiver went up her spine.

She laid the pan on the draining board while she went to the pantry to get bread, bacon and eggs and lard. They had never been short of food, she considered anxiously, though Grandma and she had contributed to this by keeping house with the greatest care, as if every farthing was the last one they had. Now, she worried. In the past if Pedro was laid off, there had always been Juan or Leo who were working. Now there was only Pedro.

It became a difficult evening, because Pedro was himself worn out. It was made worse because there was no wine in the house to alleviate the strain — one of Rosita's economies had been to do without it; and, then in the early morning, Francesca woke and howled miserably, aware, perhaps, of an extra person in the bedroom. Rosita made a mental note to move her the next day to a tiny bedroom over the hall; it was time she learned to sleep alone.

A sleepy Pedro was kind about the expected child; Rosita had been afraid that he would have been annoyed at such an early addition to his family. "Kids are sent by God," he told her; but it did not make him any happier.

19

THE next morning, while Rosita was still urging little Manuel to hurry up or he would be late for school, Pedro quickly shaved himself and washed his face at the kitchen sink. At Micaela's insistence, he gobbled a bowl of porridge, while standing with his back to the fire to warm himself. Then he grabbed his cap and jacket from the peg on the back door, gave Rosita a quick peck on her cheek, and said, "I hope to get back tonight." He hurried out of the house, to look at his damaged ship.

The previous night, as he turned over in bed before finally settling to sleep, he had told her that they would talk about their finances tomorrow; and he asked who the woman was he had met on the stairs, as he came up.

"Effie Halloran," Rosita had replied cryptically. Further explanation could wait until morning.

Now he had fled back to his ship, Rosita felt vexed. She knew that he had responsibilities there, but she needed to *talk* to him, quietly and sensibly. Then she realized that if the ship were laid up for some time, there would be too much time for discussion — and no income to discuss. She shrugged, as she turned to deal with Francesca, who was whining because she was hungry.

* * *

Under the bleary eyes of the third mate, the ship was being unloaded. They had taken a mixed cargo from New York to Charleston; there, they had picked up armour plate destined for Liverpool. The boat was teeming with men, from company clerks to stevedores, though the job was nearing completion.

The crew members who lived nearby were returning glumly to work; others would get shore leave later on.

Pedro went to look for the bosun; he had to arrange with him for innumerable small repair jobs to be done, and a lot of general maintenance which had been neglected during the voyage because of bad weather.

Perhaps it was the bad weather which had kept the U-boats fully occupied, too. It was a miracle that they had not encountered one. Off course, overloaded, too slow to be part of a convoy and obviously battered by the storm, any U-boat commandant who had spotted them would have licked his chops over them, thought Pedro grimly.

"The Ould Man's fit to be tied this morning," the bosun told him in reference to the ship's master. "And the Chief's down in the pit, giving hell to everybody in sight. The office told the pair of them to quit crying into their milk; this is no time for refits, they said; there's a war on!"

In fluent Basque, Pedro cursed all owners, and stuffed his chapped hands in his trouser pockets. The bosun grinned. He did not understand

Basque, but the tone conveyed the meaning. He said to Pedro, "They got some fellas down below looking at it; it mayn't be as bad as we think."

Pedro did not reply. He had sailed for three years in this old tub, because nothing better had offered. He had, however, been trying for a berth with de Larrinaga, a Basque family firm trading with the West Indies, out of Liverpool. Now that he had more experience under his belt, he felt that he should try again; before the war began, he had been thankful for a job; but, now, merchant seamen were in a little shorter supply and he might stand a better chance. The ship's turnaround was, however, much quicker than he had expected, so he had to defer his job-hunting.

Against the better judgement of the ship repairers who had been called in, minor repairs only were made and some rigging which had been lost in the storm was replaced.

Intent on a speedy turnaround, the owners gave short shrift to the complaints of the chief engineer about the needs of his engine room. A few days later, the ship sailed for New York, largely under ballast.

Painfully aware of the war being waged in the Atlantic and that he was serving in a ship which, as his second had remarked, was not much better than a bloody sieve, Pedro was careful not to communicate the crew's unease to his family. Rotten owners who ran rotten ships were one of the hazards of a seaman's life.

Nevertheless, he and Rosita were heavy-hearted on the day he sailed. Though she was pregnant, he would have loved to take her to bed that evening; but it was not possible with the eyes of his mother-in-law and Maria on him all the time. Sometimes, Rosita, too, wondered savagely if the two women really understood anything about human longings for the comfort of a regular sex life; how difficult it was to be faithful when your man was on a long voyage and other men looked hopefully at you. Did Maria understand the tension between Pedro and herself, as they sat gravely by the fire together, unsatisfied? The pain of loving a man so much was pain indeed.

That last evening, they had sat around discussing their money problems. Anxious that there should be no dissension between Pedro and Rosita, Micaela took the initiative in explaining to Pedro where his allotment went. As she spoke, her knitting needles flashed steadily; she was knitting her son-in-law a new navy-blue sweater.

Pedro listened without comment, while he cleaned out the bowl of his pipe with his penknife.

When she had finished, he said uneasily, "The minute I got your letters, when the pilot came aboard, I knew what you were up against. And I know you do your best — I've never seen either of you waste anything." He was grim-faced, as he drew on his cigarette. "I've been thinking that I can increase the allotment to Rosita to the maximum the company will let me. And I'll hope to give you a bit more when I dock. I have to keep some money by me, you understand. Ciggies don't cost much, because I don't buy them in England; I sometimes have to stand the lads a drink — they're my mates, and I have to live with them."

Rosita was patching the seat of a pair of Manuel's trousers; she was an excellent needlewoman, and the stitches barely showed. She looked up at her husband, letting her work fall into her lap, as he stopped speaking. He looked so tired and melancholy, as he slumped in his chair, that it hurt her. She said cheerfully, "Not to worry, luv. We'll manage somehow — with the bit extra you'll leave us. I've still got Francesca's baby clothes, so we won't have to buy anything new for the baby when it comes."

His face softened. She was a sweetheart, and he longed to cuddle her. His face lightened slightly, as he said in a rueful tone, "I won't be able to bring much in the way of presents for you."

"Tush, don't worry about that."

* * *

In the golden glow of a Canadian summer evening, Old Manuel slowly dug over a small flowerbed in his Victoria garden and thought about Pedro. He remembered his bringing him a small blue lorry that he wound up with a key. He had run into Pedro's open arms to hug him in his excitement at the present, loving the comfort of those strong arms round him and the stubbled chin against his face. That was how he had always remembered him — and always would, thought Manuel, as he stopped digging to let his aching back recover.

20

AFTER Pedro's return to sea, Manuel actively missed him. Until then, his father had been a friendly person who came and went, whom he only vaguely remembered between times. It had been Grandpa who had been the stalwart backbone of his life, and, like most backbones, had been taken for granted.

Occasionally, Manuel had nightmares, when he seemed to be flying through the air and then falling to hit the tiles of the lavatory roof. He was grateful when Auntie Maria heard him cry out and lit her candle, and, like a friendly ghost, crept across to his bed to comfort him.

One day, after noting his mother's swollen figure, he asked, "Are we going to have another baby, Mam?"

Rosita smiled. "If God wills," she said.

"Will it be a boy or a girl?"

She laughed softly. "We don't know. It doesn't matter."

* * *

But it does matter, thought Old Manuel, as he remembered this tender moment with his mother. I love Faith, but I would have loved a son, as well. I'd have taught him how to fish — and build and sail a boat — and I could've talked politics with him. He would've been a real Basque in his ways.

He could not find any irrefutable argument to confirm his idea that a son of his would have embraced his Basque traditions with enthusiasm; he simply sensed that it would have been so.

He wondered if he would have a great-grandson by Lorilyn, a boy who might have pride in his Basque forebears, who would be as handsome as Pedro and have the wisdom of Juan Barinèta.

He realized suddenly that this dim hope was why he was writing down what he remembered of his early life; he wanted his notes to be passed down to this phantom descendant. Basques were becoming fewer and were scattered, like the Jews, all over the world. He wanted with all his heart to leave on earth a child with the tough independent outlook and the physical and mental strength of his Basque forebears.

* * *

Heavy with her pregnancy, Rosita once lamented to Effie Halloran that it was great to be a man. "Away at sea — away from all the troubles at home. It's the life of Riley."

"We all has our troubles," comforted Effie. "It's no joke having a man under your feet all the time. And your Pedro's good to you."

The winter mists of 1914 engulfed the city. Around the Wapping Dock, there were no trees to lose their leaves and announce the approach of winter. It was the increasing sound of fog horns bellowing across the water which told small boys that Guy Fawkes Day was imminent.

Manuel, Brian and Joey, with a horde of other small children, began to collect bits of wood, abandoned scraps of furniture, old newspapers and wooden crates, anything that would burn, ready for the bonfire they would make on the fifth of November.

Manuel negotiated with Rosita for the loan of Francesca's pushchair in which to push the guy around.

"And what happens if you break it? I'm not having it run all over the place — for a guy!"

On her way to the outside lavatory, Effie heard Rosita's refusal, and paused to say, "Himself'd knock a handcart together for yez. All he'd need is a soap box and a couple of wheels."

George Halloran was very agreeable to being drawn into preparations for the anniversary of the Gunpowder Plot, and soon put together a most satisfactory vehicle for them.

The guy itself was made a monstrous object. The lower part of the body was made out of a pair of old overalls once worn by Grandpa. They were stuffed with newspaper, Mrs Connolly provided a hopelessly torn pullover of Pat's which was also stuffed, to make the upper part of the body; and, to Manuel's delight, Auntie Maria made a wonderful head by stuffing one of her old black woollen stockings and embroidering a gruesome set of features on it with a length of red knitting wool. A long-since-abandoned beret, which had for years been used as a hot-water bottle cover, gave the guy an unexpectedly Basque appearance.

The effigy was arranged in the soap box, and a whole string of small boys took turns in pushing it all the way up to Paradise Street, where they collected a number of pennies for it from the seamen around the Sailors' Home. They then pushed onward into Church Street and up to Bold Street, shouting to the well-dressed shoppers, "Penny for the guy, Missus," or, more belligerently, "Remember, remember, the fifth of November, Gunpowder, Treason and Plot!" The shoppers seemed to feel that grubby urchins with an improvised wheelbarrow had no right to be there, so they only got a few farthings out of them.

Stolid little Brian Wing was trusted by everyone, so he was the group's treasurer. He carefully put all the coins they collected into his marble bag, since it was not the marble season. Afterwards, they crowded into Mr Wing's steamy back room, while he obligingly counted the proceeds for them.

While Mrs Wing smiled through the steam as she ironed shirt after shirt, they decided shrilly on their fireworks shopping list. Catherine wheels and rockets were the prime favourites, closely followed by a banger for each boy, and two volcanoes.

Though Mrs Wing would have been thankful for the amount they collected, to add a little pork to their evening rice, nothing was said. Boys usually gave their mothers most of the odd pennies they earned for going messages for other housewives, or minding horses, or catching a line for an incoming boat. Money collected for Guy Fawkes Day seemed sacrosanct; it was the children's great day.

Because of the war and creeping shortages of many peacetime products, it proved difficult to find fireworks. A very small shop in Park Lane finally yielded a gratifying number, left over, perhaps, from the previous year.

The joyful little boys streamed back to Wapping, to ask Joey's father, Pat Connolly, to keep them safe from being accidentally blown up. He also undertook to build their bonfire, having acquired a reputation, from previous years, for being very good at bonfires.

"For sure," he said, "and I'll find a bottle or two to set the rockets in." Then he asked, "Have you got any spuds to roast?"

Crestfallen, they admitted that they had not; and what was the good of a bonfire without potatoes to roast?

Then Manuel announced grandly, "Me mam'll find us some," and he fled next door to make good his promise of at least twelve spuds.

"How many do you want?" asked Rosita, a little anxiously. She had a sack of potatoes in the cellar, but they had to last for months — and prices were going up at a frightening speed.

"There's five of us — and Mr Connolly — and there'll be some more on the day. Could I have twelve, to be sure?"

About four pounds of potatoes, at least. Rosita bit her lower lip.

At her hesitation, Grandma Micaela ordered firmly, "Give them him. Compared to the lot out there, we're not poor — Pedro's in work."

It was a matter of pride.

"All right," Rosita agreed reluctantly.

* * *

George Halloran's willingness to help on occasions was not the only kindness received by the three women.

Domingo Saitua, who worked on the Birkenhead ferry, came in one night, and said shyly, holding his beret between his great red hands, "Mam said you wanted a wheel put on."

Thankfully Rosita produced the push-chair and the loose wheel, and he squatted down by the back door and neatly put it on for her. It was a labour of love — he considered Rosita the most beautiful woman in Liverpool.

Another time, a pane of glass fell out of the kitchen window and shattered in the yard outside. The following day, a wizened old man, who must have been in his seventies and said his name was Pablo, came with a piece of glass, cut it to size and puttied it into the frame. "Used to have a drink with Juan often enough," he told Grandma, grinning toothlessly.

Afterwards, Rosita laughed. "I swear I never told anybody the pane was broken — I haven't left the house since it fell out!"

"Grapevine," replied Grandma, as she neatly turned the heel of a sock and Pudding tried to bat at the swiftly moving knitting wool.

"Well, I'm very grateful. Otherwise, I'd have

had to fill it with cardboard."

Numerous small acts of kindness like these helped Micaela in another way; the short visits of other Basques were a comfort to her in her loneliness. She was the oldest woman in the community and this set her slightly apart. Because of her rapidly increasing blindness, which was accepted as a natural result of ageing, she tended to sit more at home, doing jobs that did not require her to move about so much. So she was more easily approached by the Basque wives of the kind helpers; tired, harassed women, they came to ask her advice.

Aunt Maria also enjoyed the visits. The old couch in the kitchen-living-room had become her permanent bed, so that she did not have to climb the stairs. Manuel missed her and her candle in the bedroom. Lots of old people slept in living-rooms, so he did not see the significance of the new arrangement. He did notice, however, that Father Felipe visited her rather more often than he had done before Grandpa died, and that, though he encouraged Grandma to walk up to the church to attend Mass, he apparently did not expect Auntie Maria to accompany her.

"Why do we have to go to Mass, and Auntie's let off?" he asked his mother crossly, when he had been called in from a great game of Boches and Allies to be made clean for church.

"Because she's frail, dear," his mother had replied, as she scrubbed his face, hands and knees with Sunlight soap and a piece of flannel.

As he dried his face with the thin kitchen towel, he stared at the patient figure propped up on the couch, her rosary held in her listless hand. She had taken no notice of the exchange between his mother and himself.

★ ★ ★

Manuel had forgotten the tiny incident, until soon after Faith had been married.

Kathleen had always accompanied him to church, though, being a Protestant, she did not take the Sacrament. One Sunday, she said she felt too tired to walk the short distance to Mass, but that she would like to attend.

She had never complained before of fatigue without an obvious reason for it, and it was with some anxiety that he got the car out. Because parking was difficult to find and the distance not very great, it was the first time that he had ever driven to church.

It had been the beginning of the end, he thought helplessly, as had been the increasing number of visits to Maria by Father Felipe.

Kathleen had not had the consolation of priestly visits; the church had so few men that pastoral visits had, largely, become a folk memory. Instead, she had had innumerable hospital visits for blood infusions, to counteract the leukaemia which had struck her down. She had been admitted at other times for all kinds of infections, to which she had been laid open by the underlying disease. He shuddered when he remembered the lingering misery of the last years of her life, and cursed modern medicine with good old-fashioned Basque curses for extending a life not worth living. Then he reminded himself not to be ungrateful; nowadays, modern medicine could have cured Aunt Maria.

So that she, too, could die of cancer? he asked himself furiously in his distress over his suffering wife.

Distraught at the memory of Kathleen, he pushed his notes to the back of his desk, and went to the kitchen to get a glass of wine. He felt shut in, dreadfully alone. No one to talk to. None of the close neighbourliness of his youth to sustain him. He thought of Sharon, one of the very few who seemed to invite confidences; she always spoke to him if she saw him in the garden. Of course, Veronica also stopped to speak; the trouble was that she never stopped speaking! And she had her own axe to grind, he considered grimly.

He slowly put on a jacket and zipped it up. Then, slapping his beret on his head, he went out to walk by the sea.

21

GUY FAWKES Night did not turn out at all as Manuel had expected.

Pat Connolly built one of his perfect bonfires and lit it. To the pleasure of the small crowd which had gathered to watch, the fireworks all went off with appropriate bangs and whooshes. The potatoes had been roasted to blackness on the outside and steamy perfection inside. But a thoroughly frightened Manuel had clutched Jean Baptiste Saitua's hand, and had, at first, even refused to put a match to his own bangers.

He was obsessed by the nightmare scene he had witnessed at home, immediately before Jean Baptiste had whipped him away to join Pat Connolly.

Aunt Maria had begun to moan, saying that she had a terrible pain in her side. She started to thresh about on the couch; her crochet, her rosary, her smelling salts, her medicines were scattered suddenly from the tiny sidetable; her hot-water bottle and her shawls fell off the couch.

With unusual agility, Grandma had leapt up from her own chair; and his mother, after glancing quickly round, hastily deserted the washing-up, and, as she squeezed round the table, dried her hands on her apron.

"Give me a towel, quick!" Grandma shouted to her.

Rosita grabbed the kitchen towel and threw it across the room to her. A paralysed Manuel saw it turn scarlet, as his aunt doubled up and spat blood.

At that moment, Jean Baptiste Saitua and Domingo came through the unlocked front entrance to collect Manuel.

Jean Baptiste gave one horrified glance at Maria, and said immediately to the boy, "Ready to go? Let's go down to the bonfire."

Easing her way round the furniture towards Maria, Rosita said quickly, "Yes, luv. Away you go. We'll look after Auntie." She added softly to Jean, "Ask Bridget to come quick and Madeleine."

Though filled with dread, Manuel allowed himself to be led away. While he and Jean Baptiste knocked on Bridget's door, Domingo ran fleetly back to his home to get his mother.

"What's to do?" asked Bridget apprehensively, seeing the child's white face in the light of the street lamp.

"It's Maria. Go quick."

"Jesus Mary!" It was a call she had been dreading, and she fled back to the kitchen to get a clean apron.

Manuel silently walked down to the corner of Corn Hill. He was afraid to ask the big Basque what was happening to Auntie Maria, because he dreaded an honest answer. He had expected that his grandmother and mother would come to join in the fun; but he realized now that they must look to his aunt's needs. He hoped that her Guardian Angel was on the watch and doing better than Grandpa's had.

Persuaded by Pat Connolly, he obediently carried bits of wood and rubbish from a niche, in which it had been hidden by the boys, to the bonfire to keep it blazing.

Pat had stored the fireworks on top of a wall, well back from the fire, and young Vicente Saitua had been stationed near them to guard them from thieves.

Even the excitement of the rockets sparkling in the cold November sky failed to divert Manuel completely. He kept glancing over his shoulder and wondering if he dare run back home.

Jean Baptiste was well aware of what was probably going on in the Barinètas' home; his wife had sent back a message with his son that on no account must Manuel be allowed to go home.

Instructed by his mother, Domingo asked Manuel casually, "Where's little Frannie?" and was much relieved to hear that she went to bed early.

"Me mam said she was too small and would be afraid of the noise," Manuel explained.

"Oh, aye," agreed Domingo. "This is fun for big lads, like us, int it?" and this had coaxed a faint smile out of the frightened child.

Though they did all they could to make a happy evening for the children, both Pat and Jean Baptiste were heavy-hearted. Consumption was a wicked disease, and you never knew who would be struck by it next. The Basque families, better fed and slightly better housed than most people in the dock area, had no other case that he was aware of. But even the rich feared it, particularly amongst their women and children.

"It's rough on old Mrs Barinèta," said Pat, under his breath to Jean Baptiste, as he heaved some stringed bundles of newspaper into the flames. "The wife says she hasn't got over losing her hubbie yet."

"Will they call the doctor?"

"I doubt it," replied Pat. "He can't do nothing for her. It'd be more expense for the family, and wouldn't do no good. He might put her in hospital. They wouldn't want her to die there."

"They'll have to get him for the Death Certificate, won't they?"

"They'll worry about that later. Bridget'll help them as much as she can."

"Oh, aye. And our Madeleine, too. Better to die in your mother's arms, with friends round you." Jean Baptiste stepped back from the bonfire, to join Domingo and Manuel.

"Come on, Mannie," he said kindly. "I'm going to send a rocket up specially for you." He took the long-stemmed firework from the top of the wall, and squatted down, to put it into the long neck of a beer bottle as straight as he could make it stand. "Now," he said, "if you set it like that and put a match to it carefully, it'll go straight up into the air — and not into somebody's bedroom window!" He struck a match and handed it to Manuel. "Now, you light the fuse, here."

They were surrounded by a small squad of slightly older boys, who said they remembered other Guy Fawkes Nights, when rockets fizzled and then seemed to go out, only to suddenly take flight dangerously close to the faces of all of them. As Manuel put the match to the fuse, they all seemed to yelp together, "Nearly took me ear, it did."

Manuel wanted to back quickly away, but he was hemmed in by the boys' big boots round him. The rocket, however, after a preliminary spit, soared upwards, leaving a stream of red and green stars after it. It did a splendid arc, and the onlookers let out a collective exclamation.

Manuel was impressed. He watched the firework until the last green star died in Liverpool's overwhelming smog, and Jean Baptiste smiled down at him, and said cheerily, "That was the best rocket I've seen in a long time. You must've lit it exactly right."

He was relieved when the lad looked up and grinned at him.

Pat Connolly had been watching the potatoes bake in the ashes, turning them occasionally with a spade. They were now giving out a delicious smell, so he pushed them out of the fire and lifted them to the edge of the pavement to cool.

Manuel was suddenly very hungry, and Pat Connolly chose a particularly big one and split it open with his penknife. "Got a hanky?" he asked.

Manuel quickly produced a grubby piece of rag from his pocket, and the potato was carefully laid on it; a welcome heat from it permeated to his hand. Everybody wanted a potato, but Pat was careful to give them only to his own little party.

With shrieks and squeaks at the heat, the potatoes were slowly eaten with the fingers. Manuel ate all the soft inside of his potato and threw the blackened crust into the fire; but Brian Wing ate every scrap, his chubby face getting liberally blackened by the potato's well-burned skin.

Then the Catherine wheels were, one by one, nailed to a warehouse door. When lit, they whirled out a huge circle of sparks, and the children danced back from them to avoid being burned. An older boy set off a couple of bangers amid the long-skirted women who had come to see the bonfire. The jokes became raucous, as the women lifted their skirts and petticoats, for fear of their catching fire. Some of them ran up nearby steps, exhibiting black woollen stockings and bare thighs. In the light of the glowing ashes, with their long shadows dancing on the brick walls of a factory, they looked to Manuel like real witches.

The party was being taken over by grown-ups. Brian's big brother was the first to realize it, and politely and discreetly began to withdraw with Brian. Brian protested loudly and tried to kick his patient brother. Pat and Jean Baptiste nodded to each other, and Pat took the hand of a sleepy Joey. He turned to his young daughter, Mary, now a skinny eight-year-old, and ordered, "Our Mary, you take Manuel's hand. He's coming to our house tonight. His auntie isn't feeling too clever, and we don't want to wake her up with him coming home, and all."

Mary nodded. "Give me your hand, Mannie," she said; she was used to being the big sister in charge of a small brother.

He backed away from her. His face was covered with smuts and he looked as if he were about to cry. "No! I want to go home," he whined. Then, more hysterically, he wailed, "I want me mam."

Jean Baptiste swept him up into his arms, and told him peremptorily, "Your mam wants you to stay with Mary tonight. Now stop crying — you're a big boy now."

Jean Baptiste's red face looked like carved granite under his black beret. He had spoken crisply in Basque, exactly like Grandpa used to when he was cross.

Manuel's wails became a subdued snuffle.

Trotting along slightly behind Mr Saitua, Mary looked up at the unhappy face peering down at her over the big Basque's shoulder, "Mam's making hot cocoa for us when we come in," she promised.

She did not know what was happening in the Barinèta household, except that it had been obvious to her at the bonfire that something was wrong, because Rosita had not joined them. She had, however, already learned from her mother to protect Joey from some of the hard facts of the raw life around him; and now she was doing her small best for Manuel, despite her own nervousness that her mother might not be at home.

She smiled up at him and wrinkled up her nose. He smiled wanly back and stuck his finger in his mouth. He liked Mary.

22

AUNTIE BRIDGET was not at home, so Mary carefully made cocoa for them all, and they drank it while sitting on the rag hearth rug before the dying fire. Then Mary took them upstairs, ordered them to take off their outer clothes, while she took off her own dress and stockings. She then put Joey and Manuel into a double bed and climbed in after them. After a few minutes of pushing and shoving, they settled down to sleep, and the next thing that Manuel knew was Auntie Bridget's smiling face, as she shook each of them and told them to hurry up or they'd be late for school.

Downstairs, a bowl of porridge with a little sugar and milk awaited them. Pat Connolly had already gone to work; his empty porridge plate still lay on the table.

Though Bridget Connolly had been up all night and was so tired she felt fit to drop, she sent the children off with a pat on each small behind, and the injunction to Manuel that she was sending them off a bit early, so that he could pop in and see his mam.

A tide of relief went through Manuel. He had a wild hope that everything at home would be all right. Auntie Maria would smile at him from the old horsehair sofa; Grandma would be washing the breakfast plates in the chipped enamel basin in the sink, and his mother would probably be making the beds, or perhaps sweeping the staircase with a dustpan and brush.

He pushed open the front door and walked in. The house was deadly quiet. The parlour door was shut.

He peeped into the kitchen. There was no one there, and the horsehair sofa held neither Auntie Maria nor the rumpled pile of bedding which usually surrounded her. The sight of the exposed black oilcloth of the sofa made him turn white.

"Ma!" he shouted shrilly. "Mam, I'm home!"

His mother came slowly down the stairs. Her hair was a wild tangle of copper, her face white and haggard, her big blue eyes suddenly sunken and bloodshot. She winced, as she slowly descended.

Manuel stared up at her, and then whispered, "Where's everybody gone, Mam?"

Rosita reached the bottom of the stairs and sat down heavily on the second stair. She ignored Manuel's question, and pulled him to her. "Did you have a good Bonfire Night, darling?" she inquired, with a forced smile.

His eyes wandered round the gloomy stairwell, as he answered absently, "Yes."

"Good. Had breakfast?"

His eyes came back to her face. "Yes."

"It's chilly this morning. You'd better put your woolly scarf on."

She felt him tremble in her arms. "Ma, where *is* Auntie Maria — and Grandma — and Frannie?"

"Well, Auntie Peggy O'Brien invited Frannie

to play with her little Theresa, so Effie took her round the corner earlier on. And now Grandma and Effie — " She paused to sigh heavily. "Well, they're in the parlour."

Manuel glanced fearfully over his shoulder at the closed parlour door, and then looked back at his dishevelled mother. "Is Auntie Maria there, as well?"

He had never seen his mother look so ill, and, as tears welled out of her bloodshot eyes, he was appalled.

"Mam," he whispered. "Oh, Mam!"

They had been speaking in Basque, and their close communion was made more intense by their own language.

"She's gone to Heaven, lovey." Rosita wept uncontrollably into her son's serge jacket, the horrors of the night still too close.

Manuel was engulfed by such primeval fear as he was not to know again for many years; the understanding of the remorseless inevitability of death was lodged in his mind for ever. It appeared to him to be an awful monster waiting to gobble up anyone whom one loved. Creepy-crawlies seemed to be climbing up his back, and his hair rose, like Pudding's did when an alien cat intruded.

If Auntie Maria was lying dead in the parlour, how long would it be before his mother lay there — and Grandma? His mother looked as ill as Auntie Maria had done. If they both went, Frannie and he would be alone; in his consternation, he forgot his patient father, at that moment still chugging slowly across the Atlantic.

He clutched his mother tightly round her neck and felt her curls damp against his wrist.

Rosita raised her head and pushed her hair away from her eyes. "I'm sorry, dearest. Auntie Maria was mother's big sister — and I'll miss her." She again put her arms round her clinging son — she was so heavy with child that he could not sit on her lap, though he wanted to.

"I love you, Mam — and I love Auntie Maria," he said softly.

She made a valiant effort to pull herself together, despite her enormous fatigue. She pushed him a little away from her, and said quite briskly, "I love you, too — my big boy. Now, I don't want you to be too sad about Auntie Maria. You know she had a dreadful cough — and it hurt her a lot. Sometimes she would ask God to take her to Him, so that she wouldn't have any more pain." She gave another shivering sigh. "And now he's done it. And Father Felipe told her that everything would be all right — he was here last night — and he said that she was such a good woman that she would be happy with God." She tried to smile. "But we'll miss her, won't we?"

Her last words became part of an involuntary whimper, and she suddenly clutched Manuel very tightly.

"Mam! Are you hurting?"

His mother was biting her lower lip, as a long, slow roll of aching pain ran round her waist. Manuel was near to fainting with fright.

She saw his expression, and, as the pain softened, she laughed ruefully. "It's nothing really, pet. But I wouldn't be surprised if you got a new brother or sister today. Now then, you're not to worry — it's perfectly normal. When you go out, just run back to Auntie Bridget, and ask her to step in. You may have to go to Mrs O'Brien's for your midday dinner — but don't worry,"

Reluctantly he let go of her and pulled his woolly scarf from the peg in the hall, and wound it round his neck. As he opened the front door, he looked back at her, and saw that she was rubbing her back and her eyes were closed, her jaw set grimly. He wondered how he was going to make himself walk to school.

His mother was silently saying a Hail Mary, as she rubbed her back, and worrying about how to pay Bridget for two calls in less than twenty-four hours. She didn't charge much, but, in addition, Rosita felt she should send a decently big casserole over to Peggy O'Brien in thanks for her help. Normally, she considered frantically, Micaela and she herself could have managed a birth together. But Micaela was weeping her heart out on her bed. And to send for the only alternatives, a professional midwife or the doctor, was too expensive to consider.

Whether she was paid or not, Bridget would come, she was sure; they had been friends for years. But Bridget had to augment Pat's wages somehow.

Rosita held her head in her hands, as she crouched on the stairs, and cried for Micaela, for Maria — and for herself. Then she suddenly lifted her head, arched her back and moaned. Effie heard her and came running down the stairs, and Rosita accepted her help to get up to her bedroom. She feared to ask Effie to help with the birth, in case the tiny woman lost her nerve in the middle of the delivery — and Effie probably did not know about how clean a midwife must keep her hands — childbed fever, Rosita knew from her reading, travelled from mother to mother via the midwife — and it was deadly.

Perplexed and frightened, Manuel nearly fell over Mary, as he took the two hollowed-out steps in one careless bound on his way to school after leaving his mother.

He paused in surprise, and said, "I thought you'd gone with Joey." She looked pinched and cold, though she had a tam o' shanter on her head and was encased in a shabby black coat too big for her.

She scuffed one small boot against the other, and said, "Mam said to walk with yez."

"I've got to ask her to go in to me mam for a minute." He ran up Bridget's steps, pushed open the door, and shouted down the passage, "Auntie Bridget, me mam wants you."

Bridget Connolly had just gone upstairs to lie down for half an hour, before starting her housework. She swung her stockinged feet to the floor, and went to the top of the stairs, "What's up, Mannie?"

"Mam says it's the baby."

"Mother of God! At seven months?" Bridget muttered, and then shouted back, "I'll be there in a minute or two. Now you get to school. Hurry — you're late."

* * *

Little Maria, as she was called all her life, not only because she was small of stature but also to differentiate her from her Auntie Maria who was with God, was born that evening. Peggy O'Brien resignedly fed Mary, Joey and Manuel with thick slices of bread and margarine and bowls of vegetable soup at lunchtime, and more bread and margarine, with tea to drink, at teatime. She hoped that Bridget would share with her a bit of the fee she would get for the delivery; otherwise, so tight was her housekeeping, she would not be able to feed her own three children and hungry husband the following day. Yet, it never occurred to her not to help Rosita and Bridget; she knew they would be among the first to come to her when her next baby was on the way.

Late in the evening, when Peggy was beginning to feel harassed to death with so many children in her kitchen, and a very tired husband grumbling amid them, Pat Connolly came to take them home.

In answer to a question from Manuel, he told him that the baby had arrived safely; and, to the boy's relief, he was delivered to his own doorstep. He was met by a grave wraith of a grandma, who silently hugged both him and his sister tightly, before leading them upstairs to see their mother.

She was lying quietly in her own bed, looking very tired and white. Though her eyes had large black rings round them, he was thankful to see that she was not crying. A big woman in black was putting more coal on the bedroom fire. She half-turned to smile at the children. Francesca ignored her and toddled straight over to the bed. Manuel paused to stare back at her. He knew where she lived, but he did not know that she was a more experienced midwife, whom Bridget had sent for, because the baby had presented herself upside down.

As the boy moved towards Rosita, Francesca demanded to be lifted on to the bed. Laughing, Bridget laid her carefully beside her mother, where, from under the quilt, she eyed Manuel triumphantly at being allowed to be there, while he was not.

Though so young, Francesca had been acutely aware that something was terribly wrong in her small world, and she had objected strongly when she had been taken straight from her bed into Effie's room, to be hastily dressed and fed with bread and milk before being taken to Peggy's house. She had howled like a banshee as Effie pushed her doggedly in her pushchair, though she had recovered somewhat after she had been with Peggy to the corner shop to spend a halfpenny, provided by Effie, on an ounce of dolly mixtures. Now, with her mother's arm curved protectively around her, she felt safe once more.

To Manuel, the bedroom smelled peculiar — faintly like a meat stall in the market. As he bumped against the bed, his mother smiled sleepily at him, and asked if everything had gone well at school and whether Peggy had given Francesca and him some tea.

"Yes," he replied, and she stroked his head and smiled again. Then she said, "Go and look in the drawer over there. You and Frannie have a baby sister."

Obediently, he went towards the fire, which the midwife was now poking into a blaze. In front of it, set on two straight chairs was a drawer taken from the big dresser in the upper hallway. Exactly like Grandpa's coffin, he thought with a burst of fear. In the drawer, however, was a bundle no bigger than Mary Connolly's doll. A shawl that Auntie Maria had crocheted was wrapped round it, so that only a wizened red face was visible. A tiny tongue licked perfectly formed lips, and the closed eyelids looked like the small pink shells he had once picked up on New Brighton beach.

He turned to Rosita. "What's its name?"

It was Grandma who interjected immediately: "Maria, of course, after your auntie." Her shrivelled brown hands were clenched in front of her, and Manuel sensed, nervously, how distressed she was beneath her calm exterior.

"Of course," agreed Rosita immediately. "Little Maria. Now you go downstairs with your granny, and then you must go to bed."

He was astonished when his grandmother picked him up, to hold him to her and to give him an unexpected kiss. Micaela had, for some time, been telling him that he was too big a lad to be picked up or sat on her knee. Her red-rimmed eyes suddenly twinkled close to his. "Now you've got another person to add to your prayers," she said, as she put him down. "You run downstairs, while I put Frannie into her own bed. I'll be down in a moment."

Because the damp winds of winter were making the old house cold, Grandma collected his nightshirt from Auntie Maria's bedroom. She brought it downstairs to the kitchen-living-room and put it on the oven door to warm, together with the kitchen towel. Then she brought the enamel basin from the sink and filled it with warm water from the oven tap. She set the bowl on a wooden chair beside the fire. In the warm glow, he stripped and washed himself, while she made cups of cocoa for both of them. Afterwards, they sat knee to knee, he with her shawl over his shoulders to keep him warm, while they drank their cocoa together.

* * *

Looking back, Old Manuel, snug in his Victoria bungalow which boasted a fine warm bathroom, as well as a cloakroom, could not imagine sitting in its glossy pinkness to drink cocoa, in close communion with a loving grandmother, his cotton nightshirt so hot on his back that he could hardly bear the first touch of it. He had never seen Lorilyn being bathed when she was a child — or Faith, for that matter. Perhaps it was because he had been away so much — or, perhaps, an innate prissiness of Kathleen's.

Vaguely puzzled, he returned to his notes.

* * *

Without Auntie Maria presiding from the sofa, the kitchen-living-room seemed empty, though his grandmother was being wonderfully comforting. He wondered if she missed Auntie Maria as he was doing; yet, she was still in the house — in the parlour — and Grandma was, he realized with relief, still strong and well, even if she did have to feel her way round the house.

* * *

What a frightful twenty-four hours it must have been for the women concerned, mused Old Manuel, feeling very tired himself. A painful death with a subsequent laying-out with all its grief, to be followed almost immediately by a premature birth.

His grandmother must have summoned all her courage to make that evening seem cosy and normal to him; inside, she must have been storming with grief at the loss of her eldest daughter. She had heard his prayers there, by the fire, ordering him to include Auntie Maria, as well as Little Maria. As if I would forget Auntie Maria, the little boy had thought indignantly, as he got up off his knees.

* * *

Because she had a chronic disease, Burial Insurance for Maria was unobtainable, so she had a pauper's funeral. No men followed the coffin, except for Father Felipe and the undertaker and his employees. It was a sombre, black-clad procession of women, carrying small bunches of flowers, who piled into the tram that would take them to the cemetery. Only Grandma, Rosita, with Little Maria in her arms, Manuel, Francesca and Father Felipe rode in a carriage kindly provided free by Ould Biggs. It was a bitter, frosty day and all the mourners were thankful when it was over, and they could crowd into the Barinèta home for tea and cakes and a good warm.

⋆ ⋆ ⋆

Unlike Francesca, who had been a placid, contented baby, Little Maria filled the house with steady yelling for some months after she was born. Even a neglected Manuel was sometimes pressed into service to sit in a chair and rock her. All the women visitors, who came in to admire her, laughed knowingly and said she was colicky, whatever that was, and that she would grow out of it.

Manuel wished intensely that she would simply shut up. He would wake in the night to hear her screaming; and his mother looked daily more tired and sounded ever more irritable with young boys.

23

THE frazzled mood of the family was lifted somewhat by an unexpected visit from Uncle Agustin. His ship had docked in Birkenhead, across the River Mersey, and he had begged shore leave to see his family, because of the loss of his father and sister.

When Manuel came home from school and found his uncle sitting at the kitchen table, he had not, at first, recognized him; Agustin had been at sea during their last visit to Bilbao, and he had not docked in Liverpool for some time before that. Then, when the thin, saturnine man had greeted him by name and grinned at him, the boy said delightedly, "Uncle Agustin!" His relief at having a male relative sitting in his home was so great that he laughed aloud.

Though Agustin had not lived with his parents for years, he had felt keenly the loss of his father and his sister, and when he entered Rosita's house, he was very downcast. His arrival caused a fresh burst of grief to well up in his mother and Rosita, which he tried hard to alleviate by delivering affectionate messages to them both, from aunts and uncles, cousins and friends, of whom Manuel had little recollection. He told them, also, that he had just married his sweetheart — very quietly because of Juan's death. The news about Maria had reached them two days later.

He spoke in Basque, and Manuel immediately felt a close fellowship with him and with his relations in Vizcaya.

After Agustin had returned to his ship, Grandma sat wrapped in thought for some time. Manuel had heard her beg Agustin to write to her from time to time, and he had said he would.

"But he never will," Grandma said later to Rosita. "He never was any good at learning his letters." Then, perhaps feeling that she was being unfair to her eldest child, she added, "But your father always said he was a born seaman."

As Agustin left the house, he dropped some silver coins into his mother's apron pocket. It was the first money that she had received, which she felt she could call her own, since the Prudential man had brought her husband's burial money. She knew Agustin could not spare it; but she carried it for several days, jingling it comfortably in her pocket, until Rosita suggested that she buy a new, much-needed pair of winter boots with it. After some persuasion, she did this, and Manuel remembered her smiling down at their shiny, laced-up newness.

* * *

Rosita wrote to both Leo and Pedro about Maria's death and the premature birth of the new baby. Without much hope, she addressed Leo's letter to Nevada, but again there was no response. Her letter to Pedro, however, did catch up with him, and some weeks later both

Micaela and Rosita received kindly letters of real sympathy. He also said how he himself would miss Maria, who had, he wrote, always been so easy to talk to — and to please. He was glad the new baby had been called after her. Although Rosita had not told him how difficult the birth had been and how weak she still felt, he must have sensed something was wrong, because he inquired anxiously after her own health, which he rarely did.

By late January 1915 Little Maria's shrieks had been reduced to occasional spasms, and her mother began to think that, after all, she would not go out of her mind for lack of sleep.

"There's nothin' more exhausting than a colicky baby," agreed Micaela. "Now she's napping a bit in the afternoon, you must rest, too."

So Rosita retired to bed for an hour with a battered novel from the second-hand shop whenever Little Maria closed her eyes in the afternoon. As her mother said, "The front steps won't hurt, if you scrub them only every other day, instead of every day."

* * *

In the middle of a blizzard carrying heavy sleet, Pedro thankfully docked in Liverpool, to unload a cargo of raw cotton. Though they had not been attacked by German submarines, the whole crew had once again been drained by the tension of crossing the Atlantic in a slow tramp, unable to keep up with a convoy. The men were irritable and on edge, longing to get ashore as soon as they could: to get thoroughly warm in dry clothes, and eat a well-cooked meal.

Rosita met him with her usual hugs, and yet there was a restraint about her. She was not her former bubbling self.

He dropped his suitcase and kitbag in the narrow hall, and held her pallid face between his wind-chapped hands. His own weariness was forgotten. A spasm of fear hit him. In nursing Maria, had she caught the same dread disease?

She smiled weakly at him.

"You look ill," he said gently. "Are you OK?"

She sighed, and enclosed one of his hands against her cheek. "I'm not sick," she assured him. "I'm tired, that's all, what with Maria being so ill, and Little Maria screaming her head off, night and day."

He dropped his hands from her face and put one round her waist, as they went into the back room, where Micaela had discreetly waited, sitting in her rocker, to give the young couple a chance to greet each other.

Pedro went straight to his mother-in-law, and put his arms round her as if she were his own mother. "I'm so sorry about Maria, Mother," he said. He was shaken to see how Micaela had, in a few short months, aged so much; and he realized from the slightly fumbling way in which she sought to clasp his hand that her sight was nearly gone.

Both the women were quick enough, however, to prepare a fish meal for him, which, with the bottle of wine he had brought in his suitcase, cheered them all up considerably.

When Manuel came home from school, he was ecstatic to see his father. Pedro had Francesca on his knee, and the boy stood in front of him, grinning from ear to ear, scrubbing one boot against the back of the other. He longed to dislodge his sister but had learned from experience not to try to — if she were thwarted, she had a scream which would outdo Little Maria's best efforts.

Pedro laughed and caught the boy in his free arm, and Rosita said suddenly, "You're the spitting image of each other, except for Manuel's dark hair."

It was true, considered Pedro. As the boy lost his baby nose, he was acquiring a slightly flattened one with wide nostrils, exactly like his own, and the child's face was already longer and narrower, with flatter cheekbones than most children round the neighbourhood. He *looked* Basque, and Pedro swelled with pride in him.

Once Little Maria had been persuaded to go to sleep in her cot in the corner of their bedroom, and Micaela had retired to her own room, Pedro lay naked beside his wife, and grinned wickedly at her. Her hair on the pillow was a flaming background to her pale face. The blue eyes were shadowed, however, as if she did not want to look at him. He began to caress her and tried to kiss her mouth, but she turned her face away.

"What's up?" he asked surlily. She had never behaved like this before. Then, in the candlelight, he saw tears glisten on her long golden lashes. "Is something wrong, love?"

She opened her eyes and really looked at him. She said hoarsely, as if forcing herself, "I'm scared. I don't want another kid."

He stared at her bewilderedly, and she hastened to say, "I love you. I want to make love. But I'm afraid of what happened with Little Maria happening again — and killing me. You'd never believe the pain I had."

He stirred uncomfortably, some of the desire going out of him, with the unexpected disappointment. Then he shrugged. "Kids come from God," he said.

There was a sudden twinkle in her fine eyes, as her sense of humour began to surface. "They come from men, you old rogue."

He nodded. "I suppose."

She turned towards him, and her long generous curves so close to him roused him again. He wanted to take her by the shoulders and shake some sense into her; he was her husband, wasn't he? He wanted what was his God-given right. But she was speaking again. "I'm tired to death, what with being so torn with the baby, and nursing Maria — and no sleep — and Mother not able to help so much now. And then Mannie and Frannie. I couldn't face another baby."

He kept a hold on himself, torn between his own needs and her obvious distress. He closed his eyes, while she spoke again.

"I want to ask you something. You know Mary Challoner — lives in Park Lane — she's a Prottie, but she's a decent woman for all that. She was sitting next to me the last time I took Maria to the doctor. She thought she was pregnant, she told me. Then she said, 'But I've had a good run for my money — four years since the last one.'"

It took all his patience to make himself listen, but he did.

"When Maria had gone into the surgery," Rosita continued, "and there was no one else in the waiting room, I asked her what she meant — and she said her hubbie did his best to see she wasn't left with a kid.

"He covers his you-know-what with a rubber cover — buys 'em in London and in France, when he goes there. She says they still have a good time — but no baby." She propped herself up on her elbow, and added earnestly, "It's not like aborting a kid — I know women who'll do that for me — but it's terribly dangerous — and it's wrong."

Her husband responded bitterly, "Priests think any kind of birth control is wrong. Fat lot of practice they get — they'd change their minds if they had a horde of kids — I know what you're getting at."

"Couldn't we do like Mary's hubbie?" Her eyes were imploring now. She badly wanted to please Pedro, to enjoy herself.

He whistled to himself, and the candle danced in the small movement of the air, as he silently considered wife versus church. What did he really believe himself, amid the welter of teachings handed down by a celibate church hierarchy? He knew he had never, until this moment, questioned their teachings. But one thing he knew from the society around him — it was deadly easy to lose a wife in childbirth. He would, he knew, sell his immortal soul rather than lose his lovely wife, if it could be avoided.

He nodded, and ran his hand down her thigh. "I'll go shopping," he promised. "But not a word to anyone, remember. Promise?"

She smiled her old, seductive smile. "I promise," she said. Then, after a moment's hesitation, she asked, "What do we do now?"

"Don't worry," he said, as he pulled her close. "I won't go in. And I'll try to make it good for you."

* * *

Before he sailed again, there was a lot of earnest conversation between him and his wife and mother about giving Manuel a better education. They spoke volubly in Basque.

"Jean Baptiste wanted his youngest to go to St Francis Xavier's, but he had a good spell unemployed, and they couldn't do it. Manuel could be a doctor or a solicitor, if he went on into university," Rosita told him.

"University?" Pedro looked at her incredulously. "A kid from Wapping Dock?" He had had in mind keeping the child in school until he was sixteen.

"Why not?" demanded Rosita. "By the time he gets his Matric, there might be some way he could get there. Madeleine says there are a few scholarships, even now."

Pedro was not too sure what a Matric was. While he considered this lofty ambition, he sipped his mug of tea. If you went to university, he knew you could become a doctor or a lawyer and have a good house in West Derby. It seemed like a pipe dream to him. His own father had scraped money to keep him in school until he was fourteen, and had helped him to take time out from going to sea while he studied until he had got his Master's Certificate; and it had made a world of difference to his life.

But an economic downturn meant he could be out of work very easily — any seaman would tell you that — and, since his father-in-law's death, Pedro had done what he could to quietly put away a little in his own private Post Office savings book, to help tide him over such bad times.

"He could go into the Navy — that's regular. Twenty-one years, you can do."

"Humph," responded Rosita doubtfully. "If ever he's going to be an officer, he must go to grammar school, and he must learn to speak good English. Tell me, where will he learn to do that except in a better school?"

Pedro was not sure that he wanted a son who was an officer and spoke like one. Wasn't his own English good enough?

"We speak English," he said defensively. "And the lad was born in Liverpool — not like me — so he's eligible to serve in the Navy. He could work his way up a bit — they'd train him."

She replied stubbornly, "He's got to speak English — like Father Felipe talks."

"That bloody Spaniard?"

"Tush!" interjected Micaela. "How can you speak like that? He's a priest!"

After the last few nights with his wife, Pedro was feeling resentful of the Church and all its works, and Father Felipe's exquisite, carefully learned English seemed patronizing to him; even his poor attempts at Basque were annoying, as if he were trying to descend from his lofty position as a Castilian to hob-nob with nobodies. What did a priest know about real life? Pedro wondered, with all the antagonism of a Basque for a Spaniard.

Poor, overextended Father Felipe would have been sorely hurt, if he had been aware of his parishioner's lack of esteem. He would, however, have earnestly encouraged young Manuel's further education. He had already suggested to Micaela that the boy should be given to the Church; and Micaela knew that a child in the Church brought his family instant prestige.

Micaela now spoke up. "He's the eldest boy — the only boy, up to now. We should try our best for him."

Manuel, sitting at the table carefully boring holes in the last of his conkers, preparatory to drying them out on top of the oven, was dreaming of being able to smash Andrew Pilar's best one, and only half took in the conversation of his elders. He assumed that if he were sent to St Francis Xavier's, all the other children he knew, like Joey and Brian, would be going, too.

His elders decided that if they all practised the most rigorous economy, they would manage to send him.

"As well as fees, there'll be tram fares — and uniform," Rosita fretted, suddenly afraid that she was being too ambitious.

Micaela looked up from her knitting. "We'll manage," she assured her daughter serenely. She already saw a purple biretta covering her grandson's tousled dark hair. God would provide, she was sure.

24

IN 1916, when, at the age of eight, Manuel entered St Francis Xavier School, he felt very lonely; Joey and Brian showed no signs of being able to follow him. On his first day he feared that he might be the only Basque boy attending because he was the only one in his class. He soon discovered that there was a sprinkling of them in the upper classes, though they were drawn from all over the city. They ignored him because they did not know that he was a Basque — he was just another new pupil, younger than they were.

Occasionally he heard them speaking to each other in Basque, frequently making derogatory remarks about English boys who had been too rough with them, because they were slightly sallower in complexion than British boys.

Real fights were rare in the school yard, but one day proud Manuel was called a dago by a nine-year-old Scot. Furious, Manuel struck out with all his force at the scornful, freckled red face of the bigger lad. He became immediately embroiled in a fight with a known bully that he could not win. The other boys formed a circle to egg on the Scot. With his nose already bleeding, it was clear to anyone passing that, despite his best efforts, Manuel was getting the worst of the encounter.

Held down on the asphalt playground, Manuel

took a punch in the eye which made him cry out.

His cry was followed by a sharp yelp from his antagonist, who received a quick series of kicks in his ribs from a tall, thin youth standing over the pair of them.

The newcomer scowled at the ring of boys. Then he bent down, got a good grip on the back of the braces of the enraged Scot and hauled him off Manuel. He shook the boy, as he hissed into his badly scratched face, "Pick on someone of your own size, you little twerp!" He shoved the boy away into the crowd.

Lying on the asphalt, trying to get his breath, a surprised Manuel viewed his rescuer through his unhurt eye. He was even more surprised when the boy said curtly in Basque, "Get up."

The back of Manuel's head was throbbing badly where he had hit it when falling backwards. His nose was still dripping and his eye seemed to be swelling. He staggered slowly to his feet, while his rescuer snarled at the retreating boys, "Get going you stinking pack of cowards, before I tell on you." They reluctantly dispersed, taking the young Scot with them, muttering to each other as they went.

The Basque boy was several inches taller than Manuel, blond, blue-eyed and pallid-skinned. He looked Manuel up and down, and said again in Basque, "Gosh, you do look a mess. Better get cleaned up before a teacher sees you." He picked up a blazer lying on the ground. "Is this yours?"

Manuel nodded dumbly, as he steadied

himself on his feet. He felt his nose running and wiped it along his shirt sleeve. He was shaken to see a long streak of blood on the white cotton. His mouth began to tremble, and he had a strong desire to cry.

"We'll go to the cloakroom," said the older boy more kindly. "And get you cleaned up. You should have more sense to keep out of fights you can't win — he's much heavier than you."

Manuel humbly agreed. Then, as they trailed round the edge of the playground, so as not to disturb the various games of football being played with tennis balls, Manuel said furiously, "He called me a dago!"

Pale-blue eyes were turned reflectively upon him, to examine a face which already showed something of the long flat planes of cheek and jaw, an upward curving mouth with full lower lip, which would be his as a man. "Well, you're dark, but you don't look like a Spaniard," the older boy said at length. "Did you tell him you were Basque?"

"Na. He probably wouldn't know what a Basque is," responded Manuel scornfully. The blood was beginning to coagulate in his nose, and he badly wanted to blow it. The eye still stung painfully.

The other boy was grinning. He said, "Dad says nobody really knows who we are or where we came from."

They reached the cloakroom with its scuffed floor and long lines of black, iron clothes hooks. A tiny washbasin, cracked and grubby, was affixed to the far wall, and next to it hung a roller towel.

Manuel managed to pull the roller towel far enough to damp it under the solitary tap and then wipe his face with it. Streaks of blood were left on the towel. He damped it again and pressed it against the hurt eye. His nose still oozed slightly so he wiped it again.

"Don't touch it any more," advised the strange boy. "It'll dry up in a minute. Wash the muck off your hands and put on your blazer."

Manuel obediently soaped his hands and left a fair amount of greyish foam on the soap tablet and in the sink.

"You'll pass now. There goes the bell. You'd better hurry!"

Manuel gulped. He did not want to return to his classroom, but he knew he must. "Thanks," he said heavily. "Thanks for hauling Stewart off me."

"It's nothing," the boy replied, and turned to wander off to his own classroom, as if to belie his own instruction to hurry, When he had gone, Manuel gave his nose a further good wipe on the towel, put on his blazer and fled before he could be chastised for the mess he had made. He slid quickly into his desk, and was, for once, thankful for the fat boy who sat in front of him and partially masked him from the teacher's icy stare.

* * *

After his mother had washed his face for him and bathed the black eye, clucking her tongue at the damage, and he had had his tea, his grandmother was surprised at the question suddenly fired at her. "Granny, what *is* a Basque?"

Before answering him, she knitted the two stitches remaining on her left-hand needle. Then she replied with puzzlement, "Well, *we* are Basques, dumpling." Although she could barely see him, she sensed that the answer had not sufficed, that he was still in some kind of quandary, so she added, "From Bilbao."

"I know that. But a boy at school — a Basque — said that nobody really knows what a Basque is."

Micaela rested her knitting in her lap, while she considered this assertion. Then she said, "People have always moved about in the world, so they say that they come from the place their parents settled in. After a while, they become part of that place and its history. Your great-grandfather told me, though, that Basques had *always* lived in the Pyrenees and had married each other — for thousands and thousands of years, long before people wrote down their history. And nobody was able to shift us from the mountains — not Arabs, not French, not Romans nor Spaniards. We've been there since time began, so that even the stories of our beginnings have been lost." She was suddenly interested about the boy he had mentioned, and inquired, "He was a real Basque?"

"Yes — not from round here, though."

Manuel had been leaning against the side of her chair, and now he made to get on her lap. She quickly swept her four sharp needles and ball of grey wool on to the floor. The chair wobbled furiously as Manuel settled himself comfortably in the curve of her arm, and she laughed. "It's a long time since you've done that," she told him. "You're too big to be nursed. What was the boy's name?"

He grinned up at her and laid his head on her shoulder. "I don't know," he replied. Though he was proud to go to St Francis Xavier's, he had felt very lonely today, with no Joey or Brian to help him in a fight. He needed the comforting warmth of Grandma, who always had time for him. She was always there and always would be. Or would she?

Micaela felt a faint shudder go through the child's thin body. "What is it, dumpling?" she asked as she carefully stroked his hair back from the black eye.

Manuel hesitated, and then answered, "I was thinking of Auntie Maria."

His grandmother sighed. "Yes, dear?"

"I miss her — and Grandpa."

"We all do, dear." Micaela hugged him closer, as the fearsome pain of loss went through her once more. They sat in silent communion together, the chair rocking slightly under them.

There was the patter of his mother's carpet slippers, as she came downstairs. She called back up to Mrs Halloran, "Don't let the girls bother you — send them down if you're tired of them." As she hurried into the living-room-kitchen, she said in a quieter tone to Micaela, "I don't want them to spend too much time with Effie — the girls'll learn bad manners."

"Tut! Effie was a parlourmaid once — she knows her manners," Micaela immediately admonished.

Rosita shrugged, and then began to discuss the strange Basque boy.

She leaned against the sink and folded her arms, which were aching from hours of washing clothes and bedding on a scrubbing board. "There are a few other Basques scattered round the town — you do hear about them occasionally. Mostly, they've been here a long, long time."

"I was glad he came along," Manuel said with feeling; his eye was aching badly.

His mother nodded. "You know, dear, you must learn not to get into fights."

Manuel sat up straight in Micaela's lap, and the rocking chair rocked rather violently. "Stewart called me a dago," he said indignantly.

Rosita sighed. "When you're foreign, you have to ignore petty insults, my pet."

"I'm not foreign. I live here."

"Yes, dear. But you're Basque, same as Brian is Chinese and Joey's Irish."

"Are we all foreign?"

"Down here, we are."

Manuel slumped back into his grandmother's arms and gave up.

25

ABOUT a week later, they met at the tram shop, two nondescript schoolboys in grey woollen shorts, their bare knees chapped by cold, damp winds. They both wore navy-blue gabardine macintoshes, and caps with the St Francis Xavier badge on them. Each carried on his back a satchel of books required for that evening's homework. Neither boy looked particularly healthy, their complexions pale and eyes ringed.

Manuel ventured a shy grin, and the older boy nodded lordly acknowledgement of it.

A horsedrawn delivery van splashed through the puddles in the gutter. They both stepped back to avoid their shoes and socks being soaked, and the bigger boy asked, "What's your name?"

"Manuel Echaniz. What's yours?"

"Arnador — Arnador Ganivet. Where do you live?"

Manuel told him, and Arnador looked at him speculatively. Wapping Dock was where a lot of first-generation Basques lived. According to his father, they were poor and illiterate seamen working for de Larrinaga. It definitely was not what his mother would call a good address. *His* parents and his grandparents had all been born in Liverpool; they did not mix with common seamen's families, though they were quite proud of their Basque origins. He wondered, if he brought a Basque boy home, which attitude would weigh heaviest with them, that he could speak good Basque or that he was lower class.

He decided that he did not care; he admired Manuel for having taken a bad licking from a bully while defending his Basqueness. He grinned at Manuel, and asked, "How does your eye feel?"

Manuel grinned back. "It feels OK. It's a bit yellow still. Where do you live — which tram do you take?"

"I usually bike to school, but I couldn't today — I've got a couple of broken spokes — my uncle's going to put new ones in tonight. Anyway, I'm going across the water — I'm going out to tea with my cousin." He frowned, and added, "She's a girl. Awful bore."

As a cumbersome tram rolled down towards them, sparks flying from its pole when it touched a crossline, they stepped out into the street to get on it, and he added, "I live in Catherine Street. We've a flat — two floors." They swung up the winding stairs to the upper deck, and sat down together on a wooden, slatted seat at the front. As they took off their satchels and laid them at their feet, he went on, "A dentist has the ground floor. It's handy for Dad — he's a ship chandler, down on Chaloner Street. He likes to walk down the hill to work every day."

Manuel was impressed; he had never before heard of a Basque who owned his own business — he discounted the Basque shipowners in the city — to him, they were as far removed from normal life as earls or lords were. In his own small, sea-going world, everyone worked for somebody else.

"Have you got any brothers or sisters?" Manuel asked.

"One sister — Josefa. She's a nurse at the Ear, Eye and Throat on Myrtle Street — she walks to work as well. She's nearly nineteen. Have you got any?"

"Two little sisters."

"What does your dad do?"

"He goes to sea."

They spent the rest of the journey down to the Pier Head exploring their interests in cricket and who they liked and disliked amongst the teaching staff at school.

As they descended from the tram, Arnador to catch the ferry across the river, Manuel to cross the roads back to the Goree Piazzas and Strand Street to walk along to Wapping, they called cheerfully to each other, "'Bye. See you tomorrow."

He was exhilarated by the new contact, and his mother was pleased when he told her about it; a slightly older Basque friend might smooth the path through school for Manuel.

* * *

A week, two games of football in the school yard, and a number of amiable conversations later, Arnador invited his new friend to Saturday tea.

Rosita was delighted. Scrubbed until his skin was red, and dressed in his Sunday shorts and best jersey, he walked up the hill to Catherine Street and nervously pressed the lower bell of two big brass ones by the Ganivets' white enamelled front door.

He was received with mild approval by Mrs Ganivet, and, later on, by portly, bald Mr Ganivet, whose late arrival upon the scene was explained in English by his wife, who said, "He were doin' his books in the front room. Always goes over his books of a Saturday, don't you?"

Mr Ganivet gave a dignified nod.

"Now, as you're here, luv, we might as well have tea. It's ready."

Indeed, it was. While he played a game of lotto with Arnador on the gaily patterned hearth rug, he had surreptitiously watched a young maidservant lay the table and then bring out plate after plate of food. He had already formed the mistaken opinion that the Ganivets must be very rich, much richer than even the Saituas, who now had three men in the family, all working; and, when he saw the groaning table, he was certain of it. There was sliced ham with sliced tomatoes, bread and butter, scones accompanied by a huge glass dish of jam, and a big fruit cake on a fancy glass stand. There was a large silver cruet stand, in which were set a pot of mustard, a bottle of vinegar and dishes of salt and pepper with a tiny spoon in each. There were table napkins rolled into confining silver rings, and a mystifying array of knives and forks, plates and glasses in front of each chair. Finally, the maid staggered in with a tray resplendent with two linen-covered teacosies, which Manuel presumed was the tea arriving.

Despite Manuel's feeling rather overwhelmed, Mr and Mrs Ganivet were very kind to him; it was the beginning of a lifelong friendship between the two boys. At school, Arnador, one year older than Manuel, was the closest Basque in age to him. Living in the upper half of a Victorian house in Catherine Street, where there were few other children, the older boy had been extremely lonely. He was a deeply intelligent child and a born leader; he found great solace in Manuel's increasing admiration of him.

Like a Highland Scot, Manuel had imbibed from his father and grandfather a natural grace of manner and a certain pride in being what he was. To Mr and Mrs Ganivet, stout in figure and their belief that being a Basque was a gift from God, Arnador's new friend was welcome.

"His granddad was the Basque emigrant agent for years, he says," Mrs Ganivet whispered to her spouse, "and his dad's got his Master's. And his Basque is better than Arnador's; Arnie'll learn from him — it would be awful if he lost the language."

An expression of irritation passed over Mr Ganivet's round, pink face. His daughter, Josefa, refused to speak her mother tongue, and she insisted upon being called Josie by her English friends. She had said tartly to her parents that she was a third-generation Liverpudlian — she had never been to Vizcaya — so why couldn't she be like other people?

Mrs Ganivet had earnestly hoped that her

daughter would meet some nice Basque boy and would give up her nursing, to settle down and breed some more little Basques. It appeared, however, that strong-minded Josefa would end up as a formidable nursing sister, a spinster like her heroine, Florence Nightingale. Her mother had been appalled when, at home, Josefa had dared to criticize the work of some of the doctors at the hospital, and said that if she were a doctor she would do things very differently. It was wicked, stormed Mrs Ganivet, like criticizing the Pope; a woman's place was to serve, not pick holes in physicians' diagnoses or want to be a doctor herself.

Manuel was an answer to her prayers that Arnador might grow up to be proud of his linguistic group, and marry his cousin from Wallasey, who spoke perfect Basque.

⋆ ⋆ ⋆

Not for nothing were Arnador and Manuel descendants of mountain people and of whalers and other seamen; they were born explorers. They ranged around Liverpool as far as they could walk; they had so little pocket money that neither would waste a penny on an unnecessary tram fare. Once or twice, Arnador and he cycled out of the south end of the city, Manuel sitting uncomfortably on the luggage carrier of Arnador's bicycle. When he heard about it, Mr Ganivet put a stop to it — it was dangerous, he said.

"He's more afraid that I'll park it somewhere,

and wander off and it'll be stolen," confided Arnador, with a wry grin.

"But you've got a chain and lock — you lock it at school."

"It's fairly safe at school, after they've locked the front gates. Anywhere else, someone with a pair of tin snips or a wire cutter could snap the chain." He laughed, and added, "Or pick the lock in seconds."

Arnador was not at all put off by the humbleness of Manuel's home. He fell hopelessly in love with Rosita, and was delighted to eat with the family. He tolerated the two little girls, and was quite willing to put together a street cricket team with Joey and Brian, using beer bottles as wickets. He had a happy knack of adapting himself to his surroundings; when they were grown men, he once said to Manuel that he learned as much about how people functioned, while sloping round Wapping Dock and up through the tough north end of the city, as he ever did in university.

While men died in scores in French battlefields, the boys swam naked in Wapping Dock, until chased out by the watchman, and on wet days lounged through bicycle shops and Lewis's Department Store, until they were shown the door by the shopkeeper — or, in the case of the larger shops, by the shop-walker. They warmed themselves by the coke fires of nightwatchmen on construction sites, and Arnador would get into conversation with the garrulous old men who took these cold, thankless jobs. They heard wild tales from them of the days of sail or of being navvies building railways or canals, of being gloriously drunk on paydays and very hungry the day before.

Arnador taught Manuel how to avoid direct confrontations with other youngsters, how to make friendly jokes to avoid unnecessary scrapping. As they wandered into unknown territory, he also warned him against men who hung around public lavatories, or in the narrow back alleys. He was surprised that Manuel was well aware of child prostitution and the sickening diseases, deadly at that time, that he could pick up, if he allowed himself to be touched by an older man.

"Auntie Bridget told Joey and me to watch out for ourselves — and the locals to stay clear of. If you want to know anything, you can always ask Auntie Bridget, and she'll tell you flat — she doesn't hide things like some grown-ups do. She told me how babies come."

"How do they?" asked Arnador. "I've never been sure."

Manuel was surprised to find there was something he knew that Arnador did not; and he gave him a short lecture on human mating and reproduction that did real credit to Auntie Bridget's clear teachings. "She says that to father a baby outside marriage is mortal sin."

Arnador was impressed. Unlike Francesca and Little Maria, Josefa was much older than him, so he had not had the advantage of seeing a girl naked in her tin bath. He had observed from paintings of nudes in the Art Gallery that women apparently did not have penises;

but Manuel had confirmed that what some of the boys said at school was true — they really did not.

★ ★ ★

When Manuel forgot to draw his bedroom curtains one night and the light of his candle shone out across the yard, he got a different kind of lecture from his mother. She told him crossly, "I've told you before about the Zeppelins, for Heaven's sake. Remember to draw the curtains before you light your candle. They're waiting up there to see a light. A single one could bring bombs straight down on us. And that would be goodbye to all of us."

Suddenly afraid, Manuel dutifully blew out his candle and then drew the curtains. He had heard of the Germans' cigar-shaped airships that could float silently over a city and bomb it. His mother had mentioned them before. But he had recently seen a picture of one in Pat Connolly's newspaper, which proved to him that they did indeed exist — he had rather suspected before that they were figments of his mother's imagination, like Jack the Giant Killer and a number of other story-book characters. The war seemed suddenly to close in on him from a direction other than the sea.

Though no adult ever discussed the matter with either lad, they knew about the terrible losses of ships and men at sea. Wherever women congregated, in tiny corner shops, outside the church after Mass, in little groups gossiping in the streets or back kitchens, women talked in quavering voices of dead husbands, sons or sweethearts; of allotments cancelled because ships simply and inexplicably went missing; of children going hungry. They wept into their aprons or on the shawl-draped shoulders of other women, ignoring the children who stood uneasily round them or played at their feet.

Many of the women in the dock area normally wore black. To a casual observer, their state of mourning did not stand out so much as it did amongst the upper classes, whom the boys passed in the centre of the city and around Arnador's home. In fashionable shops in Church Street, Bold Street and Lord Street, however, young girls worked long hours stitching black mourning dresses and mantles. Another group trimmed black hats and, for older women, black bonnets, both with long veils to cover the faces of the bereaved. It was to become a thriving industry before the war ended.

When the headmaster rose, one morning, to report, not without pride, that most of the boys who had left the school in 1915 had given their lives for their country, the war began to breathe down the backs of the necks of the younger pupils. Though they listened quietly to the rhetoric about the nobility of giving one's life for one's country and never doubted whether it was necessary or not, the fear of death was there. In the school playground, boys boasted about which regiment they would join, as soon as they were old enough, and what they would do to the bloody Boche as soon as they could get to France. But Arnador said nothing, as his quiet orderly mind examined the whole idea of war. Manuel said flatly he would be going to sea, and felt sick at the reminder that his father was actually out there, facing submarines and battleships alike.

26

EVERY time his father docked during the First World War Manuel's tight-clenched stomach would relax, and he looked forward to their doing things together. As he grew bigger, he understood clearly that it was Pedro who maintained the household. His mother worked very hard; when she was not scrubbing floors, she was cooking, washing or driving bargains in the market. In her spare time, she knitted and mended, as she gossiped to neighbours, who wandered freely in and out of the house.

But women had only the money their husbands or fathers gave them. And without money everything collapsed. Manuel looked forward to when he could go to sea, and, when he returned, drop money and chocolates into his mother's lap. He ignored his grandma's hints about the Church and university; having to go to school until one was sixteen was a long enough stretch.

Arnador did not agree with Manuel about his future; he had his own eyes fixed on university, though he was unclear what he would study.

On his return, Pedro was invariably greeted with almost hysterical relief by Rosita and Micaela. Not for them were the grumbles of other local women about the meanness of their menfolk, or the groans at the likelihood of another pregnancy. There was an abiding love and general agreement between Rosita and Pedro, and quiet, patient Micaela had a place both in their hearts and in the home.

Manuel had little idea how lucky he was to have such a peaceful home; he took it for granted. If, when visiting his young friends, he stumbled upon a family row with dishes flying, or a wife or son being beaten, he was always alarmed and nonplussed. Rosita might shout at him for entering the house with dirty boots or slap her little daughters for being rude, but it had nothing of the ferocity he observed elsewhere.

Street fights were rare in his small corner of the dockside. Arnador said, however, that they were common in the north end of the city, particularly when the pubs closed on Saturday night. "Sometimes the police get beaten up," he told Manuel.

By silent consent they kept out of that area. Arnador was careful, and had a disarming way of dealing with people, considered Old Manuel, with some amusement. He could not recall his ever getting into a physical fight, though he could be a formidable debater, the old fox.

While Pedro was at home, Rosita's face would look a little less drawn, and Micaela would lose some of the gravity which had become habitual to her. The house would be cheered up by the friendly rumbling of Basque voices, as friends of Pedro's dropped in to see him, on their way to the Baltic Fleet.

Like most seamen during the war, Pedro had

an uneasy feeling that his time might be short. Whenever he was at home, he made a habit of taking Manuel to the park to sail his boat on the pond, or they played pelota against a warehouse wall. To the amusement of the dock watchman, who knew Pedro quite well, they sometimes swam together in Wapping Dock; it was common to see boys diving off the steps there, but it was rare to see a man. The watchman, who was supposed to keep people out of the water, sometimes turned a blind eye.

They also went across the river in the ferryboat, to explore the Wirral countryside beyond Birkenhead, or, when the tide was in, to swim in the sea at Hoylake.

One evening, Pedro found Arnador doing his arithmetic homework with Manuel at the kitchen table. He found Arnador's slightly pompous character amusing, and, when he heard from the boy that he hoped to go to the university, he was keen to foster the friendship with Manuel. If Mannie was destined for higher education, he had better have friends who also studied; he realized that Wapping Dock boys were unlikely to comprehend the necessity of hard work at school.

Manuel forgot about little Brian Wing, the last hope of the Chinese laundry, who, most evenings, sat by his mother's ironing board, while she heard him spell in English, a decrepit dictionary at hand to confirm the correctness of his efforts. His eldest brother now worked full-time in the laundry, and the next one had just gone to sea, but, with the elder boys now adding to the family income, Mr Wing wanted better things for his smallest son; the child never moved out of the steamy laundry until his homework was done.

Pedro was the first seaman with whom Arnador became friends. His father dealt with them every day in his chandlery business, as they came to buy all the requirements of a ship from rope to teapots; but Arnador was not encouraged to visit the warehouse. He was much more fascinated by Pedro's stories of his life at sea than Manuel was. Manuel had listened to his father and his grandfather talking about their lives ever since he could remember; he regarded their adventures as a man's normal life. He believed that everybody understood seagoing and docks and foreign ports — they were all part of the life you hoped to escape to the minute you could finish school and be a man, preferably not later than aged thirteen. It was as well that he did not take seriously his family's determination that he should have further education; if he had, there would probably have been an instant rebellion; he accepted the discipline of St Francis Xavier's, but he assumed it would not last for that long.

* * *

It was through a horse that Pedro made the acquaintance of Arnador's mother. Once, on shore leave, he took both boys to see the Annual Horse Parade in Lime Street. Liverpudlians flocked there to see working horses groomed to perfection, their tails and manes plaited with coloured ribbons. Their polished harnesses glittered with brightly shining horse brasses and had flowers attached to them.

Though Francesca had little idea of the reason for the outing, she howled to be taken along. As usual, she was bought off by Rosita's promise of a halfpennyworth of dolly mixtures from the corner shop. Rosita would have enjoyed going to see the Parade, too, but she earnestly wanted Manuel to have his father's company; amongst seagoing families, too many boys barely knew their fathers, except when they sat, downcast, by their empty fireplaces, unemployed.

In Lime Street, Pedro and the boys stood behind a temporary barrier to watch the heaving, shining mass of animals. While Pedro, a cigarette drooping from the corner of his mouth, gossiped with another man in the crowd, Arnador and Manuel sucked boiled sweets produced from the depths of Pedro's tobacco-dusty pocket. A few police kept the crowd orderly, so that no one was kicked by an irate horse or run over by a backing wagon.

Living at a distance from the docks, Arnador did not see as many horses as Manuel did, nor had he had the regular warnings from his mother to keep out of reach of them. He was enthralled by the sheer beauty of the animals, which were not ordinarily so well groomed. The nearest to him was a neat little carriage horse with a coat like polished coal; it was in the shafts of a light trap. The driver held the reins loosely in his lap, and tipped his straw hat to someone on the other side of the carriage. A lively exchange of jokes ensued, and the horse stirred uneasily.

Cautiously, Arnador slipped under the barricade, and approached the dark beauty.

Pedro called, "Hey! Come on back, lad."

Arnador ignored him, and patted the horse's neck.

"Arnador!" Pedro was not used to being disobeyed.

The youngster half turned, grinned at Pedro, and said, as he stretched out his hand to stroke the animal's nose, "He's OK, Mr Echaniz. He likes it."

Pedro saw the animal's lips curl back from its yellowed teeth, as it moved its head from the caressing hand. He swiftly ducked under the barrier to pull the boy back. Arnador saw the movement and reluctantly turned to obey Pedro. The irritated animal leaned forward and bit into his shoulder. The heavy teeth did not manage to bite through his jacket, but had a firm enough grip to give the boy a sharp shake.

Arnador screamed with pain. It gave another vicious shake, and then let go, as the alerted driver hastily reined it in.

As the horse tried to rear, Pedro snatched the boy away.

"You stupid bugger!" he shouted, and shoved the crying boy back under the barrier.

Nearby horses shuffled uneasily, and the crowd round Manuel pushed backwards, away from the restive animals.

In the space left, a furious, scared Pedro shook Arnador like a terrier shaking a rat. The boy cried out in pain and fright.

A constable pushed his way along the front of the onlookers. "What's this? What's this?" he shouted. "Keep back there."

Pedro cursed under his breath; the last thing he wanted was an over-zealous constable making a fuss. He let go of Arnador, and growled at the boy, "Shut up! You're not dead yet." He urged both boys towards the shops behind the crowd, muttering, "Excuse us, please."

A passage was made for them, and for the constable who followed. Arnador was doing his best not to cry, but his face was as white as Rosita's front doorstep.

Manuel whispered uneasily to his father, "Should we take Arnie home?"

As they took refuge from the crowd in a shop doorway, the constable said, "Now then. What's up?"

"The boy went under the barrier to pet a horse — and it nipped him. He's all right," responded Pedro.

Scared that the constable would demand his name and address, because he had crossed a police barrier, Arnador snuffled agreement with Pedro. "It gave me a fright," he said. "That's all."

"Lucky you weren't kicked," the constable told him, and turned away.

Arnador still looked very white, so Pedro said, "We'll take you home — make sure your shoulder's all right."

"I can see myself home," Arnador protested. He was afraid Pedro would tell his father that he had been disobedient.

"Nonsense!" Pedro eased the boys away from the Parade, and they went over to Renshaw Street, to get a tram up to Catherine Street.

When Arnador put out his hand to grasp the upright rod in order to swing himself up the tram steps, he cried out, despite his earlier protestations of being able to manage alone.

Pedro helped him on, and they sat in the downstairs part of the vehicle; young men usually went upstairs so that they could smoke.

Arnador's eyes were clenched tightly shut; the shoulder was hurting badly. Pedro regretted his burst of temper, as he saw the boy struggling to be brave. Manuel watched both of them with apprehension.

Arnador was too young to have a key to his home, so when they rang the doorbell, Betty, the maid, answered it. She viewed Pedro's handsome face with insolent interest. What was their Arnie doing with a common seaman? "Something wrong?" she asked, making no move to let them enter.

Pedro asked to see Mr or Mrs Ganivet.

"She's restin'," replied Betty, opening the door just sufficiently to let Arnador in.

Pedro's eyes narrowed. "Tell her that Mr Echaniz wants to see her."

It was an order, and she reluctantly let them into the hall. He removed his peaked cap as he entered, and she viewed with scorn his navy woollen sweater. What would the mistress think? Then she turned sulkily and flounced up the stairs. Arnador held one arm against his chest, to ease the pain, and led them into the red velvet opulence of the Ganivet sitting-room.

The boys hung uneasily round the doorway, while Pedro stood in the middle of the room, and was made suddenly aware of the bareness and shabbiness of his own home. Arnador struggled out of his jacket, and winced as Manuel helped him loosen it from his left shoulder.

Mrs Ganivet nearly ran into the room, tucking loose strands of her hair into her bun as she came. "What's wrong?" she asked, as Arnador turned his blenched face towards her.

She turned to Pedro, and he made himself known to her. He explained briefly what had happened, and finished up, "He's probably got a nasty bruise. I thought I'd better bring him home."

"Stupid boy," Mrs Ganivet exclaimed tenderly. "Take off your jersey, luv. Let's have a look."

Arnador cried out when she heaved the garment off him, and pulled down the shoulder of his undervest. There was a clear line of bruises on both sides of the snow-white shoulder where the horse's teeth had gripped him.

"Dear me!" she exclaimed. "Mr Echaniz, do sit down a mo', while I get the arnica bottle and a towel. You must have a cuppa afore you go." She turned to Manuel, "And you sit down, luv."

She pushed her son to the red plush sofa, and told him, "Arnie, dear, you rest here." She tucked a matching red cushion behind his back. "There, that'll be more comfy. Back in a mo'."

As she ran upstairs, they could hear her shouting to Betty to make some tea and put out the cup cakes.

"How does it feel?" asked Pedro of the sufferer.

Anxious not to be thought a coward, Arnador replied that it was easing. "Mother always makes such a fuss," he added in apology.

Aware of the fussiness of mothers, Manuel made a face at him.

When his mother dabbed arnica liberally over the bruises and then padded the shoulder with one of his father's big cotton handkerchiefs, so that the arnica would not get on to his jersey, Arnador drew in his breath sharply.

"There you are, dearie. Now you lean back on the cushion. You'll feel fine when you've had a cuppa cha," she told him.

She turned to Pedro, who had been watching her ministrations without comment. "It was proper kind of you to bring him home," she said. "He'd have probably been all right by himself, but it must've been scary for him — you don't expect to get bitten by a horse, do you?"

As Pedro agreed, she sat down by a little mahogany table. He half rose to go, but she saw the movement. "Stay a bit," she urged. "Betty's making the tea. It's nice to meet Manuel's father." Within her, she was acutely aware of the handsome man before her and was slightly ashamed of herself. How could a decent Catholic woman feel like that?

To cover her embarrassment, she plied Pedro

with quick questions about where in the Pyrenees his family lived and confided that her husband's and her own grandparents had come from Pamplona. As she spoke of Pamplona, she shyly changed from English into Basque, and Pedro smiled and spoke Basque in return.

While the adult conversation flowed back and forth, Manuel watched Arnador. Though his colour was better, he reclined awkwardly on the sofa. His eyes were closed and he was, for once, silent. "Is it still hurting?" Manuel whispered.

Arnador opened his eyes, and nodded.

"Sorry," Manuel muttered.

27

THE day after Old Manuel had written for Lorilyn how Arnador had been bitten by a horse, he awoke to a flawless summer morning. When he looked across the drive at the Strait dappled with sunshine, he decided that he would take the *Rosita* out in the afternoon; if the wind were right, he would sail her up the coast. First, however, he had to take the rose up to Kathleen's grave and then go to buy some much-needed groceries.

Because of the need to carry the groceries home, he took the car out and carefully drove it up to the cemetery. He did not linger there very long; just stood looking at her memorial stone, which was brightly lit by a shaft of sunlight, and then, with a sigh, went back to the car, and drove downtown to Safeway's.

In the car park, he parked carefully between a couple of trucks, and went into the shop. As he entered, a blast of air-conditioning made him wish he had put on a pullover; sudden changes of temperature bothered him sometimes.

He looked very frail as, with slow care, he moved down the aisles, picking out the things he needed. Sharon Herman noticed his entry, as she contemplated the offerings of the meat department. His frailty and the resigned droop of his shoulders moved her in a way she could not explain to herself. She quickly dropped two lamb chops into her basket, and walked towards the aisle down which he had vanished. She soon caught up with him, as he stopped to pick up a tin of coffee.

Manuel was startled by a plump, soft hand being laid over his thin brown one pushing the shopping trolley. "How are you?" asked the feminine voice.

He jumped, and looked up.

Not Veronica, thanks be to Holy Mary, but her house guest. His brown eyes twinkled amid a myriad of wrinkles, and his wide mouth curved up into his usual quirky smile, as, with some relief, he assured her that he was very well. He could not think of anything more to say, so, on the spur of the moment, she asked him if he would like to have a cup of coffee with her. She joked that the store had a small corner with a coffee machine, which was meant for the use of senior citizens — she was tired and needed to sit down — but she was really too young to sit there without embarrassment — it would be so much easier if he could spare the time to sit with her!

He laughed, and wheeled his trolley over to the corner she indicated. They filled paper cups with coffee, and sat down at a small table. Manuel put two packets of sugar into his coffee and stirred it with a plastic stick. "Bridget! That's it," he said, as he looked earnestly into her face.

She looked so startled that he had to smile again. "You remind me of someone I knew when I was a small boy. She delivered babies and often she nursed people who were sick. She actually brought me into the world. She wasn't a qualified nurse, like you, of course." He was too shy to tell her that everybody loved and trusted Bridget.

She was interested, and, because it had been in the forefront of his mind the previous evening, he told her how his friend Arnador's shoulder had been treated at home with arnica; and its partial dislocation discovered over twenty years later when he volunteered for the Royal Air Force.

"I used to carry his school satchel for him, because his shoulder hurt him — and he never played cricket again — or pelota. But I'm grateful for it," he assured her. "If he had gone into the Air Force, he would probably have been killed in the Battle of Britain — so many of them died. As it is, he's still pretty spry. Best friend I could ever hope for."

"Really?"

Manuel's face was suddenly a little wistful. "He's a great lad. I get a letter from him most months. I wish he were nearer."

"Has he ever come over here?"

"Oh, yes. He came a couple of times when Kathleen was alive. And he's been twice since — since she passed away. It's my turn to go to Liverpool."

"Are you going?"

"I hadn't thought of it — not seriously, that is."

"Perhaps you should." She did not want to point out that, at their age, one or the other of them might die quite soon.

He caught the implication of her remark, however, and considered it for a moment. Then he replied, "Perhaps I should. I won't tell Faith, though. At least not until the last moment."

"Who won't you tell?"

"My daughter Faith. She always worries when I travel. Says I'm too old."

"Live dangerously!" she advised. "Do what you want to do."

He laughed, as he turned to look at her. "You're dead right," he told her. "I will."

28

AT the eleventh hour of the eleventh day of the eleventh month, 1918, the great war to end all wars came to a finish. Throughout the war, my daily life had gone on much the same, wrote Old Manuel to Lorilyn; yet, behind everything I did, it lay like a threatening black shadow; your Auntie Francesca and I used to dread that Father would be killed, and we were so relieved every time he docked, especially when he came home a few days after the war ended. We knew then that he was safe.

* * *

On 11 November, Rosita stood on her doorstep, leaning against the doorjamb, one arm round ten-year-old Manuel, and thanked God that the child had been too young to serve in the conflict.

At her feet, on the step, sat Francesca, aged five, and Little Maria, just four. Between them sat Grandma Micaela. They were watching fireworks rocket into the sky, and riotously drunk neighbours dancing round a bonfire. Micaela could actually see nothing, but she could hear the crackle of the fire, the reports of the fireworks and the shouts and shrieks of the dancers; earlier, she had heard all the church bells of Liverpool ring out the victory. In her mind, however, she heard the frantic weeping for those who would not return home — and she saw the shocked faces of wives whose husbands had returned so badly mauled that they would have to be nursed for the rest of their lives — on minuscule pensions, if they were lucky enough to get one.

While the little girls chattered excitedly and drew her attention to scenes she was too blind to see, she fingered the rosary in her pocket. Her faith had been tried to the limit by the senseless slaughter of the war; and yet, she ruminated sadly, what hope had she to cling to, other than the belief that God knew what he was doing.

Francesca snuggled down closer to her. "I'm cold, Granny," she said in Basque.

The old woman opened her shawl and wrapped it round her little granddaughter.

The huge bonfire fell in with a crash and a rain of sparks, and some of the more noisy dancers went in a mob to the Baltic Fleet. Joey Connolly asked his father to take him closer to watch a few Catherine wheels whizzing bravely on warehouse doors. Pat agreed, and asked Manuel if he would like to come, too.

Rosita had expected Manuel to leap at the offer. But he scuffed his feet, and said he did not want to go. Though he and Arnador often played with Mary and Joey, he was beginning to feel oddly uncomfortable in his own neighbourhood. A better education and a growing awareness of a bigger and more interesting world than that of

Wapping Dock or being a seaman was beginning to make him feel cut off. At times, when playing in the street with the international collection of children from nearby, he found himself carefully silent; they had once or twice given him a hard time when he had made some ill-considered remark, which, in St Francis Xavier's, would have passed for humour.

On Armistice Night, he sensed the terrible sadness beneath the jollity of the singing, dancing people, and he felt sick.

* * *

Arnador, bespectacled and earnest, had never shared his schoolfellows' jingoistic acceptance of the nobility of dying in muddy trenches; there had to be better ways of stopping the Germans, in his opinion. He read the papers far more thoroughly than Manuel did, and observed the increasing number of discharged, wounded men on the streets, many of them dressed in hospital blue. He told his father flatly that he would never be so stupid as to volunteer and probably would not answer a call-up.

Mr Ganivet lectured him angrily that, though he was a Basque, England was his country and he should be prepared to lay down his life for it.

Afterwards, Arnador told Manuel about the ensuing family row, and said angrily, "It doesn't make sense. Who wants to be blown to bits? I bet the Germans don't."

Manuel was quite shaken by Arnador's passionate outburst. He responded promptly, by saying, "Well, they can stop fighting."

Yet, twenty years later, when the German Nazis threatened Britain, Arnador had tried to get into the Royal Air Force. Perhaps he had felt that a fundamental principle was at stake that time, Manuel decided.

* * *

One of Manuel's saddest memories of the First World War was that of Effie Halloran sobbing bitterly in his mother's kitchen-living-room, because both her boys had been killed. He had wanted to run away from grief so close to home. But he had sat at the kitchen table trying to do his homework, and chewed the end of his wooden penholder. Awful things happened to women, as well as to men, he had thought. Men went to sea and faced danger daily — that, in his head, was the essence of being a man — but he felt uneasily that the women at home had to be pretty brave, as well.

Men poured home, ships were laid up, war factories closed. Women who had worked hard and well during the war years were impatiently shoved aside and told to go back home and raise a family.

Women resented this, not only because their modest wages had given them a modicum of independence, but because for many of them earning was a necessity; they had lost husbands, sweethearts, brothers and fathers, and had, therefore, to maintain themselves. It was some time before such women were absorbed by light industry as welcome cheap labour.

The land fit for heroes was slow in arriving. Pedro's ship returned to its old routes down the west coast of Africa, and he took good care not to give a hint of his desire for a move to another company, until he was sure of a 'hit'. Meanwhile, cargoes were not so easy to come by and, to cut costs, the quality of food supplied by the owners deteriorated from poor to worse. Seamen and engine room crew were increasingly recruited from Lagos at wages much lower than those asked for by Liverpool men. The officers made little complaint; they were worried enough about retaining their own jobs, and, as repairs were deferred, how long the old tub would stay afloat.

When ashore, Pedro looked up all the men he knew who worked for de Larrinaga, most of whose crews were Basque. His friends all said mournfully that the competition was wicked; every company had its own group of men who had served it before and who were competing anxiously for any vacancies.

Pedro understood the pressure only too well. Some of the Negroes in his current ship felt themselves to be so vulnerable to unemployment that they hastened to sign on for the next voyage immediately the previous one was completed, to make sure of retaining their job; in effect, they never stepped off the ship for months at a time.

In the event, another enemy swept through the population. Spanish flu, incurable, unstoppable, took thousands upon thousands of lives, particularly amongst young adults, already thinned out in Europe by the slaughter of the war. It left those who survived the attack weakened and deeply depressed. Ships' crews were far from immune, and that was, perhaps, why a jubilant Pedro suddenly hit on a berth with de Larrinaga in the *Esperanza Larrinaga*. It had a Liverpool crew, mostly Basque.

"The wages aren't a lot better," he told Rosita. "But the conditions are. Jean Baptiste knows the cook and says he's great."

He suggested that with the small increase in pay they might manage to send Francesca and Little Maria to a good school run by nuns; the fees were not very great. Rosita was overwhelmed that he should give such consideration to his small daughters. "I can't think of anybody else who would try that hard for their girls," she told him, as she hugged him hard.

He kissed her and said, "I want them to have decent jobs — not to have to sew till their eyes drop out, like you had to when you were little."

Remembering her long apprenticeship as a seamstress, Rosita was in hearty agreement with him.

A delighted Micaela expressed the hope that one of them would become a nun.

"If she has a calling to it," replied Rosita cautiously. She had observed that her own small world of the dockside and the city centre was not returning to its pre-war pattern. The brighter girls were trying for clean factory jobs, or, better still, office work, which paid more.

★ ★ ★

Even the Church felt subtly different. A lot of her neighbours had never been particularly devout — but there was a wavering in the ready acceptance of priestly pronouncements, a sly shift in the way people addressed their hard-working Jesuit mentors — they were still polite, but not so respectful. Even her own belief had been shaken. How could one worship a God who had taken away Effie's boys, her only joy in a bitterly hard life? It was all very well to tell the poor demented soul that it was God's will — but what kind of God was he to allow men to murder each other?

As Manuel grew bigger, she worried constantly that he might fall into bad company. The church still offered a certain discipline in this regard, and she insisted that he say his prayers and attend Mass.

She was glad that he had a nice, steady friend in Arnador; only yesterday, he had brought his books to her house to do his homework with Manuel; and he had helped Francesca with the more difficult words she had to learn to spell. Two decent lads together could sustain each other.

She smiled as she went to get water and a big stick with which to clean the outside drains; she was so lucky to have Pedro and Manuel — and the girls. Best of all, Pedro had, at last, got a decent berth with a good company.

29

IN 1919 the Liverpool City Police went on strike. As a result, there was so much violence in the city that both Mrs Ganivet and Rosita warned the boys not to go near the north end of the town. They scolded almost identically. "With no police, you don't know what may happen to you — they've got soldiers on guard — with rifles, and they shot somebody last night. And see how it's raining; you'll be soaked!"

Determined not to miss the excitement, each boy told his mother cheerfully that he would be visiting the home of the other one.

In macintoshes and boots, their identifying St Francis Xavier caps stuffed into their pockets, they trudged along Lime Street to look at the London Road shopping area, which it was said had been hard hit by looting rioters. They found themselves in a fairly large crowd all going in the same direction.

They were struck dumb by what they saw; other appalled sightseers whispered to each other, as if they were at a funeral. Even Arnador seemed awed by the destruction. Though the pavements appeared to have been swept, bits of glass from shattered shop windows crunched under their feet or lay in neat heaps along the base of the gaping display windows, empty except for fluttering price tickets and knocked down shelves and stands. Behind them, the boys caught a glimpse of interiors reduced to a shambles. Some windows had already been boarded up, and, in front of others, men were at work with sheets of plywood closing off the rest from the wrath of further rioters.

They were relieved that the army did not appear to be on guard.

A solitary constable stood rigidly at a corner, truncheon drawn.

Arnador viewed him with interest. "The strike isn't one hundred per cent," he remarked thoughtfully.

Manuel whispered back. "I thought they were all out." He gazed at the unmoving constable; there was something touching in the way he stood alone, waiting for further mobs to descend on the cruelly smashed tiny businesses.

Arnador's eyes dropped, as the constable became aware of his stare. He said uneasily, "Perhaps he doesn't believe it's right to let ordinary people suffer, when it's not their fault. It could be our house — or his — next."

Manuel's eyes widened in horror. "Do you think so?"

"It's possible." He waved a hand towards a corner shop, particularly devastated. "The mob that did this probably got upstairs and cleaned out the owner's home, as well."

Manuel felt slightly sick. "Mam says that they're so poor up Scotland Road, it's pitiful. They'd take anything."

"They're very poor round Wapping Dock."

"Well, nothing happened round us."

"In the war, they sacked a German butcher's shop on Park Road." The older boy paused to watch a man hammering boards over a side window, which, somehow, still had its glass intact. Then he added, "Because he was foreign — and the enemy. We're foreign, and people would turn on us, if they didn't like what Spain was doing."

Manuel responded stoutly, "I'm not foreign; I was born here — and we're not Spanish."

Arnador smiled. "They don't know the difference. And you look foreign."

"You don't!"

"I'm fair. I blend in better — it's very convenient!"

As they climbed the hill and, with others, viewed the endless damage, a small fear entered Manuel's heart. Would people hurt you simply because you looked different? In the polyglot area in which he lived, he had never been made to feel different, except when, at school, Stewart had called him a dago. Could the brutes who had caused such chaos in friendly London Road turn on other people? If there were no police?

Sickened by his own thoughts, he was suddenly dimly aware that it was the police, taken for granted like letter boxes or lamp standards, who normally stopped people from wreaking havoc. At this moment, except for the defiant, almost heroic figure they had passed on the corner, there were no police.

"Let's go home," he urged Arnador.

They were dripping wet and they moved

towards a shop entrance, to shelter for a minute, while they decided what to do. A deep voice said sharply, "Move along there, please."

They jumped, and turned. A soldier not much older than themselves, his rifle on his shoulder, stood deeper in the entrance-way. He looked very grim.

Without a word, the youngsters moved away, and then, suddenly frightened, clattered as fast as they could through the thickening crowd, back down to Lime Street.

Actually being given an order by a soldier in khaki uniform, with a gun, confirmed their mothers' scoldings. This was as serious as the paper said it was. Soldiers were normally men on leave; they did not order civilians around; they were meant to fight wars.

Though the strike was not undertaken without cause, none of the striking men got their jobs back. New recruits, many of them Irish, were taken into the Force; this was deeply resented by many people on Merseyside, and remained a rankling grievance for half a century.

* * *

Even seventy-three years later, Old Manuel recalled how terrified he had been at Arnador's idle remark about mobs turning on people. Until then, he had always believed that a man belonged where he was born, though he could also be proud of his racial origins. Perhaps, he considered, as he carefully shaved himself one morning, it was that incident which had made him more stubbornly Basque than he would have otherwise been.

He grinned, as he peered into the bathroom mirror to dab a small nick in his chin — despite Kathleen's best efforts to convert him to an electric razor, he still shaved with an old-fashioned cutthroat. We always were an obstinate lot, he told his mirror image with blatant pride.

* * *

That same year, Brian Wing electrified the neighbourhood round Wapping by winning one of the very few scholarships then available, to the highly respected Liverpool Institute.

Struggling to keep their little laundry going, his father and mother were considered poor even by the hard-up residents around them. How could Brian have ever learned enough to do it? Manuel and Arnador wondered.

Auntie Bridget Connolly, who was credited with knowing everything about the area, soon told them that the family had given a home to a poor university student of Chinese descent, on a promise that he would tutor Brian in maths and English. The young man and the nervous little boy had liked each other; and the pair of them were so proud of their success that, according to Bridget, "When I saw 'em this mornin', they were grinnin' at each other like two Buddhas out of Bunney's gift shop." She smiled softly at Manuel and Arnador, and went on, "He looked proper nice in his uniform, he did. He's a lovely little lad."

"He'll probably be the only Chinese kid in the school," Pat Connolly remarked, as he checked the racing news at the back of his newspaper. "Poor little tyke."

"He won't have no trouble," Bridget assured him. "He's smart at avoiding it — watched him many a time I have."

Manuel and Arnador agreed. They were both intrigued at having another friend in Wapping who, like themselves, would be better educated.

The next time Manuel went up to the laundry to see Brian, Rosita instructed him to tell his small friend how happy the Echaniz family was at his success.

Brian's eyes became slits behind his Woolworth's glasses, as he grinned. He was dressed in his usual slightly large woollen shorts, handed down from his older brother. "Got any ciggie cards to swop?" he asked.

Still the same old Brian, Manuel decided with an odd sense of relief.

* * *

Pedro missed the fun of preparing for Christmas.

Manuel did all kinds of small jobs round the Pier Head and the dock, to earn pennies to buy presents for Grandma Micaela, Rosita, Francesca and Little Maria, and for his father. He caught ropes thrown by boatmen approaching the dockside; he held horses occasionally for delivery van men — horses that pulled drays were too big for him to cope with; for a halfpenny, he watched a telegraph boy's bicycle at the kerbside;

and, once, he actually watched that a motor car remained untouched, when a very well-dressed man wanted to walk down to the Pier Head to take a photograph of a ferry coming in. He shared the latter job with Brian, and they stood one on each side of this most unusual vehicle and scowled ferociously at any street kid who came to stare at it. The man gave them twopence each, when he returned and found it safe and unblemished. Both boys were ecstatic. Manuel also got a whole series of pennies from Mrs Saitua, for running her messages for her. She had caught the Spanish flu and, though she had survived it, she still had not recovered her strength, so she was very glad of his help.

Pedro docked a few days after Christmas. Since he had missed the traditional Christmas Eve feast, though he had had a Christmas dinner aboard ship, Rosita and Micaela again made some of the customary Basque Christmas Eve dishes for him, and the family enjoyed roasted bream, fried potatoes and new bread, followed by a big plate of choux pastries filled with cream and covered with chocolate. The Saituas, two sturdy Basque friends of Pedro's, the Connollys and the Hallorans were invited to visit and share the cakes.

Bottles of wine and a box of cigars were opened, and, in the ensuing merriment, even Rosita's tired, pale face began to show some colour.

Mysterious parcels were unearthed from Pedro's kitbag and hidden until 6 January, Epiphany, when they would be placed in a basket in the front window as gifts from the Three Wise Men on their feast day.

In English fashion, Manuel, Francesca and Little Maria had all hung their stockings up in front of the fireplace at Christmas, into which both grandmother and mother had contrived to put small presents. None of them seemed to remember that 6 January was still to come.

While Francesca was cuddled on her father's lap, Manuel leaned on the back of his father's chair until he reeked of smoke from Pedro's cigar. He longed to have his father to himself for a little while; but, meanwhile, he listened to a heated discussion of British and Spanish politics, interspersed with joking references to the hazards of shipboard life. Sometimes, the words poured out so fast that the Basques present broke into their own language, and everything had to be quickly translated by Rosita for the benefit of the Connollys and Hallorans, as she refilled glasses and handed round the cakes.

When Pedro asked Rosita to pour half a glass of wine for the boy, Manuel felt he had suddenly become an adult. Francesca and Little Maria promptly demanded a glass, too. Drops of wine were put into two glasses and then surreptitiously topped up with water. Everybody laughed when Little Maria carefully held her glass by the stem, exactly as Micaela did.

Even though the war was over, Bilbao was doing quite well, Pedro told them; he had gleaned this news from other Basques in his new ship, and now he floated the idea of, perhaps, going back there.

Mr Saitua made a face over the rim of his glass. "It won't last," he said. "The blasted Spanish'll drain it dry."

"There's a lot of talk of fighting for a country of our own. What do you think?"

Jean Baptiste Saitua pulled another face. "There's always been talk — but have you ever heard of a Spaniard letting go of anything he thinks he owns?"

Rosita intervened to ask her husband, "Do you think the children would have a better chance there than they do here?"

Pedro again looked to Jean Baptiste for comment on this.

The older man scratched his sunburned bald head with huge, swollen fingers. "I doubt it. My boys are in steady jobs. And Manuel could do better, if he stays in school long enough."

Pedro felt that now he was with the de Larrinaga Line he was doing fairly well himself, though one never knew with certainty when a ship might be laid up. If Manuel got into a profession, however, he would never be out of work — and the possibility of that was much greater for him in Liverpool. He nodded his head, and said to Rosita, "I believe he's right."

* * *

A day or two later, Pedro sailed again. Manuel was playing football with Brian Wing further up the street, and the two little girls had gone together to the corner shop to buy a penny block of salt for their mother. In the dark hall, Pedro held his wife in his arms, while Micaela busied herself making beds upstairs. She laid her head on his shoulder and said, with a sigh, "I wish you didn't have to go."

"It'd be much worse if I didn't have a ship to go to!" he replied. "There've been a few that have been laid up recently."

He felt her shrug slightly as she said, "I wish you could've had Dad's Basque agency. You could have had it, if you'd asked."

"There aren't that many emigrants going through, nowadays."

"Humph." She giggled suddenly, as he fondled her. "Get away with you," she told him. "Start that little game and you'll never get down to the ship before she sails. Come on, now. Let go!"

He laughed, loosed her, and gave her a quick kiss, before picking up his kitbag and tin suitcase. "See you soon, luv. Ta-ra."

She opened the door to let him out, and stood on the step to watch him swing down the road towards Queens No. 2. Then she shivered, wrapped her woollen cardigan closer round herself and went slowly indoors.

* * *

Seated in his neat Canadian kitchen, Old Manuel read a letter from his cousin, Ramon Barinèta, in Liverpool, sipped coffee, and, with half his mind, considered the steady rhythm of Rosita's work during her husband's absences.

She was always busy in the stone-floored, eighteenth-century house. He himself had loved the old lodging house and had, as a boy, never noticed its total lack of convenience; or that his grandmother was steadily becoming more frail and dependent upon her daughter.

As he grew older, Rosita had prevailed upon him to do some of the jobs his grandfather had done for her. Grumbling, he had chopped up kindling wood, and carried buckets of coal up from the cellar each day. Once or twice, he had hung out the family wash for her in the tiny back yard. His undeveloped muscles had ached, as he sought to avoid the wet sheets dragging on the ground as the freezing wind from the river caught them. He was embarrassed at pegging out his mother's bloomers and his sister's small undergarments, and he prayed, as he hung up a row of female stockings, that none of his friends would come through the door from the back alley, while he was doing it.

Now, as a very old man, he remembered with a pang his mother's scarlet hands, so swollen from scrubbing clothes on a wash board and scrubbing floors with hot soda water that her wedding ring cut painfully into her finger.

He remembered, too, with some amusement, that in a burst of compassion at her fatigue he had undertaken the fortnightly cleaning of the flues of the big kitchen range on which she cooked and which gave warmth to their living-room-kitchen. He remembered inserting the long wire brush into the main flue and pulling it out too quickly, so that the whole room had been doused in soot. His mother kept finding the thick black powder in odd corners for months afterwards.

He decided to include in the notes he was writing for Lorilyn a list of domestic tasks that he hoped that she would never have to face.

He carefully made the list. Then he wondered if a female electrical engineer would deign to do any housekeeping at all. Once he himself had qualified in a similar field and had gone to sea, he had never done any domestic work — until Kathleen died.

He chewed his thumbnail and wondered if Lorilyn might serve at sea, once she had her degree. In the middle of describing his mother's hard work, he suddenly wrote something that was a denial of his family's traditions. "I hope you will neither have to serve at sea or marry a seaman, my dear. It causes too much heartache."

She wouldn't go to sea, would she? Well, some women were nowadays doing men's jobs. He pursed his lips. She couldn't say he hadn't warned her.

He would leave the sentences in.

30

ONE miserable, overcast January afternoon in 1920, when the gas lamps in the street had already been lit, Madeleine Saitua flung open the Echanizes' back door and rushed in like a flustered hen. With her came a blast of cold air and noise from the workshops. A surprised Rosita mechanically closed the door after her and the clangour of panel beaters was sharply reduced. "Madeleine! You shouldn't come out in felt slippers in the rain; you'll catch your death!" she scolded.

Madeleine pulled out a kitchen chair from under the table, and sat down suddenly, realizing that she was still weak from the flu. She patted her big breast, as she panted to get her breath back.

Manuel had just returned from school and was unpacking his satchel, to return to his mother the piece of greaseproof paper in which his sandwiches had been wrapped; the paper would be used again and again. Now he stared at Madeleine apprehensively; it was not like Mrs Saitua to hurry about anything.

"Rosita, is it true that Pedro's ship's overdue?"

Rosita gaped at her friend. "No. I haven't heard anything." Her blue eyes were wide with shock. "They would've let us know if it was — wouldn't they?"

Manuel's heart gave a painful thud, and he

turned quickly to look at his mother. She was slowly blenching. Madeleine had not said 'late'; she had said 'overdue', with all that the word portended.

At Madeleine's precipitous entry, Micaela had stopped knitting, and lifted her head towards the sudden rush of cold air; she sensed trouble. Now, from her rocking chair close to the fire, she cackled suddenly, "They wouldn't let us know until they were sure she was lost, they wouldn't."

The women's silence after Micaela's remark scared Manuel; it was clear that none of them wanted to face the import of Madeleine's anxious inquiry.

The kettle on the fire boiled, and spat angrily. Without taking her eyes off Madeleine, Rosita told Manuel to take it off and put it on the hob. Then she asked, "Where did you hear about it, Madeleine?" She pulled out a chair for herself and sat down carefully, afraid she would fall in a faint.

Madeleine had recovered her breath, and she responded promptly, "Well, Jean Baptiste was visiting friends living in Scottie Road, and the landlord of the Throstles Nest tells him — knowing he's Basque, like. Said a couple of lads from Harrison was talking about it. He told me just now, when he come in. So I gave him his tea, and I run down to see if you was all right — if it were true, like." She leaned forward to lay her hand on top of Rosita's which was clutching the table edge. "Have you been down to the office lately?"

"No," Rosita answered her dazedly. "Allotment's not due yet." She took a big breath, and said, "The Harrison Line men could be wrong."

Manuel interjected. "I can run down to the office and ask them for you."

Rosita glanced up at the old alarm clock on the mantelpiece. "They'd be closed, luv, before you got there." She grimaced, as she added, "And you being young, they'd fob you off with some official nonsense."

"Oh, aye, they would," agreed Micaela, and again picked up the sock she was knitting for Manuel, as if to impart some sense of normality to the frightened little group.

The kitchen-living-room was so still, while Madeleine waited for Rosita to say something more, that the click of the knitting needles and the tick of the clock could be clearly heard, despite the roar of machinery and the clatter of metal sheets. Madeleine shivered.

Rosita did not know what to say. Her mind wavered between a frantic need to know the truth and the fact that the only place which could give her accurate news was shut until nine o'clock the following morning.

Watching her livid face and unable to bear the women's unnatural quietness, Manuel suggested, "First, we don't know if they really are overdue, do we? Dad could simply be late because they've had to stop for a repair or bad weather — a gale could have set them off course."

His mother's expression did not change; it was as if she were staring down a long, dark tunnel, which she did not wish to enter. She did switch her gaze towards her son, however, and it came to him vividly that she knew his father was dead.

But she couldn't know, could she? It wasn't logical. Passionately, he went on, "Maybe there's something in the evening paper. I'll go up to Park Lane and get one."

Seeing the boy's obvious anxiety, and worried about Rosita — she was far too quiet — Madeleine seized upon Manuel's idea. She leaned closer to Rosita. "Let him go up and buy one," she advised.

Rosita nodded. "There's some coppers in my purse over there, on the sideboard. Run and get one, dear."

Rosita could hear her daughters chattering, as they opened the front door on their return from school. She frowned; she must teach them not to dawdle on the way home, now that the nights had drawn in. Manuel shot past them, twopence clutched in his hand, as they called to their mother and hung up their coats and hats in the hall.

She made herself call a cheery, "Hullo," as Madeleine tried to comfort her by saying, "Even if it is late, they'll probably turn up. Pedro said a number of times what good mates he had — real experienced."

"Yes, you're right. He was very happy with them." As she forced herself to her feet, to greet Francesca and Little Maria, she realized that she had expressed herself in the past tense, and it took all her courage to suppress her panic.

She turned to the little girls and hugged them both, while she listened to the stories of their afternoon, and gave them a biscuit each to nibble on until tea was ready.

Over their heads, she looked warningly at Madeleine, and nothing more was said about the ship. Micaela needed no prompting; she knitted briskly, as she looked up to greet her burbling granddaughters.

Manuel stood in the tiny newsagent's shop and frantically turned the pages to find the shipping news, while the newsagent stood patiently behind his magazine-laden counter. "I'm looking to see when Dad's ship's due."

The newsagent took a puff from his cigarette. "In trouble, are you?" he joked.

"No. Mam wants to know."

He hastily folded the paper, tucked it under his arm and ran home as hard as he could.

The *Esperanza Larrinaga* was not mentioned in the shipping news.

31

THE rumour had spread. When, the next morning, after the children had been sent to school, Rosita put on her shawl and went down to the shipping office, there was a number of flustered women besieging the clerk at the counter. The frail-looking young clerk, only recently discharged from army hospital himself, said that the vessel was, as yet, listed only as being late. Inquiries were being made.

Whey-faced wives and mothers bowed their heads and went home to wait.

A few days later, in the newspaper, the ship was reported missing. The first half-pay allotments were withheld.

Rosita and Micaela were thrown back upon the diminished savings in the boxes under Micaela's bed. "Keep the bit you've got in the Post Office," advised Micaela. "You may not need to use it." She came from a family of fishermen, and she comforted Rosita by saying insistently, "I've seen it happen more than once. Fishing boats, and all; and you're fit to die yourself. Then the whole crew turns up weeks later in some outlandish spot. Been picked up by another small vessel — and had to go with them to whatever was their destination. And that may be what the company's thinking — they haven't written to you yet."

Manuel was refilling the coal hod by the

kitchen range from a bucket he had brought up from the coal cellar.

"But, Grandma, if they'd been found, we'd know by radio, wouldn't we?"

Grandma pulled a face. "Not many ships have got such newfangled things. For sure, if your dad's ship had it and they were in trouble, they would have sent a message, I would think. I doubt they've got a radio."

Manuel agreed. "I think Dad would've mentioned it if they'd had one."

Rosita tried to smile. "You could be right, Mam. They're safe in a boat without a radio," she said, but her mind was in a turmoil of sheer terror.

Manuel talked about it with Arnador when, as usual, he came to the Echaniz house to do his homework with him and with Francesca. Arnador had never been able to express his intense loneliness to his friend; he simply arrived with his school books most evenings, and thankfully sat down to work in Rosita's busy kitchen-living-room with the family around him. Mrs Ganivet could never understand this, and always pointed out shrilly that he had a bedroom with a gas fire of his own. He told her dully that he and Manuel worked well together, which was true.

That night, as they sat at the table together, they whispered about Pedro's ship, while, by the fire, Grandma and Rosita entertained two Basque ladies; the adults tried to keep their conversation free of reference to the feared disaster, so as not to frighten the children.

Struggling with an essay — at least a paragraph, Sister Winifred had insisted — on 'What I Did in My Christmas Holidays', Francesca caught the boys' whispers. She looked up at Manuel and Arnador aghast. "Daddy's ship's lost?" she hissed.

Manuel was jolted. He had forgotten that Rosita had not told his sisters. He quickly said comfortingly, "It's a bit late — and everybody worries about men at sea when the winter storms are here."

"Are you sure?" Her pinched little face lacked a trace of colour, as she spoke.

"My dad hasn't mentioned it," interjected Arnador. "He would know about it, and would have told us at home — because it's a Basque ship." He was sliding swiftly round the truth, trying to protect his friend's little sister.

Francesca half-turned to ask her mother what had happened, but Manuel caught her and said, "Not now. It's not fair to worry Mam."

"I want to," hissed Francesca.

"Mam's friends may have men in Dad's ship. You'll scare them!"

She stared resentfully at her brother through red-gold lashes, and said sulkily, "All right. How do you spell 'plentiful'?"

Arnador told her.

* * *

When he returned to Catherine Street, his father was sitting in a red velveteen-covered chair in their sitting-room, with the newspaper spread out on the tea table in front of him. Mr Ganivet did not like being disturbed when he was perusing the newspaper; but Arnador was sufficiently shaken by Manuel's news to ask, after he had divested himself of his outdoor clothes and hung his satchel up beside them, if he knew anything about the missing *Esperanza Larrinaga*.

"Indeed, yes. We were talking in the office about it. A terrible loss to us, if it has foundered."

His ponderous, often insensitive father seemed genuinely upset. Arnador inquired, "Do you mean to the business — or to us personally?"

Mr Ganivet looked nonplussed at the question, and then said almost indignantly, "A loss to the Basque community, of course. The crew is almost all Basque — it will be very hard on the families." He began to fold up the paper. "What made you ask about it?"

"Manuel's father's on it."

"Oh, my goodness! That's terrible! There are three children, I believe you said?"

"Yes, and Grandma — she's blind."

Mrs Ganivet came bustling in to say that her husband's evening supper and Arnador's bedtime cocoa awaited them in the dining-room, and she would be with them in a minute. She trotted out again, and Arnador said to his father, "Manuel loves his father — there's nobody like him."

The stout little man nodded absently, his thoughts already on the Cheddar cheese and crackers awaiting him.

Arnador followed him to the dining-room; he thought resentfully that he never seemed to be able to get close to his father; he could talk to Pedro more easily. As he sipped his hot cocoa, he wondered idly what his mother would do if *his* father was suddenly missing. Would he himself then be responsible for her? At fourteen? It was a shattering thought, and he wondered if it had occurred to Manuel, who was not yet thirteen.

* * *

A few days later, Micaela heard the flap of the letter-box rattle, as a letter was pushed through it. She went into the hall and ran her foot gently round the floor near the front door, until she heard the soft swish when her foot moved a letter. She picked it up and felt the ominous length of a business envelope.

"Rosita!" she called down the cellar steps. "There's a letter come."

Rosita had been checking how much coal she had in the cellar; Manuel often neglected to tell her when he brought up the last bucket of slack. Now, wild with hope that it would be a letter from Pedro, she flew up the stone steps.

When she saw the long narrow envelope in her mother's hand, she paused, too scared to take it from her.

"Here, luv," prompted Micaela, and held it out to her, while she waited for the sound of its being torn open. She tensed herself to cope with a wild explosion of grief.

She heard, instead, Rosita walk slowly into

the kitchen-living-room, pull out a chair from the table and sit down. Only then did she hear the letter being slowly torn open.

Micaela felt her way to the table and also sat down. From the alley at the back of the house, clearly over the racket of workshops, came the singsong shout, "Any old iron, ra-ags, jars or bones?"

As the sound receded down the passageway, Rosita said wonderingly, "How could such a big ship go down with all hands — without a trace?"

"Dear God! Is that what they say?"

"Yes." It was only a whisper. "They say they've searched and searched." She looked beseechingly at her mother, begging for a denial of the news. But her mother's blind eyes were closed, the toothless mouth pinched, a thin line in a bloodless face, as if she were overwhelmed.

"Mam! Mam!" Rosita screamed at her in sudden agony, and hammered the table with her fists. "Help me, Mam! Help me, Mam."

Micaela dragged herself back to her daughter's desperate pain. "My lovey," she crooned, as she made herself get up from her chair, to hold her well-loved, stricken daughter.

The awful shrieks penetrated the thin wall which separated them from Bridget's house. At the first scream, Bridget paused, her paring knife suspended over a potato. When the second one assailed her ears, she dropped vegetable and knife, whipped off her grubby apron, shoved her bare aching feet into her husband's carpet slippers, and fled next door. She had been waiting for this dread day, having heard the rumour about the *Esperanza Larrinaga*. Only yesterday, she had begun a special novena to the Virgin Mother to protect Pedro — but she knew from the frantic cries coming from next door that she had been too late. On her way out, she snatched up half a small bottle of gin, which Pat had bought cheap from a docker the day before; it was the only sedative she had in the house.

When Manuel came home from school, the house was deadly quiet. He almost tiptoed into the kitchen-living-room, past the parlour door, which was open.

By the fireplace, his grandmother sat in her rocking chair, eyes closed; she was so still that, for a second, Manuel thought she had been taken ill. By her side, in a straight chair sat tiny, shrunken Effie Halloran. Both had their rosaries wound round their fingers.

At his entry, Effie turned a lugubrious face towards him. Tears oozed down the deep lines in her wizened face. "Hush," she said. "I think she's dropped off."

Manuel carefully laid two text books on the table. He was scared. "Dad?" he asked.

Effie nodded. "I'm proper sorry, duck."

"Where's Mam?" The question came urgently from white lips.

"Upstairs with Mrs Connolly. She's havin' a little lie-down."

He turned and took the narrow staircase two at a time. He burst into his mother's bedroom. On the bed lay Rosita in the arms of Bridget. The younger woman was wailing into her friend's shoulder, and Bridget was saying, "There, there, me darling, there, there."

As the boy came up short by the bed, Bridget said softly to him, "I'm so sorry, luv."

"Oh, Bridget!" he exclaimed frantically. "What shall we do?" He began to cry hopelessly.

"You poor lad!" she replied softly. The boy needed comfort, and the little girls would be in soon. Yet, she did not want to let go of the stricken woman in her arms.

Desperately, she asked him, "Could you be a brave lad and run up to Madeleine's and ask her to come. If she's not in, get Peggy O'Brien from across the road — she's got little kids, and I don't want to ask her unless I have to."

Manuel wiped his tears on the sleeves of his blazer, as he tried to control himself. He sniffed hard. He was grateful to be asked to do something positive.

Bridget said, "Before you go, give your mam a hug and a kiss." She loosened her hold on Rosita, and with her face still buried in Bridget's shoulder, his mother lifted an arm vaguely to encompass him. He bent to kiss her and she held him for a second. She smelled of gin. Fighting back his own grief, he said, "I'll get Mrs Saitua for you."

The faded red-gold head nodded slightly.

Within five minutes, Madeleine and her daughter, Panchika, who had been enjoying an afternoon off, came running through the front door, followed by a panting Manuel. They brought with them a bottle of wine and a big loaf of bread, fresh out of the oven.

Micaela awoke from her doze of exhaustion. She felt tired enough to die herself. "Is that you, Madeleine?" she asked.

"Yes, dear — and Panchika." She went to Micaela, ignoring poor Effie, and kissed her. "We'll soon have the kettle on — and I'm going to ask Manuel to get Father Felipe."

Effie heaved a sigh of relief. It had not occurred to her to go and get a priest; she was not an ardent Catholic.

While Madeleine spoke, Manuel had stood, white and trembling, by the door of the room, with no idea what to do. During the previous few days, he had done his best to prepare himself for this situation; but all his good intentions had gone out of his head and all he wanted to do was find a quiet place in which to cry. Now he said, "I'll go now, Mrs Saitua."

* * *

"They're all out," the priest's housekeeper told him, not unkindly. "Except Father Clement. It's your dad, you say? In the *Esperanza Larrinaga*? You're the fifth one today." She nodded her wimpled head sadly. "It's a bad day for the parish. Come in, lad, and I'll ask Father Clement if he thinks he could walk down to your house — he's very frail now and it's hard for him to walk."

Manuel, cap in hand, stepped into the

linoleumed hall which shone with polish.

Wrapped in a cloak pressed upon him by the housekeeper, together with his walking stick, the old priest slowly accompanied the young boy down to the dock road. He asked Manuel to steady him by holding his arm, and Manuel respectfully did so; he had rarely touched a priest before. Priests were holy — you did not go too close to them. As they walked, the priest spoke very gently to him about the wisdom of God in all He did, and suggested that he could express his love for his father by a series of prayers for his soul. Brokenly, Manuel said he would.

⋆ ⋆ ⋆

The crowd in the Echanizes' kitchen-living-room had been augmented by Francesca, who, like Manuel had tried hard to prepare herself for this day, and Little Maria, who did not exactly understand what had happened to Daddy, but that something awful had, and was howling steadily in Grandma's arms.

At the entry of the priest, all the to-do ceased, and Manuel hastily put a chair under the old man. In a way, thought Old Manuel, tears springing to his eyes at the memory of the loss of his father, though he himself was an old man now — in a way, Father Clement had been better than Father Felipe would have been; his age and frailty commanded added respect, and his mother had knelt before him to be comforted with charm and delicacy. Her rosary had been found for her; prayer suggested; the smell of gin ignored.

"He was so good to me, Father," she told him brokenly, as she wept. And the old priest thought that he had not heard that kind of praise very frequently from bereaved wives in a parish which was both poor and harsh.

When finally he left to confer with his fellow priests about a Mass for the souls of all the men lost, the family was still weeping, but he had exorcized the hysteria. It was as if he had taken away with him some of the agony of mind and now carried it himself.

Old Manuel remembered sadly that, on that day, he would have sworn that he could eat nothing; but he had been a healthy growing lad, and he ate everything Madeleine prepared for tea, and this encouraged a tear-stained Frannie and Little Maria to eat, too. Micaela sipped tea, but refused anything to eat. His mother had been taken back up to her bed, and, with Bridget on one side of the bed and silent Effie on the other, had drunk a cup of tea as black as shoe polish with a good dash of rum in it. Mr Halloran had come in in the middle of the uproar, had gone upstairs to fetch his small hoard of spirits, and handed it to his wife. He then sat down in his room to wait, with what patience he could muster, for his wife to come up and make his tea. He was not alone in the parish; quite a number of husbands had similar waits, while their wives went to help their friends.

32

A COUPLE of nights later, after the girls had been put to bed and the dishes washed up, Rosita sat down at the kitchen table to write to Pedro's mother and father on their far-away farm in the Pyrenees, while Manuel tried manfully to concentrate on his homework at the other end of the table; Arnador had not come down to their home since the bad news; he said to Manuel that he would not intrude at such a time.

Manuel wished that Francesca was still up and doing her homework, but Francesca, terribly distressed and frantic that her mother would also be lost if she left her, had not been to school, nor had her bewildered little sister. Finally, tonight, Bridget had popped in with a pill which she carefully split into two. She made each child swallow half, and had then taken them both up to bed, telling them that they would be fine in the morning and looking forward to going to school. The exhausted girls dropped off to sleep almost immediately, and, when she came downstairs, she kissed Rosita and said the sedative was a mild one, and to send them to school in the morning.

Now, Rosita sat staring at a piece of lined notepaper. How do you tell parents that they have lost their son? She chewed her wooden penholder till its tip began to disintegrate.

Manuel's own misery and his mother's fidgeting troubled him so much that he finally suggested softly to her, "You could simply say that you are sorry to have to tell them that . . . "

Thankful to be given an opening, Rosita wrote as he directed. Micaela, lying on the sofa with her eyes closed, listened to the scratching pen, and, when the sound was replaced by that of Rosita folding up the letter, she said, "Have you given them my love and say how I grieve for them, too? Poor souls, they have only one son left, now."

"No." Rosita unfolded the letter and put the message in at the bottom of the page, and added 'With love' before her own signature, crossed it out and put, 'With all our love.' The old couple had always been very kind to her.

"Now write to my brother-in-law in Bilbao. He should hear it from us — that his niece is a widow."

At this reminder of her solitary state, Rosita broke down and cried again. Both Manuel and Micaela immediately got up to comfort her.

It was a while before her sobbing ceased and she could write to her uncle and his two elderly daughters, all of them trying to scrape a living and with worries of their own.

As she finally licked the envelopes closed, Manuel said, "I think you should write to Uncle Leo."

Back on the horsehair sofa, Micaela sighed. She said despondently, "I wrote several times in the war, and when I wrote for Christmas,

1918, the letter came back marked *Gone away*. I'd hoped that, perhaps, another clerk might make an effort to forward it — seeing that it was Christmas." She had felt intensely her lack of letters from her emigrant son; though he had difficulty, he knew how to read and write, she thought with resentment. Unless, of course, he had been killed in the war, which was a fear which haunted her.

Now, she said to Rosita, "You must be tired, dear. You could write to Agustin tomorrow."

Rosita was finding it almost impossible to concentrate, so she agreed. "One more day is not going to make any difference," she said with a sigh.

Before she could put the pad of paper and the pen and ink back on the dresser, Manuel interjected. "Mam, couldn't I write to Uncle Leo — to save you a bit? Suppose I wrote him a letter to the only definite address we've ever had for him — the one in Nevada, and put it in an envelope addressed to the postmaster there, with a little note asking if he would help us to trace him, because the matter is urgent. If the postmaster knew it was urgent he might take the trouble to inquire for us. For instance, he could ask other shepherds coming in to collect their letters if they knew him and knew where he was."

Rosita shrugged rather hopelessly. Let the boy try. She pushed the pen, ink and paper towards him. "All right. Thank you, luv."

* * *

As Manuel let the letters slip into the bright red pillar box with its royal insignia of George V, on his way to school the next morning, he prayed that Uncle Leo would reply. He was a grown man and would know what the family should do.

As he trudged through the morning rush to work, he grizzled miserably, his chin tucked down into the school scarf round his neck, so that passersby would not notice that he was crying. He presumed that he would now have to leave school and go to sea, though he had, as yet, not discussed it with his mother. He thought of the wide expanse of nothing which was the ocean — and of his father drowning in it because there was no one to rescue him — and he did not feel very brave. He was thankful to see Arnador waiting for him at the school gate.

* * *

At home, there were numerous visitors. Not only Rosita's Basque friends and other neighbours called upon her; one or two other wives of missing crew members came simply to share their common sense of despair. Among the latter was the downtrodden, woebegone slip of an Irish woman, Bridie Pilar, wife of a Filipino stoker and mother of Andrew Pilar, who still tried, sometimes, to bully Manuel, especially when he was in his school uniform.

When Rosita opened the door to her, Bridie burst into tears and flung herself upon Rosita, her black shawl flapping round her like the wings of a bat.

It took Rosita a second or two to realize who she was, but when she did, she urged her to come in and sit by the fire.

Seated in Micaela's rocking chair, Bridie rocked herself back and forth in desperate agitation, her face in her hands, greasy black hair falling forward in rat tails.

Micaela, who had been dozing on the sofa, woke up and asked anxiously who was there.

Rosita, standing by the weeping woman, told her. She herself was not certain of the import of the visit. Bridie was not a close neighbour — she lived in Park Lane. Micaela was also a little mystified, but she heaved herself off the sofa, and said, in a resigned voice, "I'll make some tea." Unerringly, she reached into the hearth for the poker. With it she located the hob on which the kettle stood, and lifted the kettle to weigh whether there was any water in it. Satisfied, she pushed the hob round with the poker till it stood over the fire. The kettle began to sing.

Rosita, with her hand comfortingly on Bridie's shoulder, watched her mother anxiously; she did not want to interfere unnecessarily, but she was always afraid that blind Micaela would get too close to the blaze and burn herself, though she had never done so.

Bridie began to shriek. "What am I going to do? And me with five boys to feed? It'll be the workie for us, it will, for sure."

At the mention of the dreaded workhouse,

Rosita shivered. It was a threat of which she had been agonizingly aware ever since she had received the news of the ship's foundering.

She said, "Don't take on so, Bridie. There'll be a compensation award; it'll give us a bit of time to find work."

Micaela put the old beret which was the teacosy over the pot. "Have you got a dad who'd help out?" she inquired. She was upset herself and her hands trembled, as she got down the mugs from the dresser.

"Me dad? He's drunk most of the time — if he's got any money. And me mam half-starved, and afraid of being beaten if she opens her mouth. And me brothers are in a state, 'cos two of 'em died, one with the flu and one in France — and that means two widows pestering them already." She gave a mighty sniff and accepted a mug of tea from Micaela. "What am I to do?"

Rosita let her arms fall to her sides and turned to sit down herself. Through long nights she had wept herself to exhaustion; now she had to give thought to the same question. The compensation would be a small lump sum, which would not last long, and she had nearly as many mouths to feed as Bridie had. And she badly wanted to keep Manuel in school, if she could.

"There'll be the Burial Insurance, too."

Micaela opened her mouth as if to say something, and then thought better of it, when Bridie said, "I haven't got none."

"Have your lads got any work?" Rosita asked.

"Andy's muckin' out the milkman's cowshed and washing his cans for him. The others sometimes bring in a few pence, runnin' messages, like. But I got rent to pay, and I'm owin' more than a week already."

Rosita thankfully sipped at her mug of tea. She began to resent having to comfort someone who was not a friend and whose boys were known pests. "Well, I'm going to let every room in this house, to start with."

"You're lucky. I've only got two rooms, and I'll lose them if I don't pay up."

When Micaela heard her daughter say that she would let rooms, she foresaw a lot of trouble. Life was difficult enough, sharing the kitchen-living-room sink and the kitchen range with Effie Halloran; to have others also using the same facilities would be almost intolerable. The thought of the noise, the inevitable arguments, and the total lack of privacy for her family left her daunted. And yet, what else could Rosita do?

As if in answer to Micaela's unspoken query, Rosita continued speaking to Bridie. "I'm going to look for work I can do at home," she said determinedly.

"What work? You nor I don't know nothing." Bridie leaned back in the rocking chair, small sobs intermittently escaping her. "He were a proper nice fella," she wailed.

"Before I was married I was a seamstress. I served my time at Cripps'. I'm going to ask them."

"Lucky for you," responded Bridie tartly. "And you're pretty — you could marry again. Many a man wouldn't mind taking on a couple of little girls — and a boy ready for working."

Rosita dismissed the suggestion with an impatient shrug. How could she face anyone but Pedro in her bed? The insensitive bitch!

Micaela swallowed. It was clear that neither woman understood exactly what her legal position was. Bridie had brought up a point which Micaela felt she should clarify. There were not too many marriageable women in the Basque community and Rosita was still young enough to have more children. She might, indeed, get an offer of marriage. It would be her best chance of a new life — when she was free to accept it.

She swung her feet to the floor and leaned towards the two widows. In her distress, she unthinkingly spoke in Basque. "There's something I have to tell you about," she began, "because it seems as if you don't know about it. Neither of you can get married again — at least, not for a long time."

Rosita turned a startled face to her mother. She did not want to remarry, but the remark was very unexpected. Bridie had not understood what Micaela had said, but she understood from Rosita's reaction that it was something extraordinary.

"What do you mean, Mam?"

"What did she say?" asked Bridie suspiciously.

Rosita quickly translated. "Why, Mam?"

"My love, your hubbie isn't yet dead — not in law."

A wild irrational hope shot through Rosita, and died.

Micaela heard her quick intake of breath, and

her voice broke, as she added, "The ship is *presumed* lost with all hands. Nobody knows for sure that it has foundered. So, unless you can produce his body, you have to wait seven years, in case Pedro or Mr Pilar turn up again. After seven years, you can apply for them to be declared dead. Now — well, you're not a widow, you are still a wife. Which means you are in limbo."

Bridie said anxiously, "Tell me what she's saying. You look like a ghost."

Micaela repeated her warning in English. Since she had lived in the seagoing community for over forty years, neither woman doubted what she told them.

Bridie burst into wild laughter, swinging the rocking chair madly backwards and forwards. "Does that mean we won't even get the compensation? Be treated like whores living in sin? And me without even bread in the house?"

Micaela felt suddenly very old; the world was too cruel. Unwilling to leave either woman without hope, she said, "I think they'll pay — because they are a good company. But they could hold off — you never know. The Prudential won't pay the burial money either, without a body with a death certificate."

At this added burden, Rosita closed her eyes. She wanted to go upstairs and crawl into bed and never get up. Grief overwhelmed her again, as Bridie continued to yell. She did not see Micaela hoist herself to her feet and cross the fireplace, to administer, quite accurately, a very sharp slap across Bridie's face.

"Hysterics won't do you any good," she told her firmly. "You've got to keep your wits about you."

Bridie's laughter ceased abruptly. "You didn't have to do that!" she retorted, as she rubbed her tingling cheek. "I've got a right to be upset, I have." Ordinary tears began to trickle forth again. "And no bread — not a crust in the house." She looked up appealingly to Micaela. "Could you lend me a shilling, luv? I haven't got nothing."

33

WHEN Pedro's ship went down, Mr Ganivet was genuinely sorry that Manuel's father was lost. It was the talk of the waterfront, as everyone surmised what must have happened to the ship. He liked young Manuel, and he asked the boy, one day, when he was having tea with his son, what his mother was going to do.

Mrs Ganivet leaned over the tea tray with its huge teacosy and pot, and said, "Now don't you worry the boy, luv."

"Of course not," her husband responded irritably, and continued to Manuel, "I'm naturally concerned about you and your mother."

"We've got a big house — she's letting rooms," Manuel answered stiffly; he thought that letting rooms was probably beneath the Ganivets. "It used to be an emigrants' hotel."

"Of course. I remember. I met your grandfather once or twice — a fine old man."

Nothing more was said, but a few days later, in the early afternoon when he could safely assume Manuel to be in school, Mr Ganivet walked along the dock road from his warehouse, to call on Rosita.

Rosita did not know who he was, when she answered the door, and was completely flustered when he made himself known. She invited him into the parlour, as yet unlet. The room was both cold and damp, so she hastened to bring him a glass of wine to warm him a little. Slowly and shyly, he explained the reason for his visit.

Though Rosita had not taken off her flowered pinafore, or had time to comb her hair, Mr Ganivet was impressed by the woman's dignity and touched by her air of sadness; she must have been a real beauty, was his first thought. His wife had told him what a fine man her husband had been, and the sight of Rosita increased Mr Ganivet's determination to do what he could to help Manuel.

Very carefully and courteously, as if he were wooing the business of a shipowner, he suggested to her that he would be happy to undertake Manuel's school expenses until he was fourteen.

"I imagine," he said, "that the boy will want to go to work to help you, but I understand he is not yet twelve and that is too young. When I was talking to Arnador's schoolmaster, the other day, I mentioned Manuel to him, and he said he taught the boy maths — and that he was good at it — worked hard. It seems to me that he should, at least, continue at St Francis Xavier's until the usual school-leaving age. He will be bigger and stronger by then."

Rosita was stunned at such an offer of help. Tears sprang up in her eyes, and her lips quivered. And he was a real Basque, speaking Basque!

She had been worried to death about Manuel. He had said he would try for a job as a ship's boy, and lie about his age. But she had told him tartly that his fees were paid until Easter — and he had not yet grown out of his latest set of trousers and blazer — so he should continue at school. Despite her deep anxiety about money, she added with artificial cheerfulness, that she and Granny would probably find his future fees from somewhere, at least until he was fourteen.

Now, by the Grace of God and a small ship's chandler, her forecast could come true.

Mr Ganivet, enchanted by her, was continuing. He said, "Boys grow so fast — I would help with his uniform, as well, of course. As long as you can manage to feed him . . . "

She felt she could take this offer of help from a fellow Basque — it would be different, she told herself, if he had been of another nationality — so she thanked him gratefully.

He rubbed his hands and smiled jovially, and she wondered suddenly if there was going to be a price to pay for the help. But he did not touch her. He finished his wine, got up and said, "I will write to you in a few days." He felt it would not be the best of manners to open his wallet then and there, and give her the money; he would post it to her.

* * *

He did not tell his wife what he had done. Mrs Ganivet was extremely good to Manuel when, increasingly, he and Arnador did their homework in Arnador's room because of the growing turmoil in the Echaniz home. She did not, however, feel it necessary to call on his widowed mother; nor did it strike her as odd that he was able to continue school. Wapping Dock was a faraway place, like China, as far as she was concerned.

* * *

To Rosita, Mr Ganivet's offer of help seemed like a miracle, and the memory of it helped to sustain her through the bitter early days of her widowhood. Behind her mourning had lurked the worrying thought that Manuel would not be thirteen until September 1921, and was, consequently, physically immature to be sent to sea, where the work was usually very demanding. At fourteen, he would have some muscle on him. He would also benefit, in the long term, from having completed the minimum schooling required by the Education Committee.

She quietly wept into her pillow, however, as her dreams of letting him matriculate and, perhaps, go to university faded and died.

34

ON his way to his wife's grave with a pink rose in a plastic grocery bag, to protect it from a buffeting summer breeze, Old Manuel thought about his mother in her years of limbo. With his own Kathleen in her grave, he could understand her anguish and despair. She and his father had been so close, despite his being much at sea. Much closer than Kathleen and he had been, he thought with regret. But then Rosita had not had to contend with such a formal society as Kathleen had; Rosita's life *was* her family which flowed gently alongside that of other families close by, where most of the little neighbourhood saw each other every day; they did not have to make appointments with each other, or give formal invitations in order to mix. There were no organized charities to be run — you simply helped the neighbours when they were in crisis — and, then, men understood that need as well — they themselves often helped, if they were ashore and muscle-power was required.

The few real rows he had had with Kathleen had been about her not being home when he returned from his travels; or, if she were at home, she went off to some meeting or other, rather than sit with him over supper to hear his adventures. He had done his best to accept Kathleen's world, because she was still the woman with whom he had fallen in love and, in bed, he could still express that love. She was trustworthy with money, too, a very important facet of married life. He grinned to himself, as he walked along; Basques at least shared the Canadians' belief in saving. She had many virtues.

As, for the hundredth time, he went over in his mind what had been missing in his married life, he felt again a sense of mental confusion, doubts as to how he had dealt with his life in Canada, with Kathleen. After he had become aware of the enormous gap in understanding of each other's background, he had stopped complaining, accepted whatever was happening as best he could, though within him had grown a terrible sense of isolation. The isolation had been mitigated while he was at sea, in company, as usual, with mates that he knew. To a lesser degree, he had been glad of the male world of designing ships, too. Only when he had retired and was at home all the time had it hit him full in the face, that men and women in the affluent society in which he found himself lived very separate lives.

"There didn't seem to be any time to do nothing very much together," he told himself. While, between voyages, Pedro sloped around in his father-in-law's kitchen, doing a few odd jobs for Rosita and Micaela, there had been a good deal of communication in an unthreatening, non-confrontational way. It had been the same with his grandfather, Manuel remembered. The old man had been very dogmatic and acted as if he were the cock of the walk, but he was aware of how the others felt, and tacit adjustments were made to accommodate the needs of his family.

Maybe it was because they were used to living on top of each other; if there were a verbal quarrel or a physical fight, it was difficult in a tiny living-room to carry on for long. He laughed to himself — there wasn't enough room! And there would always be family onlookers, who would separate the combatants and take them away to be soothed in different corners, and point out the good reasons for not fighting.

Manuel paused in his walk to take out a cigarette from his shirt pocket and light it. As he drew hard on it, he thought with satisfaction that his had been a wonderful tribe, Barinètas and Echanizes alike. He had been lucky, except for the loss of his father, and Kathleen had never faced the kind of problems that had ensued for Rosita.

At the time of Pedro's being lost at sea, there was no Widow's Pension for Rosita, though the shipping company did pay a lump sum in compensation. With five of them to feed, however, it had not lasted very long. Similarly, there had been no government pension for his grandmother, when his grandfather had been killed; Pedro had, as a matter of course, maintained his mother-in-law, though he must have hoped, at times, that Leo would return to help them.

Only in the last few months, since Old Manuel had begun to write his memoirs, had he truly appreciated the dogged courage of the two women, as they brought up his sisters and himself. Neither was ever idle — except Micaela in the last month of life — and what physical and mental stress Micaela must have endured as a blind widow, crippled by arthritis, in a foreign country — with nothing of her own!

And his mother? As she faced the devastation of her life, she had still been handsome, though with hands roughened by years of scrubbing, and a waistline expanded by pregnancies and the need to make do with a starchy diet. Though the passion she had shared with Pedro must have eaten into her very being, she had never, to Manuel's knowledge, taken a lover after her husband's death; nor did she marry again, when after seven years, she had been free to do so.

At the latter thought, Old Manuel made a face. Those were the days when, at the age of forty, a woman was considered hopelessly old; and, in fact, he could remember a swath of neighbouring men and women who had died around that age — or were invalids, living on the kitchen sofa.

* * *

As each room was let, the old house by Wapping Dock rapidly became a nightmare to live in. The women vied with each other for the use of the kitchen oven; for other cooking, they tramped back and forth through Rosita's kitchen-living-room with buckets of coal from deliveries dumped in the back yard, to build fires in the small bedroom fireplaces. From time to time, there would be bitter quarrels, as tenants accused each other of stealing their coal. At other times, they would make a tremendous dust in the tiny back yard, as they sieved cinders from the ashes to burn them on subsequent fires.

The single lavatory in the back yard frequently became choked, as tenants, unused to modern plumbing, failed to flush it. They all had chamber pots in their rooms, so that they did not have to come downstairs every time nature called. The pots were not always carried through Rosita's room to be emptied when they should have been; and the stench became all-pervading in the house.

Periodically, Manuel was faced with having to clear the lavatory. To drown the disgusting smell and to control his desire to vomit, he began to smoke, and smoking became a lifetime habit.

Rosita did not dare to ask the help of the landlord's agent to improve the plumbing, because the agent would probably have insisted on turning out most of the sub-tenants — or have demanded an increase in rent to reap some of the financial benefit.

The only water tap in the house was in the kitchen-living-room, so pails of water were filled and slopped across the room, to be taken upstairs — or to the parlour, where an elderly hospital cleaner existed as best she could.

In the days when emigrants had filled the house, it had been for very short periods; as soon as a group embarked for New York, Micaela and Rosita had been able to give the house a thorough cleaning. Many of the emigrant women had been good housewives, who left the room they had occupied immaculate. This was not so amongst the type of tenants who had to live permanently in such primitive circumstances.

Though two of Pudding's great-grandchildren hunted industriously and grew fat on their efforts, the whole dock area was cursed with rats and mice; and in a house where food was kept in every room, rodents and cockroaches began to flourish.

Rosita's greatest dread was dealing with tenants who failed to pay their rent. She had no man to threaten them, and, in any case, as the years crept on, unemployment with its consequent hardships became a city-wide, chronic disease.

She would sit by her own, often empty, fireplace, and weep to Micaela. "How can I turn Iris Mary out, with her expecting, and her hubbie with no work — they hardly eat!"

Bundled up in a blanket on the sofa, in increasing pain from her arthritis and with little heat to assuage it, Micaela would not reply, because there was nothing to say that would comfort.

Rosita continued to try for finishing work from the big dress houses in the city; but the elaborate dresses of pre-war days, with their infinite amounts of embroidery to be done and flounces to be hemmed, had given way to very short, comparatively plain fashions; and she was turned away.

35

FIFTEEN months after Pedro's ship foundered, when softer winds blowing up the Mersey heralded the spring of 1921, and the corner shop had a pile of small Easter eggs on its counter, George Halloran had a stroke and died on his bed, upstairs. Once again, the house resounded to the cries of bereavement; and the women gathered to comfort hysterical, penniless Effie, who wept not only for her husband but for her dead boys.

After the added sorrow of a pauper's funeral because Effie was behind with her burial insurance, Effie wiped her reddened eyes and said she would find a job. Micaela was thankful, because the woman was a week behind in her rent as a result of George's unexpected demise.

Even in the worst of economic times, there are jobs that no one wants to do, and, for a while, Effie toiled in a stapler's workshop in St Anne Street, where all day long she teased wool for stuffing mattresses.

She would return home, worn-out, her black shawl a mass of fluff. The same fluff clung to her hair; and Micaela said that if you touched her you could feel the fine hairs stuck to her face and arms; she began to cough, as the hair accumulated in her lungs.

By the time Effie had obtained her job, she had missed another week's rent, which was a serious problem for Rosita.

"I can't make myself turn her out," she said anxiously to Manuel, and the boy instantly agreed with her; Effie had become almost part of the family.

"If only I could get some sewing work," Rosita fretted. "It would really help. I could do it at home and watch the tenants don't pilfer food or coal — now your grandma can't see, she can't really watch."

Since her search for sewing work was fruitless, she borrowed the *Evening Express* from Pat Connolly, and finally found an advertisement put in by a firm which offered a small fortune to those who would affix green baize linings into cutlery baskets — at home. Upon inquiry, she discovered that the company, in the shape of a small, sharp-faced man called Mr Holley, would pay ten copper pennies per basket for this fiddling piecework.

The family became accustomed to her sitting at the table, snipping at the green baize, and cursing quietly when the glue made the pieces stick to her fingers. Manuel did his best to help by contributing the two shillings and sixpence a week which he earned by doing an early-morning paper round; and both he and Francesca handed over any pennies they earned by going messages for the neighbours.

* * *

Though Manuel would not be fourteen until September 1922, he could legally leave school at the end of the previous summer term. He was counting the days until he would be free to look for a job. His mother had been so forceful about the importance of his continuing in school until he was fourteen that he had obeyed her. When he had asked impatiently, how she could pay the fees, she had snapped, "I'll manage, somehow. Don't worry."

She did not want to tell him of Mr Ganivet's help, because she felt it might spoil the easy friendship between Manuel and his son. "Arnador's a good friend to him," she said to Micaela. "And I want to keep it that way."

Micaela agreed.

Deep in his heart, Manuel's desire to go to sea to help his mother was tempered by the memory of Pedro's fate; yet, he told himself crossly, most of the men in the neighbourhood faced the very real threat of injury or death, wherever they worked. But you never heard them complain about it.

He wished he could discuss this cowardice with Arnador. Arnador was very practical, however, and he knew he would say immediately that Manuel should stay ashore and try for a fairly safe job, like clerical work. And if I do that, thought Manuel fretfully, not only would I be a coward, but Mother would have to spend my wages on food for me; if I go to sea, I get food thrown in — and she can have all my wages.

* * *

One warm Friday evening in June, near the end of his last term at school, Rosita put her head down on the kitchen table and unexpectedly burst into tears.

Micaela got up from her sofa and hobbled towards the sound of weeping, while the children asked in alarm, "What's up, Mam?"

"It's the rent," she wailed. "First the collector ticked me off this morning because I couldn't pay the arrears. And this afternoon, the agent himself — Roy Fleet — came, and said if we don't pay up he'll put us out — on Monday morning."

"But we've been in this house for thirty-five years," protested Micaela, as she bent over her daughter.

"I told him that. But I've got behind since Pedro went — because the tenants don't pay me regularly."

Micaela sighed — she still could not believe the threat. "To think that Juan or Pedro did all the repairs!" she exclaimed. "Isn't that worth something?"

A very shaken Manuel bent to pick up a scared Little Maria, who was not sure what the threat was, but had begun to whimper. He held her close and whispered to her not to be afraid, while Francesca, who had been laboriously knitting by the empty fireplace, put down her pins, and sat like a small white statue, staring at him, aghast.

"Mr Fleet's not a bad man," Rosita said dully, "but he's got an owner pushing him. He knows I'm a widow — and he'll be thinking that I can't afford such a big house any more — but it's only because I let rooms that I can get by."

"What happened finally?" Manuel asked, as he mechanically patted Little Maria's back to comfort her.

"Well, he said if we could pay a pound by Sunday night, and the rest of the arrears at a shilling a week, he'd rescind the eviction order. He's given me his home address, so that I can pay it any time up to eleven o'clock Sunday night. I suppose he's trying to be kind." Elbows on table, her head between her sticky hands, she wept again. "I haven't got a pound — and neither your grandma nor I know what to do."

Her arm still round her daughter's shoulder, Micaela felt defeated. Though blind, she could feel the dampness of the house from leaking gutters and drainpipes, and she could smell the extra smokiness from downdraughts caused by a crumbling collection of chimneys. Rosita had remarked recently that, after one hundred and fifty-odd years of use, not a door handle or a lock worked properly, and every door and window rattled in the wind.

"Conor and Lily and Effie — they've all missed paying this week. They can't help it sometimes when there's no work — and Effie changed her job this week, so she's short."

"Have you got any money at all?" asked Manuel. He jumped as Francesca sidled up close to him. He looked down and winked at her, and said to her, "Don't you be afraid. We'll fix it somehow." His deep-timbered voice sounded manly and comforting.

His mother sobbed. "I've two and sixpence — your newspaper money. I have to keep that for a bit of food for us."

"Phew!"

"Lily Rawlings says her hubbie's got work for Monday and Tuesday — she'll pay me Tuesday night. They owe two weeks now, because he didn't have any work last week — and she's got morning sickness so bad that she can't go charring for a bit — till it settles down." She wiped her eyes with the back of her hands.

A small voice piped up. "What about going to the post office to get some money?" Going to the post office with Granny had recently been one of Little Maria's delights — because she sometimes was allowed to buy a halfpenny lollipop on the way back.

Her grandmother replied honestly, "The post office doesn't have any more money, dumpling."

"Could we pawn something?" Manuel asked.

"We haven't got anything that would raise a pound. I had to pawn even Granny's and my wedding rings a few weeks back, to pay for Frannie and Maria going to school."

Shocked, Manuel looked down at his mother's left hand. It was bare — and he had never noticed, he thought ashamedly. "Dear God!"

He glanced wildly round the room. "Could we at least hide the furniture, so that the bailiffs don't get it?"

"I'm going to ask Pat to help us put it in his yard — I hope it doesn't rain."

"What about the tenants' stuff?"

"They won't take that. They'll be mad,

though, when they can't find ours. Not that they'll get more than a few pence for each piece — *if* they manage to find it and auction it."

Rosita was slowly collecting herself. She looked up at Little Maria watching her fearfully from the safety of Manuel's arms, and said, "Don't be afraid, pet. Mummy's going to finish a lot of cutlery boxes by tomorrow noon, and Mr Holley'll pay me for them." She added, for the benefit of Manuel and Francesca, "He closes on Saturday afternoon."

A frightened Francesca leaned against Manuel, frozen by a gnawing dread of that vague monster, the workhouse, which everybody seemed to hold up as the ultimate punishment for being poor. Her mother's decision to work on her boxes gave her a ray of hope, and she said, "You go on with the boxes, Mam. I'll do the dishes and see Little Maria into bed."

Manuel put Little Maria down, and, after a doubtful glance up at him, she wandered back to the hearth rug, to collect her rag doll. Francesca briskly made her way to the kitchen sink and the dishes, while the youth said to his mother, "The newsagent's will still be open — I'll ask him if he'll advance next week's half-a-crown to me." He walked quickly round the table, to take down an old jacket of his father's hanging on the back door, and put it on. "When I come back, I'll go round all the tenants and try to squeeze a bit out of each of them."

His mother nodded; she had no hope of his success; but he was back within a few minutes with a shilling in his hand. "One," he said triumphantly. "All we need is nineteen more!"

The shilling was carefully deposited on the mantelpiece, while he determinedly plodded up the stairs. As he went up, he heard Little Maria gabbling her prayers at her grandmother's knee. The child finished, "Amen. Can I have a piece of bread and jam before I go to bed, Granny?"

He paused halfway up the staircase. His mother snapped, "No, you can't. Get up to bed." He turned and ran down again. Never before had he heard his mother refuse any of them food, except immediately before a meal.

"Mam!" he cried reproachfully. "She didn't have much tea."

His mother paused in her application of glue, and with brush poised, said sulkily, "I must keep what I have for breakfast."

Little Maria, halfway into her nightgown, began to cry, and Micaela shifted herself to embrace the child.

Standing in the doorway, Manuel snorted indignantly. "Mam! She's only little! You can give me a slice less at breakfast!"

He thought his mother was going to weep again, but, instead, she said resignedly, "All right. Get her a piece."

While he got the loaf out of the bread box and carefully cut a slice, Francesca stacked the washed dishes on the dresser. She was hungry and the bread smelled so good; but she felt that she was nearly grown up, like Manuel, so she did not ask for a slice herself. She watched while Little Maria climbed on to Micaela's knee, and, with a bright smile, accepted the bread. Then she went to stand by her mother, as Manuel put the rest of the loaf back into its box, and slowly turned to go heavily up the stairs again.

She said to her mother, "Mam, I could cut the pieces of baize for you, especially if you made me a paper pattern."

Rosita doubted the steadiness of the child's hand, when it was necessary to be precise. She replied doubtfully, "The divisions of the baskets are not identical, dearest; that's why it's such a slow job."

Francesca picked up the next box and looked attentively at it. "Let me try, Mam. I'll measure very careful over the box itself."

"Well, try one. Cut the baize fractionally bigger than the section — not much bigger, or we'll run out of baize. Then try the piece in the particular box, and trim it very carefully. When you've cut out a set, I'll glue it in — and we'll see how well you've done."

As Manuel climbed the narrow staircase, to knock first on the Rawlingses' room, he quaked inwardly. The young couple lived on the edge of penury; and he knew that Lily Rawlings was expecting — most mornings, when he got up, he heard her vomiting.

Rawlings was, however, much more worldly-wise than the stripling facing him. If the bailiffs came when he was out, they could easily haul out what bits of furniture *he* owned; and he knew that he would never find a more kindly landlady than Rosita. Further, Lily would need helpful women around her if the baby were to survive. Manuel's request for money — any money — had to be taken seriously.

He turned to his anxious wife standing behind him, her cotton dress tight across her stomach. "Lil, have you got any cash at all?"

She replied unwillingly, "A couple of bob — for food till Tuesday. Have you?"

He made a rueful face at her. "A tanner for ciggies," he owned up. He dug the sixpence out of his trouser pocket, and stared at it in the palm of his hand.

"Go and get your two bob — I got work for Monday and Tuesday, for sure."

"You've got to eat!"

"Ask Mrs Betts at the corner to put it on the slate till Tuesday night."

"I don't know that she will," protested the girl weepily, but she obeyed, and brought the silver two-shilling piece from under their alarm clock on the mantelpiece.

Rawlings plunked his cigarette money into Manuel's hand, and Lily reluctantly proffered her florin on the palm of her hand, hoping that he would not actually pick it up. But Manuel took it; it was her roof as well as his own that he was trying to save.

Auntie Effie greeted him with affection and asked him in. Her face fell when, seated by her minute fire, he asked her if she could pay a bit towards her rent.

"I did tell your mam I'd pay next week. I started a new job in the bottle factory — washing bottles and jam jars. Me chest is bothering me something awful, and I lost three days' before I got this job." She nervously chewed her overlong thumbnail, and Manuel noticed that a thick grime lay under all her nails, despite having her hands in water much of the last two days.

Manuel waited. Effie's mind worked like a clock about to run down.

She heaved a great sigh, and felt in her skirt pocket. "Bailiffs?" she asked.

"Monday morning," Manuel assured her. "Mam's got till Sunday night to find a pound."

He felt dreadful when she slowly counted out half a week's rent into his hand. "I were paid two and a half days yesterday," she muttered, "and I don't know what I'm going to do. Maybe, if I work Monday, the boss would let me have the money for that day."

"They will do that sometimes," Manuel said. "Pat told me once."

Conor said flatly he hadn't a cent. Not till next week. Iris simply wept, and her youngsters behind her looked like death's heads. The hospital cleaner in the parlour said crossly that she had never missed paying her rent; it was unreasonable to ask her to pay in advance.

Manuel gave up.

That Friday night, Rosita, Francesca and Manuel worked on the silver boxes until after eleven o'clock. Francesca's eyes drooped with fatigue; her back muscles and arms ached from working at a table too high for her. Nevertheless, when she heard the alarm clock go off in her mother's room the next morning, she crawled out of bed, and joined her mother at the kitchen table, to slowly snip the pieces of baize for her. As soon as Manuel had finished his paper round, he joined them, to paint the insides of the boxes with glue.

Micaela made tea without milk or sugar; the two little girls were each given a slice of bread to eat. Francesca sat looking at her slice for a moment and then slowly tore it into two, to share it with Manuel.

"You eat it up," he ordered firmly, and, when she hesitated, he told her, "The newsagent's missus gave me a cup of tea and some biscuits."

As the morning progressed, hunger bit into all of them, and they became slower.

Rosita's voice was dull and hopeless, as she said, "We have to do eighteen boxes to make up the rent — and to pay the ferry across the river to deliver the money." She laughed suddenly and wildly. "I don't know how I am going to manage next week, even if we manage to pay tomorrow."

As if to deliberately add to their torment, the noise from outside the house seemed to be even more trying than usual; the riveters, the horses and carts and the clatter of clogs and boots on the pavement seemed particularly active. Sometimes the kitchen table shuddered as the great presses in the factory behind the house worked through the Saturday shift, so that Rosita had to pause, a strip of baize in her hand, until the upward swing of the biggest press allowed the table to be steady for a moment and she could quickly and accurately place the piece of baize in the box.

By eleven o'clock in the morning, they had completed sixteen boxes. Their time was short.

Manuel quickly washed the worst of the glue off his hands, and began to pack the cutlery boxes into two cardboard containers. Though not terribly heavy, the two cardboard boxes were clumsy to carry, and Manuel said to his mother, "Wash your hands, Mam. I'll carry these up to Mr Holley's for you." His mother had not eaten since yesterday's teatime, a meal of bread and margarine, and he feared that she might faint on her way to her employer's warehouse. "Hurry, Mam. We can't risk missing Mr Holley!"

Rosita wearily dragged herself to her feet, and did as he had bidden her. "All that work — three of us doing it — for thirteen shillings and fourpence!" she said to Micaela. "And we still haven't got a pound."

Micaela nodded. Manuel said, "Well, it's better than nothing," and he carefully tied twine round the two cardboard boxes to make them easier to carry.

They caught Mr Holley, just as he was tidying up before going home. He amiably checked the boxes, however, and paid the stony-faced woman.

Outside, on the pavement, Rosita looked up at her son. She was swaying on her feet. "I'll have to use the two and sixpence you gave me for food," she said brokenly. "I'd hoped to put it towards the rent — but I can't. We must eat."

Manuel put his arm in hers to steady her, and asked uneasily, "Do you think Mr Fleet would accept a bit less?"

"Not a hope. He meant what he said." A

tear trickled slowly down Rosita's cheek. "And I can't get any more on tick at the corner shop."

That tear and the hopelessly disillusioned look in his mother's tired blue eyes were something Manuel never forgot.

As they walked slowly towards a corner shop, Manuel said, "If Jean Baptiste was in work, he'd help us."

"Certainly — but he isn't. They're only saved because their boys are older and are working."

"I could ask Mr Ganivet," suggested Manuel.

"We can't."

"He's very kind, Mam."

"He is," responded Rosita with feeling. Then she told him how his school expenses had been paid for over two years by the kindly chandler.

Manuel was stunned. "Does Arnador know?"

"I don't think so."

They paused at the entrance to the little shop. "You should have told me," he reproached her.

"I thought that if I did you would feel awkward with Arnador."

He did not answer her, because he did not know whether that would have been the case.

She said gently, "It's only a week, now, to the end of term. And you'll always be able to say that you went to St Francis Xavier's until you were fourteen. It's a good recommendation for work."

Manuel nodded bewildered agreement. It would have been even better, if he could have stayed until he was sixteen or seventeen and got his Matric. While his mother entered the shop and he waited for her outside, he stared unseeingly at the tiny window space of the shop, packed with dusty cards advertising everything from tobacco to paraffin and Sunlight soap, and tried to think of someone who could help them.

He realized for the first time how the number of Basque families in the neighbourhood had been sharply reduced by the war, when the menfolk found it safer to sail in Spanish ships out of Bilbao. Others had been able to move to more salubrious neighbourhoods, as their children grew up and began to earn. Of the remaining little community, Mr Saitua was not the only man out of work; and there were one or two families with whom they had never been friends, because Grandpa Juan had not approved of them — his polite term, Manuel suspected, for small vendettas; like anyone else, Basques could carry grudges for a long time.

He wished suddenly that Arnador was his brother, so that he could confide to him the details of the nightmare they were facing. Arnador was so sensible.

But Arnador was not a blood brother, and, moreover, Arnador's father had already helped them very generously.

Manuel felt sick with hunger and fear.

36

ON Saturday night, the family rejoiced in a meal of potatoes boiled with chopped cabbage. They cooked it on a shovelful of coal borrowed from the widowed hospital cleaner who lived in the parlour, an Irish woman who kept to herself. In fact, the family hardly ever saw her except on Friday, which was rent day, because she worked such long hours and tended to stay in bed on her days off.

Nobody went to Mass on Sunday morning. Instead, Rosita and Francesca began work on a new pile of boxes, given to Rosita by Mr Holley in return for the completed ones. Manuel did his heavy Sunday newspaper round first, and then sat down to help. Whether they saved their home or not, the family knew they must try to obtain a little money on Monday, in the hope of keeping themselves out of the workhouse; Mr Holley was their only hope.

The spectre of the workhouse haunted Manuel particularly. In a week's time, he would be looking for work, and being dressed in workhouse uniform would not recommend him to an employer; in their eyes, it would label him a shiftless ne'er-do-well. He would be wiser simply to take to the streets, he thought passionately.

Little Maria played in the street with one of Peggy O'Brien's little girls; and Micaela, wrapped in a blanket, silently nursed her arthritis. They had each had a piece of bread for breakfast. They had been unable to boil water to make tea, and this had made the women feel very low.

They had worked for a couple of hours, when their boredom was broken by an exclamation from Micaela, who was fighting her way out of the encompassing blanket. "Claire Carrandi — she would. It's not much to ask, is it?"

Rosita paused in her careful smoothing of a piece of baize. "Who?"

"The undertaker's wife. You must remember her! She's a Basque — married to Carrandi, who died of a fever in the West Indies. We were quite friendly for years. Then, when she was widowed, she married Ould Biggs, the undertaker — and that seemed to take her away, somehow."

"I do remember — when I was a young girl."

"She's nearer my age than yours. I haven't seen her in a long time. Juan gave her hubbie plenty of carting work — transporting the emigrants and their luggage down to the dock. Ould Biggs owes us plenty. Now, Sunday afternoon is a good time to go to see an old friend. Little Maria can take me up this afternoon, while you get on with the boxes. Claire will lend it."

Rosita looked a little anxiously at her mother. "Could you manage the walk up to Park Road, Mam?"

"I'm the only one who can ask her, so I'll do it — somehow."

It was true that probably only Micaela could negotiate a loan from Claire; but it was with reluctance that Rosita watched her set out, with her arm around the shoulder of Little Maria. The journey was not a long one, except for the pain that Micaela would probably experience, and the fact that she could not see.

As Rosita came back into the kitchen-living-room, Manuel sensed her worry." Granny'll be all right," he assured her, as he dabbed glue into a corner of a box. "Little Maria's good with her granny — she warns of all the steps up and down — and the traffic."

Though it did take a long, painful time to crawl up Sparling Street and along Park Lane to the undertaker's premises, Micaela's visit to Claire was not a protracted one.

The Biggses' front door was shut, and the whole place seemed locked in the calm of Sunday afternoon. Micaela told Maria to lead her down the side of the building and into a cobbled yard, where lay a couple of carts and a toast-rack horse bus, together with a dust-laden black carriage, all with their shafts up. At the back of the yard were stables in which the horses could be heard shuffling and snorting. Beside the stables were two wide doors, held shut by a large padlock, behind which rested the pride of Ould Biggs's collection, his beautifully carved black hearse with its etched glass panels.

"There's a door up some steps at the left," Micaela told Maria. "Run up the steps and bang the knocker."

Maria had to stand on tiptoe to reach the

lion's head which was the door knocker. It gave a reverberating thud, when she let go of it. She ran back down the steps, to stand by Micaela. While they waited for someone to answer, she eased her round to face the door.

An elderly maid, with long black streamers falling from her white, goffered cap, responded to the knock; Ould Biggs never knew when a bereaved client might hammer on his door, and he insisted that the maid give the right impression of solemnity.

Micaela asked to see Mrs Biggs, and was politely asked into the big sombre hall. To Maria, it was rather frightening; she wondered where Mr Biggs kept the bodies.

Claire came out of a back room immediately, and sashayed down the hall towards them. She was wearing a black, knee-length frock with a small, white frilled collar, her plump legs encased in flesh-coloured silk stockings. Her very high-heeled, black patent shoes were held in place by three cross-straps, each with a glittering black button.

Maria stared at her in fascination. She had never seen an older woman in such short skirts. Her grandmother was garbed from chin to ankle; she had not changed her style in fifty years. Even her mother still wore gathered black skirts that reached her ankles.

"Micaela!"

"Claire!" exclaimed Micaela, as Maria helped her up the steps, and led her into Claire's open arms. They kissed each other on both cheeks, both genuinely glad to meet again. The visitors were led into the dining-room at the back of the house, because, Claire explained, Mr Biggs always had his Sunday nap in the sitting-room.

Claire's last visit to Micaela had been after Juan's death; she had sent a note of sympathy at Aunt Maria's death, not sure how to cope with the fact that Maria had been buried by the City because, owing to her severe illness, she had been uninsurable. She now felt guilty that she had not visited her for a very long time. She felt worse when Micaela stumbled when seating herself, and Claire perceived that there must be something wrong with her sight; maybe that was why Micaela had not visited *her* lately.

As she rang the bell for the maid, she inquired in Basque, "Is everyone in the family all right?"

Micaela's face crinkled up in a smile. "Nobody's dead," she assured her jokingly in the same language, and Little Maria squirmed, and laughed up at their hostess.

Claire smiled back at the child. "God be thanked," she said virtuously, and then exclaimed, "She's so like you, Micaela!"

Little Maria was hurt. Surely she didn't look so wizened and untidy as Grandma did?

She was consoled by a large piece of fruit cake from a tray brought in by the maid. She sat quietly eating it, currant by currant, while the two ladies caught up with accounts of their lives since Aunt Maria had died.

Maria became anxious that her grandmother seemed to have forgotten the family's dire need of a small loan; and that she made a joke about their running a boarding-house again. "It's different from having emigrants go through — but it brings life into the house," Micaela finished up.

Maria noticed that her grandmother was cautiously feeling round for her cup of tea; she had managed to set it on the table, originally; but now, apparently, she could not judge where it was.

"Allow me," said Claire quickly, and put the cup and saucer carefully into Micaela's hand. "Are you having trouble with your sight?"

Grandma took a sip of tea and then laughed deprecatingly. "I can't see at all, except light and shadow," she admitted baldly. "I can still knit, though." She turned towards Maria, who had stolidly returned to eating her cake. "Little Maria — and Frannie have to be my eyes."

"It must be very difficult for you," Claire sympathized.

"Rosita's good to me."

Micaela's cake on its flowered plate still lay on the table. Maria slipped down from her chair, and said, "Give me your empty cup, Granny, and I'll give you your cake."

"Thank you, dumpling."

When it was handed to her, Micaela felt across the plate to locate the cake and then broke it into two. She took one half and stuffed it into her mouth. Saliva gathered at the corners of her lips, as she swallowed it almost whole.

Claire watched her in dismay. Then she jumped up and pulled the bell for the maid. "How stupid of Mary Ellen," she exclaimed.

"She forgot to put the scones on the tray."

When the maid appeared, Claire instructed her to bring in a plate of buttered scones. She said to Micaela, "Mary Ellen makes the best scones you've ever tasted — you simply have to try them."

Little Maria gave a small sigh of anticipation. Scones as well as cake?

Micaela felt that she should have told Claire not to go to so much trouble for her — but her hunger was intolerable — and Basques were very hospitable, anyway.

Three scones and another piece of cake later, Micaela remained seated for another ten minutes or so and then said that she should go home. "Come and visit me soon," she urged. "I would enjoy it so much."

Totally dismayed, Little Maria thought that her grandmother had forgotten the money they so badly needed. She did not dare to mention it herself, and felt quite frantic when Micaela told her to go ahead into the hall and put on her coat like a good girl.

The two friends embraced again, both happy to have been reunited by the visit. Micaela drew back a little in Claire's arms, and asked diffidently, "Claire, could you lend me two shillings, until I can get up to the post office to draw some money tomorrow afternoon?"

Claire replied without hesitation, thankful to assuage her sense that she had neglected Micaela. "Of course," she agreed. She loosed her hold on the old woman, and went to the sideboard, opened a drawer and took out a change purse. She pressed a florin into Micaela's hand.

* * *

Later, her husband came sleepily out of the sitting-room, trailing sheets of newspaper after him. "Who came?" he inquired.

"Micaela Barinèta — Juan's wife. You remember them?"

"Oh, aye."

"She's blind now. They seem in a pretty bad way — do you know, she was wearing a shawl — not a coat — she never did that when Juan was alive — at least, not on Sundays. Poor Rosita's husband was lost in the *Esperanza Larrinaga*, you may remember — it was in the paper, the time when I had Spanish flu. It took me such a long time to get better that I never went to see her."

Henry Biggs took his pipe and tobacco pouch out of his jacket pocket and sat down on a dining-chair, while his wife stood by him, staring into the blue flames of the gas fire and remembering Rosita's handsome husband. She roused herself to say, "Young Manuel's finishing school next week. He was in St Francis Xavier's. Must've been a struggle to keep him there — because they haven't got a wage-earner now. Nobody."

"The lad can go to sea. That'll help them." Henry lit his pipe. He then let his hand run up the backs of his wife's silk-clad legs, and tickled her gently.

"Oh, Henry!" she exclaimed. "You really are naughty!"

"It's Sunday afternoon," he reminded her, as she gave a delighted, though muffled shriek at his further advances.

37

THAT Sunday evening, Manuel saw his mother on to the Seacombe ferry, which would take her across the river to Roy Fleet's house. In her clutch purse she carried a pound in small change, and, separately in her pocket, fourpence to cover her fares, which she would pay on the other side of the river.

As the ferry backed away from the landing stage with much splashing and shuddering, he waved to her, and then stood idly for a few minutes looking at the ships anchored in the river. They ranged from small, grubby tramp steamers, with the crew's washing flapping merrily over the forecastle, to a huge Chinese freighter, so rusty that Manuel wondered how it had made the voyage from Shanghai, which, in chipped, white paint, was indicated as its port of registration. Tugs were moving a stately White Star transatlantic liner up river, perhaps to the Gladstone Graving Dock. In the distance was a single, tiny yacht, also going up river.

He was hailed by Domingo Saitua, who worked for the ferries and was waiting for the next New Brighton boat to come in. He wandered over to him, and, as the landing stage began to heave up and down under the pressure of the incoming tide, he asked Domingo what chance there was of a job on the ferries.

Stocky, beer-bellied Domingo looked him

over. "How old are you, now?"

"Fourteen," lied Manuel. "I'm leaving school next week."

Domingo straightened his navy jersey, emblazoned in white with the words *Wallasey Ferries*. He made a glum face, and said briskly in Basque, "Not a hope, lad. They like men who've been to sea. For instance, I went to sea with my uncle for a while — he was a fisherman,"

Manuel replied stoutly, "My dad and my granddad went to sea."

Anxious to comfort a boy who was his neighbour, Domingo said, "Oh, aye, they did. You're a likely-looking youngster. Try getting in with a ship's steward, who'd look out for a job for you — find you a job as pantry boy, like. Better than being a deck boy."

Manuel agreed. He could not, however, recall anyone in the Basque community who was a steward; if there had been one, he would not have hesitated to ask for help.

Domingo saw that the New Brighton ferry was coming in, so he prepared to catch a rope from it. "Good luck, Mannie," he said.

Manuel went home to do some prep for school. When ten o'clock came, he was worried that his mother had not returned, so he told Micaela that he would go down to the Pier Head again, to meet her.

* * *

The landing stage was deserted, except for Domingo, and he said that he had not seen

Mrs Echaniz land. Manuel began to wonder if, possibly, she had lost the twopence for her return journey. His aching lack of food and his increasing apprehension made him feel dizzy. He wondered what he should do if she were not on the last ferry.

As the night took over, the silence on the landing stage became oppressive. Domingo went off to attend to his work, and only the slow rhythmic plop of a tug tied up at the end of the dock or the distant sounds of voices from ships anchored in the river broke the quietness.

To his intense relief, Rosita dragged herself off the eleven o'clock ferry. He hastened forward to take her arm and ask, "Whatever happened?"

Under the brim of her out-of-date black straw hat, her eyes glittered in the rays of a lamp. "I had to walk much further than I expected to their house. They were nice to me — Roy and his missus, though. Kept me talking a bit."

As they ambled slowly up the gangway which led to the Pier Head itself, she described her visit.

"Roy was still at church, when I got there, but he had told his missus that I might come, so she stayed home. She's a nice lady, like you don't see very often, and she's got a lovely sitting-room, all in green. We had a nice cup of tea together."

Rosita paused, as they crossed the street. On the other side, a few prostitutes loitered in the shadows, their faces occasionally dimly lit up, as they struck matches to light their cigarettes. When they had passed them, she continued, "I told her what happened to your dad — she was horrified, especially when I explained how I'm a widow but not a widow. She asked if I had a job, and I told her about the cutlery boxes, and how I had applied to Cripps' and was hoping they'd find me some sewing, because I used to work for them. And I told her I'd one or two lodgers living with me — but I didn't tell her how many! I said how they'd steal from me if I didn't work at home. She was so sympathetic, I felt like crying."

They reached Wapping, where even the lights of the Baltic Fleet had been turned off. Manuel squeezed his mother's arm comfortingly, and asked what Mr Fleet had said about the rent.

"He said he thinks it'll be all right, if I don't get further behind — and pay a shilling a week off the arrears. He's going to talk to the landlord himself."

As they stood on their own doorstep, Rosita lifted her eyes to her hungry son, put her hands on his shoulders and laid her head against his chest. She burst into tears.

"Oh, Mam! Don't cry. Everything's going to be all right. You'll see."

She looked up and smiled through her tears. "Yes, lovey, we'll manage, I expect. I'm crying, with relief, and because she was so kind. It was such a relief to tell somebody. I couldn't even bring myself to tell Bridget — she's got enough worries of her own at present, what with her hubbie being out of work — though she must have guessed how hard things are with us."

* * *

Though Mrs Fleet knew that her husband had to be tough with some of the tenants for whom he was responsible, she was genuinely moved by Rosita's story of her woes, and she did not forget her.

Every Thursday afternoon, she went to Liverpool to shop and meet some of her friends over a cup of tea in Lyon's tea shop. On the Monday following Rosita's visit, she scribbled a short note to a friend she had not seen for a number of weeks; Muriel was a cutter, who had worked for Sloan, Dressmaker, ever since Mrs Ada Sloan, dressmaker, had set herself up in 82 Bold Street, in 1915. Dorothy Fleet invited her to lunch at Fuller's on the following Thursday, and when they met, she asked her elegant friend for outwork for Rosita.

As Muriel nibbled a sandwich and considered this, Dorothy said anxiously, "I wouldn't ask anyone else but you — we've known each other so long. And you did tell me, once, that you have been awfully busy for the last few seasons altering the dresses your clients bought in previous years."

Muriel's neatly pencilled eyebrows rose a little. "Yes, we still are."

"Mrs Echaniz was trained by Cripps'. By the sound of it, she's done every kind of sewing in her time . . ." Dorothy urged. "They don't have any work for her at the moment."

"Cripps' don't do as many alterations as we do — they take up a lot of time. But the client returns to us when she wants something new! So it's worth it." Muriel laughed delicately, and her jet earrings swung. She tucked a curl absently back under her small cloche hat, and then looked pensively down at her coffee. Finally, she asked, "What's the woman like to look at?"

"Clean and very neat. Shabby, though. She's still quite pretty."

"You're really quite taken with her, aren't you?"

Dorothy smiled faintly. "I suppose I am. I hate to see a bright, intelligent woman ground down. She needs work very badly, Muriel," she pleaded.

Muriel sighed. "Well, I'll try — though I'm not sure what I can do. We've more than enough outworkers, as it is. What's her house like — is it clean?"

"I asked Roy that — because of the fine materials she might be sewing. He said it always was when he was actually collecting their rent — before he got promoted to run the whole agency."

"I'd need a reference from Cripps'. Could *you* give her a personal reference?"

"Certainly." Dorothy pushed a glass dish of dainty sandwiches towards her guest.

Muriel refused another sandwich. "With these new short dresses, I have to watch my figure — flatness is the fashion now!" She slipped on her gloves, smoothing the soft leather over her long fingers, and picked up her clutch handbag. "Get me the references. Perhaps I can get her a little finishing, to see how good she is."

* * *

The following day, an astonished Rosita received a letter from Dorothy Fleet, telling her to get a reference from Cripps' and, on any weekday morning, to take it, with the enclosed reference from Dorothy herself, to the back door of Sloan's, Bold Street, so that she could be interviewed by Miss Muriel Hamilton, with a view to being given some outwork to do.

Wildly excited, she read the missive to Micaela.

"Jesus Mary!" exclaimed Micaela, pushing herself upright on the sofa. Then she said in Basque, "Make yourself as smart as you can; Sloan's are fine dressmakers, as you well know."

Manuel heard the news immediately he came home from school. He threw down his satchel, and hugged her. "It's a new beginning, Mam."

Over the weekend, Rosita's grey-streaked red curls, which normally hung untidily over her shoulders, were shampooed with Sunlight soap and combed up into a neat chignon. Then she cut a black skirt into a narrower, shorter fashion to give her a more modern appearance, and, for the sake of speed, machined it on Bridget's treadle sewing machine. Bridget lent her a plain black coat to go over it, both for her visit to Cripps' and to Sloan's.

"Aye, luv, I hope it leads to something decent for yez," she said to Rosita, as she kissed her and wished her well.

* * *

At first the work given to her was routine hemming or unpicking, but soon she began to receive more complicated work. She sat long hours at her kitchen table, which was covered with a white sheet to protect the delicate materials she stitched so carefully. At the beginning, she earned little more than she would have done lining cutlery boxes; but it was clean work for which she had been very well trained.

When he was not looking for work or writing letters of application, Manuel lined cutlery boxes for her. He was helped by Francesca. Both girls were free, now that the summer holidays had begun, and, to give their mother time for her sewing, they did many of the household tasks.

The tenants, as they passed through the kitchen-living-room, were very interested in the pretty materials of Rosita's new work; she had to reprove them sharply when they wanted to touch the delicate georgettes and fine wools.

If I can get enough work, I'll stop renting the front room, Rosita promised herself savagely, and make it into a workroom.

⋆ ⋆ ⋆

Dorothy Fleet and Muriel Hamilton often went on a Saturday afternoon to a matinée at the Empire Theatre; and, occasionally during these outings, Dorothy would inquire if Rosita continued to do satisfactory work. Her gentle reminder of Rosita's existence at the bottom of the dressmaking world eventually bore fruit.

When a cuff hand was required, Rosita was asked to work two full days a week in the workrooms.

For the first time since she had lost Pedro, Rosita had a glimmering of hope that life would improve. She jumped at the offer, and hoped that a noisy bolt which Manuel managed to put on the cellar door would prove sufficient deterrent to light-fingered tenants — Micaela would certainly hear if the squeaky bolt was drawn.

38

ON the Monday morning after Rosita's trip across the Mersey to pay the rent, Manuel left home ostensibly to go to school. He had eaten a breakfast of a slice of bread with milkless tea, Effie having boiled a kettle for them on her fire. He had no lunch in his satchel.

If his mother had not already been hard at work on her cutlery boxes, she might have noticed that he turned left along the street, instead of right; if she had seen him, she would have come flying after him to inquire where he thought he was going, since school lay in the opposite direction.

Manuel had no intention of going to school that morning. To make him less obviously a truant schoolboy to any passing police constable, he had put his St Francis Xavier cap into his plain brown satchel.

Bearing in mind Domingo Saitua's suggestion that he should find a ship's steward who might look out for a job as pantry boy for him, he was now marching determinedly along Chaloner Street to see Mr Ganivet in his chandlery warehouse. It was just possible that Mr Ganivet himself might give him a job; but, in any case, he had recalled from a conversation at Arnador's house, that the chandler sometimes did business with stewards; Mr Ganivet had been telling his wife about a steward who had returned fifty teapots, because the spouts dripped so badly on the white linen tablecloths of his First Class dining-room.

Considering that everybody the boy knew was complaining how bad times were, the Ganivet warehouse was very busy. At the loading bays, horses and carts vied with two snorting lorries trying to back in; and men in thick cotton aprons shouted to each other, while a closed pantechnicon eased out of the double gates.

He stopped one hurrying youth to ask where the office was — Mr Ganivet always referred to working in his office. He was directed to a narrow stone, corkscrew staircase which wound up through the centre of the eighteenth-century building.

At the door of his office, Mr Ganivet, his face nearly purple, was shouting at a bald-headed wisp of a man in a beige cotton jacket, who during brief gaps in the shouting said humbly, "Yes, Sir," or "No, Sir."

Manuel loitered at a discreet distance in the wooden-floored passage until the exchange petered out and the reprimanded man had zipped past him, looking very chastened. Mr Ganivet continued to stand at the door of his office, trying to regain his breath. As the high colour in his face subsided, he noticed the boy in the passage.

"Good gracious, Manuel! What are you doing here? Shouldn't you be in school?"

Seventy-odd years later, Old Manuel remembered vividly his sense of panic at the question fired at him. Of course, he should have been in school. Mr Ganivet began to roll down his shirt sleeves over his hairy arms, as Manuel gaped at him, unable to speak.

The older man turned into the littered, dusty office, glancing back over his shoulder at the white-faced boy. "Come in, come in, lad," he ordered not unkindly. "What's up? Shut the door and have a seat."

The chandler plonked down into a wooden, swivel chair beside a roll-top desk.

All the way up Chaloner Street, Manuel had rehearsed what he was going to say. Now the words tumbled out breathlessly. "I've got to leave school at the end of term, Sir, because Mam can't afford to keep me any more — I'll be fourteen in September — and I was wanting your advice, Sir, about going to sea. A friend of mine suggested I should get in with a steward, who might give me a chance. And I thought that, one day, maybe, I could be a steward myself." He paused to take breath and to glance up at Mr Ganivet.

With a pencil Mr Ganivet was tracing circles round the edge of an invoice, so Manuel continued. He had been speaking in Basque, feeling that this made a connection between himself and the man at the desk. He now said, "I remembered that you did business with stewards and cooks and people, and I wondered if you could recommend me to someone?"

He had hung his head as he spoke, fearing a quick dismissal, and all Mr Ganivet could see was the smooth dark crown of his head. "As a pantry boy," he finished hopefully.

"Humph." Mr Ganivet fiddled with his pencil. Then he heaved a big sigh, which made his waistcoat, with its gold watch chain hung with seals, rise and fall like a slow wave on the Mersey. "Well," he said, "I had hoped to see you go to university with Arnador. I believe that's what your dad hoped for you?"

"He never said anything to me, Sir, except that he wanted me in school until I was sixteen, but it's impossible; he's not here any more — and neither is my granddad." The boy raised his head, and Mr Ganivet surveyed the long gaunt face with its flat cheekbones, the wide quirky mouth and rather deep-set brown eyes. A fine face, the chandler thought, almost that of a grown man; but no sign of a beard yet. He felt uneasy about what might happen to such a fine-looking boy on a long sea voyage, if he were not under the close supervision of a more senior crew member. It would not do for him to sign on without a family man to keep an eye on him, he decided.

The silence between them deepened. It was finally broken by Manuel, who said shyly, "I want to thank you, Sir, for helping to keep me at school since Dad died — Mother told me about it yesterday. It was very kind of you, Sir, and I really don't have any right to ask you for more help — but I don't know which way to turn."

Mr Ganivet responded to the boy's thanks with a little smile, and then asked, "Do you want to go to sea?"

Manuel was surprised by the question. "Never thought of doing anything else, Sir. All our family went to sea."

Mr Ganivet nodded. The boy had obviously never had the advantages of advanced education pointed out to him; perhaps, in the circumstances, it was as well.

He put down his pencil, and said, "You were welcome to the small help with your schooling; I would've liked to continue it — but I have to prepare for Arnador's going to university — and I can't do both."

"It's not expected, Sir."

Mr Gavinet ignored the interruption, and went on, "I can imagine the difficulties of your mother, and the need for you to earn. And, of course, at sea you would be fed, which would ease her burden. Of course, you'd have to pay for your kit."

There was a knock on the office door, and the bald man in the beige jacket entered. "The cordage has just come in, Sir," he told Mr Ganivet nervously.

"Well, fill Ellerman's order. Send it in the big lorry — they're waiting on it. And hurry, man. Hurry!"

"Yes, Sir. Of course, Sir."

The door clicked shut, and the chandler turned back to Manuel. "Get me a written recommendation from your headmaster and bring it to me. Meanwhile, I'll see what I can do. I can't make any promises, and it may not be in catering. He got up from his chair, to indicate the end of the interview. "I'm not sure what I can do for you, so be thinking what else you might do."

Manuel got up. He smiled, and said with enthusiasm, "Thank you, Sir. I'm very grateful."

As they walked together to the door, Mr Ganivet smiled back, and ruffled the boy's hair. He wished that Arnador had something of his friend's warmth of character.

* * *

A week after Micaela's visit to her to borrow two shillings, Claire walked down to Wapping to see Micaela. The streets she traversed seemed smaller and meaner than they used to be when she had lived there with her first husband. The pavements were more littered, and the noise and foul odours from the factories and workshops were more intense.

As she knocked on the open door and a flustered Micaela called to her to enter, her heart sank. The house stank as it never had done in earlier years, the hallway blackened with soot from coal fires and tobacco smoke. She walked determinedly in, however, to find Micaela lying on a sofa in a muddled kitchen by an empty fireplace.

She laughed at Micaela's distress at not being able to offer her even a cup of tea, and said she had just dropped by for a moment to offer Manuel a part-time job.

She had squeezed out of Ould Biggs a Saturday morning's employment cleaning out the stables — their present man was getting old — and occasional help with putting the horse to and other odd jobs in connection with the bigger funerals, like polishing the hearse and the carriages.

Micaela jumped at it, with the thought that the boy's first wages — sixpence an hour — must go to paying back the two shillings she owed Claire.

* * *

So after Manuel had done his early-morning paper round and had had his breakfast, he went once a week to help Ould Biggs, who found him very useful, and sent for him several times during the weeks that Manuel was looking for regular work, to help with funeral processions.

Claire always gave him a huge mug of cocoa and a thick slice of bread and butter; and he would stand in the yard and gratefully consume these delicacies.

Sometimes, he would dream of a time when he would be able to keep some of the money he earned — and take Mary Connolly to a music hall matinée — and buy his mother and Bridget Connolly pretty quarter-pound boxes of chocolates.

* * *

If it had not been for the Second World War, when she joined the Forces and met a Polish soldier who married her, I might have married Mary myself, considered Old Manuel. She'd have made a good wife for a seaman. As he considered whether he should mention, in his notes for Lorilyn, the upheavals of the civilian population during the war, he was very slowly digging over his vegetable patch; the soil was waterlogged and heavy.

He paused to lean on his spade and catch his breath; digging was difficult. Next year he would get a man to do it for him. He smiled grimly to himself — perhaps he should say, if he were here next year, he would do so. He felt that time was running out, like water dripping from a leaky tank, drop by drop. Maybe he should visit Ramon and Arnador in Liverpool this year — and after a rest there, go on to Vizcaya; it would be wonderful to see the Pyrenees again.

In the midst of his meditations, he was surprised when Sharon Herman came quickly round the side of his bungalow.

"Hi!" she greeted him cheerfully. "I came to collect some stuff from Veronica's house, but she isn't home — so I thought I'd pop in to see how you are."

Old Manuel grinned at her. "Fine," he assured her. He pushed his spade into the loam, so that it would stand upright, and said, "Come in. It's getting chilly out here."

Over a glass of wine, she thanked him for a piece of fish he had left for her with one of her new neighbours in the apartment block. He smiled and shrugged. "It's nothin'," he said.

Sharon's eyes wandered round the sitting-room, while she considered what she should say next, and came to rest on a beautifully cased sewing machine, and she wondered about the woman who had sat at it, or had sat in the bay window to hand sew in a good light.

"Do you have any kids?" she asked him suddenly. "Besides Faith — you mentioned her once, I think."

The question was a personal one, and he sipped his wine, while he thought how to answer her. Then he grinned. "Only Faith — and I don't suppose she wants to be regarded as a kid. She's forty-six. I've got a granddaughter, though — she's going to be an electrical engineer, she tells me. She's at the University of British Columbia." Pride in Lorilyn made him more talkative, and he took a cigarette out of his pocket and lit it. Then, remembering that Sharon might smoke, he proffered her the packet. "Seems as if girls has gone off nursing or teaching."

Sharon refused the cigarette, and endured, with amusement, the smoke that slowly surrounded them.

He told her that he had decided to go home this summer, and she asked lightly where home was. England or Spain?

He hesitated, and then said, "Both, I guess."

They began to talk about a trip he and Kathleen had done the year before she was taken ill, and as he described it he grew slower.

He's tired, thought Sharon guiltily. I should not have come; and yet she did not want to stop his talking. As far as she knew, he had nobody to talk to.

He rubbed his eyes, and she was distressed

to see that they were filled with tears. His chin trembled, and he hastily pulled a Kleenex from a decorated box on the table beside him. "I'm sorry," he muttered. "It takes me back a bit, talkin', like."

She crossed over to sit by him on the settee, and put her arm round the bent, thin shoulders. He did not brush her off, but wept quietly into a bunch of paper handkerchiefs.

She felt a great, unreasonable anger that his daughter was not by him — or even his clever granddaughter. Such grief should have been allowed to express itself long ago. She tightened her hold on him, and he tried to control the explosion. But he could not.

"Just cry," she said very gently. "I do understand about these things."

Families don't have the experience of dealing with bereavement, she thought, trying to drown her sense that his family should have helped him more. Death isn't all round them like it used to be — or like it is with me. They have no experience to draw on.

She held him quietly, gently rubbing his back with her arm, as if he were a sick animal, until finally he drew a big sobbing breath, and said, "I'm proper sorry. I don't know what came over me."

As he leaned forward to pull some more handkerchiefs from the box, she let him go, and he added, "When I were a little kid, people died all round you; you accepted it. I should have got used to it." He shoved the damp handkerchiefs into his shirt pocket, and then went on, "Doctors was different, though, in them days. They knew you — they came to your house; and I'm dead sure they helped those in pain go more quickly. And then they stayed a while, to comfort the family like, and the neighbours came in and out to see you was all right. And the priests were there . . . " He cleared his throat, and said in a less wistful voice, "If you had to manage without a doctor, there was always neighbours to help — like Bridget — I think I once told you about her."

She smiled softly. "Yes, you did," she said. "And don't worry about crying. Even men should cry good and hard sometimes. And we're friends, aren't we?"

"For sure," he said, as he slowly stood up in front of her. He had a desperate need, suddenly, to go to the bathroom, but he was too shy to admit it. After her last remark, she had playfully held out her hand to him, and now he slowly shook it to cement the friendship. When she rose, feeling that she was dismissed, he held on to her hand and then leaned forward and gently kissed her cheek.

"Thank you, my dear."

She smiled again, and asked, "If you go to Liverpool, have you any family there to take care of you?"

"I've got Ramon, me cousin. I'll stay with him. And I've got me old friend, Arnador Ganivet — better 'n a brother, he's bin to me, all me life."

"Go soon," she advised, and kissed his withered dark cheek, and left him.

39

MANUEL'S hopes of help from Mr Ganivet began to fade, and there seemed to be hordes of boys vying for jobs as errand boys or office boys in the city. He haunted the Sailors' Home in hope of picking up a berth as deck boy or pantry boy, without success.

He discussed with his mother the idea of applying to de Larrinaga on the grounds that his father had served them. He was surprised when she did not immediately agree. When she did answer him, she said heavily, "His discharge book went down with him."

When he protested that they would have a record in their offices, she told him uneasily that it did not seem to be a good idea. She was, in fact, superstitiously afraid of history repeating itself, and that he would go down like his father; the idea was ridiculous, and she knew it, but she could not shake it off. She said, "Well, you know, he wasn't with them very long."

He could not shift her.

* * *

Mr Ganivet had not been idle, however. He had spoken on the boy's behalf to two regular customers, and the result was that, in September, a few days before his fourteenth birthday, he sailed in a large freighter, as galley boy. The ship was carrying a mixed cargo for Havana and the southern United States. He was under the tutelage of the chief steward, the cook, two galley men and a cabin steward, none of them very patient.

Old Manuel often laughed when he remembered the first time he went to sea, proudly armed with his own discharge book and a straw-stuffed palliasse for his bunk. He had considered himself the most overworked, bullied youngster ever to sail in a ship, though he might have had a different opinion had he had a father to tell him what to expect. As a little boy he had been taken down to the docks to see his father's ship and he had sailed to and from Bilbao; but being a member of the crew, he found, was different; he had forgotten that, though it might be considered romantic to go to sea, it was a rough and dangerous occupation, where men had to be able to depend on each other a great deal. Further, he had spent the last few years mainly amongst women and gentle priests which did not help his adjustment to the harsh reality of seafaring.

In truth, though the freighter was an old, coal-burning ship, it was well run; and Mr Figgin, the steward, despite being an accomplished nagger, took good care to see that he was not sexually abused or knocked about on the long, slow voyage.

The cook, an ageing black man with a strong Glasgow accent, was good-natured, and supplemented the indifferent food supplied to the crew with bits left over from the officers' mess. Manuel soon learned to call these small treats 'ovies'. It seemed to Manuel, however, that everyone was quick to cuff him if he lingered too long in his journeys up and down companionways and along the heaving passages, often armed with slopping mugs of tea for officers on duty.

If, when sweeping or scrubbing, he missed a corner, the galley man would upbraid him in the richest of Liverpool language. Anxious to keep in with the cook, he learned to peel his way through sacks of potatoes at a commendable speed, and to wash dishes without chipping them as the water in the sink sloshed about with the movement of the ship. He also learned to watch carefully, during bad weather, that he was not hit by a boiling saucepan skidding off the stove; a ship's galley could be a very dangerous place. He hated every job he was given.

The dark, silent, morose cabin steward called Jimmy was of uncertain racial origins. He came from Swansea, and, when he did find reason to speak, he had the sing-song accent of South Wales. When the boy was sent to help him, he would be ordered to fetch this or carry that — as if I were a Labrador dog, Manuel thought indignantly. Helping Jimmy, however, took him into the officers' quarters, and, when he saw them, he decided that compared with being crew, an officer's life must be pure paradise.

He confided this observation to Jimmy, one day, when he was helping to strip bunks and sort washing. "One day, I'm going to be an officer," he told him.

Jimmy managed a faint smile. "That don't come to folks like us," he said.

"My dad had his Master's," responded Manuel, as he watched Jimmy deftly tuck in the corners of clean sheets.

"Humph. You got to have schooling for that — and be white."

Manuel was startled. Schooling, yes — but white? All his life he had played with boys of every race, and he knew that below decks crews were often coloured. He had assumed that there were no officers amongst them because they lacked education. "But why?" he asked, his arms full of sheets that Jimmy had thrown over to him.

"Don't ask me. I've sailed in this old tub for years. When we dock, to make sure I keep *this* berth, I always sign on again right away for the next trip. And I don't even go ashore that often. I might never get another 'sight'. And why, Sir? Because I'm as black as the coal in the hold. Pass me them pillowcases."

"That's not fair!"

"First thing you learn at sea, lad, is to keep your place and be a good mate to the other fellas. And keep your head down — and don't say too much."

Once having broken the barriers of his self-imposed silence, Jimmy had many friendly conversations with Manuel. He taught the boy how to fish — fish was a welcome addition to a crew's austere diet. The man was a walking book on fish, Old Manuel once ruminated, and had given him a life-long interest in them.

He was not allowed ashore at Havana. The chief steward demanded a special clean-up of the galley. As he scrubbed and scraped caked-on grease, Manuel seethed with frustration. He had found the confinement hard to bear and had been looking forward to going ashore for a walk and to post letters to Arnador and his mother.

He formed the idea of jumping ship at the next port, which was Houston, Texas; but the chief steward, wise in the ways of youngsters, put him in the charge of the ship's carpenter who was going ashore to stretch his legs. Fuming, the boy trudged along to Woolworth's with the easy, amiable carpenter, to buy a pair of socks. Rousing himself, Manuel purchased three bead necklaces at five cents each and a small brooch, the latter for Grandma Micaela who did not wear necklaces.

Since Houston was a Prohibition area and the carpenter was no great drinker, he took Manuel to a soda fountain, where he was introduced to the glories of an American sundae.

He had never seen such a wondrous concoction, a halfpenny ice cream being the limit of his experience. He waded through layers of cream and nuts, ice cream, chocolate sauce — and a cherry on top; and wondered what other delights the United States could offer — once he got away from the carpenter, of course.

The soda fountain, however, was well known, and two other members of the crew wandered in to drink coffee and eat ice cream. Flanked by three adults, Manuel knew he would not be able to slip away. Hooked for ever on American ice cream, he went regretfully back to the ship.

A letter from his mother awaited him, full of love and instructions to remember that he was a good Catholic boy — and a Basque — Basques were always honourable and upright. Brian Wing had dropped by to inquire about him, and Arnador had written to him.

He received Arnador's letter when he docked again at Liverpool.

40

AFRAID that Manuel might spend his wages, or be robbed of them before he arrived home, Mr Figgin insisted on accompanying the boy to his own doorstep and handing him over to Rosita, who answered his knock.

He told her that the boy had done well, and that he would see that he was taken on again in a few days' time. He refused a cup of tea, and went off to catch the overhead railway train to Dingle, where he lived.

Delighted to see that Manuel had gained weight, his mother hugged him; and Francesca and Little Maria came running down the stairs to bounce around him, as he slung his kitbag on to the floor — exactly as his father used to do, Rosita thought with a pang.

He hugged them all — and wondered why they seemed to be blocking the entrance to the kitchen-living-room.

As he unbuttoned his jacket, Rosita looked up at him, and said in faltering tones, "I've bad news for you, dear. And some good news, too."

At her words, the girls suddenly stood still, and looked as if they might cry.

Manuel stared apprehensively at the three of them, and then asked, "Grandma?"

"Yes, dear. The funeral was last Friday. It

was a heart attack, the doctor said. She went quite suddenly."

"Oh, Mam!" He took her into his arms again and she clung to him for a moment, and then she said firmly, "We're not going to cry too much, are we, girls? Granny was very, very old — and she wished to go to God."

Manuel hastily picked up his cue. He squatted down in front of the girls and put an arm round each, as he said, "You're right. We'll remember Granny when she was all cheery and energetic — and we'll be thankful that she won't be blind any more." He grinned at their solemn white faces and pulled them close to him. "She'll be able to see the angels now!"

Bless his heart, thought Rosita thankfully.

The idea that Grandma could now see was a new one to the girls, and Francesca said in wonderment, "Of course, she will," and their faces lightened.

Their mother said, with false brightness, "And now we've got a tremendous surprise for him, haven't we?"

Their solemnity gave way immediately to excitement. "Yeth," breathed Little Maria, whose front teeth were not yet quite full-grown and gave her a lisp. She pulled Manuel towards the kitchen-living-room. "Come and thee!"

Laughing, he allowed himself to be tugged down the passage, rather expecting to find that Pudding now had half a dozen new great-great-great-grandchildren by the current cat.

Then he was in the tiny old room, and was

stunned by what he saw in the light of the oil lamp on the table.

In Grandma's old rocking chair sprawled a thin, long-legged man with close-cropped greying hair. The poor light of the lamp made his face look darker than it was and showed the deep lines which only a hard life could carve.

For a second, he thought his mother had taken a lover, and he was stung by jealousy. Then his eyes widened in disbelief as the man rose shyly from his chair.

"Uncle Leo!" he shouted, and flung himself into the stranger's arms. "Jesus! I'm glad to see you."

While they hugged again, Manuel was aware of a faded check shirt covering an iron-hard body, of tired but dancing brown eyes, and hair prematurely grey. This was not a man who had made a fortune in America. But, God, how good it was to see him.

"Where've you been? What happened?" Manuel asked as they laughingly surveyed each other. "It's amazing — you're here! I can hardly believe it."

"Well — it's a long story. I've told your mam all about it." He let go of Manuel, and sat down again, to pick up his smouldering cigarette which had been poised on the edge of Aunt Maria's little table. Francesca came to lean against him; she had been badly shaken by the loss of her grandmother, and it felt comforting to have this big, slow uncle here, a man whom Rosita and Manuel obviously loved. Little Maria must have been of the same opinion, because she shoved past Francesca so that she could clamber on to Leo's knee.

"When did you arrive?" Manuel's voice was muffled by his navy-blue sweater which he was hauling off. A good fire was making the room too warm.

"Last week." He was quiet for a moment, and then said, "I missed Mother by a day. We always leave things too late!"

Manuel said a little accusingly, "She always hoped you'd come home."

"I should've written — I know that now. With Agustin in Bilbao, it wasn't right not to." He cleared his throat, as if it were hard to get the words out. "I always assumed Pedro and Father were here, though." His thoughts reverted to Agustin, and he added, "Rosita's written to tell him about Mother."

Manuel stood near him, his back to the fire, while Rosita filled the kettle at the kitchen tap. "Why *didn't* you write?" But when there was no reply and he glanced at his uncle's face he was surprised to see his eyes closed and his jaw clenched. Rosita made a small negative signal to him with one hand, so he remained quiet. She said, "Come to the table, luv, and you, too, Leo. The meal's all ready — I read in the paper when the ship would dock — so I was able to cook for you."

He whistled when he looked at the spread table. Only money from Leo could have provided this. "You've been busy," he said, and grinned at her.

As Manuel sat down in his father's old chair

at the table, he felt that he was re-enacting his father's return from a voyage. After three and a half months' absence, he felt a strangeness, a sense of being distanced from his family. It seemed as if he had been away from them for half his life — like Uncle Leo had. In his head were jumbled a myriad of impressions, about which he longed to talk; and yet, beside the absence of Grandma and the arrival of Uncle Leo, it all seemed too petty to talk about.

Rosita was saying, "I got your letter from Houston — and Arnador dropped in to say he had had one from you. He thought that, if I hadn't heard, I would like to share his letter. Kind of him, wasn't it? He stayed quite a while." She filled the teapot and came to sit at the table with them. "Tell us how you got on?" she asked, and turned to scold Little Maria for taking two slices of bread at a time.

He muttered that, yes, Mr Figgin, the chief steward, had looked after him — too well. He was very bossy, he added, with memories of being escorted ashore by the carpenter.

He caught a twinkle in his quiet uncle's eye, and knew that he understood — he must have come home from sea when he was a boy feeling much the same. But where had he been more recently? Doing what? With whom?

Rosita refilled his tea mug and said, "Arnie'll be down tomorrow night to see you — he had to go across the water this evening — to his cousin's."

"Good." For once, he would have something of interest to tell Arnie; usually, it was his infinitely curious, infinitely observant friend who introduced the subjects of their discussions. He said to Leo, "I think I'll have about a week home. I've got to see Mr Figgin tomorrow."

Uncle Leo said unexpectedly, "We'll talk about that tonight."

Manuel was a little surprised by the remark. He'd got a ship, hadn't he? The chief steward had been positively benign on the last day, and had said that he could hope to be taken on again. He had four pounds twelve shillings and sixpence in his pocket for his mother, and would be going back to earn some more for her. It was peculiar that he had been home only an hour; and yet he was ready to return to his much-hated shipboard life, to tell Jimmy, in their tiny mess, about Old Figgin seeing him all the way home, and have a good laugh over it.

Buoyed up by this sudden sense of independence, he pushed back his chair and went into the hall to open up his kitbag.

He took out a small Woolworth's bag, and said to Francesca, who had followed him down the hall, "Blue's for you, and red for Little Maria."

She snatched the bag from him and danced joyfully back to the kitchen-living-room to explore the contents with Maria.

He took out two more little bags, and stood in the dark hall for a moment, wondering what to do with Grandma's present. Then he went slowly back to the family, and handed one of the paper bags to Rosita. "I hope you like it," he said shyly.

Rosita took out a long, pale-blue necklace of china beads. Her eyes brimmed at the memory it evoked of her husband. She got up and came round the table to give the boy a kiss. "It's beautiful," she said, as she wound it round her neck. Manuel recollected that that was exactly what she had always said to his father, and he grinned with pride.

"What's in the other bag?" asked Little Maria, and the grin was wiped off his face. He slid a pretty little brooch with a silver finish into his hand. "It was for Granny," he told his small sister. He leaned forward to show it to his mother. "Would you like it, Mam?"

Rosita's lips quivered, and she hesitated before answering. Then she said, "You know who I think would love to have it? Auntie Bridget. She was so good with your gran, and she laid her out. I think she'd love to have it in memory of Grandma."

Bridget thought it was wonderful.

41

HE would never forget the walk with Uncle Leo that he took that night through the deserted streets of Liverpool, ruminated Old Manuel, as he fried bacon to go with a tin of beans for his supper.

He had remembered dimly the young man who had kissed him on the back of his head, before going out to climb into the horsebus waiting to take him down to the dock, to a ship and to a new life. He remembered him as particularly tall and thin, even at a time in his young life when adults appeared to be all legs. As he walked, that momentous night, he was surprised to discover that he was nearly as tall as Leo.

They had sat for a while in the old churchyard of St Nick's — the seamen's church — and had then wandered down St Nicholas Place to take a look at a Cunarder at the Princes Landing Stage; and all that time, Leo talked.

He talked as if he had had no one to confide in for a very long time — and he probably had not, considered Old Manuel, chewing on a bacon rasher as he waited for his beans to heat. Uncle Leo had spoken in Basque, sometimes pausing to hunt for a half-forgotten word, sometimes pouring out an idea in a quick, rumbling flow.

At first, they had walked in silence, until Manuel asked shyly, "Did you get any of

Granny's letters — or the one I wrote to the postmaster in Nevada?"

"Other than two when I first went out, and I answered those — no, I didn't get any — that is, not exactly." He grinned at the youth beside him. "But I *heard* about your letter — so I came home." He relapsed into silence while he stopped, hands in pockets, to watch a Furness Withy boat being moved downstream, its lights winking at them like distant stars.

"I'm thankful you've come, anyway," Manuel ventured. "Will you be able to stay with us?"

Leo rocked gently on his heels. "I want to." He spoke absently, as if his thoughts were elsewhere. "Provided I can get a berth." The December wind was chilly, and he pulled up the collar of his jacket.

Manuel nodded, and then asked, "What did you mean when you said you had heard about my letter?"

"Well, it was strange. I heard through a Basque AB we took on at Corpus Christi — I was working in Argie boats. He'd come down from Colorado, in hope of shipping out on a British boat — he was a Liverpool man like us — though I didn't remember him at all. While he was hunting for a ship in Corpus Christi, he met two other Basque lads from Nevada, who'd got just as fed up with the place as I had. They'd tried all kinds of jobs and finally quit; and, like me, had decided to go back to sea." He paused to light another cigarette, and then went on, "One night in a bar they were talking about how Basques were scattered all over the world;

and they told him about going into a post office in some goddamn awful place in Nevada, where they had spent a night, and reading a letter pinned up on a notice board. It was from a kid in Liverpool telling the postmaster about his uncle, Leo Barinèta — how things were bad in Liverpool, and he was trying to trace him. They remembered it, because they had sailed out of Liverpool, en route from Bilbao to Nevada; and they remembered that the Basque agent there was called Barinèta.

"When this lad shipped with us and heard my name, he came and told me. Simple as that."

"Jesus Mary! Had they stayed in our house?"

"I don't know. Heaps of youngsters went through our house."

"So you came home?"

Leo stopped to ponder, while he watched a laundry van inch through the gate to the Princes Landing Stage. Then he said, "It wasn't that simple. I couldn't come right off. Reckoned I'd sign off next time I got to Corpus Christi — which was a regular port for us. I was fed up with Argies anyway. I knew that if I then went to Galveston or Houston, there was a good chance I'd find a British ship short of crew — if anybody's going to desert a British ship, they'll do it there — or in New York."

Manuel's conscience gave a small jolt, as he remembered his own intentions at Houston.

"But why didn't you look for a British ship when you gave up in Nevada? Then you could've come straight home."

"Well, you know how it is. I didn't want

to come home and tell the Old Man that I'd made a wrong decision; he thought Nevada was paradise on earth — but he'd never been there! I only stuck it for six weeks — there was almost a war going on between cattle ranchers and sheep-herders — and we were being harassed by gangs of cowhands. I couldn't stand the bloody sheep either — stupid buggers."

"Mam wrote to you when Grandpa was killed."

"So she said. I never got it, though — I'd moved over to try Colorado by then, I think."

"Grandma was never the same after he died."

"I can well believe it."

"You know, you could've written to us," Manuel upbraided him, his expression resentful below the black beret he was wearing.

Leo made a wry mouth. "I'm hopeless at writing. I kept thinking I'd do it when I was settled. It took years, though. Kept trying different jobs — but an immigrant is dirt — even if he can speak three languages — and all you get is labouring jobs. I was out of work, so I came down to the coast, and shipped on the first freighter that looked anything like — and it wasn't a bad ship; I've been sailing out of Bahia Blanca for over six years now. And I suppose I was settled. To be honest, it was as if I'd never lived in England. Like a lot of emigrants, I was looking forward all the time — not back."

Listening to his uncle, Manuel had been leaning against a fence, watching basket after basket of laundry being shoved into the side of the liner. Now he transferred his gaze to his uncle. Leo's face was set, with the same closed-off expression that Manuel had noticed when he had first arrived home. He looked like Uncle Agustin — who never wrote either. "Are you all right, Uncle Leo?" he inquired.

Leo shook his head, and then said slowly, "Yes. I'm all right. I lost the wife about a year ago, and sometimes it hits me again — especially because of finding Mother gone, as well."

"Wife?" Manuel looked at him with complete astonishment. He had always imagined his uncle to be a footloose bachelor. "What happened? Was she a Liverpool girl?"

They turned to walk along the Princes Landing Stage, past the empty, folded-up gangways which served the ferryboats. In the lamplight, Manuel anxiously watched the play of expressions on his uncle's face, while the man got a hold on his feelings.

"I'm sorry," he said to Leo. "You must feel like Mam did when Dad was lost." He was tremendously curious about this newfound romance, and he ventured, "Tell me about her."

Leo was, in truth, glad to tell someone about his loss — he had not bothered Rosita with it, as she unburdened to him her stories of years of struggle and grief written all too clearly on her lined face. Sometime he would tell her, but not for the present.

He found it difficult to express to an untried stripling the unexpected happiness he had found when he had met Consuelo, and the appalling emptiness when she had died. He threw down his cigarette butt and ground it under his heel. Then he said, "I met an Argie girl, first time I docked in Bahia Blanca; she and her mam were selling fruit in a little street market. I was just a deckie then, an AB, and I'd been signed off. I was alone and I'd a bit of money to spend, and wondering what to do next, though I expected to rejoin the ship in about three days' time. She said she knew by my clothes that I was no Argie; she thought I was American, so she tried her bits of English on me. She was a pretty little thing, all curves, if you know what I mean?" Manuel nodded; he knew because his interest in girls was growing daily.

"Well, she and her mam were surprised when they got an answer in Spanish, and we joked quite a bit. Then, when I went down to the ship, they had a cargo and were going to sail again in two days' time. So I signed on, and away I went. But I didn't forget her. Next time we docked, I walked up to see if they were still in the market. And they were."

He looked at Manuel, and the boy was glad to see his eyes suddenly twinkle. "Now you should know you don't play around with Spanish girls; they often have strong-minded dads and brothers! Anyway, her mam settled it, by asking if I'd a place to stay when I was in Bahia Blanca — seeing as how I seemed to be sailing out of the port regularly — I'd told them I was a Basque, originally from Liverpool. Now, I told her, I was in a sailors' lodging house and wasn't too happy about it, so she said she had a spare room where I could safely leave my gear — and stay when

I was in port. I didn't know then that she had *three* daughters with no dowry money to marry off!" He suddenly laughed at the recollection, and his whole character seemed to change; he lost his quiet withdrawn look, and was suddenly very much like his father, Juan Barinèta, who had always appreciated a joke.

Manuel chuckled. He said, "She was trusting, wasn't she?"

"She'd got me weighed up. She was a wise old owl. And Consuelo and I got along fine, no doubt about that. So I married her," he finished simply, "and we lived in with her family — and it worked quite well, because I wasn't under their feet that much; and when I was there, the girls spoiled me rotten!"

"I bet they did," agreed Manuel. "No father around?"

"No. Nor brothers. The father took off when they were young, and their ma had managed to bring the girls up herself — and nice girls, they were." His face went dark again, as he said, "Then we were hoping for a baby and we began to watch out for a place of our own near her mam, so she wouldn't be too lonely while I was at sea. I wasn't worried about her, because her mam was there." He sighed. "I was away, and she was about four months — and, one day, so her mam told me, she suddenly went down with fever — fevers are common there, because the land is swampy and they don't have much in the way of drains or clean water. Anyway, I came home to a grave and three demented women."

“That must’ve been awful.”

“Oh, aye. There were a few other deaths in the neighbourhood, and my guess is that it was cholera — it kills that quick, you’d never believe it. The others were lucky they didn’t get it.”

Manuel put his arm round his uncle’s shoulder. He shuddered. Cholera had visited Liverpool in times past.

Leo felt the shudder, and said, “It’s the way life is, lad.” Though the remark indicated resignation, the tone did not. Then, making an effort, he said firmly, “But I didn’t bring you out to talk about me. I want to think about your mam and the girls — and you. Let’s sit down here a minute — I wanted to speak to you first, before I talk to your mother.” He indicated a seat at the end of the landing stage, and they sat down. “Now, what I had in mind is . . . ”

It was obvious that Leo had been thinking hard during the week he had been with Rosita, and that he had been distressed by the obvious discomfort of having lodgers intruding on her all the time. He suggested that he should live with them in a cheaper, smaller house — if they could find one with three bedrooms, and he would make Rosita a regular allotment. “Somewhere up in Toxteth, maybe — where she wouldn’t be too far from her dressmaking or her friends. How does that sound to you?”

It seemed wonderful to Manuel, as the sickening sense of responsibility which had haunted him for years seemed to ease at the thought of having another man to share it. He said, almost boastfully, “I’ll be able to make her an allotment as well."

"Oh, aye. But that's what I really want to talk to you about. The way you are, you aren't going to get anywhere much. I want you to do as well as Pedro did, and go to technical school in January, if they'll take you. Take some kind of engineering, so you can work ashore when you get older. A lot of fellas do that, if they get the chance." It was cold sitting on the bench, so he shoved his hands into his pockets. "I got a bit saved for when Consuelo and I got a place — and a bit for the baby that was coming. I can use this to start you off — and Rosita and I could feed you, I expect."

"Don't you want to get married again?" Manuel asked baldly.

"I thought about that. But it's unlikely I'll meet another Consuelo." He smiled at the boy beside him. "If, by chance, I do, we'll worry about it then." He took his hands out of his pockets and rested them on his knee. They looked big, callused and capable. He muttered, "I doubt I will.

"Saitua was saying the other night, when he came in, that you're the brightest lad here amongst the Basques. I want you to go to technical college, and then do courses between going to sea — and we'll have a qualified engineer in the house before we know it."

He stood up, and clapped the shoulder of the astonished boy, whose life had been changed in five minutes.

"Come on, now," Leo urged. "It's very late — and Rosita's going to scold us for being out in the cold for so long." He struck a match on the heel of his shoe; and in the tiny flame, Manuel saw his eyes twinkle, as he said dolefully, "Have to behave ourselves now, because Rosita's going to boss the pair of us."

42

MANUEL'S new home was in a decent, tree-lined street of working-class homes in Toxteth. The front room had a small bay window which jutted straight on to the pavement, and, when Rosita managed to buy a second-hand treadle sewing machine, she put it in the window, so that she had a good light for her sewing. Increasingly, however, as Sloan's realized her skills, they tended to employ her for full weeks in their workrooms, which meant that, between her wages and Leo's allotment the little family felt quite prosperous. While in college, Manuel worked in his spare time at various odd jobs, and was able to bring home a little additional money to Rosita.

The house was much closer to Arnador's apartment than their previous home had been; so, while he was still at school and Manuel was attending technical college, they often worked together on the living-room table in the evenings, and were of help to each other.

Anxious to be thought grown-up, Francesca and Maria sometimes claimed the other end of the table to do their modest assignments. As they all grew older, they would, at the weekends, frequently play cards together or go for walks in the parks. When Manuel finished college and went to sea, as a very junior electrical engineer, and Arnador was doing his first degree at Liverpool University, the boys spent a lot of time together during the periods Manual was ashore.

At first sight, it seemed as if their lives would diverge, as Arnador was drawn into the university world, and the young men pursued their vastly separate careers. It was not so. They had the easy association of brothers who liked each other, without the natural jealousies of blood brothers. Manuel was aware of how easy it could be for a man at sea to get cut off from friends ashore, and he made a particular effort to keep in close touch with his friend. To Arnador, Manuel was as much part of his life as his family was, and he automatically included his friend in his social life, if Manuel were in port. Because of the tight Basque connection, with its ties of language and culture, Rosita, Leo and Mr and Mrs Ganivet frequently asked the boys to meals; and birthdays, Christmas and Epiphany were days when a special effort was made to see each other.

When she was sixteen, bright, intelligent Francesca, with her delicate red curls and flawless skin, obtained a post with Boot's Cash Chemists, to work behind their cosmetics counter. Boot's had an exceptional staff and a job with them gave a girl a certain prestige. Once she had some experience, Francesca was encouraged by modest promotions. Rosita saw to it that her black dresses were always perfectly cut, her white collars starched and neat. She loved her work, which led to a career in cosmetics lasting a lifetime.

A year later, her more prosaic sister went into a bakery as an apprentice. She enjoyed what she was doing and became a skilled confectioner, much in demand to decorate elaborate wedding and birthday cakes. She had a merry, teasing way with her, and had lots of admirers.

Manuel and Arnador explored the world of women together. They were careful not to commit themselves to any particular one, mainly because they both knew that it would be some years before either of them could afford to keep a wife and family.

For fear of finding himself permanently entangled with a girl, Arnador refused to go out with female fellow students. He would say scornfully to Manuel, "They're husband-hunting — and I suspect that their mothers watch them like cats." Then he would add unkindly, "And what's more they're boring!"

So they laughed, and picked up girls at dances or in cafés. They played cricket with scratch teams, attended football matches, got drunk, and, altogether, did not allow their studies to weigh them down too much. With other male students, they sat around in pubs and cafés, eyeing the girls, and argued politics hotly over pints of beer or cups of coffee.

It was during one of these rather shallow debates, at the time when, in Germany, Adolph Hitler was rising to power, that Arnador soberly forecast another war. In fact, neither he nor Manuel was the least surprised when the Spanish

Civil War broke out, though it was Arnador who said sadly, "This is only the prelude."

A number of Liverpudlians, including some Basques, went to Spain to fight General Franco. Neither of the friends was keen to go, Arnador because he felt Franco would win and Manuel because he knew he must help to maintain his mother and Uncle Leo when they grew too old to work.

* * *

Those were good times, thought Old Manuel wistfully, despite the thundering of European dictators and the shadows cast by the war in Spain, not to speak of the worry about his relations caught in the conflict. His and Arnie's lives seemed to be set on hopeful courses, and they had all the optimism of youth.

As he remembered, he was looking down at the huge fountain in Butchart Gardens, a few miles out of Victoria. Jack Audley and his wife had persuaded him to join them for dinner in the restaurant in the Gardens. Though crowded with tourists, he had enjoyed the riot of colour that the Gardens presented. Now, however, he was very weary, his legs ached and he needed to take a pill to assuage the pain. His mind was tending to wander, and he wished suddenly that Arnie was beside him.

Arnie was now eighty-five! Manuel found it astonishing, regardless of the fact that he was eighty-four himself. Arnie's sister, Josefa, was even older — a formidable harridan in her nineties, with whom Arnie now made his home. When he was young, Manuel had, on the few occasions when he met her, been afraid of her as she swept into the Ganivet house, so sure of herself with her starched uniform rustling round her. During the war, she had suddenly become more human to him, when, as a result of a passionate encounter with a Royal Air Force Pathfinder much younger than herself, she had shocked everybody by becoming pregnant, something which had not become obvious to her family until after her Pathfinder had been shot down over Hamburg. Pathfinders' lives, during the war, had been nearly as short as those of merchant seamen, Old Manuel reckoned.

She was forty-one years old and well advanced in her nursing career. She was totally distraught because she could not bring herself to seek an abortion. Her parents were shocked beyond measure. They had rallied round her, however, as had her nursing colleagues; and Josefa subsequently picked up her career again after six months' quietly given leave — surgical nurses were worth their weight in gold at a time when wards were filled with casualties. Her mother tenderly babysat her solitary grandchild, a girl who was christened Josephine.

Josephine was now an accomplished concert pianist. She was unmarried, and, when she was not on tour, she enlivened Josefa's and Arnador's retirement by making her home with them, and contributing a share to the upkeep of the household.

She had been good for her Uncle Arnador,

who was now a Professor Emeritus at the University of Liverpool, considered Old Manuel. She encouraged him to take a bus down to his department twice a week, to read the journals connected with his subject, and continue his interest in the vagaries of human population.

As the fountain sprayed him lightly with water, Old Manuel chuckled. He still felt that it was lucky that Arnador had been a demographer; it meant he could understand and take an interest in his friend's discipline. If, for example, he had become a physicist, Manuel admitted that he would have been sunk.

"What are you laughing at?" Jack Audley asked. He was bored with watching the fountain; but his wife had involved herself in a long conversation with a Japanese visitor, who had come specially from Osaka to see the Gardens. The Japanese spoke English well, and Mrs Audley was encouraging him to take a look at the Japanese garden which formed part of Butchart Gardens.

Manuel turned to him. "I was thinking about old Arnie. Remember him? He's been to stay with me a few times."

"Sure."

"He had a funny career. He counted heads all his life — like, whole populations. From his figures, he can often forecast what's likely to happen to a country — or even an individual, like whether you'll get work or not. He makes me laugh because he's better than a gypsy coming to your back door to tell your fortune."

"Humph." Jack Audley did not believe him;

he was also feeling grumpy. He said deflatingly, "Don't get any gypsies out here."

Manuel was irritated. Sometimes, he got from Jack an annoying reminder that, though he had been in Canada for years, he had alien roots and different formative experiences. It made him feel at a loss, when his interests were summarily dismissed — even a tiny one, like a knowledge of gypsies.

It's time I went home to visit Arnie, he decided, feeling quite as grumpy as Jack. Jesus! How his legs ached!

43

IT was only when she went to live in Toxteth that Rosita understood how much the small community in Wapping had supported each other. Apart from the crises that they faced together, the daily casual contacts in the narrow streets and the freedom to walk in and out of each other's houses had, over many years, knitted them inexorably together. Now, even to go to the cinema with Madeleine Saitua entailed sending a note by post to arrange a date, where once Rosita would have run up the street to ask her and to enjoy a cup of tea with her. Even worse, Bridget and Pat Connolly's house had been condemned by the city authorities as being unfit for human habitation, and they had been moved out to a soulless new housing estate, called Norris Green, on the edge of the city.

"I have to take two trams to come and see you. I might as well live in China," Bridget had remarked bitterly, on one of her rare visits to Toxteth. "Our Mary and Joey are that miserable out there, you'd never believe it."

Though her new neighbours were civil enough, Rosita was never able to establish a closeness with them. As she said sadly to Bridget, "I expect it's because my kids are grown-up. You get to know people through the children playing with each other."

Bridget agreed. "Perhaps that's why I can't take to Norris Green," she said.

* * *

When Old Manuel looked back on the nineteen-thirties, he marvelled that he had managed to get through college; and then, like Uncle Leo, go to sea steadily through the worst Depression of the twentieth century. Neither man had been paid very well nor were their living conditions aboard ship particularly good, as shipping companies struggled to survive. Nevertheless, by pooling their resources with Rosita, they came home at the end of each voyage to a house that was warm and comfortable by the standard of the times.

Sometimes Old Manuel laughed quietly to himself, as he remembered those times. Not all seamen spent their earnings riotously when they were ashore. Rosita and Uncle Leo had been absolute Tartars about his saving money. Just like Grandma Micaela, Rosita drew their allotments and collected the residue of their pay for them when they arrived home, gave them each back some pocket money, took out an agreed amount of housekeeping and banked as much as she could, against the day that one of them failed to get a ship. She dealt similarly with Francesca and Maria, when they began to earn.

Uncle Leo never married again, though, for many years, he had a widowed lady friend whom he solemnly took out for a drink every Saturday night that he was in port.

It was too comfortable to last, Old Manuel thought, with hindsight. Life never remains static; it's almost impossible to forecast anything — unless you are a demographer, of course!

* * *

In 1937, with the family bank account in a healthy state, Rosita and Leo had persuaded him to stay ashore for a time, and add to his qualifications by taking another course or two at the College of Marine Engineering.

He had agreed, and, thanks to a lot of reading while he had been at sea, he was not finding the work too difficult. Walking home from college, one June afternoon, whistling 'Happy Days Are Here Again', he was feeling very content. He was looking forward to going to the Playhouse with Arnador; since they both had to be careful about money, they always sat in the sixpenny seats at the back of the balcony.

As he turned into his own tree-lined street, basking quietly in the late afternoon sunshine, he stopped dead.

In front of his home stood a black car, a very rare sight in Toxteth.

His heart jumped. Was it a doctor's car? Had something happened to Maria? As a baker who worked nights, she was the only one at home in the daytime.

Galvanized by sudden fear, he sprinted down the street.

The front door was open. He shot inside, and was met by a flood of voices speaking

Basque and the sound of a howling child. To his astonishment, his way to the living-room, whence the noise came, was blocked by a customs officer, fidgeting uneasily, cap in hand.

He looked round, as Manuel halted behind him.

"Whatever's up?" Manuel demanded, a little breathlessly.

At the sight of the new arrival, the customs officer's face showed considerable relief. "It's some of your family from Bilbao — we're on our way to the hospital . . . " Without a word, Manuel pushed impatiently past him, and was dumbfounded by the scene before him, though everything seemed rather dark after being in sunlight.

A woman was lying on Grandma Micaela's old sofa, and by her knelt a man. On the hearth rug stood a tiny, filthy toddler with black curly hair, screaming hard. As Manuel entered, the child lost his unsteady balance and flopped to the ground, looked around him, and heightened his screams. By the table, stood Maria in her dressing-gown, her hair tumbled from sleep, tearing up a white pillowslip, as if her life depended upon it.

Thoroughly scared, Manuel exclaimed, "Christ! What's happening?"

The kneeling man looked up. Out of a face blackened with dirt, a pair of tortured, blood-shot eyes stared at him. Manuel did not know him and turned, in bewilderment, to his sister.

She was quickly folding the white cloth into a pad, and she said in a frantic tone, "Thank God you've come, Mannie!" She gestured towards the sofa. "Quanito and Carmela have escaped from Bilbao. They've brought little Ramon to us, while they take Carmela up to the Royal. She's in such pain that I'm just making a quick bandage to put over her face before they go."

Manuel turned to the settee. His eyes had adjusted to the shadows of the room, and he could hardly believe what he saw. One side of the woman's face did not look like a face at all.

All the flesh seemed to have been ripped away, to expose a glimpse of bone or teeth. Though blood had clotted in some places, in others there was a soggy, yellow mass. The forehead, the chin and the neck were red and very swollen. Whether the eye was there or not, he was not sure; the swelling was too great. She seemed hardly conscious, though she was moaning.

He looked again at the man. "Quanito?"

The man nodded. He seemed ready to collapse, too.

Maria impatiently pushed the men back. "Give me space," she ordered. She leaned over Carmela and said softly, "I'm going to sponge the good side of your face. Then I'm going to put a pad over the wound; it's wetted with salted water. I'll put my summer scarf round it to hold it, until you get to the hospital." She spoke in Basque.

The woman fought her weakly, but Quanito

held her hands and whispered comfortingly to her.

Not knowing what to do, Manuel turned to the toddler, who had ceased to scream and was now sobbing hopelessly. He picked the child up and was promptly kicked for his pains. He persisted, however, and held the child close to his shoulder while he tried to hush him.

The patient young customs officer, who had edged into the crowded room, said to Manuel, "We could not get the lady to relinquish the child. She insisted on coming into the house with it, though I doubt she really knows what she's doing. Otherwise, I would have had her in hospital by now. I had a real shock, when I saw her, poor thing."

Manuel nodded. While Maria murmured to Carmela and Quanito, he inquired of the officer, "How did they come?"

The man replied, "In a fishing smack — we've had a few like that. There were seven of them in the boat. They landed not more 'n an hour ago." He glanced across at the tableau by the sofa, and said softly, "The medical officer took one look at the lady, and asked for a car to take her to hospital immediately. I was just going off duty, so I got the job."

"It's very good of you," Manuel responded, as he patted the back of the sobbing child.

Her face a mask of anxiety, Maria stepped back, and Quanito asked Manuel brusquely, "Help me lift her back into the car." He did not know who Manuel was, but supposed him to be family.

"Of course." Manuel turned and bundled the little boy into Maria's arms. He told her that he would go up to the hospital with Quanito, and once Carmela had been seen by the doctors, he would find a public telephone and phone Rosita at Sloan's, and ask her to come home.

Maria clasped the child to her and commenced to rock him gently, though she looked very distraught. Manuel could see that she was trembling.

"Mam'll come quick, I'm sure," he said.

He and Quanito eased Carmela into Grandfather Juan's old carving chair, which had arms to it. By this means, they carried the wounded woman to the edge of the pavement with a minimum of handling her. The customs officer held the car door open while they eased her inside. She felt very hot and she moaned as they moved her. Quanito crawled in with her, to hold her upright, and Manuel got in beside the driver.

The worried young customs officer took off like a racing speedboat, his hand on the horn. He used the horn every time he approached a white-coated policeman at a corner, directing traffic, and the constable, seeing the uniform and sensing a crisis, stopped the traffic so that they could pass over the intersection. Much to the ire of a porter, who seemed to think they should have parked elsewhere and walked into the hospital, they followed an ambulance and drew in behind it.

The man was more civil, however, when the customs officer climbed quickly out. Here was

Authority. A stretcher was sent for, while the officer ran inside, to capture a nurse and explain that the Port Medical Authority had sent them an emergency case.

Thanks to the customs officer's efforts, Carmela was carried straight in, to be seen by a doctor and then admitted.

Quanito was not allowed to accompany her. Nearly beside himself, he was sent with Manuel to wait in a crowded waiting room. The customs officer inquired if they would be able to get home again all right, and when Manuel said they could go by tram, he said goodbye. Both Quanito and Manuel thanked him profusely for his help.

The numbers in the waiting room slowly declined as the evening approached. Finally, when they were the only two left, a passing nursing sister stopped to ask what they were doing there.

Manuel stood up and explained that they were waiting for news of Quanito's wife. A perplexed Quanito glowered beside him; he spoke no English, but he sensed that the sister did not approve of them. It was not surprising; Quanito was still wearing the clothes in which he had tried to rescue his family from under the ruins of their home. Covered with dust, he had then got wetted down with spray while in the fishing boat. With little water in Bilbao, he had not had a wash for a week and smelled very badly.

"You'd better return in the morning," the nurse said coldly.

Manuel's lips tightened. He drew himself up

to his full height, and said belligerently, "My cousin has just come from Spain — Bilbao. He has lost almost his entire family in the air raids, and his wife is terribly wounded. They have been through hell. Hell, do you understand! Please tell me where I can inquire."

A nursing sister was not used to such speech from the lower classes, and she flushed with anger. Then she asked suddenly, "Bilbao? Spain? How extraordinary! What's her name?"

"Mrs Carmela Barinèta — from Bilbao."

She looked again at Quanito, and then said, "Wait here. I'll inquire."

She swept away in a rustle of starch, and they sat down to wait again. Quanito leaned back against the wall behind the wooden bench on which they were sitting. "I wish I'd thought to ask Maria for a glass of water. After so many days of little to drink, I'm dried out."

"I'll ask for you," Manuel said, and he got up and went to a desk at the other end of the big room, where a young woman was writing busily.

"Could I have a glass of water?" he asked.

She glanced up impatiently, and then across the room at Quanito. "I'm not here to run around getting glasses of water," she told him. "You should think of these things before you come."

Furious, Manuel made an obscene gesture at her, which, mercifully, she did not appear to notice. He walked all round the edge of the room, in the hope of finding a lavatory, where he could get water. If there was one, it was well hidden.

He returned angrily to Quanito. "No luck," he said. "Blast them."

"It doesn't matter," Quanito replied, and closed his eyes.

Until that moment, Manuel had forgotten to telephone his mother. He looked at his watch, and realized that Rosita would now have arrived home. He had been so anxious to support Quanito and Carmela that he had forgotten Maria and the baby. To help the time of their waiting pass, he had inquired what exactly had happened in Bilbao, and was horrified by the reply.

"All the family in Bilbao is dead, except us," Quanito had hoarsely whispered to him. "It's sheer luck that we're still here. You see, everybody thought that Bilbao could hold out indefinitely against Franco's armies — we'd wear him down and break out and take the countryside back again. But we hadn't counted on the Germans helping him."

"Germans?"

"Sure. It was the German Luftwaffe that bombed the hell out of us, not to speak of being shelled by German guns. Other towns had fallen. But they weren't fortified like Bilbao is. We couldn't shoot planes down with the guns we had, though. So they swept down on us and dropped bombs wherever they fancied — and machine-gunned the streets." He stopped for a moment, as if hit by acute pain. Then he went on with an effort. "We've held out for nearly six weeks — but, I tell you, the city can't take much more."

He again stopped, and Manuel thought he was going to cry. But instead he sighed and turned to face Manuel. He said brokenly, "Father and mother — your aunt and Uncle Agustin — and my younger brother; Great-uncle Barinèta and our two cousins — three old people — all of them died in the ruins made by one bomb. I couldn't believe the wreckage when I saw it. We lived in the next street, and when I heard the crash, I ran through the raid to see if they were all right. The neighbours came, and we all worked like demons trying to get them out. Then the broken wall of a warehouse at the back of them teetered. We ran for it — and down it came. And that was that." He looked down at his torn, filthy clothing. "I've never had a chance to change my clothes since it happened."

Manuel shivered. "My God!" he muttered.

Quanito cleared his throat. "That's not all of it. You know I had two other boys older than Ramon?"

Manuel did not know. He said apprehensively, "Did you?"

"Yes. When the raid seemed over, they wanted to play in our street — they were tired of hours of being in the cellar. So the wife let them out to play by the doorstep."

"Not them, too?" Manuel whispered in horror.

"Yes. Out of nowhere, a plane suddenly dived, and machine-gunned the street. Took my boys and two of a neighbour's. We buried them together in an old churchyard nearby — it was the only place we could dig in. My lads were only three — twins. Then, on the way back to our house, they began to shell us."

"Was that how Carmela got hurt?"

He nodded. "We started to run for home, and a piece of shrapnel hit her. Took that whole chunk out of the side of her face. I got her home — but she was in agony. So we laid her in the cellar, and the other couple stayed with her and Ramon. I ran like mad for the nearest doctor — and his house was flat! I was nearly out of my mind. I thought, I'll never be able to get her to a hospital, with all hell let loose — and she so badly hurt."

"What did you do?"

"I went back home. And then the idea came to me, to try to get down the river and over to England — to you people — because we lived right by the river — in the Old Town.

"As soon as it was quiet again, my friend and I put what food and water we had into my boat. We brought two lodgers living with my neighbours with us. Between us, we bandaged Carmela and carried her down. And we came out by night — without lights, though a lot of fires tended to light up the water. I began to think we'd never make it."

"It must have been terrifying."

"It was — especially for Carmela, particularly when her mouth swelled up. She couldn't even bear to cry."

Manuel shivered. These things didn't happen to you or your family, did they? The newspapers didn't tell you about people like Quanito; so you imagined that they must be managing through the reported battles. He said nervously, "Mother wrote to Uncle Agustin — your father — a couple of months ago suggesting he should bring the family to Liverpool."

"I know — but we didn't seriously think that Bilbao would fall. It's a fortress of a place — but we didn't count on German bombers and long-range cannon."

In the bleak hospital waiting room, the two men had almost given up hope of hearing anything about Carmela. Even the supercilious woman at the desk on the far side of the room had departed, turning out most of the lights. Then the door opened and the nursing sister hurried across the empty room. She was wearing her cloak, as if ready to go home.

She said quickly to them, "Mrs er — Barin — what is it? Your wife has been put under sedation and is comfortable. You may come in tomorrow to see how she is."

Quanito watched the faces of the other two, and saw from Manuel's expression that all was not well. His face darkened under its coat of dirt, and he asked anxiously for a translation, as the nurse began to move away. Afraid Quanito might make a fuss, Manuel hastily thanked the sister and told Quanito that the nurse had done her best. As they moved out of the hospital after her, he gave a fuller translation, and Quanito shook his clenched fist at the black stone frontage of the hospital. "She's my *wife*," he hissed at Manuel. "Surely I can see her?"

Manuel did his best to comfort the man. He said, "She'll be sound asleep under sedation, and the doctor will probably have her in surgery, as soon as she's a bit rested."

Quanito bowed his head and accepted what he did not seem to have the power to change, and Manuel took him home by tram. The few passengers stared at such a wreck of a man accompanied by a young man decently clad in a tweed jacket and grey trousers.

* * *

At home, a startled Rosita had been faced with Maria standing in the doorway, looking for her, while she rocked a grubby, dozing child in her arms.

"Good gracious, luv! Who've you got there?" Rosita exclaimed, as Maria turned back into the hall so that she could enter.

Maria babbled out the story of the day, while a work-weary Rosita took off her hat and coat and hung them up. Then she peeped at the tear-stained little face against Maria's breast, and exclaimed, "Poor little lamb. Maybe he'd sleep for a while, if we put him on the sofa and wrap a shawl round him. Which one of theirs is this? Ramon?"

"Yes. The baby."

"Where are the other two?"

"They're gone, too, Mam."

"Oh, God!" Rosita pulled out a chair and sat down suddenly, as Maria carefully laid Ramon on the sofa, and shook out a shawl which normally lay folded on the back of it. As she tucked the shawl round the child, he stirred, put his thumb in his mouth and then seemed to drop off to sleep.

"Agustin?" inquired Rosita shakily, as Maria turned to face her.

"Dead. He was home from sea, and one bomb took him and his family, and Great-Uncle and his family next door but one."

Maria had held up very well until then. But now she began to cry, while her mother reeled visibly under the blow of her news. "Don't cry, luv," she said to her daughter in a pitifully small voice. "We've got to be the brave ones, and help them." Inside, she wished frantically for Bridget, to help her bear the grief.

"Holy Mary. Give me strength!" she prayed. She made herself get up and put the kettle on the gas stove, which she lit with a match. Then she went to her daughter, and held her and crooned to her, just as Micaela had done for her in years past. "Frannie'll be home soon, and she'll help us," she comforted the younger daughter. "We're going to have a good strong cup of tea, and then you go back to bed for a while. I'm going to make a big supper. I bet Quanito hasn't had much to eat these past few days — and he's got to keep his strength up. Thank goodness, I've plenty of fish in." Then she added brokenly, "Poor Carmela! Poor woman!"

Maria continued to cry for a little while and to hold on to her mother. "Come on, my dove. You have to go to work at midnight," Rosita said. She mopped the girl's eyes with her hanky, and then inquired, "Has little Ramon had anything to eat?"

"I got a cup of hot milk into him — but that's all."

As her mother made tea and then poured it, Maria sat down and, speaking softly so as not to wake Ramon, she expanded on the tragedy which had struck their extended family. She said, "Quanito was so thankful for the kindness which they received, once they came over the bar and were spotted. There've been other small boats coming in and the pilots were watching for them, when they went out to other ships. They brought mostly kids with one or two priests looking after them. They've been sending them to Basque camps. I suppose that's what they'll do with the neighbours who came with Quanito."

Rosita took a big gulp of tea. She gestured towards the sofa, and replied firmly, "Well, that little chap's never going to a camp. He stays right here in this house — and so do Quanito and Carmela, until they want to go home."

Maria smiled faintly at the intensity of feeling in her mother's voice. She could guess that Rosita was already working out how to squeeze three more people into the little house. Comforted that her mother was now in command and that Francesca would be home soon, she finished her tea and agreed to go back to bed.

When Francesca returned from work, Rosita told her of the tragedy, and she immediately set to to help her mother make the evening meal. In the middle of this, Arnador arrived on his bike, which he parked in their back yard. He knocked at the back door and entered without waiting for a response.

Expecting to pick up Manuel and walk down to the Playhouse, he was very shaken to hear their dreadful news.

He sat for a few minutes with Rosita, while Francesca continued to peel a pile of potatoes, and expressed his sympathy at such a tragedy. Then he said he thought he should get out of their way. "I think I'll go back home to tell Mum and Dad and Josefa — I know they will feel a deep sorrow for you. I'll drop by tomorrow evening to inquire how Carmela is."

Very soberly, he let himself out of the back door and wheeled his bike through the yard entrance.

Rosita returned to cutting up fish and breading it. "He's such a nice lad," she said. Francesca nodded. Within herself, she was sick with horror, and she would have been glad if sensible, reliable Arnador had stayed a little longer.

When Manuel and Quanito returned about eight o'clock, Francesca was whipping mashed potatoes, and Rosita had a pot of hot fat on the back of the stove waiting to receive the fish. Bread, cheese and a bowl of Australian apples graced the table; a bowl of tinned peas was keeping hot in the oven.

Rosita did not know what to say, as the apparition which was Quanito entered her living-room. Was that dried blood on his jersey? She opened her arms, and he went into them like a child who had been lost. He said, "I'm so tired."

She held him, while dry sobs shook him. Then

she said gently, as she led him to a chair, "Sit down here a minute. I'm going to give you a big glass of decent Basque wine, to set you up a bit. Then Manuel'll take a bowl of hot water upstairs for you, and you can wash yourself, and take those clothes off." She turned to Manuel. "Mannie, you go and get out a pair of your pyjamas for him and your dressing-gown."

Without bothering Quanito with a single question, she soon had the family round the table. She herself held a whimpering Ramon. She made a joke of feeding him with well-mashed spoonfuls from her plate, and, after a moment's hesitation, he seemed to accept her soft, Basque voice, and ate. When she saw that he had a fair number of teeth, she gave him a piece of fried fish in his fist to feed himself. She pressed more wine on his father, and Manuel, remembering his thirst in the hospital, brought a jug of water to him.

After Manuel had taken Quanito upstairs, to sleep in Uncle Leo's bed, Rosita asked Frannie to get a bowl of water and put it on the table, and she tackled the job of cleaning up Ramon, who was in a disgusting state. She washed the little boy while holding him on her lap. She had no children's clothes to put on him, so a towel was torn in half to make two clean nappies and then she wrapped him in the shawl from the sofa. As she worked, she played with the child, and finally made him gurgle and smile.

Together her daughters stripped her bed, to put an old oilcloth tablecloth under the bottom sheet, to preserve the mattress from Ramon, who was, as yet, far from watertight. For several nights, he shared Rosita's bed, until the second-hand shop in nearby Granby Street was able to provide a small truckle bed for him.

When Ramon had been topped up with as much hot milk as he would accept, he was laid in the bed, still in the shawl, and Rosita lay by him until he slept. Then she went downstairs again. She was immensely tired herself, but she had, somehow, to plan for the next day. She had no time to grieve.

Downstairs, she found Manuel describing the details of the family in Bilbao to the two young women huddled on the sofa together. The only relation whom the girls had seen before was Uncle Agustin. They knew he had a wife and sons, and that one of his sons was married and had children. But, except for Francesca's visit as an infant, neither girl had been to Bilbao, so they were not well acquainted with their cousins. Manuel told them, "Quanito knew our names, though when he first saw me he did not know, for certain, who I was!"

"What are we going to do, Mam?" Francesca asked. "I can't believe what happened to them — it's too awful to face."

"It happened," Rosita assured her. "And Carmela is obviously very sick." She examined her needle-pricked left hand, and heaved a great sigh. "Well, as I said, they'll stay with us for now. Just how I cope with tomorrow, I'm not sure."

Her children stared at her. They understood the complication of having a small boy to care for, when all of them went to work — or, in Manuel's case, to college; and Quanito would, tomorrow, want to go immediately to the hospital to see his wife.

After an uneasy silent pause, Manuel said, "I could miss my morning lectures — I could get a pal to give me his notes to copy — so I could take Quanito up to the hospital. He doesn't know the city — and it's two trams."

Rosita flexed her aching fingers, and said to Manuel, "If you and Quanito could watch Ramon first thing tomorrow, I'll run down to the phone box and phone Sloan's. Thank goodness, Miss Hamilton doesn't retire until next year. I can tell her what's happened, and say I'll be in on Monday. It's Friday tomorrow, so I'll only lose a day and a half. It'll give me a chance to talk to Quanito and, maybe, get up to the hospital to see Carmela."

Maria spoke up. "If I can get a few hours' sleep when I come off shift tomorrow morning, I can watch Ramon, so you could get up to the hospital in the afternoon. Then Mannie can get to his afternoon lectures."

The coming of Ramon had already begun to alter their lives. In her heart, Rosita feared the little lad would soon be motherless, and she knew that, at a stage in her life when she needed the most peace because her menopause was upon her, she was going to have to bring him up. She had no idea how she was going to do it.

44

THERE were no sulpha drugs in those days to save Carmela from a dreadful death, thought Old Manuel sadly. By the time she had medical attention, she was in a shocking state. Twenty-four hours after her arrival in Liverpool, she died of septicaemia.

Because Quanito was penniless, her funeral expenses were paid from Rosita's and Leo's bank account. Later, proud Quanito's fishing smack was auctioned to pay the dues incurred by its presence in the Mersey river. He insisted upon giving Rosita the balance of the money raised by the auction, in part payment of the funeral costs.

Immediately after his wife's death, he nearly went mad. For hour after hour he raved of vengeance, vengeance on Franco and his Spaniards and on his German allies. He swore by Almighty God that he would make them pay for the death of Carmela and their beautiful sons and for his entire family. Again and again, he swore it aloud.

On that awful evening, Manuel and Arnador finally made him so drunk that he did not come round for thirty-six hours. When he did regain his senses, he was deadly quiet. He sat with a fretful Ramon on his knee, frozen with grief.

Rosita, almost constantly in tears herself, fluttered round him, trying to comfort him with food and with tender promises to be a mother to his small boy — though God only knows how, she thought to herself. There was room in her small home to house both father and child, if the British would allow them to stay in Liverpool, she assured him.

* * *

As refugees, Quanito and Ramon were reluctantly allowed to stay temporarily in Liverpool; and, when Manuel, Leo and Quanito happened to be in port at the same time, the back bedroom was rather crowded. Ramon was comforted by his truckle bed being pushed close to Rosita's, and he was spoiled to death by Francesca and Maria, as well as Rosita. He thrived on it.

Until the Spanish War was over, Quanito found a berth with a small Basque shipping company sailing out of Liverpool to the West Indies. After the vicious conflict was ended early in 1939, Quanito applied for British citizenship; but he had not been in the country sufficiently long to be considered for it. He was, however, given permission to reside with his son in Liverpool. He thankfully accepted this.

When travel was possible, he went back to Bilbao to see if his home still stood. He left Ramon with Rosita, and crossed the English Channel by ferry and went by train to his home city.

Rosita received a postcard to say that he had been to see his old home, but it had been pulled down as unsafe and was now a heap of rubble surrounded by a temporary fence.

After that, he vanished and Rosita never heard directly from him again.

From time to time, a shy Basque seaman, carrying a verbal message, would arrive on the Echaniz doorstep. He was always invited in, fed and plied with wine. Then the news was whispered to them.

Quanito was up in the mountains with the Basque Separatists, who were fighting for a country of their own. They had blown up the car of a Spanish general — with the general inside it. They constantly harried Spanish businessmen until, in fear of their lives, they left Basque cities. They picked off informers and any Spaniard unlucky enough to come within the sights of their guns. They had had to bury some of their own men and some were in prison — but not Quanito, who, though very daring, was also very smart, the seamen said.

Rosita wrung her hands. "When are they going to stop?" she asked an older man, who was one of the messengers.

"When we have a country of our own," he replied with a shrug. "When we've seen their cities burn, as ours did. Who's going to accept Spanish rule, after all we've been through. We'll never give up."

Each night visitor brought a small sum of money for the maintenance of Ramon. Rosita accepted it and banked it for the child; none of the family inquired from what source Quanito had acquired it. Rosita asked Manuel or Leo to change the foreign currency, since seamen often had such money to change, and the transaction would not cause so much comment as it might have done if a woman undertook it.

Even after the commencement of the Second World War, Quanito did not forget them, and money continued to arrive. Rosita took to writing anonymous small notes to her nephew, saying that Ramon was thriving. She asked the messengers to pass them on, if they had the opportunity. She never knew whether Quanito received them.

* * *

Encouraged and cosseted by three women and two men, the boy knew little about his parentage until he was about ten. In the meantime, he was simply told that they had died in the Spanish War. As far as he was concerned, Rosita was his mother and Uncle Leo was cast as father. Manuel was the big brother who played endlessly with him, when he was home, and brought him presents from foreign places.

Ramon's lack of a birth certificate worried both Leo and Rosita. They tried to adopt him, since he was their grand-nephew; his mother was dead and his father, they told the authorities, had deserted him.

They were immediately caught in floundering red tape. First, the Spanish Government and the Spanish Roman Catholic Church were anxious for all refugees to return to Spain, and Ramon and his father were refugees; the fascists felt it was insulting that many Basques did not wish to return to live under their oppressive regime. Second, the would-be parents were brother and sister, not husband and wife — it was, therefore, an unstable home declared the British, and, even if the child was an orphan, it was not wise to place him in it.

Patient Leo said angrily to Manuel, one day, that he wanted to scream at the woman dealing with the case. When he heard this, Arnador gave them the name of a good solicitor. Quite a lot of their precious savings were expended on his fees.

It took time, but the solicitor proved his worth. Ramon got official permission to reside permanently in the country and to apply for citizenship when he was aged twenty-one. Meanwhile, Rosita and Leo were declared his official guardians. It was not what his elders had wanted — but it worked.

* * *

Perhaps it was as well that Ramon's situation had been formalized, because eighteen months after the Second World War broke out his wrathful father became internationally famous. Still an ardent Separatist, he travelled secretly to Madrid, and neatly shot dead two German diplomats visiting their fascist allies. It was the first of a number of German assassinations carried out by an unidentified crack shot, believed to be a Basque, until, in Argentina, he missed his target and, unintentionally, killed an eminent Argentinian. Cornered on a roof top by the Buenos Aires police, he must have decided that this was the end, because, rather than be captured, he shot himself.

Long in their graves, his father and mother, his extended family, and his beloved Carmela and their sons had been methodically revenged. Few Basques grudged him such a reprisal.

45

IT was obvious to Rosita that she could no longer work full-time at Sloan's, now that she had Ramon to care for, so she begged an interview with her old mentor, Miss Muriel Hamilton, and explained the situation to her.

"I need to work," she explained, "and I love working for Sloan's. But now I've got young Ramon . . ."

Rosita's exquisite work with a needle was more precious to her employer than she imagined. Younger women coming into the trade were not nearly as well versed as their mothers had been. Miss Hamilton hummed and hawed, and agreed to provide work for her at home. Rosita would not earn nearly as much, but, added to what the rest of the family was bringing in, she knew she could manage.

Neither Miss Hamilton nor Rosita foresaw the havoc that would be wrought in the women's clothing industry by the war, hovering on the horizon, and the consequent rationing.

Because she was at home more, Rosita began to notice that Maria was being courted by Madeleine Saitua's younger son, Vicente, and she was very upset about it.

"You're too young for him," she stormed at her daughter, one night after Ramon had been put to bed. "He must be at least fourteen years older than you are. Do you want to be a widow for half your life?"

"Don't be silly, Mam. I'm nearly twenty-three. I know what I want." Maria fought back stubbornly. "He's always been in work — being a carpenter, he can work ashore or in a ship. What's the matter with him?"

There was nothing the matter with him, except that he was thirty-seven years old; and Rosita knew it. She had known him for most of his life, and Madeleine Saitua, now a widow, would be a kindly mother-in-law. Sulkily, she returned to a collar she had been embroidering for Sloan's.

Boiling with rage — and yet made fearful by her mother's remarks about widowhood — Maria went out to meet her beloved and go to the cinema, before going on nightshift.

Later on, when Francesca returned from a meeting of an amateur dramatic club to which she belonged, she found her mother sitting dejectedly in Grandma Micaela's rocking chair, the *Liverpool Echo* unopened in her lap.

Aware of how tiring Rosita was finding the care of Ramon, she inquired a little anxiously, "Are you feeling poorly, Mam?" She sat down on a straight chair facing her mother. Rosita thought she had never seen her look more beautiful.

The older woman sighed, and told her about Maria and Vicente.

Francesca laughed. "They've been going together for over a year now. Didn't you know?"

Rosita made a face. "I suppose I didn't notice

him amongst all her other hangers-on!" She sounded tart.

"Come on, Mam. Vicente's as nice a fellow as you can imagine. He'll treat her like a princess. Isn't that better than being misused by a younger, more thoughtless chap?"

"She says she wants to be engaged. He's asked her."

"Tush, Mam. Let them be. We don't know what lies ahead of us. It's better for her to be happy now." She took the hat pins out of her hat and laid them on the table, while she removed her hat carefully from her head. "Be agreeable to their getting engaged — and see what happens. It may not last."

"But, Frannie, when she's forty-five, he'll be fifty-nine and close to the end of his life."

"That could leave them over twenty years of contented married life!"

Rosita frowned, and then laughed suddenly. "You're wicked girls — you always defend each other! And what about you, young lady? When are you going to get yourself married?"

"When a nice Basque asks me," replied her daughter cheerfully. "Maria and I are agreed — we both want Basques for husbands — Grandpa and Daddy were such golden examples, that neither of us can consider anybody less!"

At the mention of Pedro and Juan, her mother smiled at her. Her smile was sweet, and she said, "If you do as well as I did, it'll be good."

So no more was said to Maria about her choice of Vicente, and within the month she had a modest diamond ring on her finger.

* * *

It seemed to Rosita that the family had hardly got its collective life adjusted to their joint sorrows as a result of the Spanish Civil War, when the Second World War was upon them. As Basques, they had a better knowledge of what it might entail than most of the population of Liverpool; and all of them worried about Ramon, who, by the age of approximately two years, had had enough of conflict to last a lifetime.

When war broke out on 3 September 1939 Manuel was nearly thirty-one years of age. Though he was now a refrigeration engineer in ships carrying fruit, and usually had a neat small cabin of his own — which he had promised himself on his very first voyage, he remembered with amusement — he was not paid very well. Like many during the Depression years, he had not thought seriously of marriage, because he, like Leo, had a commitment to help maintain the existing family home; to take a wife and start a new family could cause endless problems. Besides, Arnador was still single, and free to range with him as a fellow bachelor.

A year older than Manuel, Arnador had at last established himself as a lecturer at the University of Liverpool, after doing post-doctoral work in Manchester. But even university staff were not paid that well, he confided to Manuel.

Manuel was at sea when war was declared, but he docked a couple of weeks later, and came up to Toxteth to see his mother in a brief shore leave. Perhaps, because the fright of the declaration of war tended to make some people look around them more and re-evaluate their lives, he noticed how greatly Rosita seemed to have aged; her red mane of hair had grown sandy-looking with the white in it; she was stouter and her movements slower. She greeted him cheerfully, however, with her usual ebullience, and Ramon toddled round after her, chattering all the time — speech which had to be translated for Manuel by his amused great-aunt. "He's trying that hard to talk, bless him," she told Manuel.

Manuel's and Leo's homecomings did not often coincide, though Leo had been home once since Ramon's arrival. At that time, he had not seemed to have changed much. He was a bosun and enjoyed his job — he never seemed to change ships. He had gone bald and put on some weight under his navy jersey, and, sometimes by a turn of his head or a hand gesture, he reminded Manuel of Grandfather Juan. He had been badly shaken by the news of the loss of his brother and the Bilbao family, and he had been completely in agreement that Ramon and Quanito should stay with them as long as they wished.

* * *

It had been expected that immediately upon the declaration of war, the city would be heavily bombed, and Rosita had received instructions from the newly appointed air raid warden about her being evacuated to the country with Ramon. If the boy had been at school, he would have gone with his teachers; the schools would be closed.

"As if I'd leave you to be bombed!" Rosita said to Francesca and Maria. "I'll make a bed for the little lad under the cellar steps — that's the safest place in the house, according to the air raid warden. The poor little lamb isn't going anywhere."

So Ramon spent most nights, during the years of the war, sleeping soundly under the cellar steps, amid the smell and dust of the coal ration.

The evacuated children drifted back from the country in such numbers that the schools had to be re-opened. In the meantime, Ramon learned how to put on a gas mask.

Men were called up, further disorganizing businesses, which were trying to adjust to producing articles required for war, rather than for peace, amid stiff rationing of resources. Women in factories began to earn very good wages and to find that there was little to spend them on.

Rosita suddenly found she was getting dozens of requests from young women in the immediate vicinity to make dresses for them. Most of the material presented to her was undoubtedly obtained on the black market, but she was also asked to recut dresses bought in second-hand shops or to make blouses out of men's shirts, skirts out of men's trousers — as brothers were called up and trustingly left their civilian clothes hanging in the wardrobe at home.

At first she refused, but the young women were prepared to pay so much more than she had ever earned before, that she decided to leave Sloan's, who were having their own problems, and concentrate on this new, very lucrative business.

In 1940, Ramon was sent to school in nearby Granby Street, and she had more time. Her sewing machine in the front room whirred throughout the war, as she put money away for a better education for Ramon.

The boy grew up to be a typical Liverpool lad, unusual only in his ability to speak two languages. He played football, and, as he grew bigger, was always importuning for money to go to football matches. He became a sturdy boy with wavy black hair and a fair skin; and he blended into the amorphous mass of the population of the great port. Few would have guessed that his father had been a famous guerrilla, fighting a murderous battle of revenge against the fascists.

* * *

On the outbreak of war, Vicente obtained a special licence, and he and Maria were quietly married in St Peter's Church by an aged and sad Father Felipe. Francesca was the bridesmaid and Domingo Saitua was the best man. White-haired Madeleine Saitua put on a pretty wedding breakfast for them in her house, at which Domingo's wife and daughter, Rosita and Ramon were the only guests. Manuel and Leo were both at sea. The newly married couple went to live with Madeleine, who said rightly that she had more than enough room in her house.

* * *

Three months later, Boot's regretfully told Francesca that their cosmetic trade would be almost wiped out by the lack of stock; they hoped she could find another post more closely connected with the war effort and would return to them when the conflict was over.

Disconcerted, she discussed with Rosita the idea of volunteering for the Forces. "I don't have any particular skills, Mam. I don't know what else to do."

Her mother took off her spectacles and rubbed her eyes. She glanced doubtfully at her beautiful daughter; she did not want the girl in uniform — uniforms were for men. "You can speak and write three languages," she reminded her.

"I've never found them a commercial asset," replied Francesca, with a wry grin.

Rosita picked up a reel of cotton and carefully rewound a piece of thread on to it — appropriately coloured cottons were beginning to be in short supply. "Look, Boot's have given you two weeks to find another job. Mannie'll be docking in a few days, and I would like you to discuss it with him before you do anything drastic."

In the event, it was Arnador who settled the matter with one word. He said, "Censorship!" He and Manuel were of one mind; neither of them wanted Francesca in the Forces, a very common state of mind amongst the male population, when their own sisters were involved!

Encouraged by the young men, she applied to the Censorship Office and was sent to Glasgow. When, on 18 December 1941, the call-up of women was announced, she found, like many others, that she could not change her job without Government permission. She found the work so interesting, however, that she was happy to stay there. "And it is vital to the war, Mam," she told Rosita.

* * *

Similarly, Arnador himself was co-opted by the Government to do highly secret work intercepting and translating radio messages and telephone calls, where his knowledge of Spanish and Basque was invaluable.

Because he was convinced on moral grounds that this was a war which had to be fought, he had on its outbreak volunteered for the Air Force; to his astonishment, he had been turned down because of a partially dislocated shoulder, the result of the bite he had received from a horse, as a boy, an event which he had totally forgotten.

* * *

Rosita and Ramon were a comfort to each other, as they took shelter under the cellar steps during air raids, and they gave thanks to God each time Manuel and Leo came home from sea.

46

WITH sorrow in his heart, Old Manuel tried to write something of the war for Lorilyn, to make her understand its personal impact, something separate from lists of battles. Just as Rosita used to do, he chewed his ballpoint pen, as he considered his healthy, lively granddaughter. She was not unlike her great-aunt Maria; she had the same dark colouring and vivacity, the same impatience with small obstacles in her life — dear Little Maria, who had had fifteen months of happy married life, before a direct hit in an air raid on Madeleine's house, so near the target of the docks, had killed not only Madeleine herself, but also Vicente and Maria, who were expecting their first baby.

He put down his pen, in order to rub his aching arthritic fingers. Thoughts of his sisters made him feel so lonely that he wanted to weep. The loss of Maria had broken his mother's heart, and Manuel himself had not been able to believe that someone so lively, so close to him, could possibly be dead. Francesca, too, had been stunned by it. She came down from Glasgow to comfort her mother; but wars were such that they took little note of personal grieving, and Francesca had had to return to her work, and leave Rosita and Ramon to comfort each other as best they could. That same night Manuel went back to sea — it was pure chance that he had been in dock on the night of the tragedy. There was no individual funeral because there was nothing much left to bury. A communal service was held for all the victims of the incident and the bits were buried in a communal grave.

The old man remembered all the fine women who had filled his young life, Grandma Micaela, Rosita, Francesca and Maria, dear delicate Aunt Maria, Bridget Connolly, Peggy O'Brien, Effie Halloran, Madeleine Saitua and vague ghosts of his Bilbao cousins and his Echaniz grandmother.

With the weakness of great age, he let the tears run. Then, telling himself not to be an old fool, he took off his glasses and wiped them carefully. As he put them on again, he saw almost with shock, that he had not included Kathleen, his dear wife of many years, or Faith, who doggedly did her best for him even now, or Lorilyn, in whom he put his hopes for the future.

He sighed, as he leaned back in his swivel chair. He had loved, still loved, Kathleen, and Faith and Lorilyn, too. But they had understood little or nothing of the world from which he had come; they belonged in another place, nice, sanitized, wealthy . . . But often dull, he considered suddenly.

He went to have his afternoon nap. Before lying down, he stopped in the kitchen to get a glass of water and take one of his pills. It seemed to him that, lately, his damaged legs had ached a lot more than they used to, though ever since the day he had been carried into the hospital at

Halifax, he had had to take an occasional pill to ease the pain. As he stood leaning against the kitchen counter, waiting for the pill to do its work, he told himself he was lucky; he could easily have had to have his legs amputated.

⋆ ⋆ ⋆

After his nap, he made a cup of coffee and took it to his desk. He would tell Lorilyn how he met her grandmother.

I was torpedoed off the coast of Nova Scotia, he wrote. It was the second time — the first time was near the coast of Northern Ireland; but we managed to get the lifeboats off, that night. This time, we weren't so lucky and had to cling to a raft, with several men on it. The water was so cold, it was a miracle some of us survived — you probably know how the icebergs drift down from the North Pole in the western Atlantic; their chill seems to permeate the water all year. Some convoys had a rescue boat, to pick up men like us, after the convoy had extricated itself from the submarine attack. Ours did not, and, of a necessity, the convoy — what was left of it — had to continue on its way to Liverpool; otherwise they might lose more ships, while searching for men in the water. The last ship in the convoy passed right by us.

By chance, Joey Connolly was an able seaman on the same ship, and he, too, was clinging to the raft. Because he was obviously weakening, two of the men tried to heave him on to it. He was far gone, however, and he slipped into the sea and we lost him, young Joey who never learned to cheat at marbles.

Some fishermen risked their own lives to rescue the three of us still alive when they spotted the raft. They took us into a Newfoundland outport. The few inhabitants opened their doors and came running; they took blankets from their beds to wrap round us. We were nearly smothered in oil, and the women washed our faces as best they could, and then spooned hastily heated canned soup into us, while we waited for transport to Halifax, Nova Scotia. It seemed like eternity, waiting for medical help.

A team of doctors and nurses was ready for us, when we did arrive, and we were stripped and washed and the damage assessed. Though the doctors had by that time had a fair amount of experience of resuscitating patients like us, one died.

Thinking about it, Manuel mentally doffed his beret to the Halifax doctors and nurses. Thanks to them, he still had a pair of legs.

In the night, when the sedation was wearing off, I must have made some sort of a noise, because the night nurse left her desk and came to my bedside. Fair, brisk and capable, she arranged pillows round me to ease the weight on tender parts, and she sat a few minutes with me until I must have dozed off.

And that's how I met Grandma Kathleen. I fell in love at first sight — not that I expected to live to do anything about it — I was sure I was a goner — I hurt everywhere!

* * *

He did not write that he had cried that night for Joey and for Auntie Bridget Connolly, whose heart would be broken when she got the news.

47

IT was several months before he was passed as fit, plenty of time in which to woo his night nurse. It was with reluctance that he joined a British ship sailing from Halifax, in convoy, to Liverpool. As before, the convoy was attacked by German submarines. Two ships were lost, and one damaged, but he himself was lucky this time.

When he walked up the tree-lined street to his home, he found Uncle Leo sitting on the doorstep in the spring sunshine, reading the single sheet evening newspaper.

Manuel dropped the small suitcase given him in Halifax with a few clothing basics and some toiletries, and grasped his uncle's hand. They hugged each other until every distressed muscle and joint in Manuel's body began to ache all over again. Both of them had been under the same intolerable stress for months and months and did not need to say much to each other to understand. Leo had not actually lost a ship under him, but he had had a number of uncomfortable encounters with subs.

"We'd no means of knowing when you'd dock. There's never a word of shipping news in the paper. Come in, lad. I docked yesterday — real lucky to see you."

As he took off his jacket, Manuel asked after the family and was assured that everyone was well, and that Arnador had left a telephone number with Rosita for him. "He's gone to Manchester to be some sort of a back-room boy for the Government," Leo explained.

"Any air raids?"

"Oh, aye. But not much up this end — the north end's taken a beating, though."

After a long, Basque-speaking evening with the family, where he seemed to have held Rosita's hand for hours to reassure her that he was, indeed, there and was well again, Manuel said he thought he should go out to Norris Green, the next day, to see Bridget and Pat Connolly about the loss of Joey.

"Yes, you must go. She came to me when Maria and Vicente . . . " Words failed her, and she clutched Manuel's hand even harder. "She's taking Joey's death very hard. She'd love to see you."

* * *

The next morning, with a heavy heart, he made the long tram journey out to Norris Green, and did his best in a hopeless situation.

* * *

That afternoon, Ramon played truant from school to be with Manuel. They went down to the Mercantile Marine office, where he had to arrange for a new discharge book, and to inquire for a ship to Halifax, sailing fairly soon. He was told that it would be some days before he got his new book, and the clerk promised to bear him in mind for a likely ship.

Afterwards, they walked along the landing stage to look at the river, crowded with shipping, and to catch up on their news.

Kathleen was constantly at the forefront of Manuel's mind, and one problem in regard to her was troubling him; she was a Protestant and he was a Roman Catholic, a very serious matter in Liverpool.

After he had heard about Ramon's prowess in the school football team and how many pieces of shrapnel had just missed hitting him during the air raids, he asked the boy, "Do the kids get at you for being Catholic or speaking Basque?"

Ramon laughed. "I never tell them — they don't ask anyway. If the class goes into church for something special, I go along. What does it matter?"

"I'm glad for you. Do you think you'll get a scholarship to the Institute? Mam said she thought it was possible."

"I dunno. I'll try. Uncle Arnie says he'll coach me when I'm old enough."

* * *

That evening, Manuel asked Rosita what the feeling was about Catholics in the city. She thought it was an odd question, but she answered, "Well, for sure, you can get a job in a Prottie business now — and that wasn't always easy. They'll take anybody now. Remember when they used to ask what your religion was when you applied for a job? Well, not any more."

She smiled up at him impishly, and added, "When the bombs are dropping on you, Catholic and Prottie alike, you just think to comfort each other — you don't think, 'Is she a good Catholic?'"

If anyone as devout as his mother could say that, Manuel decided, times were really changing. Perhaps there would no longer be bloody religious riots in Liverpool, as there had been before the war.

* * *

The whole family had a good laugh that evening, as Manuel collected every big copper penny that anybody had, so that he could telephone Arnador in Manchester and Francesca in Glasgow from the public telephone box at the end of the road.

Francesca was delighted to hear his voice, she said. She told him that, for once in her life, being trilingual was proving an asset. "When the nuns realized that Maria and I could both speak a little Spanish — because we'd heard it at home and in the Church, like you did — they pushed us to take it as a subject. And I thought it was such waste of time! But nobody's interested in cosmetics at present, so it's a lifesaver for me."

She sounded happy, and said she was sharing a flat with a Scottish lady, who had been the governess to a rich Egyptian family and had learned good Egyptian Arabic. "She's a wonderful old bird — and she works in the same building as I do. We have a good time together."

Arnador sounded lonely in his Manchester flat. He did not say exactly what he was doing, but told Manuel that he worked long hours — and that it was just as well. He would be glad when he could go back to his own kind of work, and get a decent post.

It was not like Arnie to complain, so Manuel stayed on the phone until the very last penny had been expended and he had been cut off. It was then that he thought of writing to Arnie once a month without fail, to keep his spirits up.

Arnador responded with alacrity, and they kept up the habit for the rest of their lives. We put the world to rights — by mail, thought Old Manuel with a wicked grin. And we're still doing it.

As he slit open Arnador's latest epistle, he chuckled to himself. Before he went back to sea, he told his mother about Kathleen. "I'm going to ask her to marry me," he told her.

They were sitting on the cellar steps, while outside an air raid raged noisily, and Ramon snuffled softly in his bed beneath the stone steps. Leo had already sailed.

Rosita did not answer immediately. She was glad enough that the boy had found someone at last, but a sharp fear pierced her, and she asked, "Where will you live?"

"Probably in Halifax," he replied. "It depends on her. I've been earning better since the war began — things are more expensive there — but they've got everything, Mam — not like us here."

She nodded. She felt suddenly old. With Little Maria gone and Francesca in Glasgow and now Manuel, it seemed as if there would be no family any more. And for what else had she struggled and fought?

She made a tremendous effort, as, in the candlelight, Manuel turned to look at her. She patted his hand, and said, "She sounds a lovely girl, dear. I hope I shall be able to meet her."

"Of course you will, Mam. When the war's over, you and Uncle Leo must come to stay with us. And probably I'll be docking in Liverpool regularly — and be able to see you."

⋆ ⋆ ⋆

But Kathleen had other ideas. They were married while the war still raged; and she continued to nurse. But once peace was declared, she persuaded Manuel to move to Montreal, where he could go back to college to study — this time, marine architecture — while she continued to work.

⋆ ⋆ ⋆

It was the autumn of 1953, when he was already in a good post as a marine architect, before Rosita was able to come to see them. In the years immediately after the war, half the world was trying to get home again, and reasonably priced passages were hard to obtain. It was a stroke of luck that Arnador managed a visit before she did. He had been to a conference in Chicago, and returned to Britain via Montreal.

Faith was six, Manuel remembered, preparing to begin school that September. He took a week off to be with his friend. To give Kathleen some relief from the child, they took her up to Mount Royal, and she played with the dog, while they lay in the summer sunshine and poured out their souls in Basque.

It was then that Arnador told him that he had always loved Francesca and that they were going to be married shortly. "Rosita seems very pleased," he said. "And my mother is delighted — she's expecting a few Basque grandchildren. Neither Frannie nor I have the courage to tell her that we don't want any children. Frannie wants to continue with Pond's — she loves her job — selling Hope, as she calls it, to plain women.

"Neither of us is that young, anyway — I couldn't ask her until I had a tenured position — something to offer her."

"I suspect she would have married you if you hadn't got a bean. Frannie's like that."

"Well, I can take care of her, now." He was sprawled on the grass, and he turned to face his friend. "It'll be great being brothers-in-law!"

Manuel laughed. "For sure. We're as good as brothers, anyway."

After he sailed, Manuel missed him badly.

* * *

Kathleen looked forward to Rosita's visit with no little trepidation. She could not visualize what Rosita would be like.

She kept Faith with her in the car, while Manuel went down to the dock to meet his mother, having thought mother and son might appreciate being together for a few minutes.

When Manuel saw Rosita coming down the gangway of the liner, he had been shocked. Dressed in dead black, she looked like a small dark wraith. She looked elegant, as always, but under her hat, her pageboy hairstyle was snow white, and she peered at him through plastic-rimmed spectacles, her face wizened like a walnut shell.

"Mannie!" she exclaimed softly, and he took her in his arms. For a moment she murmured endearments in his ear in tremulous Basque, and then she asked, "Where's Kathleen — and little Faith?"

"In the car," he said. "She was afraid of Faith getting knocked about in the rush to meet the boat."

Though Rosita looked frail, she was very alert. When first meeting Kathleen she was kind but wary, concentrating on Faith, who, at first, clung to her mother; this grandma was not at all like the brightly clad grandma who came on the train from Vancouver.

Once they reached their apartment and she had carefully hung up her best black coat and hat and had drunk a dreadfully weak cup of tea with no milk in it, Rosita looked around the living-room. She was generous in her praise, as if no one else in the world had managed to produce such a pretty child or so cleverly arranged such a nice apartment. She finally succeeded in persuading Faith on to her knee, and slowly produced a whole family of tiny golliwogs out of her skirt pocket. They were beautifully made and just the right size to inhabit Faith's new doll's house. From the very bottom of the pocket she drew out an old-fashioned paper poke of dolly mixtures and handed them to the child. Together they spread out the tiny coloured sweets on the coffee table to be admired and tasted.

At the sight of the little bag of sweets, Manuel's throat contracted. He remembered two other little girls, long ago, kneeling on a rag rug and, regardless of dust, spreading out halfpennyworths of the same sweets, each trying to be first to claim the heart-shaped ones.

On the whole, the visit went very well. Kathleen learned to cook some good Basque dishes, and Rosita revelled in the plenitude of food in the shops.

At the end of a month, they saw Rosita on to her ship, promising to visit England soon, but Kathleen never did; she always seemed to have some good reason why she should not. So Manuel went over, shortly after Rosita's visit, to attend Arnador's and Frannie's wedding, and to be the best man.

* * *

A few months later, he went for his mother's funeral, five days in a ship, which seemed to crawl.

* * *

Ramon was in his last year at the Liverpool Institute. He had said firmly that he did not want to go to university, and, although Arnador thought he could do it if he wanted to, the boy said firmly that he would rather go to work.

One icy February day, in 1954, he came home from school, to find Rosita apparently asleep in Grandma Micaela's rocking chair. She had sewing resting on her lap, and the needle was dangling. Thinking that the needle might fall to the floor and that someone might tread on it, he went quietly towards her with the intention of pinning it back into the doll's dress she had been sewing. It was then that he discovered that she was not breathing.

He was a sensible youth, but he had never seen anyone dead before and he was afraid. Behind his first primeval fear was another terror — that of being alone, bereft.

He backed away, trying not to panic.

Francesca, that was it! He ran into the kitchen, and found Rosita's change purse in its usual place in the kitchen drawer. He took out all the pennies it contained, ran out of the house, forgetting to shut the front door, and went to the public phone box to call Francesca.

Because she was in town arranging a special

promotion for her company, in Lewis's Store, there was no reply.

Ramon put down the phone and stood shivering. Then he picked up the battered telephone book and found the university number. He asked the telephonist who replied to his call if she could trace Dr Arnador Ganivet, Demography.

Mercifully, Arnador was not lecturing, so he came immediately, tearing down the street on his old bicycle, known to the family as the Flying Bedstead.

While Ramon dithered behind him, he checked that Rosita was indeed dead. Then he sent the lad with a written message to the doctor on Parliament Street with whom, Ramon said, Rosita was registered for health care. "Not that we've ever had to call him," Ramon assured Arnador.

The doctor was resting for a little while, before his evening surgery. He got up immediately, however, picked up his bag and bundled Ramon into his rusty Austin Seven, to drive the boy home.

While Ramon had been away, Arnador had picked up the thin shadow of a woman, who had been his friend since he was nine years old, and very gently taken her upstairs and laid her on her bed. As he stood panting by the bed, getting his breath back, a slow grief overwhelmed him, almost as if it were his own mother who was there. He bent and closed the already half-shut eyes, and then kissed her on the cheek.

Then he went downstairs to the kitchen to

see if he could find some wine. When Ramon returned with the physician, he was slowly drinking a glass. The kettle was singing on the gas stove to make a strong cup of sugary tea for Ramon.

The doctor concluded that it had been, in layman's language, a silent heart attack which had caused such an obviously quiet death.

After he had gone and a very white Ramon had drunk the tea which his adopted uncle proffered, they went back to Arnador's house, to await the return of Francesca from work. To keep the boy busy, Arnador asked him to help to prepare the evening meal, and when Francesca opened the front door with her latchkey, she could smell fish frying.

Arnador handed the frying pan over to Ramon, and went to the hall to greet his wife and tell her the news.

She looked at him, stunned, and then burst into tears, to cry helplessly in his arms. Ramon turned off the gas ring on which he had been frying the fish, and came into the hall. When he saw his weeping cousin, he burst into tears himself, and Arnador, himself distressed, hardly knew which to deal with first.

Francesca turned to him and hugged him to her. "You must stay with us, darling, until Uncle Leo comes home. Then we'll think what to do."

It was comforting to Francesca to have Ramon with them, and even better when Manuel arrived.

When, six weeks later, Uncle Leo arrived, he

had already received the news of his sister's death by cable, kindly sent through the office of his shipping company. He had had time to think what they should do, and he asked Ramon if he would come back and live in Rosita's house with him, if he got a job ashore.

Since to Ramon, Leo had always been his father, he agreed and they lived together until, at the age of twenty-one, he brought home a happy-go-lucky girl called Julie to be his wife and look after the pair of them.

* * *

After leaving school, he had obtained a job in the accounts department of an insurance company. He was quick at figures and had had a couple of promotions by the time he married, but he disliked the daily confinement in a tiny office.

On the first anniversary of his marriage, he took Julie to a Chinese restaurant for dinner. It was a beautiful place and not one that they would normally go to. Afterwards, while Julie went to the ladies' room, Ramon went to the cash desk to pay the bill.

It was presided over by a stout, elderly Chinese, who first glanced at the young man, and then stared at him, as he took his credit card. After saying that he hoped the young couple had enjoyed their meal and being assured that, indeed, they had, the Chinese said, "I know you, don't I? But I don't think you've been here before?"

Ramon stared back at the amiable Chinese,

and assured him that he had not seen him before.

They laughed, and the Chinese looked down at the credit card as he put it into his machine.

"Barinèta!" he exclaimed. "I bet your grandpa lived by Wapping Dock! There's a real likeness — that's why I thought I knew you. Are you any relation to Manuel Echaniz? I used to play with him when I was a little boy. My name's Brian Wing."

Ramon had never heard of Brian, but, when Julie rejoined her husband, she found herself invited to a table behind a fine ebony screen. Wine was brought, while Brian poured out the stories of Manuel and himself. Ramon's credit card was returned to him, with an absolute refusal of payment for their dinner, and anxious inquiries were made as to Manuel's whereabouts.

Brian was a widower with one son and two married daughters. He owned two restaurants and a small wholesale fish business. Though his son managed the restaurants, his wife had always kept the company's books and he missed her help sorely.

After a most interesting hour together, the young couple went home. A few days later, Ramon went to see Brian again, to ask for a job as bookkeeper. The salary was not much more than he was getting, but he gradually undertook the supervision of the wholesale fish business.

When Brian died, Ramon bought the fish business from Brian's son, using the money which Rosita had saved for him and had left him on her death. At the time of Old Manuel's proposed visit to him, he had also established a retail outlet, which Julie helped him to run. Their one son helped to run the wholesale side. No matter how many baths the family took, they all smelled slightly of fish — but they were quite prosperous; and the odour from the source of their prosperity did not seem to worry them very much.

48

ALTHOUGH he had been retired for many years, Arnador still belonged to the academic world; as Professor Emeritus, he could always go over to the university and find someone to discuss the latest trends in his discipline.

On the other hand, there were days when Old Manuel felt as if he had lost the art of intelligent verbal communication. Since Kathleen's death, he had, at times, been beside himself with mental loneliness. Though he had not been as close to his wife as Pedro had been to Rosita, they had managed to get along amiably when he was at home. Even as a marine architect, however, he had been away for protracted periods in various shipyards, and this had been her main complaint during their marriage. "It's all very well for you. You've the company of men you work with. Unless I'm nursing, I can get quite lonesome," she would say.

"But you do all kinds of things," he would reply helplessly. "You're hardly home when I'm home." He would watch her go off to a tea party or to preside oyer a meeting of some kind, when all he longed to do was to take her to bed, before Faith got home.

It took him a long time to understand that her attitude to their sexual relationship was different from his, though he had, at times, from the beginning felt a stiffness in her response. Sex was way down at the bottom of the list of things to do as far as she was concerned.

Sometimes he laughed ruefully to himself. Was he any different, he wondered, from other men in that it was always at the *top* of his list.

When he went home to Liverpool, which he had done from time to time, some of the tension and frustration which lay uncomfortably at the back of his life in Canada left him. He was more relaxed, though he was never unfaithful to his wife. It seemed to help him to speak Basque in a Roman Catholic world in Liverpool. Without effort, he understood the subtle nuances of tone and gesture.

He still enjoyed feminine company, he considered, as long as its name was not Veronica. He rather wished that he had not cut himself off from Kathleen's circle of friends immediately after her death; he could have visited them occasionally and enjoyed conversations with their husbands as well. It was too late, however, to do much about it now. And only this morning, he had collected his plane tickets from the pretty Pakistani girl in the travel agency. In two weeks' time he would be in Liverpool with Ramon and Arnador — and they would not stop talking for the whole month he proposed to stay there! Blessed thought!

Meanwhile it occurred to him that young Sharon had been looking a bit peaky last time she had popped in to see him. He wondered if she would like a day's sailing in the *Rosita*. On

Sunday, if she were free, they could go up the coast and have lunch somewhere. And she, at least, would be interested in the details of his trip to England; she had urged him to take it. He would phone her this evening.

He chuckled to himself. He still had not told Faith that he was going. She was going to be so annoyed with him when she found out.

* * *

Sunday proved to be a perfect day for sailing; not too hot and with a steady gentle breeze. Sharon insisted on bringing a picnic basket as her share in the expedition, and they sat on the rocks in a tiny cove to eat their lunch, while they watched speedboats and other yachts taking advantage of the lovely day.

She was, as he had expected, enthusiastic about his proposed visit, and she asked him who looked after his house while he was away.

"Well, the post office holds my mail, and Jack Audley'll pick up the circulars from off the step — if he remembers. He's done the lawn for me once or twice, when I've been away." He hesitated, and then told her, "I'm not too happy about askin' him this time — he's been complaining of a pain in his chest lately, and I know his wife wants him to see the quack."

"Oh, don't worry. I'll do your lawn for you. Would once a week be enough?"

He was embarrassed. "I wasn't meaning to ask you," he assured her. "Doing lawns is a man's job. It can wait until I get back."

She brushed back her hair from her face, and replied firmly, "No, it can't. Unkept lawns are the first things looked for by thieves — a lawn that hasn't been cut signals that the owner is away. I'll do it. Your yard's a pleasure to be in."

He grinned at the compliment to his garden, and shyly accepted her offer.

"I'll give you a key to the house, so you can go in and get a drink if you like. I keep the wine in a rack in a cupboard next to the fridge."

She laughed. "You'll probably find me flat on my back on the sofa, when you get back — dead drunk!"

He looked her up and down, pretty as a picture in her blue jeans and white T-shirt. "That would be no hardship," he said with one of his slow chuckles.

Her eyes twinkled as she accepted the implied compliment. She handed him another sandwich, and then asked, "Have you told your daughter about your trip?"

He made a face. "No. I'll phone her the day before I fly."

"You are naughty!"

"I will not have her run my life," he responded with sudden fierceness. "She means well — but it is very irritating to be lectured at my age."

Sharon did not attempt to alter his decision. She suggested instead that he leave Faith's telephone number with her. "So that I can give her a call if anything goes wrong in connection with your house — a break-in, for instance." Inwardly, she thought it might be interesting to hear from Faith how she felt about her father some time.

"That's a good idea," he agreed. "Can I give her your name and number?"

"Sure."

As he munched his sandwich, he ruminated over the arrangement, and then he said, "You're a true friend."

She lifted her glass of wine towards him. "I hope so," she said.

49

IT was with his usual sense of relaxation and freedom that Manuel emerged from Customs at Manchester Airport, to see Ramon running towards him, pushing his way rapidly through a straggling crowd of others on similar errands.

Now in his fifties, Ramon was a stout man with a mass of greying curls bouncing round a bald pate. His shabby, working macintosh ballooned behind him as he opened his arms to embrace Manuel. They hugged each other and got in the way of other, less demonstrative, passengers, and wiped tears from their eyes, as they climbed into the fishy aroma of Ramon's delivery van parked outside; the blue van had white frothing waves painted along its sides, and *Barinèta and Son Fresh Fish Daily* proudly above them.

During the drive to Liverpool they spoke Basque to each other, and the dear familiar idioms poured out, like water from a fireman's hose. There was a fine, warm affinity between them as if they were much closer in age than they actually were.

As the van bumped its way into Aigburth, the Liverpool suburb where Ramon had bought a little house, Manuel felt a surge of pure happiness, and he forgot the aching loneliness of his life in Victoria.

When Ramon's wife, Julie, heard the van pull up at the gate, she hurried to the door and flung it open. She was nearly as stout as her husband and, despite liberal applications of perfume and scented talcum powder, still smelled slightly of fish. Her tiny feet, in high-heeled patent-leather pumps, took her surprisingly quickly down the path to greet her guest, of whom she had long since grown very fond.

Again, he was hugged and kissed, then dragged into the little home, to be seated by the sitting-room electric fire, and have a glass of wine thrust into his hand, until the kettle had been boiled and tea made. "Aye, it's good to see you," Julie assured him.

Old Manuel leaned back in the small fireside chair, and looked around the comfortable room, with its bookshelf, its radio on a side table and television set in the corner. Without hesitation, he said, "It's good to be home."

He felt as if he had just docked after a long and tiring voyage.

* * *

Much later, when Julie had gone up to bed and he and Ramon were seated comfortably in the sitting-room finishing a cup of cocoa each, pressed upon them by Julie, he asked Ramon what he felt he was, now that he was older, Basque or English?

Ramon laughed. "I'm not sure," he said. "I don't know any other place, except Liverpool. The wife and I did a bus tour of Spain once — but Bilbao wasn't on the itinerary, so I've never been there. Julie was tickled pink that I could speak some Spanish, though; learned it from Francesca. I've got one or two Basque friends — Uncle Arnador, for one — he comes regularly to see me, and we talk Basque together. The wife thinks we're *both* learned. Don't disillusion her!"

"What about your boy — young Leo?"

"Ha! Pure Scouse! I used to tell him about his grandfather, Quanito Barinèta, and how he avenged his grandmother's death. But the Spanish Civil War doesn't mean anything to him, any more than the Second World War does. They were just dates to learn in school. He's married now and off my hands, though he works for me." In further explanation of himself, he said, "Being a Basque is like being a Welshman whose parents were born in Anglesey; he'll say, as I would, that he's a Liverpool man — but you can bet he'll belong to the Welsh Society — and sing like a lark! The Welsh is still there."

Manuel laughed. "How's your singing in Basque?"

"Lousy. The Basque may be still there, but . . . Uncle Leo was the last person I ever heard sing the old Basque songs — he could hold a tune well, God rest him. I can still put a beret on properly, though!"

Uncle Leo was the only person in our family who died in hospital, remembered Manuel suddenly, and he shuddered visibly; it was the last thing he wanted to happen to himself. Better to be run down and finished in one blow.

The mention of Uncle Leo brought to mind Rosita and his sisters, particularly Francesca, who had been the last of the three women to die. She had died from injuries sustained in a train accident, when, in 1963, she had been returning from a visit to her company's head office in London. As recorded in a long, heart-rending letter from Arnador, it was as well that she did die from her injuries within forty-eight hours of the accident. 'Not only was she badly crushed, but her lovely face was hopelessly disfigured,' he said.

It had taken old Arnie — and himself — a long time to get over that, if either of them ever really had. And, sometimes, considered Old Manuel sadly, another bright spirit, Little Maria, danced in the back of his memory, to haunt him through a sleepless night.

He and Ramon talked a little while longer, and then Ramon took him up to his bedroom, where Julie had turned on the electric fire in case he was cold.

* * *

When, afterwards, Ramon climbed into bed with his wife, she was still reading a novel, and he said regretfully to her, "He's gone that thin; he looks as if a breath of wind would blow him away."

Julie looked up from her love story, and said prosaically, "He's feeling his age — like Uncle Arnie."

50

IT was a joy to Manuel to walk into the spacious lobby of the Adelphi Hotel in Liverpool, to see his old friend waiting for him. Arnador was leaning on a walking-stick, but with such self-assurance that onlookers could be convinced that he did not really need such support. They greeted each other warmly. In some ways it was barely necessary to talk; after seventy-six years of friendship, carefully nursed through wars, depressions and uneasy peace, they knew each other more intimately than did men who lived closer to each other. Both Manuel and Arnador believed that you could express ideas and feelings in letters which you would never mention face to face.

They were to dine together, and, once they were seated in the restaurant, they spoke Basque, with old-fashioned idioms and exclamations no longer heard in the streets of Guernica or Bilbao or Pamplona. Although Arnador had had the advantage of speaking Basque with his wife, Francesca, and with his ancient sister, Josefa, his language was as outdated as was Manuel's.

Manuel inquired after Josefa's health, something he had forgotten to do when he had telephoned Arnador on his arrival at Ramon's. He was told that she was still quite spry. "Her daughter — my niece, Josephine — you know her — keeps an eye on both of us, when she's not on tour with her Chamber Music Group." He laughed when he added, "She's not that young herself — must be over fifty now."

"Does she speak Basque?"

"No, despite Grandma Ganivet's best efforts when she was small."

"My Lorilyn's the same. I suppose it's the first thing that goes, with immigrants."

Arnador carefully poised some green peas on his fork, and then, before he put them into his mouth, he replied philosophically, "It has to go — children want to be like the others round them — and they know that they must speak English to get a job."

After a good dinner, and a bottle of wine split between them, they retired to the lounge for coffee. It was a fine Edwardian room, full of gilt and mirrors. The coffee drinkers already there seemed small and insignificant, drowned in the room's huge proportions. After a while, Arnador began to fidget, and he remarked, "It's too damned quiet. Let's go over to the Big House. We could have a drink there." He put his coffee cup down and pushed it into the middle of the small table in front of him, as if to discard more than an empty cup.

Manuel hastily drained his cup, and got up. He beamed at Arnador, as he also rose, carefully using his stick to balance himself. In spite of being very bent, his head thrust forward from years of study, he still gave an impression of height. Manuel had always been shorter than him and was still fairly upright in his carriage, though half a bottle of wine and a liqueur had made his balance a trifle uncertain, and he held on to the back of a chair for a moment before setting out across the vast carpet to the door.

Arnador had insisted on paying the restaurant's bill and for the coffee.

They tottered down the marble steps and across the fine lobby, oblivious of the stifled giggles of the girls behind the reservation counter; berets were not seen too often in Liverpool any more.

Chattering expansively in Basque, they descended a series of front steps, once trodden by kings and princes, and walked slowly along the pavement, to cross a narrow street to The Vines, known to seamen as the Big House. It seemed a long way to both of them, and they sank thankfully into mahogany chairs in the bar, to sigh with satisfaction at a glittering array of bottles and mirrors and to notice and remark that the Victorian Walker paintings were still hanging there. This had been the haunt of seamen, flush with pay, since before they were born, and they opened their coats and settled back happily for a long session.

After a couple of measures of the best Jamaican rum that the house could provide, they fell into conversation with two retired excisemen, full of wild stories of their adventures in search of taxes. When the excisemen left they grinned at each other. The soft lighting glanced warmly off the fine wooden panelling; and the rise and fall of Liverpool voices around them added to their sense of well-being. Arnador said comfortably, as he looked around, "Just like old times!"

"Remember when you were seventeen, and you bet you could get me and Joey Connolly into here and buy us both a drink?" Manuel asked. "And we got kicked out in short order, because we were all too young — and you stood outside and called them everything you could think of — in Basque?"

Arnador giggled, like a young girl. "Of course I remember. I'd more courage in those days!" He took another sip of his rum and savoured it, before letting it slide down his throat. "I'm getting old, Mannie!"

"That's why I made this trip. Feeling old myself. Don't have the steam I used to have," Manuel replied with studied solemnity. "Felt I might not be able to do it — next year." He ruminated on this sad fact, and then added dejectedly, "Wish I'd never left Liverpool. Could've brought Kathleen here."

"Come on. You live in a lovely place."

"Boring. Full of old people," Manuel announced with the certainty of the very drunk.

They had a heated and laborious argument about why one man's boredom was another man's paradise; and Manuel invited Arnador to come with him, when he returned to Victoria, to spend the rest of the summer with him. "I've still got a car — take you all over the island," he promised. "Beautiful to look at — you're right there. And good fishing."

Arnador considered this offer, and then responded dampeningly, "We've already done it." He stopped, to collect words which seemed to be fluttering disorientingly around his brain. Then he suggested, "We could go to Vizcaya from here. Strange — but I've never been there — and, come to think of it, neither did Frannie."

"Except when she was a baby." Manuel drained his glass, as he remembered a little boy looking down into a flawless, fairytale valley, from a shepherd's hut. "Most beautiful place I've ever seen. And I've seen most places." He sighed heavily. "Let's have another drink."

While another two rums were ordered, the idea of going to Bilbao began to be discussed between them. "We could stay in a hotel there," suggested Arnador, "and take bus tours wherever we wanted to go. Easier than trying to rent a car — I've not had a driving licence for years, anyway."

And so the idea grew. They planned to meet the following day for lunch and then go together to Thomas Cook's to discuss the details of the journey.

"I want to go down to Wapping," Manuel announced suddenly. "Never seem to get there when I come on a visit. Ramon always wants to go to Wales or up to the Lakes, when I suggest it!"

"That's easy," responded Arnador promptly, though his speech was slurred. "Remember the Baltic Fleet? Josephine mentioned recently that it's a very nice restaurant, now. We could meet there for lunch, and you can see your old home." He stopped to yawn mightily. "And then we can go into town and see about going to Spain. Haven't been down to Wapping since your mother went to live in Toxteth."

When the barman called, "Time, gentlemen, please," and put a white cloth over his beer pumps, they could barely stand on their feet as they got up from their seats.

"Like me to call you a taxi?" asked a barmaid as she quickly mopped their table.

They looked at each other, and giggled foolishly as they clung swaying to the edge of the bar.

"Yes, please," Manuel said to the girl. "Wanna go Aigburth — and then Grassendale, for this gentleman."

* * *

That night, helped by a laughing Julie, it was with a huge sense of satisfaction that Manuel climbed the stairs to bed, while singing an unprintable song in Basque.

* * *

Around two in the morning, moonlight flooding into the room woke him.

Though his jacket and shoes had been removed, he still wore the rest of his clothes. An eiderdown had been tucked around him. He had no idea where he was.

Disoriented, he found it difficult to breathe, and his mouth was dry and foul. He felt he was suffocating, and he threw off the eiderdown.

It did not help.

He lay very still, taking short breaths, while his brain went round and round like a roundabout. Where was he? And why was there such a sense of weight on his chest — as if old Mr Wing was pressing his big iron down on him?

He began to be frightened and to sweat. Maudlin tears ran down his face.

"Drunk!" he suddenly recollected. "Very tight!"

He must have made some slight noise, because a rumpled Ramon in striped pyjamas came quietly into the room, bringing with him the usual slight tang of fish. "You all right, Mannie?" He came over to the bedside and peered down at the old man.

His presence was comforting. Manuel whispered, "Could you open the window — and give me a drink of water?"

Ramon took a glass of water from the side table and Manuel sipped it eagerly, while Ramon steadied him with an arm round his back. Then he laid the old man back on his pillow, and went to open the window.

The cool night air flooded in, and Manuel immediately felt easier. "Bevvied," he announced carefully to the younger man, and closed his eyes.

"It were just like holding a bird," Ramon told Julie the next morning. "No weight in him at all."

* * *

Resplendent in a red silky-looking dressing-gown, Julie woke Manuel about nine o'clock the next morning. She carried a steaming cup of tea.

He smiled weakly at her, as he eased himself slowly upright. He felt tremendously, overwhelmingly tired.

"How's your head?" There was a gurgle of laughter in her voice.

"Fine," he answered truthfully, as with a trembling hand he took the cup of tea from her. "We drank good stuff. I feel a bit tired, that's all." The effects of the rum had not yet worn off.

While he drank the tea, she sat down on the bed. "What do you want to do today?"

He grinned his wide, slow grin at her over his cup, as he told her about the luncheon engagement. "Would you like to come?" he asked her.

"I can't. It's Friday," she said regretfully. "I've got to help Ramon and young Leo in the shop. Funny how a lot of people still eat fish on Fridays — but never go near a church! And we're one of the few places, now, that still sells really fresh fish — so we get a big crowd — I should be down there now."

She made him promise to take a taxi down to Wapping. "I'll leave the telephone number on the kitchen counter for you," she said.

* * *

Manuel was resigned to the idea that Liverpool had altered greatly since the days of his youth;

but he was ill-prepared for the shock, when his taciturn taxi driver drew up in Hurst Street at the entrance to the Baltic Fleet. Before descending, he paid the driver. When the man had left, he stood, bewildered and forlorn, with his back to the restaurant, surveying, with unbelieving eyes, the view across the narrow street.

He could not locate a single familiar landmark, except that at the side of a narrow road leading off Hurst Street to his right, a rusty street sign, hanging by a single bolt on a block of stone, declared *Sparling Street*. Other than that, there was nothing but rubble, which had been used to fill up the cellars of the demolished buildings. It was like the scene of an air raid, a tumbled sweep of brick, stone and concrete, through which a few blades of grass and dandelion leaves announced that, one day, nature would repair the damage.

His head bent towards the gusty wind, he slowly walked round the tiny Baltic Fleet, which stood alone beside the huge highway along which the taxi had brought him. He wanted to see what lay across the roaring river of traffic.

Where once had been the Salthouse Dock, there was a car park, and beyond it he could see the familiar bulk of the Albert Dock Warehouse. The great walls that had protected the docks had gone. Slightly to his left should have been the Wapping Basin. If it were still there, he could not see it through eyes blurred with tears.

Since he was early for his appointment with Arnador, he walked slowly back along Hurst

Street and up and down the traces of the tiny side streets.

After carefully pacing distances, he saw what he had been looking for; two steps leading from the narrow pavement up into the rubble — and, a foot or two away, two more steps.

He stood looking down at them, feeling dizzily confused and very tired. After a few moments of hesitation, he squatted down on one of the steps, and rested his arms on his knees. Then he put his head down and cried, cried on his mother's doorstep, and cried again because the next doorstep was that of Bridget, who had comforted them all.

Not a soul passed him, not a vehicle went up and down the narrow lanes which had been his childhood playground; the Baltic Fleet was locked in pre-lunchtime calm.

After a while, he took off his spectacles and wiped his eyes with a paper handkerchief, and then cleaned his glasses before putting them back on. He stared down at the street where he and Joey Connolly, Brian Wing and Andy Pilar had played at marbles or flicking ciggie cards, or, later with Arnador, had played cricket with a couple of beer bottles as stumps, much to the alarm of various beshawled housewives, who had visions of the ball going through their windows.

Except for the traffic roaring along the busy new road, which once had been the dock road, there was no noise, no thudding machinery, no horses' hooves, no clanging bell of the railway train that used to run along the other side of the street under the overhead railway — no overhead railway, either.

Old Manuel picked up from the side of the step on which he sat two tiny shattered pieces of brick. He looked at them in the palm of his hand, and then slowly slipped them into his pocket. Nothing left, he thought, except the memories in my head — and in Arnie's head.

He was thankful to see signs of life in the Baltic Fleet; a curtain was flicked straight; the door was set ajar. A taxi drew up and discharged Arnador, who, as the taxi left, went towards the restaurant's entrance. Then, spotting Manuel struggling to get up from his doorstep, he grinned and waved.

Manuel was truly glad to see him, but found it difficult to hurry amid the ghosts which swarmed around him.

* * *

They had an excellent lunch with a good wine, and Arnie listened attentively to Manuel's expression of shock at what he had seen. Arnador had taken one glance at the carnage wrought by time and city planning, and said he really did not want to walk around it.

They sat smoking for a while over a brandy each, Manuel still looking a little disconsolate. Anxious to cheer up his friend, Arnador suggested that before making their proposed visit to the travel agent, they should go across to the new Albert Dock complex to look at the Maritime Museum.

The brandy and the suggestion had their effect. "All right. Let's go," agreed Manuel. He was determined not to further spoil his time with Arnador by being depressed. He got up quickly and the room whirled around him. He shouldn't have taken the brandy, he decided ruefully. It took more time than you would think for rum to work its way out of your system, never mind downing brandy so soon after it. He unsteadily beckoned for the bill, and insisted that it was his turn to pay.

As they stood in the entrance, they both carefully put on their berets, last reminders of a once vibrant Basque community for whom the Baltic Fleet had been the great meeting place.

Teetering on the edge of the pavement, they viewed cautiously the fast-moving traffic, which lay between them and the Museum. Then, picking what seemed to be a quiet moment, they began carefully to cross the wide road, lane by lane.

⋆ ⋆ ⋆

"I never saw neither of them, I didn't," cried an almost incoherent driver of a huge lorry laden with containers for Seaforth Dock. "They was masked by another lorry," he wailed, to a shaken young police constable not yet enured to the results of traffic accidents.

As the constable jotted down notes in his notebook, and another constable waved slowing traffic onwards, the driver tried not to look at the ambulance crew gently wrapping up the remains of a lifelong friendship.

He saw instead, two berets blown by the wind, scampering over the ruins at the side of the road, to come to rest on what must have been a doorstep. The wind whined, and it seemed, for a moment, to be the sound of the high-pitched laughter of old men enjoying a joke.

The frightened man shivered; the place felt haunted.

Selective Bibliography

Ancona, George, *Freighters* (Thomas Y. Crowell, New York, 1985)

Behrens, C. B. A., *History of the Second World War. Merchant Shipping and the Demands of War* (HMSO and Longman Green, London, 1955).

Carr, Raymond, *Modern Spain* (Oxford University Press, Oxford, 1980).

Collins, Roger, *The Basques* (Basil Blackwell Ltd, Oxford, 1986).

Forester, C. S., *Brown on Resolution* (Pan Books, London, 1963).

Keefe, Eugene K., *Area Handbook for Spain* (The American University, Washington, DC, 1976).

Lane, Tony, *Grey Dawn Breaking* (Manchester University Press, Manchester, 1986).

Lane, Tony, *Liverpool: Gateway of Empire* (Lawrence and Wishart, London, 1987).

Laxalt, Robert, *In a Hundred Graves* (University of Nevada Press, Reno, Nevada, 1972).

Laxalt, Robert, *Sweet Promised Land* (University of Nevada Press, Reno, Nevada, 1986).

Legarreta, Dorothy, *The Guernica Generation* (University of Nevada Press, Reno, Nevada, 1984).

Middlebrook, Martin, *Convoy* (Penguin Books, Harmondsworth, 1978).

O'Connor, Fred, *Liverpool: It All Came*

Tumbling Down (Brunswick Printing and Publishing Co. Ltd, Liverpool, 1986).
Robinson, A. R. B., *Chaplain on the Mersey, 1859 – 67* (A. R. B. Robinson, York, 1987).
Scott, Dixon, *Liverpool* (Adam and Charles Black, London, 1907).
Spanish State Tourist Department, *Spain* (Spanish State Tourist Department, Madrid, date unknown).
Taylor, J. E., *Of Ships and Seamen* (Williams and Norgate Ltd, London, 1949).
Unwin, Frank, *Reflections on the Mersey* (Gallery Press, Neston, 1984)
Waters, John M., Jr., *Bloody Winter* (D. Van Nostrand Co., Inc, New York, 1967).
Whittington-Egan, Richard, *Liverpool: This Is My City* (Gallery Press, Liverpool, 1972).

Other titles in the Charnwood Library Series:

PAY ANY PRICE
Ted Allbeury

After the Kennedy killings the heat was on — on the Mafia, the KGB, the Cubans, and the FBI . . .

MY SWEET AUDRINA
Virginia Andrews

She wanted to be loved as much as the first Audrina, the sister who was perfect and beautiful — and dead.

PRIDE AND PREJUDICE
Jane Austen

Mr. Bennet's five eligible daughters will never inherit their father's money. The family fortunes are destined to pass to a cousin. Should one of the daughters marry him?

THE GLASS BLOWERS
Daphne Du Maurier

A novel about the author's forebears, the Bussons, which gives an unusual glimpse of the events that led up to the French Revolution, and of the Revolution itself.

CHINESE ALICE
Pat Barr

The story of Alice Greenwood gives a complete picture of late 19th century China.

UNCUT JADE
Pat Barr

In this sequel to CHINESE ALICE, Alice Greenwood finds herself widowed and alone in a turbulent China.

THE GRAND BABYLON HOTEL
Arnold Bennett

A romantic thriller set in an exclusive London Hotel at the turn of the century.

SINGING SPEARS
E. V. Thompson

Daniel Retallick, son of Josh and Miriam (from CHASE THE WIND) was growing up to manhood. This novel portrays his prime in Central Africa.